Multi-award-winning author .... novels featuring strong heroin.... and the bad guys who fear them. ... until she married a Texan without reading the fine print. Now she lives halfway between Houston and Galveston and embraces the humidity. When Leslie's not writing, you might find her camping at a lake, fishing pole in one hand and a book in the other. Visit her at lesliemarshman.com, Facebook.com/lesliemarshmanauthor, Instagram.com/ leslie_marshman or @lesliemarshman on X (formerly Twitter)

Karen Whiddon started weaving fanciful tales for her younger brothers at the age of eleven. Amid the gorgeous Catskill Mountains, then the majestic Rocky Mountains, she fuelled her imagination with the natural beauty surrounding her. Karen now lives in north Texas, writes full-time and volunteers for a boxer dog rescue. She shares her life with her hero of a husband and four to five dogs, depending on if she is fostering. You can email Karen at kwhiddon1@aol.com. Fans can also check out her website, karenwhiddon.com

RESOLUTE BODYGUARD

LESLIE MARSHMAN

MURDER AT THE ALASKAN LODGE

KAREN WHIDDON

MILLS & BOON

First Published in Great Britain 2024
by Mills & Boon, an imprint of HarperCollins*Publishers* Ltd
1 London Bridge Street, London, SE1 9GF

www.harpercollins.co.uk

HarperCollins*Publishers*
Macken House, 39/40 Mayor Street Upper,
Dublin 1, D01 C9W8, Ireland

Resolute Bodyguard © 2024 Leslie Marshman
Murder at the Alaskan Lodge © 2024 Karen Whiddon

ISBN: 978-0-263-32231-6

0524

MIX
Paper | Supporting
responsible forestry
FSC™ C007454

This book contains FSC™ certified paper and other controlled sources to ensure responsible forest management.

For more information visit: www.harpercollins.co.uk/green

Printed and Bound in the UK using 100% Renewable Electricity at CPI Group (UK) Ltd, Croydon, CR0 4YY

RESOLUTE BODYGUARD

LESLIE MARSHMAN

To Red

For all the times you've been an unofficial
background brainstormer.

Chapter One

"We call Nathaniel Reed, Your Honor."

Nate strode to the stand and swore to tell the truth before sitting on the hard wooden seat. It was a late Friday afternoon, and he gazed at the sea of faces filling the small courtroom. The divorce trial of Skip and Mitzi Stoddard, the reigning high muckety-mucks of Boone County, was the biggest attraction to hit Resolute, Texas, in years.

The day had been long, the room growing ever warmer as the two lawyers tried to corral their clients and avoid contempt charges.

"Mr. Reed, did you witness an altercation between my client and her husband on September twelfth of this year?" Mitzi's attorney asked.

"I did." But he hadn't planned to testify on Mitzi's behalf when he tried to break up a physical fight between the couple in the Chute's parking lot.

"Please tell us what happened that night." The out-of-town attorney who specialized in newsworthy divorces gave Nate a smarmy grin.

He thinks he has this in the bag.

"As I walked toward the restaurant, I heard arguing and saw Mr. and Mrs. Stoddard beneath one of the parking lot lights. He pushed her, she slapped him and then he punched her in the face."

Gasps swept across the room like the wave at a sports stadium.

"What happened next?" the attorney asked.

"I rushed over to see if Mrs. Stoddard needed help, but before I reached her, she'd landed a punch of her own. I separated them, but they both told me to mind my own business."

"To clarify, Mr. Stoddard laid hands on his wife first. Correct?"

Having worked as a bodyguard before opening his own security-and-protection company back in California, Nate had been trained on how to testify at trials. "Their altercation began before I saw them, so I have no way of knowing who started it."

Mitzi's attorney angled a glare at Nate.

Skip's deep baritone broke the silence as he jumped to his feet. "See? I told you she started it."

"Counsel, control your client." Judge Harmon always gave one warning. But never more than one.

Skip's lawyer, famous throughout Texas for winning felony cases, pulled on his client's sleeve in an attempt to yank him back into his seat.

"I didn't start it. He did!" Mitzi stood and pointed at Skip. "And he threatened to kill me."

Her attorney rushed back to their table. "Sit down *now*."

Judge Harmon banged his gavel.

"The hell you say." Skip turned to face her.

Mitzi took a step toward Skip, and her lawyer wrapped his arms around her waist from behind to hold her back. She pulled at her attorney's hands, her long nails digging bloody trails across them.

Judge Harmon banged his gavel. "Order! Order in t he court!"

Mitzi broke free and charged Skip, who slid around the far side of his table. Mitzi followed him, and both lawyers ran to separate their clients. The bailiff, a middle-aged woman who was as much a courtroom fixture as the judge, rushed to intervene.

Mitzi slapped Skip.

Judge Harmon stood, an angry frown on his reddening face. Nate hoped the judge's blood pressure medication was working.

Skip threw a punch meant for Mitzi. She ducked, and her attorney took it on the chin.

Judge Harmon banged his gavel again and again. "Bailiff, take them both into custody. Seeing as it's Friday, they'll be spending the weekend in jail. We'll attempt this again next week."

Mitzi straightened and slugged Skip with an uppercut that sent him sprawling backward into his lawyer.

Cassie Reed, Nate's sister and the Boone County sheriff, raced from the public viewing area to assist the bailiff. Nate glanced at the judge, now an alarming shade of maroon, before he swung over the edge of the witness box and ran to help. The bailiff fought to get Skip off his attorney, while Cassie moved behind Mitzi to cuff her. But the woman was too quick, lunging for the bailiff's sidearm and pulling it from its holster.

"Gun!" Cassie yelled.

Mitzi swung the barrel toward Skip and pulled the trigger a second after he dove back to the floor. Nate tackled the woman, grabbing the gun from her hand as they landed in a tangle of limbs. At the same time, a piercing shriek filled the room. Everyone froze, and Nate looked toward its source. The shot had grazed the court reporter's arm. But instead of looking at her own wound, the stenographer's look of horror was turned toward the judge.

Judge Harmon lay collapsed across his bench, one arm outstretched, his gavel teetering on the edge.

Cassie tossed Nate zip cuffs for Mitzi, then helped the bailiff flip Skip onto his stomach and cuff him before calling for an ambulance and deputies. "Nate, I need you." She headed toward the judge.

Putting nothing past the woman he'd just cuffed, Nate sat her in a chair and used another pair of ties to secure her to the attorney's table. Then he followed his sister behind the judge's bench, where she checked for a pulse.

"He's already gone." Cassie held the chair while Nate maneuvered the portly judge, a fan of weekly church pancake-and-bacon breakfasts, back into it without letting him slide to the floor.

They examined him for holes and blood, then agreed he hadn't been hit by the bullet ricocheting.

"Heart attack?" Nate asked. "He was passing maroon and approaching burgundy when I joined the melee."

"Maybe. Might have been an aneurysm or a stroke. We'll let the medical examiner tell us."

Another commotion in the courtroom caught Nate's attention. His brothers, Chief Deputy Adam Reed and Deputy Noah Reed, strode down the center aisle and took possession of the Stoddards.

Nate surveyed the room. All four Reed siblings, two cuffed spouses, one frazzled bailiff, a winged court reporter and a dead magistrate.

He looked at Cassie. "We're gonna need another judge."

SARA BENNETT STAGGERED into her penthouse apartment and dropped her briefcase and purse on the entryway floor.

Kicking off her heels, she detoured through the kitchen for a glass of wine on the way to her fashionable, yet comfortable, living room.

After another ten-hour day as a Travis County prosecuting attorney, she looked forward to the weekend. Not that she wouldn't still be working, but trial prep at home in athleisure and fuzzy socks beat a day at the office in a suit and heels every time.

She'd just settled onto her couch when a text notification chimed on her cell phone. Sara fished it out of her blazer pocket, glanced at the screen and cursed, her hand tightening around her wine glass.

enjoy ur weekend while u can

She had no idea who was texting her, taunting her. Before joining the district attorney's office, she'd been told things like this—angry phone calls and emails—could happen. What bothered her was that she'd been receiving the texts for several weeks, and they were coming in on her personal cell.

Most likely, they had nothing to do with her job. Probably a wrong number who never figured out their mistake. That was what she'd convinced herself of anyway.

Sara gazed through her living room's wall of windows. Austin's lights glowed in a view stretching out before her, Friday's nightlife just starting to spring into action. And she didn't mind one bit enjoying it from the comfort of her home. Put her in court, questioning a witness in a criminal felony case, and she didn't miss a beat. But stick her on a bar stool in a club trying to make small talk with a stranger, and she disappeared like a redacted sentence in a legal brief.

When her cell rang with "I Shot the Sheriff," she answered it on speaker. "Cassie. What's happening out in the boondocks these days?"

"Oh, you know, the usual. Drunk-and-disorderlies at the local dive bar, speeding tickets in school zones, the plaintiff in a divorce trial shooting off a gun in the courtroom and the judge dropping dead from a heart attack."

"Good one." Sara wandered into her bedroom, tossed her phone on the bed and slipped out of her skirt and jacket. When Cassie stayed silent, she asked, "You're joking, right?"

"I wish. Happened last Friday—craziest trial I ever witnessed."

After dropping her blouse in the laundry basket, Sara pulled on a pair of leggings and an oversized fleece top. Grabbing her phone, she padded back out to the couch. "Who was the plaintiff trying to shoot?"

"Her husband. Thankfully, she missed him but winged the court reporter. It was sometime during the brouhaha when the judge collapsed."

"I may be prosecuting violent offenders in a big city criminal court, but li'l old Resolute always sounds way more exciting." Sara sipped her wine. "Did I tell you I've been assigned my first murder trial?"

"You sound enthusiastic." Cassie's tone sounded the opposite, which disappointed Sara. Usually her friend was her biggest cheerleader.

"I am. It feels good to finally be respected by my boss. For so long, he handed me cases he considered less important. But my conviction rate's impressive, if I do say so myself." She was proud of that rate—not because of the high number, but because the people she put away deserved to be off the streets.

"You always *were* focused on your goals. Your grandfather must be so proud of you."

Sara smiled at that.

"So… I guess I should tell you why I've called." Cassie cleared her throat. "I was hoping I might entice you to take a break from lawyering and come be our replacement judge."

Sara hadn't known what to expect, but it definitely wasn't this. "I've already got a job I love, Cass. And I wouldn't even qualify. I haven't lived in Boone County for the last six months."

"We might have a way around that. Since you officially became involved with the Boone County Youth Program eight months ago, Bree's been receiving mail addressed to you at her place. You'd just need to change your driver's license and voter registration immediately."

"Cassandra Reed!" Sara's voice rang out in her high-ceilinged penthouse. "Are you telling me that you, the most by-the-book stickler I've ever known, are saying you're willing to go *around* something? Bishop must be rubbing off on you."

"I need to run it past the county commissioners, but I'm sure we can make it work. I just wanted to ask you first." Cassie's voice dropped into a whisper. "And off the record, my husband's ability to skirt the rules as a PI might have influenced me a little."

Sara wandered out to her balcony and gazed at the carpet of lights beneath her. She wanted to do her friend a favor, but not at the cost of her own career.

And then there was Nate. Cassie had told her a while back that he'd spent a good portion of the last year or so in Texas, but she hadn't mentioned if he was back in California now. Sara hadn't seen or talked to him since their brief fling a decade ago and wasn't sure how she felt about seeing him now—if he *was* still in Resolute.

She did think about him, though, and probably more often than she should. She'd discovered those first-love feelings and memories never quite disappeared completely, and every time Nate crossed her mind they still tugged at her heart.

"I'm honored that you thought of me, but there's gotta be someone down there who wants the job. What about whoever lost the last election?"

"Judge Harmon has run unopposed every four years for the last thirty-two. No one down here wants to be— Oops. Guess I shouldn't have said that last part. Seriously, you'd love it. There's even a house that comes with the job, so you won't have to rent a place. And it would only be until the next election takes place in a few months."

It wasn't the judicial position Sara was working toward, but it *was* a judgeship. Was accepting the offer enough to give up her career with the DA's office?

Was it enough to risk facing her unresolved emotions about Nate? She'd never told her friend about sleeping with him during that spring-break visit. Maybe because he was Cassie's little brother and Sara had worried it would damage their friendship. Or maybe because she'd always felt a little guilty about how she'd ended things with him.

Sara swallowed the last of her wine. "I'm sorry, but I have to say no. My life is perfect right now. I love living in the city. Plus, I've got a big trial coming up, and there's no way I can back out of it. It'll be the biggest one so far in my career."

"Well, I tried."

"I do appreciate you thinking of me. It's just not a great time to break my momentum at work."

"No worries. I'm glad everything's going so well for you. You're still invited for Thanksgiving if you want to come down and overdose on family."

"Thanks. Sounds like you'll have quite a crowd this year, what with all the pairing-up y'all have been doing lately."

Cassie chuckled. "Yep, the Reed family is growing. But we always have room for you."

Sara gave up on her friend volunteering information about Nate and bit the bullet. "Is Nate still in town for the holidays, or did he have to go back to the coast and miss the feast?" *Hopefully that sounded casual rather than interested.*

"I think he has a quick round trip planned, but he'll be here for Thanksgiving. Unfortunately he'll be heading back to California permanently in December, so he won't be home for Christmas." Cassie sighed. "It's been nice having him around. I'm going to miss him."

"What a shame." *I'll have to face him if I go for Thanksgiving.* "Turkey Day's not for another three weeks, right? Let me check my trial schedule, and I'll let you know if I can make it." Sara's phone beeped with an incoming call. "I have to take this. Talk soon."

She ended one call and accepted the new one. "Hello?"

"Hi, Sara. It's Alton."

She went back inside and closed the sliding glass door to cut off the background traffic noise. Calls from the district attorney were always important, especially on a Friday night. "Alton. What can I do for you?"

"It's about the Singleton trial coming up."

Relieved that she could speak confidently about her preparation, Sara smiled. "I've finished all the—"

"I'm sorry, but you won't be first chair. I'm prosecuting the case."

"I'm almost finished with the trial prep. I planned on working all weekend so next week could be devoted to jury-selection details."

"I appreciate all your hard work, Sara. But I've been instructed to take over."

Sara controlled her anger. "Will I be second chair?"

"I can't have an ADA who accepts plea deals anywhere near the case. It's a delicate situation."

"I've rarely made plea deals, and I definitely had no intention of making one in this case. Singleton belongs in prison." She paced as she spoke. "Look, Alton, I'm ready for this trial. And you know how much it means to me."

"I know. And I *am* sorry. But I just got off the phone with the governor, and he wants an experienced prosecutor who will send the defense attorney home in tears every night. Apparently a senator has been in his ear about this trial." He sighed. "It's all politics, Sara. Nothing against your work or you personally. I promise I'll assign you the next murder trial we get."

She could almost hear the unspoken part of that sentence: *that doesn't involve politicians.*

"Messenger everything you have at home on the case to my home tonight. I need to jump on this immediately."

"I'll do it as soon as we hang up." Sara ended the call before she damaged their working relationship with words she'd regret.

She strode into the kitchen, grabbed the bottle of wine and returned to the couch. Damn him. She refilled her glass and took a long drink of the cold Riesling. She wouldn't cry. She never cried. But she sure as hell wanted to punch something. She'd been working on the Singleton case for months, along with other smaller cases. And now she was supposed to just hand over her piles of investigation and preparation to her boss, who would waltz into the court-room with a slam-dunk case?

She didn't want to do it, but she would. She had to. Because the scumbag defendant needed to be locked up. Because she wasn't about to get blamed for Alton losing the case due to lack of preparation on Sara's part. And because she just wasn't wired that way.

As she walked across the room she called up her favorite Etta James album on her cell and connected to her living room soundbar. Returning to the couch, she picked up the remote for her gas fireplace and turned it on. Listening to the soulful blues, staring into the real flames dancing among the fake logs, Sara considered her options. She wasn't one to make spur-of-the-moment decisions. Her entire life had been planned with care since the day she turned fourteen.

If she swallowed her pride and went back to her heavy workload of small cases, she had Alton's promise of a future murder case. Plus, she enjoyed working with him. She'd made it a practice to never burn bridges behind her, and she dreaded setting fire to the one she had with Alton.

On the other hand, if she took the position in Boone County now, when she returned to Austin with a judgeship added to her résumé her opportunities would be wide open. She could be one big step closer to her dream of being a district judge, like her grandfather had been. Except in Travis County, home of the state capitol.

She grabbed her cell and pulled up her favorites list.

Cassie answered with, "Please don't tell me you can't make Thanksgiving."

"Oh, I'll be there." She would just have to deal with Nate if he was home for the holiday. And if he was still basically living there, well—like Pops always said—never trouble

trouble until trouble troubles you. She took one more sip of liquid courage. "And about that judge vacancy…"

NATE STROLLED INTO the kitchen of the Reed ranch, and all talk ceased. No family dinner had been scheduled, yet Cassie was leaning against the counter, discussing something with Adam and Noah.

"We were talking about how hard it is to find someone to take Judge Harmon's place," Cassie said.

"Have you talked to the county commissioners yet?" Nate picked up the open can of nuts on the counter and shook some into his hand. "Surely someone must want the position and was just waiting so they wouldn't have to run against Harmon."

"I *have* talked to them. But so far no volunteers have stepped forward." Cassie popped a cashew into her mouth. "But it's only been a week since Harmon died. We'll find a replacement."

Nate shrugged. "If they want me to testify for the divorce trial again, it better happen soon. I'm still heading back to California in a few weeks, and I'll be out there indefinitely this time."

"I'm not sure Mitzi's lawyer will call you again as a witness. He wasn't happy with your magnificently vague answer last time, and I'm not sure it matters now that she's charged with attempted murder and aggravated assault." Cassie crunched another nut. "If she doesn't accept a plea deal, her trial for the new charges will be handled by the district court, and we'll all be called as witnesses. But that won't be happening any time soon."

Adam tasted the chili he was stirring, adding in more spices, and changed the topic. "So you think this big contract coming up will put Reed & Franklin Security on the map?"

"We're already on the map, bro." The only thing Nate got defensive about was his company. He and his partner, Matt Franklin, had busted their butts to bring in elite clients who needed bodyguards, security and protection. And word of mouth had done its magic in record time. "But this contract is with a big company with an even bigger budget. We'd be able to hire more security professionals and expand the business."

"I'm proud of you." Cassie's eyes filled with big-sister love. "Dad would be, too."

Nate bit his tongue, not wanting to ruin the evening. He and their father had butted heads often, which was why he'd left town shortly after high school. It was enough that his sister and brothers believed in him. "Did I miss the memo about a late family dinner tonight?"

"It's just siblings. And since when is seven thirty late for any kind of Reed dinner?" Adam put a pan of cornbread into the oven. "At least I don't have to make a special veggie chili for Bishop." He raised a brow toward Cassie.

"Hey, not my fault my husband's a health freak. Speaking of health, isn't it about time to toast ours?"

"Past time, if you ask me." Noah retrieved four longneck bottles of beer from the fridge, pried off the caps and passed them around.

They tipped their bottles toward each other and drank.

Nate finally registered the otherwise quiet house. "Where are Rachel and the kids?"

Adam straightened from checking the cornbread. "She and Bree had some youth program business tonight, and they decided to go out for dinner afterward. And Martina wanted some time with her grandkids."

"Like she doesn't get some every day babysitting." Cassie laughed. "You really lucked out in the future-mother-in-law lottery with her."

"Tell me about it. She loves taking care of Daisy, but there's not much conversation happening with a one-year-old. Now that Brad's in kindergarten, I think she misses spending all day with him." Adam looked at his siblings, all three standing around doing nothing. "Y'all better get cracking on the toppings because this chili is just about ready."

A flurry of cheese grating, jalapeño slicing and table setting commenced. By the time the cornbread and pot of chili were set on the table, everyone was seated except Adam. He ladled his famous Texas all-beef-no-beans chili into bowls and passed them around.

Cassie's phone rang while she was still blowing on her first steaming spoonful. "Be right back." She disappeared into the kitchen.

A few minutes later the brothers heard a whoop, then Cassie returned with a triumphant smile on her face.

"We not only have an additional guest for Thanksgiving, but we've got ourselves a judge."

"That was Sara?" Adam asked.

"Yep." Cassie scooped that first bite of chili into her mouth, following it with a nibble of cornbread.

Noah let out a loud laugh and looked at Nate. "Bro…"

There was only one Sara who Cassie would invite to Thanksgiving. The Sara who was a lawyer in Austin. The same Sara who'd stolen his heart before breaking it more than ten years ago. "Are you talking about Sara Bennett?"

Cassie nodded. "You remember her, right? I brought her home for spring break one year." She took a sip of beer.

Oh, he remembered her all right.

Sara's rejection had happened when he was admittedly immature, when the rest of his life had been in turmoil. He'd felt like a fool, and whether or not she even remembered, he couldn't forget.

Cassie frowned. "It's too bad you'll be leaving for good so soon after she gets here." Then the frown turned into a smile. "But at least you'll have Thanksgiving together."

"Ah, just like Paris." Noah was the only Reed who knew about Nate and Sara's brief romance during her long-ago visit. "You've always had spring break, but now you'll always have Thanksgiving."

Nate avoided his brother's eyes. This was one of the times having a twin in tune with his thoughts sucked.

"When's she arriving?" Adam asked.

"Monday." Cassie reached for her beer. "I hope it's okay—I told her she can stay here until the judge's mansion is ready for her to move into." When Boone County was established in the late 1800s, the first county judge had built an enormous, stately home within walking distance of the courthouse. With no relatives, and serving until his death, he'd deeded the house to the county on the condition it be offered as a home to every subsequent Boone County judge. "We'll need to sort out and pack up Harmon's personal effects and have the place cleaned."

Adam nodded. "We've got the room."

"Perfect." Cassie grinned.

"Yeah. Just perfect." Nate rolled his eyes mentally when no one but Noah caught his sarcastic tone.

His sister looked at him. "It'll give you two a chance to get reacquainted. I think you're the only one who didn't see her when she was here for the youth center ribbon cutting this summer." Cassie pushed back her chair and scooped a second serving of chili into her bowl. "I'm looking forward to catching up with her myself. I guess she's got some juicy stories she can't wait to tell me."

Chapter Two

"Hi, Sara."

The handsome man who opened the Reeds' front door smiled, and Sara forgot to take her next breath. Nate's angled cheekbones and strong jaw had replaced the softer features of his younger self, but she'd recognize him anywhere. Especially since she'd cyberstalked him a little.

Her lips automatically curled into a return smile as she finally sucked in air. "Nate. It's been a long time."

Nate opened the door all the way. "Come on in. I'll grab your luggage for you." He took a step toward the porch as she crossed the threshold.

Turning to face each other so there was room to pass, Sara inhaled his scent. No longer a teenage boy wearing his father's Old Spice to impress a girl, Nate smelled of fresh air and sun-dried laundry.

"There's no need to get it right now." She lifted her gaze, meeting his dark brown eyes. "I may stay at a hotel instead." She moved past him into the living room.

"Unless you want a long commute, the closest you'll come to a hotel are a few rundown motels between Resolute and Victoria. We do have Doc's Motor Court here in town, but I think you'll be more comfortable staying at the house."

"Hmm." Sara gazed at the well-worn leather furniture and wooden beams overhead. More rustic than she was used to, but charming. She'd loved this house the last time she'd stayed here, mainly because of the feeling of family she'd experienced for the first time in her life.

Her own parents had been self-absorbed while playing at being jet-setters, leaving it to the nanny and housekeeper and cook to raise their daughter. But the Reeds were like the families she'd read about in books as a child. The type of family she'd always longed for, even before she'd met them.

"Then I accept the invitation to stay here, as long as I'm not intruding." Sara sat on the couch, unable to relax until Nate sat across from her in a leather recliner. But then she couldn't pull her eyes away from him. He'd had a great physique even when she had first met him. The Henley he wore now revealed even larger biceps than she remembered. His chest, a broad expanse of muscles, stretched the shirt wide before it narrowed and clung to what Sara would bet her favorite pair of Louboutin heels were granite-hard six-pack abs.

"Big change, moving down here," Nate said. "Was it hard giving up the DA position in Austin?"

She hid the momentary spark of surprise that ricocheted through her brain. Though she'd thought of Nate often and Cassie had given her infrequent updates about the Reed brothers' lives, Sara had never imagined *him* knowing anything current about her life.

"It wasn't an easy decision. I enjoyed being a prosecutor. But I'm looking at this opportunity as a means to an end." She brushed at a piece of lint on the sleeve of her cashmere sweater. "And you? Your security company seems to be doing well."

His dark brown eyes widened, and she mentally kicked

herself. Cassie had only mentioned that he had his own business, and that was a few years ago. Sara had kept up with Nate's success by occasional online sleuthing.

He straightened in his chair. "It is. The last year's been difficult, with me spending so much time in Resolute. But between my partner in the office in California and me working remotely—as well as racking up frequent flier miles between here and there—we're still growing." The pride in his voice was clear.

"How did you decide on a career in security?" None of the articles about Nate or his company had mentioned its owner's path to success, other than the note in his bio about a background in security.

"I sort of fell into it." He crossed a boot onto the opposite knee, his thumb tapping a soundless rhythm on the chair arm as he seemed to run out of words.

Lord, save me from lulls in small talk. "How does someone fall into a career like that?"

"I headed west after I graduated, eventually got a job in Vegas as a bouncer. That led to a stint as a bodyguard with a security company. After learning everything there was to learn about the business, a buddy and I opened our own company in Southern California."

"You left Resolute when you were eighteen?" Sara willed her cheeks not to blush as the blunt question left her mouth. Being slightly older than Nate had seemed a big deal back then.

"I turned nineteen that June." His steady gaze bored into her. "A few months after we met."

So he *did* remember. Sara bit her tongue, refusing to be led into a discussion of their past. Best to just forget it. They were older now, wiser, traveling crosswise paths.

"Would you like some iced tea?" Nate's smooth baritone voice yanked her back to the present.

"I'd love some."

He disappeared into the kitchen as Sara sank back into the past.

Despite her instincts telling her she should, she didn't want to forget the past—that week, that night. It had been the first time anyone besides her grandfather had made her feel valued for just being herself. Not for being a good student or an overachiever. Not for being wealthy or having semi-famous parents.

But when spring break had drawn to a close, she'd panicked. She had seen the passionate look in Nate's eyes and known what was coming, just as she'd known she had no time for love. No desire for it. Not when she'd already sacrificed so much, worked so hard. Her life plan had already been set in stone, and she wouldn't allow it to be derailed. Especially by something as capricious as emotions. Still, she never wanted to forget what those emotions had felt like, however briefly they'd lasted.

Sara's phone dinged with a text notification, and a frustrated sigh escaped her as she pulled it from her purse. She'd had several during the drive from Austin, all from her boss. Make that *ex*-boss. And each one a question he could've answered for himself if he'd just read the case notes and research she'd sent him.

But when the screen lit up this time, it wasn't the district attorney.

u can run but u cant hide ill find you

A chill ran up Sara's spine, its icy tendrils reaching out, wrapping around her lungs, squeezing the breath from her.

The other texts she'd received from anonymous numbers had been annoying but harmless. She'd blocked them in the beginning, but each time they continued from new numbers.

This text seemed targeted at her, its message especially disturbing since she'd just left Austin.

Nate set a glass of tea on the table next to her, and still focused on the text, she startled.

"Everything okay?" Nate returned to his recliner.

"Sure." She tossed her phone back into her purse. "The DA I worked for keeps asking me questions about the case I was handling." For some reason, Sara didn't want to tell anyone about the texts. At least, not yet. She needed to think about it, poke it and probe it, try to figure out who was sending them. And why.

Nate's phone rang. "It's Cassie." He answered, and his side of the conversation consisted of a series of *uh-huh*s, *okay*s, and one *sure*. As he ended the call, he met Sara's eyes. "She's stuck on a case out in the boonies and won't make it home as early as she'd hoped. She asked me to take you over to the judge's mansion and see what you think about living there."

"Great." Relieved that she wouldn't be forced to make small talk all afternoon while the troubling text swirled in the back of her mind, Sara took a long drink from her tea, then stood. "Let's go."

As she buckled herself into Nate's passenger seat, she paused. "Wait, did you say *mansion*? Cassie just called it a house."

The corners of Nate's mouth kicked up in a wry grin. "It was considered a mansion in its day."

"How old *is* this place?"

"I wouldn't want to ruin the surprise for you." Nate

glanced at her, a sparkle in his eye. "But hey, it's free." He laughed as he turned from the Reed property onto the public road.

Good Lord. What have I gotten myself into?

Chapter Three

"This is it?" Sara stared out the passenger window at a huge house, set well back on an overgrown lot, about a half mile south of town. "You weren't kidding about its size."

Nate grinned. "It may not be the prettiest house around, but it is big. And that's probably the only drawback about this place—the maintenance. The judge in residence is responsible for the utilities and upkeep. Harmon obviously wasn't taking care of the grounds."

Assuming she'd inherited her parents' lack of nurturing skills, Sara had never owned so much as a single houseplant. "How big is the lot?"

"The house itself is on half an acre. The county owns the lots on either side, each one also half an acre. But they maintain those."

"Or maybe they don't." Sara's gaze drifted to the weeds and wildflowers as far as she could see. Maybe Judge Harmon had just decided to let his yard blend into the rest. She opened her door. "I'll look into local grounds-maintenance companies. Let's hope the interior looks better."

Since this was a temporary position, it made sense to stay here. But the mansion emitted a haunted-house aura, and Sara could imagine curtains of cobwebs and bats in the attic.

She started toward the long concrete walkway to the front porch.

"Wait." Nate grabbed her hand, his touch igniting a warm, tingling sensation. "Let me go first. I want to keep an eye out for rattlers and scorpions."

Eying the overgrowth on both sides of the path, she said, "Be my guest." Living on the top floor of one of Austin's tallest apartment buildings, most of the unsavory pests she'd run into were in the courtroom.

She followed Nate up onto the wraparound porch, and after he unlocked the front door, she walked into a dark foyer. The formal living room to their left was just as dim, and Sara strode across to the front windows and yanked open the heavy drapes. Dust motes danced in the bright sunlight, and she coughed from the stale smell.

After a quick look around at the dated furniture, Sara caught up with Nate, who had flipped up a light switch and wandered off to the right of the foyer. She found herself in an old-fashioned parlor, filled with uncomfortable-looking chairs and a matching love seat.

"Seriously, when was this place built?"

"I don't remember the exact year, but sometime in the late eighteen hundreds." Nate pointed at a small embroidered stool with silk fringe hanging from all four sides. "And it looks like some of this stuff came with the house."

"If not all of it." She dragged her finger through a quarter inch of dust on a hobnail glass lampshade. "Apparently the previous judge didn't spend much time in these downstairs rooms."

"His kids moved away when they became adults, and I imagine after his wife passed, he didn't need all this space."

Nate surveyed the rest of the room. "Harmon was known to be a bit of a tightwad, so I doubt he had anyone come in to clean very often. Also probably why so many furnishings weren't updated."

Sara grimaced as she walked back to the foyer and took in the intricately carved staircase leading to the second floor. "I'm going upstairs."

Nate joined her before she reached the first landing. "Cassie was right about getting a professional cleaning crew in here."

"So he was a widower?" Sara paused at the top of the stairs and peered down the hallway in both directions.

"Yes. His wife died a long time ago. I remember my dad making us all go to the funeral." His tone softened. "First time I saw a dead body."

Her quick glance caught Nate's somber expression. Sara had no idea how many bodies he might have seen since but suspected he was thinking about his father, who'd been murdered the previous year. Wallace Reed had been the county sheriff for probably about as long as Harmon had ruled from the bench.

"I'm sorry I couldn't make it to your dad's service." She wanted to offer a hug but didn't. Best not to complicate their new, tenuous relationship with mixed signals. "Cassie mentioned that Wallace named you as the executor of his will."

"Go figure, right?" Nate twisted his mouth to the side. "I was the only one who didn't get along with him, and he chose me. I don't know…maybe he knew what a pain it was going to be."

"If he left a will, what's making it so difficult?"

"My mom. Dad never divorced her after she left. I doubt she would want anything from his estate since she obviously didn't even want us." He ran his fingers through his hair. "But the probate court ruled that we have to make every possible effort to locate her and get a signed affidavit stating she has no claim."

"Do you know where she's been all this time?"

"I've got Bishop looking for her." He gave her a half-hearted grin. "One of the good things about Cassie marrying a PI."

"Do you know why your dad never divorced her?"

Nate's half smile disappeared completely. "She broke his heart. I think at first he kept hoping she'd come back. As time went on, he probably just didn't want to deal with anything concerning her. So now I have to deal with it." He ran his fingers through his hair again. "That's why I'm flying back and forth so much. If not for handling the estate and trying to help Adam, Noah and Cassie with their grief, I'd have been back in California right after the funeral."

Heading toward the doors to her right, Sara suddenly stopped and faced Nate. "Maybe that's why your dad chose you as the executor."

His brows pulled together. "What are you talking about?"

"You said you stayed to help the others with their grief. What about *yours*?"

"I grieved." Nate shrugged. "But I'd never been as close to Dad as they were."

"Perhaps he knew you'd have to spend more time here, which would give you all a chance to reconnect." She arched a brow. "And maybe he knew you could deal with his estate without being overcome by emotions."

He shook his head. "Wouldn't that mean he thought I didn't love him?"

Sara tipped her head, searching his face. "*Did* you love him?"

Nate scoffed. "Of course I did."

"Have you been able to take care of his will without wallowing in grief?" When she didn't receive an answer, Sara added, "I think your father understood you better than you think. And trusting you with his will was his way of showing that. Showing that he loved you. That he knew you loved him."

While Nate stood as if his boots were nailed to the floor, Sara continued on to the first door and opened it, allowing him a moment to digest what she'd said. She entered a small bedroom, dust covers draped over the furniture. More doors opened onto similar rooms.

She turned and retraced her steps to where Nate still stood. "You going to help me check out the rest of the rooms, or what?" Without thinking, she grabbed his hand and tugged him toward the primary bedroom, trying to ignore the warmth of his fingers as they wrapped around hers.

NATE HAD FOLLOWED Sara's career online for years. But the posted pictures—professional headshots with perfect hair and full makeup—didn't hold a candle to the woman pulling him down the hall.

Her chin-length pale blond hair hung loose, framing her face—which, unless he was going blind, looked completely free of makeup. In jeans and a sweater, though a little upscale for Resolute, she looked ready for a hike in the woods. Exactly like the fresh-faced college student he'd never been able to forget.

Seeing Sara again proved less awkward than he'd imagined. So far, he had managed to avoid becoming tongue-tied in her presence. But he also hadn't planned on spending the whole day with her.

Fortunately, he'd be gone for the next two days, and after that she'd be living in the judge's mansion. Aside from

Thanksgiving next week, they'd have little reason to run into each other before he returned to California for good. If he could just hold on to his cool a bit longer, they'd be out of each other's lives. Their paths were not aligned. Never had been, never would be. And he was fine with that.

As they entered the main bedroom, his nose twitched at the musty scent of the old house combined with dirty clothes piled on a chair.

"This room's going to need some changes." Sara opened one of the two wardrobes standing like sentinels on either side of the bathroom. "I guess if they're deep enough to hold Judge Harmon's suits, they'll work for my clothes. But it's going to be an adjustment from a walk-in closet."

"You could always buy some clothes racks and turn one of the smaller bedrooms into a closet." Hanging around Resolute with too much time on his hands, Nate had resorted to watching home-improvement and DIY shows.

Sara's eyes widened. "That's a great idea. Of course, I won't need as many dress suits here, especially with wearing a robe in court."

"Rumor had it that in the heat of summer, especially when the justice center's air-conditioning had a hard time keeping up, Harmon only wore a T-shirt and boxers under his robe."

She scrunched her nose. "Remind me to buy a new robe." She ambled into the bathroom. "Ooh, they updated in here."

Detecting a sarcastic tone, Nate poked his head into the en suite. "Impressive." A claw-foot soaking tub took up one corner of the large room, adapted to hold a shower head at one end. A plastic shower curtain hung behind the tub. His gaze rested on the sink countertop, littered only with the grooming items of an old man. It reeked of loneliness.

They returned to the first floor and headed to the back

of the house, passing a large formal dining room to their right. The kitchen was on their left, the attached breakfast room behind it featuring a wall of windows looking out on a field of weeds and wildflowers.

Sara flashed a bright smile. "This room will be wonderful once the grounds are cleaned up. But I need to take a better look at that kitchen."

Sara eyed the appliances, her mouth set in a firm line. Though updated since the house had been built, they resembled those of the 1960s instead of the twenty-first century. "I wonder if the wattage can withstand a microwave and an espresso machine."

"We'll check before you plug anything in, but I'm sure they've kept the electrical panel current."

Sara laughed.

Nate raised his brows, puzzled.

"Electrical panel? Current?" She lifted one shoulder in a half shrug. "Hey, it was your pun."

Nate couldn't stop from rolling his eyes. "Unintentional, I assure you."

"Whatever happened to your sense of humor? You used to have a great one." At Sara's reference to the past, an uncomfortable silence descended. She developed a sudden interest in the avocado-green gas stove.

Silently agreeing the past should remain in the past, Nate crossed the kitchen and opened a door. Behind it was a utility room/pantry that sat next to the breakfast room. It held a washing machine, drier and a freezer, and the walls were lined with mostly bare shelves.

"Why is it so cold in here all of a sudden?" Sara leaned in through the doorway.

"Broken window. Be careful—there's glass all over the floor." Nate tipped his head toward the large opening on the outside wall. "I'll board it up before we leave, and we can get a replacement installed when I get back."

"How long do you suppose it's been like this?" Sara wrapped her arms around herself.

"I'm sure it happened since the judge died. Probably kids throwing a ball or something." He glanced around at shards of glass and muddy footprints. "There's no ball, and the window frame is free of glass, so they probably crawled in and retrieved it."

While Sara found a broom and swept up glass, Nate went to the detached garage, converted from the original carriage house, to hunt for a temporary window repair. He didn't want to worry Sara, but something felt off about his kids-with-a-ball theory. Between the high foundation of the house and the height of the window, not to mention no parks or other homes nearby, it was far more likely a vandal had broken out the window.

Nate blew out an exasperated breath. Regardless of who it had been, he'd suggest that Sara remain at the Reed ranch until he had time to check things out more thoroughly.

Coming up with nothing useful, he moved on to a large shed behind the garage that housed a riding mower and other landscaping tools. Finally finding a board large enough to cover the hole, Nate grabbed it, a hammer, nails and a collapsible ladder and rounded the outside of the house. As he propped the ladder against the wall, he noticed a mess of footprints in the ground below the window. More disturbing was the square impression amid them, as if someone had climbed up on something to see inside.

Nate climbed the ladder and began the mindless task of pounding nails, but his mind wouldn't quit working. Nothing of Judge Harmon's appeared to be missing, and other than the glass, no damage was apparent inside the home. So what had this mysterious Peeping Tom been up to?

After the board was in place, Nate returned everything else to the garage and looked around again. Nothing cube-shaped in there seemed strong enough to hold a person's weight. He checked the backyard, then went into the unlocked greenhouse. Besides dead plants in clay pots, standing in rows like gravestones in a cemetery, he spotted an upside-down wooden crate. The boards didn't even flinch when he stepped up on it. Flipping it upright, the top edges were brown with dried dirt.

And just like that, his idea that Sara stay at the Reed house until he returned changed from a suggestion to a demand. He didn't know what was going on here, but it spiked his bodyguard Spidey sense. While he was in California the next day, he'd grab one of his company's state-of-the-art security systems and install it when he returned.

He might've wanted the source of his reawakening emotional turmoil to be out of his life, but he sure as hell didn't want any harm to come to her.

Chapter Four

Early Wednesday morning, Nate sat at their round kitchen table and watched Sara tiptoe from the staircase to the front door, where she set her sneakers.

She turned around and tiptoed halfway to the kitchen before she looked up. "Agh!" She froze for a moment, then continued into the room. "You scared the daylights out of me."

Nate chuckled. "You're quite the early bird, aren't you?"

"Looks like you win the worm, though." Sara took a mug from the cupboard, filled it with steaming coffee and joined him at the table. "I thought you weren't due back until this evening."

"I finished my business meetings sooner than planned and caught an earlier flight. I got in late last night." He'd returned from California ahead of time with the intention of getting the window replaced and alarm installed today. That way Sara could move into the mansion on Thursday, and his life could return to normal. Having her under the same roof, a mere twenty feet away as he'd tried to fall asleep the past two nights, was too much of a distraction for him. *Out of sight, out of mind.* "Did you go back over to the house yesterday?"

"No. I spent most of the day touring the justice center with Cassie, checking out my courtroom and cleaning out the desk in my chambers. After four decades as a judge, Harmon had quite the assortment of personal belongings in his drawers. Not to mention petrified food crumbs, dust bunnies and things I'd rather not mention before breakfast." Sara grimaced. "And I ordered a couple of robes, so I'll be ready to take the bench as soon as I'm sworn in."

The front door opened and closed, and Cassie strode into the kitchen, her Western boot heels clomping across the hardwood floors. "Mornin'."

"Not everyone's awake yet, sis." Nate gave her an admonishing look.

"Well, they should be." She eyed the stairs. "Adam needs to handle the department briefing this morning while Sara and I start packing up Harmon's stuff in the mansion." Her lips pursed, as if disappointed that speaking his name didn't make the second-oldest Reed magically appear. She rounded on Nate. "What are *you* doing here?"

"I live here."

"He got back early," Sara added.

Cassie smiled. "Good. You can help us."

Nate shook his head. "Sorry, I'll be installing a full security system over there today."

When Sara frowned at him, he tried to play off his concern. "Best to err on the side of caution." He cringed internally at the cliché, but he didn't want to alarm her.

"We need to get going." Cassie glanced at her watch. "The cleaning crew will be there soon."

"Thank goodness. I can't wait until the dust and dirt are gone from that place." Sara scrunched her nose in a cute way, and Nate decided he liked it when she did that.

He leaned back in his chair and looked at the two women. "Looks like y'all dressed for the job."

Cassie had on worn denim jeans and a T-shirt. Sara wore a pink shirt tucked into what looked like another pair of designer jeans. Nate almost laughed at the image of a city mouse and a country mouse. But neither of these women were meek little mice. Not by a long shot.

Sara rose and led the way to the front door, where she wriggled her feet into her sneakers without untying them. Nate followed behind Cassie, grabbing his keys on the way out. "I'll stop by that new bakery and grab a box of kolaches on my way over. I should get to the mansion just about the time all the heavy lifting's done." He gave them a Cheshire cat grin when they glanced back at him, all four of their brows raised in a *you'd better be joking* look.

"What?" He was all wide-eyed innocence.

Cassie headed toward her cruiser, raising her hand in an uncharacteristic middle-finger salute. "Make sure at least half are jalapeño sausage with cheese."

"And make sure they're fresh," Sara tossed over her shoulder.

Nate blew out a heavy breath as he closed and locked the front door. Definitely not mice. Whatever the opposite of mice was, that was what those two were.

"THIS IS THE last from the dresser." Sara dropped an armload of T-shirts and rolled pairs of socks onto the bed.

While Cassie packed them into an already half-filled box, Sara rechecked every drawer in the room, both wardrobes and took another look under the bed.

"Looks like we're finished in here."

"Good." Cassie taped the box closed. "This wasn't as hard as going through my dad's stuff, but I'm glad we're through."

They found Nate in the dining room downstairs. A large box of pastries and a pile of napkins sat on the end of the dining room table.

"You buy out the store?" Cassie asked as she picked up a rolled sausage kolache with a napkin. She mumbled something else, but it didn't make it around the mouthful.

Nate grabbed an open-faced one with fruit. "I got enough so the cleaning crew can help themselves, too."

Sara shot him a covert glance, impressed that he'd thought about the others who'd be working here today. As his head pivoted toward her, she dropped her eyes and examined the Czech treats, finally choosing a sausage-filled one. "Thank heavens you got coffee, too." Picking up a to-go cup, she sipped the steaming hot brew, striving for the extreme daily allotment of caffeine she was used to.

A knock on the door announced the cleaning crew's arrival. Sara directed two upstairs to start on the main bedroom and bath. Two more headed into the kitchen, and the other three dispersed to rooms downstairs. Meanwhile, Nate began opening the many boxes he'd brought with him.

"All of these are for the alarm system?" Sara asked.

"I've got cameras, glass-breakage monitors, the alarm panel, backup battery—all kinds of good stuff." Nate smiled up at her, and her mind shut down for a second.

Cassie cocked her head, eying her brother. "Don't you need a Texas license before you can install a security system *in* Texas?"

"Cool your jets, sis. I've got a licensed friend coming by to do the wiring. He'll make sure we're legal."

One of the women working in the kitchen appeared in the dining room doorway. "There's a broken window in the utility room."

Nate continued to unbox cameras. "I boarded it up the other day. The glass guy should be here soon to replace it."

"There's no board over it now." The woman seemed unsettled, her hands wrapped around each other as if she was washing them. "And I guess you've already seen the graffiti on the wall in there?"

"What graffiti?" Sara managed around the small bite of food in her mouth. She headed for the room behind the kitchen.

As she read the message written in garish red spray paint on one of the walls, the blood drained from her head and pooled in her feet. This wasn't the work of ball-playing juveniles. This was from the creep who'd been texting her.

told you id find you

Sara raised one hand to her mouth, her skin icy to the touch.

"The hell?" Nate spent more time studying Sara than the wall. "You look like you've seen the grim reaper."

"What's going on, Sara?" Cassie snapped pictures of the graffiti and empty window opening with her phone. "Do you know who did this?"

Shaking her head, Sara turned and trudged back to the dining room. Cassie dispersed the cleaning crew to other rooms before she and Nate followed.

"I've been getting some weird texts for a while now." Sara fished her phone out of her pocket. "I figured they were just wrong numbers."

"What's weird about them?" Nate asked.

"Up until this week they weren't threatening, they just gave me the creeps." Sara scrolled through her texts. "But Monday I got this one shortly after arriving at your house."

She read the last text out loud: "'You can run, but you can't hide. I'll find you.'"

Cassie held out her hand for Sara's phone. "Have you replied to any of them?"

"No. I didn't want to engage with whoever's sending them. I was afraid even if it was a wrong number, replying might encourage them." She passed her phone to her friend. "I've tried blocking the numbers, but I didn't delete any of them."

Cassie handed the phone to Nate after she'd read all the texts. "We need to arrange security for you. I can make sure one of my deputies is with you at all times. And maybe you should just stay at the ranch instead of—"

"No. I'm not going to run scared, and I refuse to disrupt your family's lives by hiding out in their house. Uniformed deputies attached to me by the hip will only draw more attention. I haven't even been sworn in yet. The county commissioners would probably suggest you send me packing and find another judge."

Cassie crossed her arms over her chest. "As the local sheriff, it's my responsibility to protect the judge of Boone Co—"

"No, Cassie." She planted her hands on her hips. "I don't want to start out on the wrong foot with the whole county. I'll be fine with Nate's alarm system."

Her friend's eyes narrowed, and Sara couldn't tell which way she was going to lean. Finally, Cassie gave a short nod. "Fine. But I *am* going to file a report so we've got a record of this." She jabbed a finger in Sara's direction. "But if anything else happens, I'm doing what I think best."

Sara nodded back, though at the moment she doubted her agreement mattered to her friend, the quintessential sheriff.

"Your swearing in is Monday. Between now and then,

you need to rack your brain for possible suspects. People you prosecuted who went to prison, anyone you know personally who may have a grudge against you, ex-boyfriends whose hearts you broke… I don't care how unimportant they may seem."

Still reading Sara's texts, Nate's gaze jerked up at Cassie's words.

Sara nodded her agreement. "I haven't been able to think of anyone so far, but I'll keep trying."

"Good. And I want you to stay at the ranch until we find whoever's doing this." Cassie took Sara's phone from Nate and gave it back to her.

"I appreciate the offer, but I don't want to impose any longer than necessary. I'm moving in tomorrow so I can get settled and be ready to hit the ground running next week." Sara stood. "End of conversation."

Without taking sides in the discussion, Nate went back to opening boxes. "While my buddy gets this system wired in, I'll go pick up a can of paint to cover the graffiti."

"Thank you. I'd prefer not to look at it every time I walk in there." Sara already felt safer because of all Nate was doing to help her.

"I'm finished packing Judge Harmon's stuff." Cassie picked up one of the boxes they'd brought down from upstairs. "Let's get these in my car. I'll have Helen ship them to his family."

As Nate shoved the last box into the back of the SUV and closed the rear door, Cassie approached Sara with a newspaper in hand.

"I almost forgot to show this to you. You made the front page." Cassie grinned as she held the paper open. "It's just the *Boone County Register*, but I checked online and several other newspapers picked it up. Including the one in Austin."

Sara skimmed the article, naming her as the new county judge. It included a brief biography of her, mentioning her stint as an Austin assistant district attorney. She loved the idea that her ex-boss, who always read the digital edition of the Austin paper, would see this article.

Do you miss me now, Alton?

But as Nate read over her shoulder, another thought occurred to her. She glanced at the top of the page. Sunday's edition. "I wonder if this is how he found out where I am." She met Cassie's eyes and watched as realization dawned.

"It might be. Dadgummit! I should've thought of that."

"Just because you're the sheriff doesn't mean you can connect two completely unrelated things at the drop of a hat. Plus, you just found out about the texts." Sara gave her friend a warm smile. "And I haven't heard that word in way too long."

All three laughed at Cassie's aversion to hardcore swearing.

"Listen, call me immediately if you get another text, okay?"

"I will." The immediate shock from the graffiti had worn off. Sara was certain, between Nate's alarm system and her best friends in town being law enforcement officers, that whoever was bothering her would disappear back beneath the rock they'd crawled out from under.

"And Nate, you don't have to leave town for good until December, right?"

"Yeah?" He drew the word out as if he knew he wouldn't like Cassie's reason for asking.

"Good. Since Sara refuses to stay at the ranch, I want *you* to stay with *her.*"

Nate stared at his sister as if her words made no sense, and Sara's gaze bounced between the two.

Cassie twisted her mouth to the side. "You're a body-guard, right?"

"Yeah, but—"

Poking a finger into her brother's chest to accentuate her words, Cassie said, "I'll have Helen set you up as an approved vendor for the county, with authorized expenses. Because as of this moment, you're officially guarding Sara's body."

"Oh, I don't think that's necessary." Sara's cheeks warmed with embarrassment.

Cassie waved her hand in the air. "Y'all know how I meant that. And yes, Sara, it *is* necessary. You don't want deputies in uniform hanging around? Then you get my brother, the bodyguard."

After Nate made a few false starts with a reply, Cassie planted her fists on her hips and leaned toward him. "Do you *not* think she could be in danger? Do you *not* think she'd be a heck of a lot safer with you protecting her?" She turned her head slightly and gave him the side-eye. "Do you *not* want to do me this favor that will put me in your debt?"

When Nate agreed to do Cassie's bidding, Sara withered on the inside. One of the main reasons she hadn't wanted to stay at the ranch was to avoid Nate. Now she'd be sharing quarters with him. A man with a life waiting for him in California. A man she still found hard to resist. Not for the first time, Sara wondered exactly what she'd gotten herself into.

"OF COURSE, CASSIE." Nate muttered under his breath as he attached a motion-activated light beneath an eave. "Anything for you, Cassie."

He'd been reluctant to become Sara's bodyguard, and

with good reason. He couldn't miss the California meeting for the contract he'd worked so hard to land. And then there was the bruised-ego thing from when the older, sophisticated college girl had stolen his heart, then forgotten about him when she left town. But the Reeds always had each other's backs, so for Cassie's sake, he'd grudgingly agreed.

What really stuck in his craw was that his sister was right. Sara *could* be in real danger, and she *would* be safer with him providing personal security. His main objective until now had been to keep as much distance as possible between him and the woman Sara had become. To stop wondering if her lips still tasted as sweet, if the scent of her skin would still drive him crazy.

But the graffiti upped the ante. In the past, he'd protected an array of clients, and he'd always kept it professional. Holding in his temper when guarding some loathsome billionaire who'd considered him nothing more than a hired gun. Keeping his fly zipped when semi-famous starlets had tried to lure him into their beds.

With his integrity on the line, Nate was always able to set aside his personal opinions—as well as ignore momentary temptations—in order to do the job. Regardless of everything else, leaving someone in the path of peril when he could protect them went against his core beliefs. He'd do the same with Sara. But God help him, his sister had no idea what she'd asked him to do.

"Nate?" Blake, the Texas-licensed alarm installer, stood next to the ladder.

Nate looked down at his friend. "Yeah?"

"Two questions. You want the main control panel in the attic? And how many keypads and where?"

"If the attic picks up a strong-enough signal, then it will work. Otherwise, wherever you think best." Nate shielded his eyes from the late afternoon sun's glare with one hand. "Keypads by the front and back doors, and one in the master bedroom."

"Got it." Blake looked at a paper in his hand. "You sure you want glass sensors by *every* window on the ground floor? The alarm will go off if any of them are opened."

"Yeah, but it won't if someone breaks the glass. There's a box in the dining room with more than enough of them."

Blake scoffed. "Hey, I'm not arguing. You're the one paying for my time." He disappeared around a corner of the house.

Over the past year, Nate had tried a few times to convince Blake to move out to California and work for Reed & Franklin Security. Alarm installations had picked up as crime increased, and his friend was one of the best. But Blake had no desire to leave Texas.

By dinnertime, the window was replaced, the entire alarm system was working and the graffiti was hidden behind two coats of primer. Sara walked into the sparkling-clean kitchen as Nate crouched over the paint can and pounded its lid on.

"Where have you been hiding?" He looked up at her dirt-smudged face.

"I found the door to the attic stairs and went exploring. Even with all the weird stuff taking up space, I'll have plenty of room to move some of the old furniture up there if I decide I just can't live with them. I'm assuming, since they don't belong to me, I can't donate them to a charity. Or a museum." She rolled her eyes, then gave the wall a critical once-over. "I thought you were going to paint it white, not just prime it."

Nate followed her gaze as he stood. "Even though white's the best choice, Cassie said you might want to pick out your own color."

"Really?" Sara beamed. "We get to pick out paint chips?"

"Well, I was thinking *you* could, but since I'll be your shadow for the duration, I guess *we'll* get to." He stepped closer and rubbed his thumb across a black streak on her cheek. "I think the point of bringing in a cleaning crew was so you wouldn't have to."

"Oh." Her grimy cheeks blushed, and she covered them with her hands. "I felt useless sitting around, and I didn't mind helping. But I must be a mess."

She didn't look like a mess. Even covered in dust and dirt, Sara was beautiful. But saying that out loud would blur the line between professional and personal conduct. "You look fine." He checked the clock on the wall. "We better get to gettin'. Adam will have dinner on the table soon."

"Give me a minute. I can't leave looking like this." Sara opened drawers until she found kitchen towels, then held one under the faucet. After scrubbing her face with it, she asked, "Better?"

Nate took the towel from her. "You missed a few spots." Stepping closer, he wiped gently at a speck of dirt on her temple. Her eyelids closed as he tipped her chin up to get at the streak along her jawline.

While he cleaned away a grimy dot on the tip of her small, straight nose, the smattering of freckles across it fascinated him. He paused, and she opened her eyes. They were a light blue, more inviting than pictures he'd seen of the Caribbean Sea. Forcing his feet back a step, Nate willed away the heat building inside of him.

But holding back would take a will of iron. Even though he'd had some difficult, dangerous jobs in the past, this one would definitely win the blue ribbon in Assignments Best Not Taken.

Chapter Five

Friday morning, Sara turned off her alarm and luxuriated in the new king-size bed she'd ordered online earlier in the week. No matter how short a time she'd be in Resolute, she refused to sleep in a small bed with a saggy mattress. Adding a set of sheets had been a good move, since she definitely wouldn't use the old sheets and pillowcases already in the house.

Nate hadn't seemed to mind the furniture in his room. He'd chosen the one closest to hers. For security reasons, he'd said. Didn't mean she hadn't spent far too much time attaching far too much meaning to the choice.

Speaking of security, he'd turned the breakfast room into command central. A folding table had been added to hold multiple monitors. Several showed live-action footage from four cameras each. One large screen showed what was happening as seen from *all* the cameras, and a few more were set up to zoom in on one zone at a time.

It all seemed a bit much for a few creepy texts and one wall of graffiti. Then she remembered how unsettled she'd felt and was secretly glad for the overkill. One thing was certain—she wouldn't be wandering around the backyard in her pajamas anytime soon.

After stretching and yawning for a few minutes, she zipped through her morning bathroom routine, got dressed and headed downstairs. The scent of coffee drew her to the kitchen, where she poured herself a cup from a percolator.

"That's the only thing I could find to make coffee in." Nate stood in the entrance to the breakfast room. "You might want to add a coffee maker to your shopping list."

Sara managed to swallow a small sip before dumping the bitter brew into the sink. She should have brought hers along from Austin. But when she'd heard the word *mansion*, she assumed there'd at least be a decent coffee machine. "Already on there." She was looking forward to today's trip to Victoria. Along with the espresso machine and more sheet sets, she had a long list of other essentials—at least, essential for her—that the mansion lacked. Not to mention a second list of groceries that she doubted the local store carried.

"You ready to go?" Nate set his cup in the sink.

"I am if there's a fast-food joint on the way. I'm not used to starting out my day with no caffeine." After pulling on her jacket to ward off the early morning chill, she grabbed her keys from the long console table in the foyer.

"There is, and you don't need your keys. I'm driving."

"Look, I appreciate you protecting me, but I'm perfectly capable of driving." Sara raised her brows. "Or does it threaten your masculine ego to ride shotgun while a woman drives?"

Apparently not to be outdone, Nate's single brow arch gave off a tuxedoed super-spy vibe. "My masculine ego thrives when I'm in a passenger seat. It leaves my hands free for other things."

Her gaze dropped to his hands, her mind picturing his arm lying across the center console, his fingers on her right thigh. She cursed her fair skin when her cheeks started to burn.

"But not when I'm on duty. I don't question your ability behind the wheel, but if the need arises for evasive driving, I doubt you'll match my skill."

"Fine." She set the keys down. She was irritated by him calling the shots, aggravated by her brief but sensual imagining and extreme caffeine deprivation. When her stomach growled, she settled on hangry. "But I need food and coffee. Now."

A smile toyed at the corners of Nate's mouth, which irritated her even more, and when he opened the door Sara breezed past him.

He escorted her to the garage, where he'd parked his truck. Her vehicle was parked in the street due to a single-car driveway and, as Nate had explained it, so no one could tamper with his—nothing personal. "After I open the door, wait for me to clear it before you go in."

The garage doors were locked, and the building had no windows. Using her abilities learned during court trials, she waited patiently without rolling her eyes or heaving heavy sighs. From an early age, Sara had been in control of her own life. Apparently Nate had become a bit of a control addict himself—at least, when he was working security.

With the graffiti gone and the alarm system installed, her fear had dissipated. But if Nate insisted on playing bodyguard and shadowing her every step, fine. She'd see how much he enjoyed her day-long shopping extravaganza. He wouldn't know what hit him.

NATE RELAXED BACK against the vinyl booth seat and exhaled while Sara gave the Busy B Café's menu a quick look. Then she picked up her phone, and her thumbs hadn't stopped moving since.

"Something urgent?" Raised in a family of law enforcement officers, he was used to phones being answered during meals. But her phone hadn't rung, and he was starting to feel ignored.

Without lifting her eyes, Sara replied, "Hmm?"

He had to hand it to her, her focus was impressive. A glance at his watch told Nate they'd shopped for seven hours straight and hadn't even made it to the grocery store. With nothing to cook at the mansion, Sara had insisted they eat here before hauling home her truckload of purchases. She was just lucky he had a crew-cab pickup. Leaving expensive stuff in an open truck bed while shopping for more expensive stuff was never a good idea.

Marge, owner of the Busy B and gossiper extraordinaire, set two mugs on the table. "You kids want coffee?" She smiled knowingly at his slumped posture against the booth seat. "Looks like *you* need some, Nate."

He nodded. "Marge, this is Sara Bennett, our new county judge. Sara, Marge here—"

Sara finally looked up from her phone. "Marge!" She stood from the bench seat in one smooth move and hugged the older woman. "It's so good to see you again."

"You too, honey." Marge set the coffee carafe down and took hold of Sara's shoulders, giving her a once-over. "You look fit as a fiddle in a bluegrass band. I heard you were comin' to town on a temporary-permanent basis."

Nate filled his mug from the carafe. "And I guess you two already know each other."

Both women looked at him as if he'd had two heads.

"Of course we know each other." Marge scoffed. "Cassie brought Sara in here years ago when she came to visit y'all."

"And I made sure to stop by for one of Marge's magic milkshakes when I was in town this past summer for the youth center grand opening." Sara gave Marge another hug before she slid back onto her seat. "Highlight of my trip."

Marge beamed as she picked up the carafe. "So what'll it be tonight? Coffee or a milkshake?"

"Umm…" Sara glanced back at the menu.

Nate piped up. "I'll have a double cheeseburger with fries. And the coffee."

"That sounds good. I'll have the same, but just a single. Fries and a chocolate shake."

"Comin' right up. I'll send over a couple waters, too." Marge winked at Sara as she picked up the menus. "Seein' as my shakes are so thick, you can hold 'em upside down without a drop hittin' the tabletop." Her laugh accompanied the squeak of her orthopedic shoes on the linoleum floor as she headed for the kitchen.

"I could've kept shopping until the stores closed if I hadn't gotten so hungry." Sara studied Nate, her lips twitching. "But you look exhausted."

Hoping the steam from his coffee was infused with caffeine, Nate inhaled it as he stared at her over his mug. "Can't imagine why."

Sara Bennett would own a gold medal if shopping ever became a competitive sport. First, they'd gone to the free-standing stores that carried linens, small kitchen appliances, electronics and items to organize all the other stuff she'd bought or was about to. While she had pointed to or handed him items, he ferried them to the cart, which she'd left for him to push. Just in case he needed to practice his evasive maneuvers, she'd told him.

Then they'd gone to the mall. Who knew one place could have so many shoe stores? Granted, she did need more appropriate footwear for country living, and her sensible choice of work boots that would stave off a rattler's fangs, along with a fashionable pair of Western boots that didn't scream *city slicker*, impressed him. But only the threat of accompanying her into the dressing room—for her own safety, of course—had put the kibosh on clothes shopping.

"Need a top-off?" April, the newest server in the diner, stood ready with a fresh pot of coffee and a shy smile. Marge had hired her after Rachel, Adam's fiancée, quit to work full-time with the county youth program. She was young and, according to Marge, had a huge crush on Nate.

"Please." He pushed his mug closer to her and gave her a friendly smile.

When the server reached for Sara's mug with her brows raised in question, Sara held her hand over it. "I appreciate you offering, but I'm waiting for one of the best chocolate milkshakes in the world."

April nodded. "OMG. Aren't they the most delicious things you ever tasted? We get to eat for free after our shifts, and I *always* get a milkshake." Her grin was almost too big for her face. "Just a milkshake." As she spoke, her gaze kept drifting to Nate.

"Now you're just making me jealous." Sara grinned back. Once April moved on to the next table, Sara shifted her gaze to him, her smile now smug.

"What?"

"I think she likes you."

"Who likes him?" Marge set their plates on the table.

"The waitress who just stopped by." Sara aimed her little twisted grin at the older woman.

Marge took a quick look around the room. "April? Oh, sure—I've told him that." She placed a milkshake in front of Sara, then glared at Nate. "And I've also told him I won't allow any cradle robbing of my employees."

Nate dropped the french fry he was holding onto his plate and met Marge's eyes. "And I've told Marge I have no interest in her employees."

"Then reserve that thousand-watt smile and dimples-to-die-for for someone you *are* interested in." Marge let out an exaggerated sigh. "I swear, every time that girl waits on you, her mind disappears for the rest of the day."

Nate pressed both hands to his chest. "How is this all *my* fault?"

"Nate's right, Marge. He can't help it that he's so darn adorable." Sara unwrapped her straw. "And to be honest, he didn't even look at her."

"Well, that's a good thing. Keep it that way." She turned and winked at Nate, then headed toward the front counter.

Sara frowned. "I don't know Marge very well, but I can't believe she thinks you'd flirt with someone that young."

"She doesn't." Nate chuckled. "Marge is Cassie's adviser, Adam's biggest fan and Noah's defender when it comes to his antics. Me, she likes to tease. As soon as she noticed April's interest in me, it became her latest favorite topic."

"How old do you think she is?" Sara sucked milkshake through her straw.

"April?" He shrugged. "I don't know. I'd guess eighteen, nineteen." He took a bite of burger and chewed while Sara looked up at him from beneath hooded eyes, still sucking on her shake.

She was probably getting at something to do with age and…flirting and maybe something else, but for the life of him he couldn't concentrate enough to figure it out. Her pursed lips surrounded the tip of the straw that she held between her thumb and first two fingers. And with each draw, her cheeks disappeared inward. He shifted slightly on the bench, watching her throat work as she swallowed.

Then, apparently oblivious to the effect she'd just had on him, she said, "So, about the same age you were when I met you." Her brows pulled together in a troubled frown.

"There's a hell of a difference between three years and ten or eleven years." Nate set his burger down and wiped his hands on a napkin. "Is that why you ghosted me after spring break? You thought you were *robbing the cradle*?"

Sara glanced past his shoulder. "Let's discuss this another time."

An elderly man stopped at their table and after a small nod toward Nate, turned to Sara. "Excuse me for interrupting your meal, but are you our new judge?"

"Yes, I'm Sara Bennett." She reached out to shake hands. "It's nice to meet you, Mr...?"

He pumped her hand. "Dodson. Fred Dodson."

"Nice to meet you, Mr. Dodson."

"Please, call me Fred." As Sara eased her hand out of his, he continued. "I must say, you're a sight easier on the eyes than old Harmon was." Still leaning toward her, Frank winked. "I hope we'll see you at the weekly church pancake breakfasts. We've got an open seat for you at the mayor's table."

"Thank you very much. I'll need to check my schedule." Patting her stomach, she added, "And I'm afraid I wouldn't fit behind the bench if I indulged *every* week." Sara chuckled, and the old man ate it up.

"Aw, hell, if Harmon could fit back there, ten of you could." Frank laughed. "Well, I better let y'all get back to your dinner. And I'll look forward to seeing *you*—" he pointed at her "—at breakfast." He shuffled back in the direction he'd appeared from.

"Talk about robbing the cradle," Nate muttered, and Sara choked back her laughter until Fred was out of earshot. When it finally broke loose, Nate joined her.

He'd assumed the town wouldn't be receptive to a citified female judge after almost a half century with a good ol' boy on the bench. But it was impressive how well Sara was already managing to connect with the locals. Marge, April and Fred Dodson loved her. All of his siblings loved her.

Now Nate's only problem, besides keeping her safe, was to avoid downing the Sara-Bennett-love-potion drink mix. Because Lord knew it would be a disaster to fall in love with her. Again.

DURING THE DRIVE home from the diner, Sara refused to let Nate's silence dampen her mood. "I can't believe I got everything on my shopping list today."

"Except food." His droll tone made her chuckle.

"We can zip back over to Victoria tomorrow morning and take care of that." She pulled her phone out of her purse. "I don't suppose there are any grocery stores that deliver to Resolute."

Nate looked at her with a blank expression. "From Victoria?" He scoffed. "You sure you can survive here for a few months?"

She rolled her eyes. "Like you don't enjoy *your* creature comforts when you're in California? Yet you seem to transition pretty smoothly from expensive suits to jeans and T-shirts."

The truck bumped over the edge of the driveway, and Nate shifted into Park but left the engine idling. He shifted sideways to face her. "I don't wear expensive suits unless I have to. And how would you know what I wear in California?"

For someone who spoke with precision in a courtroom,

every word weighed and measured before it left her mouth, Sara couldn't seem to keep her foot out of said mouth when it came to small talk with Nate.

"I must have seen a picture of you on Cassie's phone." She tried to pass the fib off with a shrug. "Not that it matters." She crossed her arms when his eyes narrowed. "My point is I'd wager I can adapt to my environment just as well as you can."

Nate held her gaze a moment longer, then opened his door. "Stay in the truck until we're parked inside." He climbed out, surveyed the front yard, then unlocked and opened the garage.

Even with the embarrassment from her verbal blunder, followed closely with aggravation at being ordered around by him on *her* temporary property, Sara couldn't pull her eyes away from Nate. The muscles across his broad back flexed and stretched as he lifted the heavy door, and unbidden memories surfaced. Memories she'd tried to erase for years.

Nate got back into the truck and eased it forward into the garage. Sara jumped out the second the engine cut off and grabbed a few bags from the back seat. As she strode toward the house, he rushed to keep up.

"You can't just take off like that." He unlocked the front door, ushered her inside and disarmed the alarm. "Stay here while I clear the house."

"Seriously? Wouldn't the alarm have gone off if anyone broke in?" Sara continued into the dining room, where she set her purchases on the table.

"Damn it!" Nate did a quick walk-through of the downstairs before returning to her. "You *have* to do what I say if you expect me to keep you safe."

About to vent her frustration, Sara realized she was

going about this all wrong. "You're right. I'm sorry." She headed for the front door.

"Where do you think you're going?" His long legs got him there before her.

"To get my stuff out of your truck."

"No. You stay inside, where I know you're safe." Nate, obviously thinking he had the upper hand, smiled at her sudden cooperation. "I'll bring in the rest."

Sara nodded in agreement, and while Nate carried in load after load of bags and boxes, she remained at the long table, unpacking everything.

"Did you have to buy the biggest, most expensive coffee-and-espresso machine in the store?" he asked as he walked into the kitchen.

"You'll thank me tomorrow morning."

"You're going to contaminate that shiny new toy with our old, stale coffee?" He trudged past her for the ump-teenth time.

Sara glanced up from the new towels she was sorting into stacks. "Darn, that's right—I've got fresh coffee on my grocery list. Oh, well. You'll thank me *Sunday* morning."

"Whatever you say," he muttered.

Who's following whose orders now?

A few minutes later, the garage door closed with a thump, and Nate delivered the last of her purchases to her. He disappeared into the kitchen, then returned with a flash-light. "Back in a minute. I just need to check something."

Finally ready to acknowledge her exhaustion, Sara collapsed onto a chair as the front door opened and closed. She should've felt guilty about making Nate do so much of the heavy lifting, but this whole protection thing seemed more unnecessary by the day. She hadn't even gotten a text since the one on Monday. And having to answer to someone constantly, especially in her personal life, got her hackles up.

The door opened and closed again, the alarm panel buttons beeped and Nate's quick footsteps carried him into the room. "We need to go upstairs."

"I'll wait here if you feel a need to *clear* the second floor. I'm bushed."

"*Now*, Sara." He rounded the table and pulled her into a standing position. "I want to check the security footage."

"Why?" The bold confidence in her belief she was safe left her like the air in a popped balloon. "What's wrong?" She allowed Nate to grab her hand and lead her up the stairs.

"Someone slashed all four of your tires."

Chapter Six

"All rise!"

Tuesday morning, Nate was standing in the judge's door-way, watching Sara enter the courtroom, her blond hair shining in the light pouring down from the high windows. After driving back to Victoria on Saturday morning for groceries, they'd hunkered down in the house for the rest of the weekend, careful to stay out of each other's way.

"Boone County Court is now in session. The Honorable Judge Bennett is presiding." The bailiff looked out over a packed gallery of gawkers, her stern voice at odds with the general atmosphere of curiosity and comical anticipa-tion. The spectators, not just from Resolute but the entire county, were here to see the new judge in action as well as watch a trial about geese.

Sara took her seat, and the bailiff finished with, "Be seated."

Nate slipped in and took up a position off to the side of the bench. A perfect spot to see the entire room and still be close enough to protect Sara if the stalker tried to get to her.

The attorneys approached the bench to speak quietly with Sara, and Nate scanned the room, studying every face, searching for furtive movements. His eyes still burned from the long hours on his computer over the weekend, investigating Sara Bennett. She didn't have social media accounts—most likely a smart move for a prosecutor. But inmates with contraband cell phones managed to post in various places, and the comments he'd found about Sara made his fingers curl into a fist.

For some reason, his usual ability to compartmentalize work and his personal life was failing him. He'd like to blame it on exhaustion, but Sara was right—the new espresso machine was amazing, and he'd spent the past weekend running searches on a full tank of caffeine.

During breaks from his research, he'd reviewed recorded footage from the property. The only item of interest so far had been the short, stocky person on foot approaching Sara's car shortly after they'd left to go shopping. But the guy had successfully hidden his identity by wearing a hoodie pulled over his head, and with no other houses on that block, he didn't have to worry about explaining the ski mask that covered his face.

And whenever Nate gave his eyes a break from the monitors, he had spent the time calling Cassie and Adam. Requesting arrest and court records for everyone Sara had prosecuted took time and resources he didn't have.

"Bailiff, please bring in the plaintiff and defendants." Sara's clear voice, sharper and louder than the one she used when off the clock, silenced the murmurs filling the room.

What would normally have been the jury's entrance was opened for Abby Parsons and Ray and Ruth McNulty. Apparently the court personnel had to switch things up due to the crowd in the hallway still trying to get a seat.

Nate didn't know a lot about judges trying civil cases, but he figured there had to be a learning curve. Sara had no experience in that and hadn't had much time yet to study up on it. He hoped today was a success for her, even while keeping his expectations low. And those expectations bottomed out when the McNultys entered the courtroom, each leading a goose by a short red leash.

His gaze shot from the geese to Sara, and he rolled his lips between his teeth to keep from laughing out loud. She managed to cover her mouth with a finger as if in deep thought, but her wide eyes gave away her shock. While the defendants took their seats, she shot Nate a sideways glance. All he could do was smile.

One corner of her mouth twitched behind her finger.

Abby Parsons's lawyer began his opening statement. It seemed this case dealt directly with the situation involving Noah and his then partner, now fiancée, Bree, from earlier this year. Their call out to the McNultys about a trespasser held at bay by a gaggle of geese had been Bree's first experience with the ornery birds. It was a hilarious story Noah still enjoyed teasing her about.

But the disclosure about the Widow Parson's affair with Ray McNulty didn't come out until the defense attorney's statement. The spectators, most of whom already knew about the extra-marital relationship, still oohed and aahed as the juicier details were revealed. They'd come to watch the new judge, but two live geese and adultery now held their attention.

Taking the stand, Abby vowed to tell the truth before launching into a fabricated version of the day Ruth's geese had attacked her. The room filled with giggles and snorts as she described Ruth McNulty leading her gaggle of geese in an assault on the poor, defenseless widow. "And what's more, I did *not* have an affair with Ray McNulty."

Even if Nate hadn't heard the goose story directly

from Noah, Ray and Abby's affair was public knowledge around Resolute.

As Abby began recounting all her alleged injuries, Sara said, "Thank you, Mrs. Parsons. I've already reviewed the list you submitted through your attorney. If there's no other *new* testimony, I'll hear from the defendants now."

Abby rose. "I'm sure if Judge Harmon was still here, he'd be much more interested in *my* side of the story."

"That may be, Mrs. Parsons. Then again, I've heard Judge Harmon was a stickler about perjury and procedures." Sara lifted a brow toward the geese. "It seems we're playing a little fast and loose on both today."

Nate mentally applauded her, and based on the nodding heads and murmurs, it looked like quite a few others were as well.

Cassie slipped into the courtroom and stood against the back wall. When she asked *How's it going?* by raising her brows, he gave her a thumbs-up.

Ruth McNulty now sat in the witness box, one of the geese on her lap.

"Is that one of the geese that allegedly attacked the plaintiff?" her lawyer asked.

"Yes. This is Greta."

"Why do you have her with you today?" The attorney kept his distance.

"To show that my geese aren't aggressive unless they're being threatened or they're protecting me." She ran her hand across Greta's back. "The only reason they chased that bi—"

"Mrs. McNulty." Sara's loud interruption caused the goose to twist its neck and stare at her. "Watch your language in my courtroom."

"Sorry, Your Honor." Ruth ducked her head, the picture of contrite. "The only reason my babies chased Mrs. Parsons was because she'd trespassed onto my property. They're kinda like guard dogs. They know who belongs there and who don't, and *she*—" Ruth pointed at Abby "—don't." Her venomous glare was far more convincing than her apologetic expression just seconds earlier.

Abby glared right back.

"That harlot was trying to meet Ray for a *sexual rendezvous* when my geese just did what they're supposed to do," Ruth continued, skirting the edge of profanity. "Protect me from nasty predators trying to get their hands on what's *mine*."

Abby stood, hands on hips. "She's the one who sent me the message to come over, pretending to be Ray." She stomped one high heel on the hardwood floor. "That's entrapment, you old windbag."

Greta hissed and slipped off of Ruth's lap, loose leash trailing behind her. Before the bailiff could reach the bird, it took off at a waddle-sprint toward Abby, its wings spread wide. Abby's high-pitched shriek echoed through the courtroom as she clambered up onto the attorney's table. Ray's goose yanked loose from his tether and headed down the center aisle, hissing at spectators. When one woman jumped up and ran for the door, the goose pumped its head up and down, then took chase.

Chaos erupted.

"Good grief." Nate kept his eyes trained on Sara, not liking the sudden bedlam and what it meant for his ability to protect her if needed.

He watched as Sara picked up her gavel, ready to bang it for the very first time. Probably something every judge remembered for the rest of their life.

But when she pounded the gavel on its base, it exploded

in a cloud of smoke and sparks. Nate raced toward the bench, vaulting the witness stand to tackle Sara to the floor and cover her with his body.

"Are you all right?" His hands patted down her robe, searching for hot sparks. "Were you burned?" Satisfied she was unharmed, he stopped his body search and looked into her fear-filled eyes.

Her lips parted and closed a few times, but she seemed unable to speak.

A few minutes later, Cassie crouched down next to them. "Nate, is she okay?"

Sara's frozen gaze shifted toward her friend. "Isn't this how the last judge died?"

"Not exactly." Nate shifted to his knees and pulled Sara into a sitting position. "What the hell happened, Cass?"

"It looks like some sort of chemical was applied to the gavel. Or its base. Or both." Cassie's nostrils flared, and Nate knew she was mentally berating herself for this happening to her friend under her watch.

So was Nate.

"Noah's collecting all the pieces in an evidence bag. We'll have Forensics examine them, identify the substances." Cassie stood. "I had the bailiff clear the room and I told the McNultys and Ms. Parsons that you'll reschedule their trial, but no geese allowed next time."

Cassie nodded.

"Nate, we'll wrap up things here while you get Sara home." Tracking everyone's movements, she didn't look at him when she asked, "You want a deputy to accompany you?"

"Couldn't hurt." He wrapped his arms around Sara and lifted her to her feet.

Cassie nodded and headed back toward the almost empty gallery.

Nate, arms still around Sara, walked her into the judge's chambers and closed the door. She leaned against him, her body trembling.

Why is my *heart racing?*

He'd been in shoot-outs, run off roads and chased by a pack of man-eating dogs with a lower pulse rate. The only variance in this situation was Sara.

"You're in shock." He steered her toward a chair. "You should probably sit—"

"I don't want to sit down." Sara stepped out of his arms. "And I'm *not* in shock. I'm furious!"

Nate expelled a heavy breath. "I cleared that courtroom, but I didn't pick up the gavel. I should have, and I'm sorry."

"If you had, you might've been seriously hurt." Sara's eyes softened. "I'm glad you didn't."

"But that's my job. I promise, I'll get to the bottom of this."

"*You* will?" Sara's eyes morphed back into icy blue glaciers. "This was *my* moment, my first time on the bench, damn it. And some sick jerk with an unknown vendetta ruined it. And if that wasn't enough, that was my grandfather's gavel he blew up. Pops gave it to me when he retired as a symbol of his faith in me, in my plan to become a judge someday." Her eyes filled with tears, but she blinked them away. "I'm going to find that sorry excuse for a human being, and when I do, he won't know what hit him."

And apparently I still suck at reading women's emotions.

Sara began unbuttoning her robe.

Nate gestured toward it. "At least that didn't catch fire."

"And do you know why?" She arched a brow, a satisfied smile playing on her lips. "Because this tropical wool material—" she shrugged out of the robe and held it toward him "—that you thought was ridiculously expensive is not only comfortable in any climate but also flame retardant. Unlike that cheap polyester one you suggested."

If there was one thing Nate had learned during his short-term relationships with women, it was when to keep his mouth shut.

"I need to splash some cold water on my face, then I'm ready to go."

"Wait!" Nate strode past her, chastising himself for not having cleared the restroom the minute they'd entered her chambers. He pushed the door open, flipped on the light and froze.

The message he saw in the mirror had been written on the wall next to the door. He tried to fill the doorway so Sara wouldn't see it, but it was too late.

"Nate?" She was right behind him, trying to shove him out of the way. "What is that?"

He stepped into the restroom so she could get past him, then they both stared at the wall. This message looked like it had been written by a finger dipped in red paint, but the metallic scent told Nate it was blood. The fact it wasn't dry yet meant they'd missed the stalker by minutes, if not seconds.

still got all your fingers?

Chapter Seven

"You ready to roll?" Sara handed Nate a cup of coffee when he walked into the kitchen. Having just finished her first week as a judge, she was more than ready to spend the weekend whittling down her to-do list.

Nate scrubbed his fingers through his hair, leaving tufts sticking out in every direction. "*More* shopping? Every day after court, we've run by the hardware store or general store to pick up something else for your master plan to make over the house. What else could you possibly need?"

"I'll show you." She took hold of his shoulders, turned him about-face and nudged him across the hall to the dining room.

Nate walked along the table, taking stock of all the small sample cans, paint swatches and assorted supplies. Large gallons of paint sat on the floor along the wall. "Let me guess—you changed your mind on the colors and want more samples."

"Not yet." Sara waited for him to turn around, then thrust her hand out from behind her back, holding a paint roller. "This is for you. Get it? Ready to roll?" She snickered.

Nate lowered himself onto a chair and set his coffee mug

on the table. "You're really going to put to me to work on a Saturday? There's a hockey game I was planning to watch."

Sara folded her arms across her chest. "If I have to stay cooped up in this house indefinitely, except for being chauffeured back and forth to the courthouse, I intend to fix it up to my liking. And if you're going to stay in this house to protect me, you're darn right I'm putting you to work."

After glaring at her for a moment, Nate's shoulders sagged in resignation even while the set of his jaw remained mutinous. "Fine, but I'm having breakfast first."

"That's a good idea." Hiding her satisfied grin, she added, "We both should start the day well-fueled. I'll have whatever you're having."

He didn't utter a word, but as he passed her on his way to the kitchen, his comical side-eye said it all.

"Thank you," she called after him in a sweet voice.

He mumbled something she didn't catch, and she decided it was best that way.

An hour later, plastic lay across the kitchen appliances and counters, tape covered the natural-wood moldings, and Nate was indeed rolling. He stepped back from the wall and tipped his head to the side. "I still think we should just paint it white."

"White's boring. A kitchen should be happy and cheerful." Sara stepped back from the wall she was working on, admiring the pale yellow.

"This isn't what I'd call sunny."

"It doesn't have to burn your retinas to brighten a room." She set her roller in its tray. "This is the perfect shade. Like a few drops of juice from a lemon were squeezed into a can of white paint."

Nate rolled his eyes. "Two words—*resale value*."

"Where'd you come up with that?" Sara handed a bottle of water to Nate before unscrewing the cap on another for herself.

"I told you," Nate said, carefully cutting a line of paint around the windowsill. "I've watched a lot of DIY and house-flipping shows."

"First of all, I'm just moving in. I shouldn't have to be considering resale value." She rolled her eyes, even though he wasn't looking at her. "And second, this house will never be sold. It's the judge's mansion, remember? The next judge can paint the walls whatever color they like."

After a few minutes of silence, with each of them facing opposite walls as they painted, Nate said, "You really were impressive in court this week. Would never have known it was your first time on the bench."

Was Nate extending an olive branch?

"Thank you," Sara replied without turning around. More silence before she continued. "You've been doing an excellent job at keeping me safe. I can see why your company is so successful."

"It's been easy since you started cooperating more." An awkward pause, as if he realized how that sounded. "But thanks."

"At least there haven't been any texts lately." Sara wasn't sure if that was a good or bad thing. She didn't miss receiving them, but oddly, the more time that passed with no stalker incidents, the twitchier she became.

She held her breath whenever her phone beeped. She peeked outside from between parted curtains before stepping through the front door. And it infuriated her. She resented having her life disrupted by a veritable embodiment of evil.

After inhaling and exhaling a few deep breaths, Sara brought her thoughts back from the dark side. Having no control over the stalker situation, she needed to focus on things she *could* control. And one of those happened to be the house. She found the idea of living here for a few months without making it at least somewhat her own unacceptable.

When they were finished painting the kitchen, Sara asked, "Want a sandwich for lunch?"

"Sure." Nate put everything with paint on it into a bucket. "I'll take these outside and hose them off."

Sara juggled an armload of sandwich makings to the dining room table from a cooler she'd loaded earlier. With most of the kitchen covered with plastic tarps, she'd planned ahead. By the time Nate came back in, two plates of food rested on new placemats and Sara sat patiently in front of one. She'd set two bottles of iced tea on coasters.

"Wow. This looks great." He slid into the chair across from her and picked up half of his sandwich in one smooth move. "You know, I think you were right about that yellow after all. It does make the room more cheerful."

Sara opened the bag of chips and shook some onto her plate. "Exactly. The white felt drab."

"And the best thing about it—" he shoved a chip in his mouth "—it coordinates so well with the green stove."

She chuckled. "You jest, but maybe that's why I chose yellow."

After a few minutes of silence while they ate, Nate said, "Mind if I ask you something?"

The bite of sandwich sliding down Sara's throat landed in her stomach like a rock. In her experience, any question that needed permission to be asked usually led to an uncomfortable conversation. "Ask away."

"Why is becoming a district judge so important to you?"

Sara toyed with a chip on her plate. Her career choice

certainly had nothing to do with her parents. Their only influence had been setting an example of what *not* to do with her life, and she avoided discussing them whenever possible. It might've been water under the bridge, but it was filthy water.

"I guess for me, it started when I was a kid. Some of my happiest moments were during the summers I spent with my grandfather. Back then he was a district judge in Hudson County, northwest of Austin, and he often let me go to court with him when I was staying there." She looked up to find Nate watching her as if hanging on her every word. "I loved everything about it. The stately old building, the reverential silence in the courtroom—even the desk in his chambers, always neat and orderly."

Nate nodded as if he understood. "So you wanted to make him proud by following in his footsteps?"

He doesn't get it after all. And she wanted him to understand it, to understand her. "I'm not going to lie and say his pride in me means nothing. But that wasn't why I wanted to become a judge." She sipped tea, searching for the right words. "Pops has always been a virtuous man, with a strong moral compass. He was a fair and honest judge, strict but also compassionate, making sure justice was served but not abused. *That's* what motivated me to become a judge. I don't want to just squander my life away, accomplishing nothing of value. I want to make a difference in the world, like he has."

"He sounds like one hell of a man." Nate's sincere tone warmed Sara. "I'd like to meet him someday."

"He is." Sara smiled. "And you might if I can convince him to come visit me while I'm here. And, um, if you happen to be in town at the same time."

Nate popped another chip into his mouth. "The day you

arrived, you mentioned that taking this *county* judge position was a means to an end. You really compare living in Resolute to paying your dues?"

Sara puffed out her cheeks, annoyed with herself. She hadn't meant to belittle Nate's hometown. "I didn't mean it that way. There's nothing wrong with being a county judge in a small town. I guess I'm looking at this as a stepping stone on the way to the goal I've had since I was twelve."

"Then this doesn't *have* to be a stepping stone. I get that there are different types of courts, but you've already attained your dream of becoming a judge. And a respected one in record time, no less. Seems like everywhere we've been around town, folks like you. You've got friends." His lips kicked up at the corners. "You even have your very own lemonade-painted house. Who in their right mind would leave all of that?"

"Big talk from a man about to move to California." Sara kept her tone light, but she watched Nate closely. Since he'd be heading back to the Golden State soon, why did he care if she stayed in Resolute or not?

After pushing his plate back, he tapped a beat on the table edge with his thumbs. "Well, technically I already moved there. I'm just returning."

"Why there? What's the SoCal pull that you can't resist—the weather, the wealth or the women?"

A full-bodied laugh broke out of Nate. "I just happened to be on the West Coast when I started my company." He stood and stacked the dirty plates together, effectively ending *that* portion of their conversation without answering her second question.

What a hypocrite. Clearly it was fine for the big, bad bodyguard to poke into her personal business, but when it came to revealing anything about himself, all he gave her was a cold shoulder.

Fine. Who cares what the attraction to California is about?

Apparently she did. When she couldn't shut out the images of gorgeous, tanned women with big assets in tiny bikinis lounging by pools, she changed the topic. "I'm thinking after lunch, we should move the *definitely don't want downstairs* curiosities and whatnot into the attic before we start painting the breakfast room." She watched for his reaction. For someone used to paying professionals for physical labor, she wasn't sure how far she could push Nate before he decided enough was enough.

"Give me five minutes to check the score for the game, then I'm all yours." He disappeared upstairs.

True to his word, he met her in front of a door at the opposite end of the hall from the master. It opened to reveal the attic stairs, and she led the way up to a space that stretched across the entire house. They easily stood upright, only needing to duck down where the slanted roof met the walls.

"Hmm. Looks like most of the *curiosities* are already up here." Sara picked up a bowl fashioned from a box-turtle shell.

Nate pointed at a bunch of old dolls sitting on a table, eyes open. "Those are downright creepy."

"Think those are creepy? You should see this." She waved him over to an antique cradle. Moth-eaten blankets filled the spaces around a doll. "I took a Victorian-history class in college. That's a grave doll."

Nate stared inside the cradle. "As in comparison to a happy doll?"

"It's a wax effigy." Talking about it made her mouth suddenly dry. "An exact likeness of a child who died. Possibly the son of the man who built this house."

"Maybe this stuff should be given to a museum or something." He met Sara's gaze. "I sure as hell wouldn't want to live here knowing this was right over my head."

"I'll check into that. Maybe Cassie knows." Sara moved a faded seamstress form against a wall. "Don't you think it's strange none of the other families who've lived here since got rid of this stuff?"

Nate shrugged. "Maybe it's all cursed and if you remove it from the house it reappears, ready to take revenge on you." He let out an evil laugh and grabbed Sara from behind.

Surprised, she let out a small shriek and swung her arms up and back. The knuckles of her left hand made contact with his face, and Nate grunted. Sara spun around to find him holding a hand over his eye.

"Don't worry." He lowered his hand, tears flowing from the eye. "I'm fine."

"I wasn't worried. And it serves you right. You almost scared the bejesus out of me." Sara peered closer at his eye, the white part completely bloodshot. "But you should probably go rinse it out, make sure there's no dirt in it." She rubbed her hands along the sides of her thighs, realizing how dusty they were.

"I'm really—"

"Please. Rinse it, then go watch the rest of the hockey game. I can move stuff up here by myself."

"Well, if you're sure. It *is* burning a little."

"I am. Go." Sara urged him toward the stairs.

He turned, and she noticed the very corner of his mouth twitch. She'd been had. But she wouldn't get mad, she'd get even. The court was closed all week for Thanksgiving, and Nate Reed was about to spend the next four very long days with a honey-do list.

Chapter Eight

Sara and Nate pulled up to the ranch just before noon on Thanksgiving Day. She leaned to look past him from the passenger side of his truck. "Interesting," she said. "They leave the door open so anybody strolling past can come in, or am I special?"

Nate shrugged. "Between the nice day and everything that's cooking in the kitchen, Adam most likely opened the doors for ventilation." He must have caught the flat expression on her face because he added, "And yes, you are definitely special."

She'd been half joking, half fishing for a compliment, so his answer warmed her. When they stepped from the truck, delectable aromas washed over them.

Nate inhaled. "Mmm-mmm. Glad we skipped breakfast and left plenty of room for all the good stuff."

Sara carried the holiday flower arrangement she'd insisted on buying since she hadn't been permitted to bring a side dish. It had been her solution to not showing up empty-handed. Her stomach grumbled. "You're not kidding, but what on earth is that racket? Sounds like a herd of baby elephants inside."

Nate chuckled. "Welcome to your first Reed holiday

meal. Not sure if you'll survive to tell stories about it, but it's guaranteed not to be boring."

"I don't doubt that for a minute."

A moment before they stepped into the doorway, Noah announced their arrival. "Sara and Nate are finally here."

"How does he do that?" Sara asked Nate.

"Even though we're not identical, we have that twin sixth sense."

Cassie came up to her and threw a welcoming hug around her shoulders. "What a beautiful arrangement."

Sara handed over the floral centerpiece, giving her friend a wry grin. "My contribution since you wouldn't let me bring anything else."

"There's just so much food already. Seemed pointless to add more. But thank you. Give me a sec to make room for this on the table."

After Cassie dashed off, Sara followed Nate's lead and hung her jacket on the overloaded coat rack near the front door. The place was packed. Bishop and Bree were fighting over the TV remote, arguing about which teams would win today's football games. Rachel and an older woman stood at the base of the stairs.

"Sara." Rachel waved her over. "This is my mom, Martina."

"I've heard a lot of good things about you." Martina, holding the sound-asleep Daisy in her arms, smiled at Sara.

"Thank you." A blush warmed her cheeks. She gazed at the slumbering one-year-old, a rush of some unfamiliar feeling she couldn't even name running through her. "I don't know how anyone can sleep through all this racket."

"Thank God for small favors," Rachel whispered.

Daisy's older brother, Brad, played on the floor with toy

cars. Occasionally he'd leap to his feet, pound upstairs, then return with another one.

Noah was fetching drinks for everyone, and she assumed Adam was in the kitchen. That meant with the addition of her and Nate, there were eleven people. Bigger by far than any family holiday she'd ever been to.

"Have a seat." Noah handed her a glass of white wine. "Nate mentioned you like the Hill Country Riesling, so there's plenty chilling in the fridge."

"Indeed I do." She took a sip. "Thank you." Finally, something to smooth the edges of her social anxiety. Although everyone here was so friendly that most of her uneasiness had already disappeared.

Sara chose to sit in the oversized leather recliner, while Nate squeezed his rather large frame onto the couch between Noah and Bishop, a groan escaping him.

"You sound like you used to in the morning after a high school football game." Noah handed him a beer.

"Pretty much sums up how I feel." He squirmed on the couch as he tried to find a more comfortable position.

Sara favored him with an evil grin, knowing she was the cause of his aches and pains.

He turned a hard eye on her. "I've spent the past five days painting walls, hauling stuff up to the attic and rearranging furniture."

Sara widened her eyes in feigned innocence. "All this complaining about a few tiny chores. If I'd known what a baby you'd be about it…"

"Well, he is the baby of the family." Noah chuckled, earning him a glare from his younger-by-three-minutes twin.

Bishop uncrossed his legs to avoid resting his shoe on

Nate's knee, laughing as he did. "Guess I shouldn't ask how the bodyguarding is going."

"No, you shouldn't. It's not going much better than it was when Sara got here. There haven't been any texts or incidents for the past week, which is putting us even more on edge." Nate rested his head against the back of the couch and closed his eyes, giving Sara a moment to notice the worry lines and creases on his face, deeper than just a week ago. For the first time, she appreciated that her troubles were his troubles. "We're hunting one very persistent, very invisible stalker."

Bishop sipped from a glass of iced herbal tea. "That's what Cassie was telling me. She usually leaves her job at the office, but this one's got her frustrated. She mentioned she wants to talk to you both later. Something about reviewing prison records."

So, her troubles were Nate's troubles. And they were Cassie's, too. And Adam's and Noah's. And that meant to a lesser degree, their significant others as well. And all this time Sara had thought she was in this mess by herself.

Having an entire family behind her was something new, and she found the notion both pleasing and embarrassing. It wasn't like she was related by blood or was even a significant other. And she'd always fought her own battles. And yet...

"Good. Hopefully she and Adam have uncovered something we can work with." Nate scooped a few pecans from the bowl Noah was holding and popped them into his mouth. Then, completely changing the subject, he asked Bishop, "Any luck tracking down our mom?"

Cassie walked back into the room and placed the flowers on a beautiful hand-hewn fireplace mantel. "Sorry, Sara.

We can move these to the table after we eat, but there's going to be way too much food on it during dinner."

"That's fine. I didn't even think about that." Center-pieces had worked on her childhood dining table because the dishes and people had been fewer. She'd gladly trade elegant flower arrangements for loving people any day of the week.

Bishop nodded in response to Nate. "I've got a possible lead, but I'll have to travel to check it out." He smiled apologetically at his wife. "But Cassie prefers I don't leave until after the long weekend."

"Probably for the best. Traffic's always crazy on holidays. Keep me posted." Nate stood. "Noah, want a beer?"

"Bro. It's not about want, it's about need. And I do need one. Gotta have one with football, and today is all about football." Using the remote, he changed the channel from one game to another amid a chorus of protests. "Hey, chill out. Just checking on the score. I'll flip it back."

Bishop scoffed. "I think today is about more than just football."

"Oh, you mean the parade?" Noah's straight face dissolved into laughter.

"I'll bring you a beer." Nate left them to debate the meaning of Thanksgiving and headed toward the kitchen.

Not entirely sure why, Sara got up and followed him. Maybe it was the strange, unreadable look on his face as he walked from the room. He seemed preoccupied with something, and she didn't want her stalker problems to ruin the day for him.

She moved through the kitchen with simmering pots on the stove, pausing to breathe in the mouth-watering aromas before continuing through the open door to the back patio. Nate was pulling an iced-down bottle of beer from a galvanized tub near the back door, so she strolled past him and took in the backyard activity.

Rachel played catch with five-year-old Brad while Martina stood in the shade, holding the now wide-awake Daisy on her hip. Adam sat in a patio chair, gazing at the idyllic scene with a smile on his lips. Sara vaguely remembered Adam from her first visit. Seemed that Mr. Serious, as she'd dubbed him then, had wound up with his high school crush and her two adorable kids.

Sara had never given any thought to having children. No reason to when she'd never been in a relationship long enough for it to be a consideration. Besides, she had no idea how to be a good mother, and she sure as hell wouldn't risk subjecting her own kids to a childhood like hers had been. She might not've been consumed with international partying, like her parents, but her focus was centered solely on her career. The idea of having children had always been a distant, hazy concept—one better considered in that mythical place called Someday Land.

Martina set the toddler down, and as the little girl grasped her grandmother's finger and tugged her toward Brad, an unfamiliar twang of maternal longing hit Sara square in the chest. Chalking it up to Daisy waddle-walking in her cute fall outfit, she quickly shook off the feeling and poured herself another glass of wine from the bottle some brilliant person here had set in the icy beer tub.

"Hey, Nate," Adam said. "Why don't you grab a chair for Sara and the two of you sit with me a spell?"

While Nate stepped away to comply with his older brother's request, Sara took the moment alone with Adam to say, "Nice family you have."

"Crazy, isn't it? One day I'm single, and the next I'm almost married with kids. But I'm one lucky son of a gun.

Martina is the perfect future mother-in-law, Brad and Daisy are great and Rachel...well, she's my world."

What would it be like to be someone's world?

Nate joined them, carrying two chairs. Once they were settled, Adam took a pull on his beer and the three of them chatted a while, his eyes never leaving Rachel and the kids. Then he asked Nate, "Anything new on the stalker?"

Nate cringed. The gesture was barely noticeable, but she marked it. "Not a damn thing, but my gut's telling me the bastard hasn't left the area."

"That's what Cassie and I think, too. We have some possible candidates to go over with you two, but to be honest, we're not convinced any of them is our guy."

Sara's hope deflated, but like Nate, she worked on not letting it show. "We could at least eliminate some of them, couldn't we?"

"That's the plan." Adam stood.

"Maybe after dinner?" Nate suggested.

"Or between football games. We'll play it by ear." Adam lifted the grill's lid, revealing an assortment of vegetables. "I thought I'd get off easy this year, roasting the turkey and everyone else bringing side dishes. But nooo, I have to make Bishop his special grilled veggies to go with his turkey."

"If this family didn't put sausage in the dressing and bacon in the beans, I wouldn't need anything special." Bishop leaned over the grill and inhaled. "But I'm kinda glad you do because your grilling skills are amazing, Adam. So very, very amazing, just like you." He wrapped an arm around Adam's neck and planted a loud kiss on his brother-in-law's cheek.

"Whoa." Noah joined the group, laughing. "You're barely

back from your honeymoon, Bishop. And already cheating on my sister?"

Cassie leaned out through the kitchen door. "Honey, please stop flirting with my brother before we all wind up on a reality show."

"Sorry, Cassie. But you know I can't help myself." Bishop failed miserably at keeping a straight face. "Adam's grilled veggies are just so special."

Everyone on the patio cracked up as Noah dropped onto the chair Adam had just vacated, a longneck bottle in one hand. "Bro, I thought you were bringing me a beer. Guess if I want something done around here, I have to do it myself."

Nate scanned the yard. "Where's Bree? I haven't seen her since we got here."

"Her sweet potatoes weren't quite ready, and she figured since the ovens here were already being used, she'd finish them at the casita."

"So, how's it going with you two?" Nate asked his twin. "Y'all like living in Adam's old cabin?"

"Are you kidding? That place is *sa-weet*. We told Rachel she's welcome to come watch the sunsets anytime she wants." Noah gave him a lopsided grin. "Long as she doesn't bring Adam along. He might decide he made a mistake and never leave."

Noah explained to Sara that years ago their older brother had moved into the largest of several cabins on the Reed property and spent a considerable amount of time and money renovating the place. Unfortunately, though large, it only had one bedroom and Rachel had two kids. So despite his affection for the place, Adam had moved back into the main house with his new family. And Noah and Bree had been the recipients of a cabin worthy of a cable-network renovation show.

Everyone laughed at Noah's story except Nate, and Sara wondered why.

Fifteen minutes later, Bree returned with her famous praline sweet potatoes and the meal began. Everyone moved back inside to the dining room and took their seats. Rounding the table with a heavy platter of carved turkey, Adam held it for each person while they served themselves.

Sara held a spoonful of sweet potatoes over her plate, searching for an empty spot. With her past holidays shared with only one or two people, she'd never attended a true family Thanksgiving dinner before. Apparently her eyes were three times the size of her stomach. She would've felt ashamed of the mountain of food in front of her, except everyone else's plates were piled higher than hers.

"White meat okay?" Adam set the platter on the table next to her. When Sara nodded, he covered her side dishes with slices of turkey. "Next year, remember to leave room for the main dish. Though I will admit, everything tastes pretty good all mashed together."

She couldn't believe she'd forgotten about the turkey. "I can see why you didn't want Nate and me to bring more food," she said to Cassie. "I'm surprised the table can support all of this as it is."

"Believe it or not, Adam used to make everything himself." Cassie scooped Rachel's cheesy green beans with bacon onto her plate. "I never thought he'd relinquish control like this."

Adam snorted. "If the twins were cooking, I wouldn't have. And we all know the only thing you can make is a trip to the diner for one of Marge's homemade pies."

Cassie shrugged. "Hey, I play to my strengths and acknowledge my weaknesses. I'm not now and never have been a cook."

"We can all attest to that." Noah looked at Sara. "If Adam hadn't taught himself to cook at the tender age of ten, we'd all have perished from malnutrition before puberty."

Laughing, Sara passed along the sweet potatoes and took a long drink of cold white wine. Between the heat outside and all the bodies inside, Adam had finally turned on the air-conditioning, but it was still fighting to lower the dining room's temperature.

As the meal continued, she realized the anxiety that had bothered her when she'd first walked into the house had dissipated. Typically, she avoided large gatherings because she abhorred small talk and, worse, sitting alone while everyone else talked and laughed and had fun. That same fear had grabbed her today, but between family anecdotes and good-natured teasing, she'd forgotten about being nervous.

Across the table, Nate's brown eyes twinkled as he raised his glass toward her in a silent toast. She lifted hers too, her lips curving upward. The heat that filled her had nothing to do with the stuffy room or the wine. It was the warmth of family. Of friends. Of Nate.

"...wouldn't share his toy, even then." Martina finished a story about Brad, and everyone laughed. Sara pretended to. She'd been lost in Nate's eyes instead of paying attention.

"You've got to pick up the pace, Sara." Noah poked his fork in the air toward her plate. "You snooze, you lose around this table."

"I'm about to be snoozing—between all this food and wine." She wiped her mouth with her napkin. "If you don't have doggy bags, I'll just take a piece of foil over my plate."

Cassie laughed. "Trust me, there's more than enough to send some home with everyone."

"Ladies, y'all outdid yourselves with your most excellent side dishes." Adam raised his glass. "I hereby declare all future holidays will forever be potluck."

"To potluck." Everyone toasted.

"And here's to Adam." Bishop held his iced tea aloft. "For all the meals he's cooked by himself, as well as his meat-free variations."

Everyone chanted, "To Adam."

Sara raised her glass along with everyone else, but her mind wasn't in the room. The holidays since becoming an adult that she hadn't been able to spend with her grandfather, those days she'd thought she enjoyed alone in her apartment, lounging in sweats and binge-watching TV while eating delivery from upscale restaurants paled in comparison to this gathering. But how could she have known? Without this experience, she might never have discovered, even if for just one day, what it was like to be part of a loving family.

But now that she had, she was afraid she'd never be content without one.

STANDING AND TAKING a well-deserved bow, Adam checked his watch. "Are you ready for some football?" he shouted.

"Football!" came the enthusiastic reply, and the crowd rose from the table and moved toward the living room.

Nate looked back when he noticed Sara wasn't next to him. She still sat at the table, a perplexed expression on her face.

"Um, shouldn't we put away the food first?" she asked.

"Ha! What a rookie you are, Sara." Reaching past her, Noah shoved a piece of turkey into a roll, dipped it in gravy and held a napkin beneath it. "Trust me, by the time half-time rolls around, everyone will have made at least one trip to the table for leftovers. Tell her, bro."

"He's right." Nate held up an empty wine bottle. "Want a refill?"

"I'm not sure if I should. I don't usually have more than one glass."

"It's a four-day weekend. Live a little."

She deliberated for a moment. "Why not?"

They went into the kitchen, and Nate grabbed another chilled bottle, popped the cork and refilled her glass. Then he headed outside to grab himself another beer, pleased when she stayed with him instead of joining his family in the living room.

"Listen, I'm stuffed to the gills." He patted his belly. "Do you feel like taking a walk? Help settle some of this food?"

Sara nodded. "That would be great. If I sit down now, I'm afraid I'll be asleep in an instant."

"We can't have that. It would be embarrassing for you if everyone heard how loudly you snore."

"What? I do *not* snore."

"Really? Then the noise I hear coming from your room at night must be a grizzly bear driving a bulldozer." Nate fought a smile. "I'm going to have to climb up on the roof and tack down the shingles you've blown loose."

"Hardy har har. And here I thought Noah was supposed to be the funny one." She laughed.

He gave her a sheepish grin. "I have my moments."

"Not enough of them." She ducked her head, her smile lingering.

"Touché."

He liked her this way, with her hair down, having fun. "Come on," he invited with a head nod. "Let me show you around the place."

The day had cooled now that the sun was dropping, but it was still warm enough that neither needed a jacket. He set a leisurely pace as he led her around to the front, down the driveway and out across the land that surrounded the main house.

Sara turned in a circle, taking it all in. "There are so many trees on your land."

"Mostly live oaks and mesquite. And then we've got all those fruit and pecan trees behind the house." About to tell her about the creek running through their property, he snapped his mouth shut. Sara already knew about the creek. About how good its cool water felt on a warm day. About the grasses and wildflowers along its banks, tall enough in the spring to conceal two young lovers.

She studied his face. "Why don't you like talking about this?"

He worried she'd read his mind and pretended to be confused. "About the ranch?" Nate prided himself on his ability to be reserved, to project an impression of aloofness. A necessary survival skill learned while growing up at odds with his father's wishes. So what was it Sara thought she saw when she looked at him?

"Not just the ranch." When he didn't reply, she added, "It's your face that gives you away, you know."

"Remind me not to play poker with you." He chuckled. "So, what exactly is my face telling you?" He continued to smile, although the direction of this conversation made him feel like a long-tailed cat in a rocking chair factory. To gird himself, he lifted his beer and took a drink.

"When Noah was explaining about why Adam moved back into the main house, your face shut down. When he talked about moving into Adam's cabin with Bree, you grew distant." She arched a brow. "When you were watching Rachel play with the kids, your eyes glazed over and you disappeared completely."

Stunned, Nate tried to gather his thoughts. How had Sara homed in on his…what? Wistful regret? Bittersweet longing for something he'd deemed unnecessary? No one else had ever noticed, let alone thought to ask him about it.

He paused then, not sure how much to explain. Did he even want to wade into the muck of his feelings on the matter? He glanced at Sara and found her watching him, like she really wanted to hear what he had to say. It could have been the wine that made her glistening eyes appear interested, but he preferred to think it was because she cared. And seeing that concern, his inhibition slipped away.

"I've always felt like the odd man out in my family. The one who didn't want to be a deputy. The one who couldn't join in on dinner conversations because they revolved around law enforcement. The one who came home from California for holidays, only to envy my siblings' tight bond with our father and each other, their private jokes and common interests."

He shrugged as if trying to convince himself he was immune to the hurt. "I created a barrier between myself and the others through the decisions *I* made."

And today that realization had become a huge clear bubble surrounding his amazing extended family, leaving him on the outside looking in. His siblings had all found their perfect matches, with Adam bringing kids and a future mother-in-law along for the ride. Even Sara had looked like she belonged here more than Nate.

"It's never too late to change things, if you really want to." Sara's compassionate smile almost did him in. "Come on, let's take that walk."

They strolled together in companionable silence, each alone with their own thoughts. When Sara stepped on uneven ground and lost her balance, Nate grabbed her arm to steady her.

"Lord, I'm such a klutz."

She looked up into his eyes, that signature blush of hers covering her cheeks. Convincing himself that he didn't care about her anymore was a losing battle. He lowered his head slowly, giving her time to say no or push him away. But she didn't. Her soft lips met his in a long, tender kiss, an almost perfect reenactment of their first one so many years ago.

He finally pulled back. "We better head back to the house before we're labeled antisocial."

"Or worse, anti-football." She coughed out a small, nervous laugh and dropped her gaze.

But Nate took her hand as they headed back to the house, and this time the silence between them swelled with unspoken emotions.

WHEN THE BREAK came between games, a synchronized flurry of activity took place. The table was cleared, leftovers packed into the fridge and dishes rinsed. Nate couldn't help but chuckle to himself. While it was usually the twins' job to do the dishes, Noah would get stuck with it all tonight.

With only minutes left until the next kickoff, Adam huddled with Sara and Nate. "Cassie and I want to meet with you at the sheriff's office tomorrow to go over the list of possible criminal suspects. It's just too crazy here today."

"Clearer heads. I agree." Sara nodded.

Nate scrutinized her expression, wondering if she was referring to the alcoholic beverages or their kiss.

"We've got pie," Cassie called. "And coffee."

Everyone gathered around the dining room table, which held four varieties of the sweet dessert.

"What's your poison?" Noah asked Sara as he handed her a small plate.

"All that refined sugar is exactly that—poison," Bishop said, and the entire group groaned.

Noah rolled his eyes. "Cassie, make that health nut shut up."

"Believe me, I've tried."

"With so many to choose from, I'm having a hard time deciding." Sara rounded the table. "Y'all must really love pie."

The others looked at each other and broke out laughing.

"What's so funny?" Sara looked around, confused.

"You kinda had to be there," Noah said.

"Noah's obsession with pie almost killed Adam and Rachel's chance for their happily-ever-after." Nate pulled her closer and whispered, "I'll tell you the details later."

"Now that you've piqued my curiosity, you better." She slid a small piece of pecan pie onto her plate.

Settled again in front of the TV with dessert and coffee, the group watched, yelled and cursed their way through the second game.

Sara sat between Nate and the couch arm, leaning into him as the food, wine and fun seemed to take its toll on her.

"How 'bout I take you home?" She tilted her head to look up at him.

"I have a better idea." He touched the end of her nose. "How 'bout *I* take *you* home?"

"That's a much better idea. I should've thought of that." Sara pushed off from Nate's thigh and the armrest to get to her feet. Addressing the room, she said, "Thank you all for the wonderful Thanksgiving."

Cassie hugged her before Nate steered her to the coatrack and started to help her with her jacket.

"I don't think I need that." Sara pressed her hands to her cheeks. "I'm pretty warm."

"Humor me." After she was zipped into hers, Nate pulled on his jacket and opened the front door.

"Whoa. It *is* cold out here." She huddled up against him in the truck while they waited for the engine to warm up.

He didn't regret kissing her. Not one bit. But now he needed to focus on the reason they were together. He was her bodyguard; she was his client. Period.

Nate sighed. They'd be alone in that big house tonight, the desire ignited by their kiss burning a hole straight through him.

It was going to be one long, lonely night.

Chapter Nine

On the drive home from the Thanksgiving shindig, Sara basked in a warm feeling of belonging. The raucous conversations, family anecdotes and chaotic fun had nearly overwhelmed her, as her only experiences with holidays while growing up had been awkward meals with her self-absorbed parents. And that was only when they'd been in town. Most years as a child she'd spent quiet Thanksgivings with her grandfather, and she still did. And though she loved that old man to the moon and back, Reed family shindigs were incredible.

She still felt a little guilty about not spending the holiday with him this year, but Pops had encouraged her to join her friends. Despite approaching ninety, he'd assured her he'd be around for next year's holidays.

Her mind drifted to another topic, and she murmured, "Hmm."

"Hmm, what?" Nate asked. The clean, woody scent of his cologne was working its magic on her.

"I was thinking about that story Cassie was telling about the first time she had a meal with Bishop. Those two seem like oil and water, yet somehow they make it work. I wonder what their secret is."

"Oh, I don't think they have a secret. They fell in love, and the rest…" Sara felt rather than saw his shrug. "I guess they just compromise."

"You mean like whether to have steak or tofu for dinner?" She chuckled. "That's a pretty big compromise."

Within the intimate darkness of the truck, Nate's deep laugh rumbled. "Yeah, like that." He paused. "You're in an awfully good mood."

"Well, I won't lie, I did have a few glasses of that most excellent Riesling." And the ambrosia had melted away her normal reticence, filling her with confidence.

"A family favorite. Made right here in Texas at one of the local Hill Country wineries." He glanced at her, a streetlight illuminating his teasing grin. "And how exactly do you define *a few*?"

"Hmph. You're my bodyguard, not my father." Not that her father had ever advised her about public conduct. And he sure as hell hadn't set a good example for it, either. But Nate was right. She'd probably downed almost a whole bottle all by herself. She normally stopped after one glass and couldn't remember the last time she'd felt so relaxed. So happy. So warm.

Definitely not since those texts had started coming. But having Nate around dissipated her concern and made her feel safe. *I could get used to this.*

"Are you hot?"

Nate's question caught her off guard. "Hot? Me?" She checked the side window next to her and found it a little steamed up. "No, I'm fine. Why do you ask?"

"You're fanning yourself."

Sara dropped her hands into her lap, her face ironically burning with embarrassment. Thank goodness it was dark. "Habit," she lied. "When I drink too much."

Okay, I'm most definitely feeling warm, but it has little to do with the wine. Not with Nate sitting so close. Close enough that she could reach out her hand and touch his rock-solid bicep or jean-encased thigh. For days now she'd tried to stop her inquisitive mind from imagining what it would be like to touch him. Not an accidental brush against him or his arm around her shoulder after a traumatic incident. But to really *touch* him. She sucked in a breath.

"Funny, I've never noticed you fanning yourself before."

"Well, I do."

"Good to know."

The mirth in his tone would have normally bothered her. But even if he was teasing her, he wasn't laughing *at* her.

As Nate turned down the street that led to the judge's mansion, Sara leaned her head back and tried to cool her jets. Not all the way; just enough that she wouldn't flame out. While her libido calmed, her mind wandered again to the time when she and Nate had hooked up before. Had she felt the same overwhelming need for him back then?

The attraction had been there, still…in her mind something seemed different, something elusive about her current emotions.

"You enjoy yourself today?"

Did he even need to ask? "Yes. It was a first for me."

Her comment clearly confused him. "First what?"

How could someone like him understand what her world had been like? "First large family gathering on a holiday. Usually, Thanksgiving and Christmas were just my grandfather and me. The last time I experienced this much commotion and fun was the last time I was here. I absolutely loved it."

"I thought maybe we were too much for you."

"Not at all. I was a bit apprehensive at first. I had

the mistaken impression—probably from too many TV shows—that family get-togethers were rife with feuds and gossip. But your family is just how I remember them. With a few new faces, of course." She kicked herself mentally for bringing up the time she'd walked away from him.

Ever the gentleman, he ignored it. "I'm glad."

His words were soft, and she realized in that moment just how important her answer was to him. *I may be wine-happy, but I'm beginning to understand why what I'm feeling now is different.*

With the younger version of Nate, she'd been content with a fling. But with the adult Nate, she wanted… Well, she wanted more.

Ironic, how easily she'd once dismissed Nate's own desire for more. Although of legal age, he'd been a teenager, and teenagers seldom knew what they wanted. Still, she must have hurt him far more than she'd imagined.

His life these days was rooted in California, which meant *more* wasn't in the cards, but there was no reason why she couldn't have the here and now, was there?

Heat flowed through her body, a heady mixture of desire, need and determination. She'd seen Nate observing her when he'd thought she wasn't watching. Those smoldering looks aroused her in ways she couldn't describe. And he wouldn't have eyed her that way if the feelings weren't mutual. For all that he pretended otherwise, he wasn't made of stone.

They reached the driveway and parked, and that fast the carefree Nate she'd seen earlier in the evening disappeared and protector Nate emerged. "Stay here, doors locked, until I clear the garage."

"Aye, aye, captain." She knew the routine and hated the need for it. Hated how this damn stalker was affecting her very existence. Redecorating the house had provided her with a brief sense of empowerment, but the work was nearly finished. She needed to find another way to feel in control of at least one aspect of her life.

She inhaled the lingering scent of Nate's cologne, and the solution was obvious.

NATE MADE A QUICK, thorough search of the garage before dashing back to the truck. He didn't like leaving Sara out in the open, locked vehicle or not, but this was the safest way. Parking inside, he locked the garage and led her inside the house, his head on a swivel.

With the front door locked, he took hold of her shoulders. "Stay here while I clear the house."

No *aye, aye* this time, but she did give him a compliant salute. Nate swallowed against the lump in his throat. Tipsy Sara was as alluring as hell.

He returned from his sweep to find her exactly where he'd left her, leaning against the doorframe, eyes closed, humming to herself.

Dang if she didn't make it hard to stay professional.

She seemed unaware when he stood inches away from her. So close, he could watch her heartbeats pulse in the hollow of her throat, identify the subtle hint of citrus and spice on her skin, see the smattering of pale freckles across the arch of her nose.

He reached his hand forward, brushing her cheek in a feather-like touch just as her eyes drifted open and gazed directly into his.

"I like your cologne," she whispered, a lazy smile curling her lips.

"Um, thanks." He keyed in the code on the alarm panel just over her left shoulder.

"Oh." Her smile faltered. "You're just setting the alarm."

"I am." His tone was as soft as hers. He locked eyes with her, gauging her reaction to his nearness. The signals she'd been giving him all night were undeniable. He wanted to respond, to give them both what they wanted.

But this wasn't how he conducted business. This wasn't how he treated Cassie's friends. Hell, this wasn't how he treated women in general. He backed away. "I'm going to check the monitors."

"Why, if the house is clear?"

"To see if there was any activity while we were gone."

"Oh."

Was that disappointment he heard in her voice? Practically speed walking to the breakfast room where he'd set up the monitors, he spent way longer than necessary reviewing camera footage for the stalker. No sign of the bastard. At least one thing was right tonight.

After enough time had passed that he thought she'd be asleep, he heard soft footsteps behind him.

"Nate?"

He turned around and stopped breathing. Her face was scrubbed clean, her feet bare. Like some dewy-eyed innocent, Sara stood framed in the doorway, her white silk robe backlit by a kitchen light. If she wore anything underneath it, he saw no evidence. What he could see, quite clearly, were the outlines of her pert nipples. "I thought you were going to bed."

"That's my plan." She bit her bottom lip, and Nate shifted in his chair.

"What's stopping you?"

"You are."

"Me? I'm not stopping you. If you want to go to bed, go. I'll turn off the lights in here."

Sara sighed. "I must not be very good at this."

"Good at what?" Nate felt like a jerk trying to play dumb. Her signals hadn't been mixed tonight, and he knew what Sara was leading up to.

Her head tilted to one side as if in deliberation. Then she straightened. "I want to go to bed *with you*."

And there she was, the confident woman Sara had been at twenty-one, taking charge of their first night together.

Nate stood, searching for a way to stop something that would not end well for either of them. "Look, this kind of thing happens all the time. Perfectly normal. A client often comes to feel affection for the person protecting them. Trust me, the feelings will pass. Best to ignore them."

Sara glided farther into the room. "Nate?"

He stood rooted, completely transfixed by the image of her swaying hips and flowing robe. He forced out a gravelly reply. "What?"

She floated up to him and placed the flat of her hands on his chest. "I don't want to ignore the feelings. And I don't think this has anything to do with protector infatuation."

She gazed up at him, her wide, trusting eyes hopeful with anticipation. Her lips parted as she drew breath. "Kiss me, Nate."

And he was undone.

He slid a hand behind her neck, cupping her head and pulling her closer until their lips almost touched. "You have no idea what you're doing to me."

"Oh, I think I do."

Her arms wrapped around his waist until her body was flush with his, her soft curving warmth the perfect counter to his hardness.

"Sara, you're making it impossible for me to—"

"Am I?" She rose on her tiptoes and brushed her lips lightly against his. "I want this, Nate. I want you."

Their lips remained touching, and he breathed her in. "There's no future in this." His words were muffled against her.

"I know."

"I'm leaving soon for California."

"I know."

"Sara…" He took possession of her mouth.

She parted her lips, and the sweetness of her tongue, thrashing with his, had him pulling her even more tightly against him.

Her hands slid under his shirt and ran the length of his back, then slipped lower. He let her have her way, not daring to break their kiss, not daring to touch her in return for fear she would realize her mistake.

And then she pulled away.

Nate's groan reflected the agony of the break, both mentally and physically.

Breathless herself, Sara's chest rose and fell as she reached out and took his hand. Without a word, he followed her as she led him upstairs to her bedroom.

Soft music played, several candles were lit and the bed covers had been turned down. This seduction of hers was not the result of too much wine. It was careful and deliberate. And if inspired by their days of close proximity, he no longer cared.

She let go of his hand, turned to face him and dropped her robe.

Seeing a naked woman was nothing new to Nate. But Sara standing nude before him with her shoulders back and head held high…this was something altogether different.

Her assertive stance, in stark contrast to her bare-skinned vulnerability, called to him on a primal level.

He wanted her, wanted to devour her until she was a part of him. At the same time, he was consumed by an overwhelming need to be gentle, to explore the exquisite contours of her body with unhurried care and skill.

He chose the latter.

As Sara reached for his belt and unbuckled it, Nate pulled his shirt over his head and tossed it to the floor. His shoes and the rest of his clothes soon joined it, and he scooped her up into his arms.

He laid her back on the bed and stretched out beside her, propping himself on one elbow while his other hand traced the contours of her face, her neck, her shoulders. Continuing downward with his caresses, he palmed her breasts and gently teased her nipples before tracing a line down her flat belly. Though she parted her legs for him, ready for his touch, he continued down, stroking the insides of her thighs before trailing back up to her navel.

Sara's hand grabbed hold of his wrist, her eyes locked on his. "Touch me."

And without waiting for an answer, she slid his hand right where she wanted him, her eyes not closing until Nate dipped into her wetness.

He kissed the column of her throat, her collarbone, her breasts. His tongue teased her nipples while his fingers continued to caress her.

When the scent of her arousal became too much to take, his kisses moved south. And there he lost his mind to the experience. Tasting Sara, drinking her in, inhaling her essence until he groaned with need.

Sara arched against his mouth, her fingers tunneling through his hair, holding him to her. Her breaths became shorter, faster, until a low moan escaped her and she trembled from the force of her orgasm.

Nate worked his way back up her body, cherishing every inch of skin on the way. Then her smoldering gaze pierced his heart and released a long-suppressed passion for this woman.

A satisfied smile on her face, Sara pushed Nate onto his back.

Memories surfaced of Sara as a college student, taking command of their first sexual encounter. For some reason, she'd needed to be in charge even back then.

She crawled across the bed like a leopard on the prowl and opened the nightstand drawer. She returned, and rising onto her knees, she opened the small foil packet in her hand, straddled him and rolled the condom down his hard, erect length. With a seductive smile, she leaned forward and, bracing herself with her hands on the bed, she began a slow and steady ride.

Her heat, her scent, the very feel of her soft skin sliding against his drove him mad, his decision to go slow evaporated by his burning need for her. As she continued to ride him, he laved at her nipples, grabbed hold of her bottom and matched her downward movements with hip-lifting thrusts that drove him deeper inside her.

As if not willing to relinquish control to him, Sara's inner walls tightened around him and released, tightened and released, again and again. Her nails dragged across his chest as her body stiffened, taking him with her to heights he hadn't known existed.

Sara collapsed on top of him, and they lay that way, legs intertwined, Nate's arms around her. She nestled her head against his chest with a sigh of contentment.

An unfamiliar sense of affection filled him. An emotion

he'd never connected to sex before—or if he had, he'd forgotten about it. Enjoyable, but dangerous. He was leaving town in a couple of weeks, and Sara would eventually go back to Austin when this judging gig was done.

Becoming attached was not an option.

THE NEXT DAY, Sara's eyes fluttered open to find morning sunlight bathing her room in hues of gold. That and the lingering scent of lovemaking produced a broad, sated smile. She blushed, remembering her wanton behavior. Seducing Nate, then her unrestrained reactions to his maddening touch.

Their night together had reawakened feelings for Nate she'd convinced herself were long gone. She slid her hand across the bed in search of his warmth and comfort, but his side of the bed was empty.

His side of the bed. Hmm, she liked the sound of that.

Sara slipped out of bed and into the shower. As she lathered her breasts, her belly, between her thighs, the memory of Nate's hands caressing her skin sent aftershocks of pleasure through her. She was sore in the best possible way yet still brimming with need. She wanted more. More sex. More Nate.

Dressing casually, Sara headed downstairs and found Nate at the breakfast table, staring at camera footage. When she rested a hand on his shoulder, he glanced up.

"Morning, sleepyhead." He swiveled the chair, snaked his arm around her waist and hauled her into the V between his legs.

"I did sleep well." Sara ran her fingers through his hair that was still damp from a shower. "What time did you get up?"

Nate pulled her down until she was sitting on his thigh

and nuzzled her cheek with his whiskers. "Not that long ago. You looked too peaceful to wake."

A sly smile appeared. "I wish you had."

"We would've spent the whole day in bed if I had, and you know it." He cupped the back of her head and gave her a deep, gentle kiss.

Standing, she said, "As much as I'm enjoying this, I really need some caffeine."

"I've got your favorite coffee loaded in the espresso machine, ready to go."

She leaned down for one more kiss, then ambled into the kitchen. Nate followed her with his empty mug, ready for a refill. When she pressed the button for coffee, the intoxicating aroma from the black elixir of life filled the air.

I wouldn't mind waking up to this treatment every morning.

"I need to finish reviewing the nighttime footage before we meet up with Cassie and Adam to go over what they've turned up on your case." Nate leaned against the counter while they waited for her mug to fill.

"Great—that'll give me time to review my upcoming court cases." Since the goose trial, she'd only dealt with a few traffic-ticket arraignments, the courtroom closed to spectators at Nate's insistence. Insistence that normally would have annoyed her, but not nearly as much as the trepidation she felt every time her text notification went off. "So, leave by nine o'clock?" She picked up her coffee and chanced scalding her tongue with the first sips.

Nate set his mug on the small platform and refilled the coffee module. "Hate to admit it, but this thing does make the best coffee in town."

She cocked her brow, her way of saying *told ya so* without words. In the back pocket of her jeans, her cell phone chirped with an incoming text. She pulled it from her pocket.

"It's probably Cassie making sure we still plan to meet," Nate said.

"It's not from Cassie." Sara tapped the screen to open the text from an unfamiliar number. Her body went rigid, the coffee she'd just swallowed churning in her stomach.

Nate tensed at her reaction. "What is it?"

"It's from *him*." Sara held up her phone so he could see her fresh horror. "According to the *Victoria Chronicle*, I'm dead."

Chapter Ten

Nate strode into the small conference room in the sheriff's department, Sara beside him. "Have we got an update for you."

Cassie and Adam, sitting next to each other at one of the tables, looked up.

"Update on what?" Adam asked.

Nate took a chair across from them as Sara slid into the one next to him.

"The latest text from my stalker." She fished her phone from her pocket and forwarded the text with the obituary to Cassie and Adam, then rested her forearms on the table, her hands shaking. He wanted to wrap an arm around her shoulders, reassure her that he'd protect her. But no public displays of affection while they worked.

Cassie read from the screen. "'Sara Diana Bennett...born in Austin...an unremarkable career with the Travis County District Attorney's Office...briefly served as a county judge during which she incurred a series of unfortunate incidents that led to her death...survived by her grandfather, Archer Bennett...no service, flowers or donations." She looked up. "This is in one of the Victoria papers?"

"Also posted on Obituaries.com for the whole world to

see." The quiver in Sara's voice matched the tremble in her hands.

"It could be in other newspapers as well," Nate added. "All he had to do was mark which ones he wanted it to appear in on that one website."

"Doesn't the website have to verify the facts before they distribute it?" Adam's tone was incredulous. "At least the fact that the person is actually dead?"

"Apparently the website only cares about getting paid." Sara crossed her arms over her chest.

Cassie set her phone down. "We'll get to the bottom of this. I'll see if the website has a phone number attached to it. One way or another, we'll get ahold of someone there and find out who submitted the obituary, how they paid for it. We can backtrack from there."

"If they're located in the US, you might need to wait until Monday. Holiday staff doesn't usually include anyone who can actually deal with problems." Sara's lips formed an adult pout that, in profile, made Nate pause.

He hadn't known someone could be so angry and so cute at the same time.

"For now, let's start working on why we're here," Cassie suggested. "Getting distracted by this creep's latest antics won't help us identify him."

"I've done background searches on the names you gave me." Nate eyed his sister. "But I'm assuming you were able to access a lot more info than I could." He pulled his laptop and several file folders from his computer bag.

They were set up in the small conference room that the deputies used for morning briefings. Adam and Cassie had turned one of the tables lengthwise so they could face each other and see the front of the room without anyone turning all the way around. Cassie powered on her laptop and held out a hand for one of Nate's file folders. He passed them out, keeping one for himself.

"Once we cross-reference the criminal records we obtained with your searches, I'm hoping some possible suspects stand out." Cassie logged into the department portal.

"I'm glad you were able to request the records as part of an investigation." Sara opened her own computer to take notes. "I have a feeling if *I'd* requested a list of all my cases, the DA's office might not have obliged so quickly. Alton wasn't too happy about my quick departure." She opened the file folder Nate had handed her.

"Just so you're aware, they did want to know why we requested the list." Adam gave her a sympathetic smile.

Her brows rose. "What did you tell them?"

"That someone appeared to be harassing you and we wanted to eliminate possible threats from your court cases." Cassie shrugged when her friend's mouth dropped open. "I wasn't about to lie. And it got us the records."

"But I didn't want anyone up there to know anything about this." Sara's disappointment was palpable.

Adam frowned. "Why?"

When Sara didn't answer, Cassie piped up. "She doesn't want this to reflect on her stellar reputation in Travis County. She doesn't want her ex-boss, who stole her last case out from under her, to be glad she took off before this stalker became *his* problem to deal with." Glaring at Sara, she added, "But she doesn't seem to realize her life is more important than some smug DA's opinion of her."

His sister could be blunt. Without thinking, Nate wrapped his arm around Sara's shoulders in a comforting move. But when she smiled at him and placed her hand on top of his, he caught a knowing glance between his siblings. Nate gave her shoulder a gentle squeeze, then removed his arm.

He wasn't about to explain his and Sara's relationship to them. He was having trouble explaining it to himself.

Nate had figured his memories of what had been ten years ago, his imaginings of how things would be if they ever reconnected had been blown out of proportion over time. But if anything, his fantasies paled in comparison to last night.

He might not have gotten Sara completely out of his system yet, but there was no harm in them enjoying each other's company in order to do so, at least until he left for California. Both he and Sara could take this time to distract each other from the unpleasant reality of her stalker and get closure on what had happened between them years ago. A win-win in his book.

Cassie shared her laptop to the huge monitor attached to the front wall, opened the folder Nate had given her and flipped through printouts of his searches, sliding the criminals into the same order as she had them arranged on her computer. Closing the folder and laying a few pages on top of it, she announced, "Arthur Jenkins."

Adam, Nate and Sara extracted the same pages from their folders while Cassie read from the screen. "...charged with aggravated assault, attempted rape, resisting arrest. As he was being led from the courtroom after being sentenced to twenty years—"

"He bellowed that he was going to kill me." Sara's tone was flat, her eyes blank. "It was the first time someone threatened my life." She blinked, then refocused on their small group, a tight smile stretching her lips. "But it wasn't the last."

Nate took a moment to digest that. He regularly guarded

people who were in fear for their lives, but they were clients and that was his job. Hearing that someone he cared about had been threatened affected him on a deeper level.

Reading from his notes, Nate ran through personal details he'd learned about the man. "Divorced before his arrest, no children, no living relatives."

"He's had absolutely no visitors since he was incarcerated." Cassie scrolled down the page. "After getting beat up several times, he joined a gang inside the prison for protection."

Sara tapped her pen against her pad. "The only way he could have sent someone after me is if he did it through the gang. I'm not sure the price he'd have to pay for something like that would be worth it to him."

Cassie moved on to the next name. "Brandon Barlow. Sentenced to ten years for violation of a protective order, stalking, assault."

"Stalking?" Nate's eyes widened. "Sounds like he should be at the top of our list."

"I remember him," Sara said. "He was specifically obsessed with his ex-wife."

Nate jotted a note on his Barlow printout before reading from his research. "Aside from the ex-wife and two kids from the marriage, his parents live in an Austin suburb, and he has a brother in that area who's single."

"Next up, David Dillon. Arrested for driving while intoxicated. A search of his vehicle revealed his own personal pharmacy. He had amphetamines, ecstasy, cocaine and enough Oxycodone to make it a first degree felony. It also happened to be his third DWI, making that also a felony under the state's third-strike law." Cassie's lip curled with disgust.

"Sentenced ten months ago to thirty years. He's had

several visitors—the most frequent one being his sister, Joan Dillon. David had no prior arrests, and Joan's record is clean."

"Parents deceased. Sister's his only living relative," Nate added.

"He was the most recent to threaten me when he was sentenced." Sara raised one shoulder in a semi-shrug. "But there were others between Jenkins and Dillon. Guess it comes with the job."

For the next three hours, they repeated the process, sorting the convicts into piles based on their likelihood of being a suspect.

When they finished the last name and slid their piles back into the file folders with the most likely group on top, Sara stretched her arms over her head and sighed. "How did you compile this particular list? I remember the names of some nasty people I prosecuted who weren't included."

"We eliminated everyone who's died." Cassie closed her laptop. "We did extensive research on the ones who've been released from prison. Talked to their parole officers, followed up on their residential situations, jobs, whatever we could find. We made a separate list of those, and a few were in this group." She tapped her folder. "We consider the others unlikely. For now, at least."

"What if this doesn't have anything to do with your job? At least, not with people you sent to prison?" Nate had already discussed this with Cassie, who'd insisted on starting with the convicts. "Was there anyone you worked with who might have a grudge? A coworker who asked you out, and you refused? A defense lawyer who lost to you one too many times?"

Sara pursed her lips as she considered his questions. "I have no idea about defense attorneys. A lot of these trials involved public defenders, and for the most part we keep things civil between us. No one at work wanted to date me that I'm aware of. And the only case that might have inspired jealousy in the other ADAs would have been the murder trial." She scoffed. "If it was that, I'd think they'd have stopped bothering me after Alton took the case for himself."

"But those are all possibilities we should look into." Adam massaged the back of his neck, a habit he had when frustrated or considering a problem. "Sara, you should start a list of every defense attorney you can remember going up against."

"That's easy. My calendar shows dates and attorneys for every trial."

"Perfect." Adam glanced at Cassie. "If we get a list of all employees in that district attorney's office, could you sweet-talk Bishop into using his investigative skills to help us check them all out?"

"There are a lot of employees, especially if you go beyond the assistant DAs and consider legal assistants, clerical staff, everyone else." Sara massaged her forehead. "It would take forever to check them all, and that's if you can even get a list."

"We'll get the list—don't you worry about that. And I'm sure Bishop will be willing to help cull it." Cassie met Sara's gaze. "I know you haven't been dating anyone recently, but I'm going to need a list of everyone you've gone out with for at least the past year."

Sara flicked a quick side-glance at Nate, her cheeks flushed as if she'd just come in from a blizzard. He tried to deny to himself that discussing the men she'd dated bothered him. But it did. Even rationalizing that they both had pasts—and they had no future together—didn't help.

"I'll get with you later on that." Sara's glare at Cassie said a whole lot more than her words.

Must be one hell of a list. His stomach did an unfamiliar flip.

SARA DRAINED HER wine and held out her glass for a refill. They'd come to the Reed ranch straight from the justice building after Adam had suggested grilling steaks for dinner.

"You sure you don't want to wait a few minutes? That one went down pretty fast." Holding the bottle, Nate eyed her like a bartender about to cut her off.

"You're supposed to pour one out for the dead, right? Well, that's what the first glass was. Rest in peace, Sara Bennett." She cocked a brow. "But instead of pouring it out, I poured it in. No sense in wasting good liquor." When Nate still hesitated, she blew out a frustrated breath. "I'm *fine*. And I will drink this next glass slowly and enjoy it as an alive person should."

With a full glass and Nate by her side, Sara wandered out to the patio. The warm weather still held, and she hoped the combination of good weather, food, wine and company would pull her out of her funk.

"You okay?" Cassie asked. "You look a little pale."

"Gotta admit, reading your own obituary in the paper isn't a great way to start the day." Sara dropped onto the patio chair next to Cassie's and set her glass and phone on the side table. "I've had chills before. But this was different—the sensation of rime ice instantly coating my bones, freezing me from the inside out." She wrapped her arms around her, shivering at the memory.

"I can't imagine. But the good news is you're alive."

Cassie raised her glass toward Sara. "And I aim to make sure you stay that way."

"Cassie, I need help in the kitchen," Adam called through the back door.

As her friend headed into the house, Sara pondered the possible identity of her stalker. Outrage filled her every time she considered the idea that someone she knew, or at least had crossed paths with, was doing this. If they had an axe to grind with her, they should've had the guts to face her instead of playing this passive-aggressive game.

A few minutes later, Cassie held the door for Adam, who carried a platter loaded with raw steaks. Bishop, who must have just arrived, followed him with a large bowl of what Sara presumed to be veggies.

Cassie reclaimed her chair. "The aroma out here is about to drive you out of your mind."

"I feel useless just sitting here." Sara hated not contributing, but she didn't want to get in the chefs' way. "I'll do the dishes."

"No, you won't." Cassie pointed a finger at Nate. "He will be cleaning up afterward."

"That's the only reason they invited us. So I can do the dishes." Nate rolled his eyes.

"That's the only reason we invited *you*," Adam said. "We invited Sara because we like her."

Despite her head throbbing from anger and frustration, Sara smiled. She was enjoying their easy banter. She would have enjoyed it more without the dark cloud of her own obituary hanging over her. She needed to find the person wreaking havoc on her life.

But just for this evening, she needed serenity. She picked up her glass, kicked off her shoes and strolled across the lawn, scrunching blades of grass between her toes. The feeling took her back to her grandfather's home, where she'd played with abandon in his yard of thick St. Augustine grass.

By the time Sara strolled back to the others with a grin on her face, her stress had pretty much evaporated.

"Feel better?" Nate asked her.

She nodded. "Definitely."

"Y'all better be at the table because everything's almost ready." Adam pulled the steaks from the grill, setting each one on a plate.

Everyone scrambled to the patio table.

"Where are the kids?" Bishop delivered the plates to the table, setting the only one with a fish fillet instead of a steak at his place.

"Still at my mom's." Rachel brought a platter of steaming baked potatoes with her and slid onto her seat. "Brad wanted pizza, and Mom accidentally promised him he could have it. I'll go get them later, unless they crash before I get there. In that case, Mom will be stuck with them all night."

"That might not be a bad thing." Adam waggled his brows at Rachel, who blushed.

"How does someone *accidentally* promise pizza?" Bishop set the bowl of fire-roasted vegetables next to the grilled corn for everyone to share.

Adam laughed. "Have you met Martina?"

"Everything looks amazing." Sara picked up her ear of corn, inhaling the elote seasoning on it. "And I love Mexican street corn." She took a bite, her mouth exploding with flavor.

Nate sat across from her, his eyes crinkling with amusement when she smiled at him. She hadn't noticed his tiny laugh lines before, and she liked them. They made him look more like the fun guy she'd met way back when.

As she had yesterday, Sara felt like she belonged here with these people. Like part of their extended family. A sense of tranquility settled over her like a warm cloak on a cold night. She joined in on the conversation, enjoyed every morsel of food and got a kick out of Nate's jokes and stories.

But in the back of her mind, she wondered how long this contentment would last.

Chapter Eleven

After several days with no new texts or incidents, Sara began to wonder which was worse: waiting for the other shoe to drop or the shoe actually dropping. The week after Thanksgiving had been quiet, with only a few traffic tickets to deal with. She'd come to the justice center almost every day nonetheless, organizing the filing cabinet and credenza and making the space feel more *hers*.

Now, on this chilly first Monday morning in December, she sat in her chambers reviewing the court docket. An eviction dispute, several DUIs, a few misdemeanor-assault cases from fights at a local bar called the Dead End and an elderly woman who went out in her front yard every full moon, holding her purse open and calling out "Fill 'er up" while turning in circles. Unfortunately she did it buck naked, and her neighbors had finally had enough. Not exactly the felonies Sara hoped to preside over someday as a district court judge. But at least some of them were... intriguing.

Nate, sitting in a visitor's chair and tapping away on his laptop, had already cleared the courtroom and left the bailiff standing guard inside the entrance. He glanced up and caught her watching him. "What?"

"Just curious if anyone's catching your attention on there." She tipped her head toward his computer. Cassie had received the list of the DA's Office employees from Austin several days ago, and they were working their way through it with hopes one name would pop off the page and this nightmare would be over.

"Nothing yet." He tapped his thumbs on the chair's arms.

"I wish I could've helped more." The entire list had been given to Sara first. Her job had been to review every name, looking for anyone who might've had an issue with her. She hadn't found any, so Cassie had then divided it between herself, her brothers and Bishop so they could research each employee. "It'll be a waste of so much time if he isn't even on that list."

"But worth the time if he is," Nate said. "And in the meantime, Cassie and Adam are also doing deep dives into the most likely criminal prospects."

A staccato knock sounded against the door, and Nate crossed the room and cracked it just enough to see who it was before backing up and opening it for Lorinda, Sara's judicial assistant, to enter.

"Sorry to interrupt." The woman walked briskly to her boss's desk and held out a small manila envelope. "This just came for you."

As Sara reached to take it, Nate barked out a sharp, "No!"

Sara jerked back her hand as if she'd burned it, and the assistant froze in place, her mouth and eyes wide. After pulling two tissues from the box on her desk, Nate used them to take the envelope from Lorinda without directly touching it.

"Didn't mean to scare you, but we don't know what

might be in it." Nate set it on a side table across the room. "Do you have any latex gloves?"

"Judge Harmon always kept a box of them in our storage closet in case anyone brought evidence in here." Lorinda disappeared in a blur.

Sara joined Nate. "You think it's a letter bomb or anthrax or something?"

"I'm not taking any chances." He met her eyes. "Why don't you step into your restroom and close the door?"

"Nate—"

"Please don't fight me on this. Just let me do my job."

Lorinda returned, handed him the box of gloves and what looked like a small portable scanner on the desk. "This is letter-bomb detector. Judge Harmon requisitioned it a while back, but we've never used it."

She showed Nate how it worked, then skedaddled out of the office and closed the door behind her. Nate donned a pair of the gloves, and Sara retreated into her private bathroom before she had to be told again.

Sara closed her eyes, held her breath and murmured a prayer that Nate didn't die while protecting her. Unable to hear anything through the closed door, her mind sought out every conceivable tragedy that might be happening to him.

She was about to crack open the door and take a peek when Nate called to her, "It's safe to come out."

"Was it anything deadly?" she asked.

"I'm not sure what it is." Nate glanced up from what looked like pictures in his hands. "There was a small rip in the envelope, so I used that to confirm there were no powders inside. The scanner showed no explosives, so I opened it up without compromising the adhesive, labels or stamps."

Sara stood next to him and looked at the pictures of an

older man as Nate flipped through them. The man leaving a house, coming out of a store, sitting in a diner.

"Let me see those," she said, grabbing his arm.

Nate held them out of her reach. "Put on gloves first. We may be able to get fingerprints off them."

Her hands damp with sweat, she forced them into gloves and grabbed the pack of pictures. A gasp escaped her as her stomach took a nosedive. She studied the envelope. No return address, but it had been postmarked in Cooley, Texas. Her legs turned to rubber, and she collapsed onto the closest chair.

Nate dropped to a knee in front of her. "What is it? Do you know the man in those pictures?"

Her mouth was as dry as the Chihuahuan Desert, and she could only nod for a moment. With the pictures gripped in one hand, she took hold of Nate's arm with the other, her nails digging into his skin. But he didn't even flinch. Just waited her out until she could find her voice.

"It's my grandfather." Sara's throat threatened to close again, and she gasped for air. "And the envelope was mailed from Cooley, Texas, where he lives."

NATE STOOD IN the middle of his sister's office, listening to his siblings' discussion. As soon as they'd realized her grandfather was being targeted, Sara had asked Lorinda to reschedule today's court cases. Then he'd rushed Sara to the sheriff's department within the justice center. Cassie, Adam, Noah and Bree had joined them to hash out the best plan going forward.

Cassie paced from her desk to the window and back. "I can call the Hudson County Sheriff and ask him to provide protection for your grandfather."

"I don't like the idea of leaving his safety in the hands

of a stranger." Sara shook her head. "And knowing Pops, he'd tell the sheriff he's fine on his own."

"The only other option is to have him come here," Adam said.

"Yes! I'd feel much better if he were here with me. Except we'd have the same problem. Pops will blow off the potential for danger and stay in Cooley." Sara's gaze roamed across each face in the room, coming to rest on Nate's. "Unless someone goes there and brings him back."

Silence reigned for a moment while everyone's eyes turned to Nate.

"Why are you all looking at me? My job is to keep Sara safe, and I can't do that if I'm three hundred miles away."

"Closer to two hundred." Noah cringed a little when Nate spun toward him. "Maybe two twenty-five?"

Sara stepped closer to him. "Please, Nate? I know he'll be safe with you."

He didn't like this plan. He didn't leave the side of someone he was protecting until the job was finished. And catching Sara's stalker was far from over.

"The only reason I asked you to keep Sara safe was because she didn't want us hanging around her all day and drawing attention." Cassie raised one brow in that big-sister I'm-in-charge look that Nate hated. "But that won't be an issue today. You'll be gone half a day at most. We'll keep her right here in my office until you return with her grandfather. One of us will be with her the entire time."

But cool fingers of reason coiled around his arm, halting him. "Please, Nate." The pleading look on Sara's face damn near ripped his guts out.

Pale blue eyes that normally sparkled were now dull with worry, her face drawn and colorless. With nothing more than a look passing between them, his fury hardened into stone-cold resolve. Whatever it took to end the madness of this stalker, he'd do it.

Whatever it took.

Because when he gazed down into those anguish-filled eyes, everything faded away except one inevitable reality—he would face down the very demons from hell if it made Sara Bennett happy again.

"All right, I'll do it. I'll get your grandfather and bring him here to you. Okay?"

Tears of what he hoped was relief rolled down her ashen cheeks as she nodded.

"Good. Now, the pictures the stalker took are from a distance, so why don't you give me a good description of your grandfather."

Sara recovered quickly. She brushed away her tears, glancing around as if embarrassed in front of the others. "He's tall, about six-three. And broad." She held her hands out on either side of her shoulders. "He's developed a bit of a beer belly since he retired, but don't ever mention I told you that. It's a sensitive subject."

Nate cracked a small grin. "I'm sure I can avoid bringing it up in conversation." That was the easiest promise he'd made in days.

"Basically, he's a larger-than-life pillar of dignity in snakeskin boots and a Stetson." She smiled back. "You two will get along great."

SARA WAS ON the phone to her grandfather as soon as Nate agreed to go get him. "Hi, Pops."

"Well, I'll be. And here I was, just thinking about you. Guess we've still got that Bennett mind-mojo going for us." His cheerful voice made her smile, despite the situation. "How's life down there in Boone County?"

Pops had been the first one she'd told, after Cassie, about moving to Resolute.

"I'm fine for the moment, but something alarming has been happening in my life, and I'm worried it might have spilled over into yours."

"Tell me what's going on." Her grandfather's tone changed to one of concern.

"It seems I have a stalker. Don't get upset—I'm okay. Cassie's brother Nate is a bodyguard, and he's been protecting me." As Sara filled him in, she massaged her forehead, dreading what she had to tell him next. "The thing is, we think he's been watching you, too. I received an envelope of pictures this morning. Pictures of you, your house. Nate's going to fly up there this afternoon and bring you back here so he can protect you, too."

"Hold on now, kiddo. These days, dirtbags like that can pull pictures from the internet and alter them digitally. I've seen the technique used before in intimidation schemes. Besides, this old man can take care of himself." His attempt at reassuring her fell flat.

Having a strong-willed, independent grandfather would make it difficult for her to convince him, but she had to make him understand the danger. She'd have to tread lightly, however. Pops didn't like being told what to do.

"The pictures were dated the day before yesterday. Can you remember what shirt you had on then?"

"Let me think." Pops paused. "Hmm, wasn't a shirt. It's been cool lately, so I was wearing my new green sweater. A pullover. First time I've worn it, and let me tell you, it's softer than a baby's backside."

Sara swallowed past a tightness in her throat. "With a shawl collar? Just enough of a V-neck to reveal your white undershirt beneath it?"

There was a long, drawn-out silence as Pops processed the information. "I'd rather you keep that bodyguard close to you. I'll call a couple buddies at the police department, ask them to do drive-bys of my house." He chuckled but the sound lacked the rich timbre of genuine amusement. "Give them something to do besides writing traffic tickets. Anyway, you know I don't much like to travel these days."

"Pops, the sheriff's department is treating this very seriously. They believe it's a credible threat, as well as a dangerous one. I'm afraid having a couple of local police buddies do a few drive-bys isn't going to cut it." Sara's voice shook from pent-up fear, and she paused to take a calming breath. Without a doubt, Pops was the single most important person in her life, and to lose him...

With her eyes burning from unshed tears and her voice continuing to quaver, she decided to change tactics and appeal directly to his heartstrings. "I couldn't live with myself if anything happened to you. You get that, don't you?"

Sara let her plea sink in and then hit her grandfather with a one-two sucker punch. Deliberately pushing away her fear, she replaced it with the full force of her determination to keep the one person who'd always been there for her safe. "I understand that you're not going to like hearing this," she said, using the stern, no-nonsense tone she used as a judge when passing down a sentence, "but I'm not asking you to come here. I'm telling you. Nate Reed will be coming to get you, so pack a bag. I've given him your cell number, and he'll be texting you with the details."

Then, to soften the sting of her harshly delivered demand, she repeated words of affection they had shared since she'd been a small girl: "I love you all the way up to the highest sky, all the way down to the deepest sea."

Her grandfather blew out a heavy breath. "Damn, you

drive a hard bargain, but if it'll let you rest easier, I'll do it. You know I'd do anything for you."

Relief flooded her. "I do, so I have one last favor to ask. Let one of those police buddies of yours drive you to the airport, okay? Just to be on the safe side?"

"Can't wait to see the looks on their faces when I request a chauffeur." His chuckle was genuine this time and drew a small smile from her in return.

"See you soon, Pops. I love you."

"Love you more, kiddo."

AN HOUR LATER, Nate jogged onto the tarmac at Victoria Regional Airport, where a twin-turboprop Beechcraft waited for him. He believed his siblings would do everything in their power to keep Sara safe. But he had no intention of being away from her any longer than necessary.

He'd called in a favor from country-music superstar Byron Cain, whose home was in Texas when he wasn't touring the country or recording in California. A few years back, Nate had helped Cain extricate himself from a particularly volatile situation, and the star had been more than happy to let Nate use his private aircraft in return for the favor.

As Nate closed the distance to the plane, a stout December gust ripped at his windbreaker, and he cursed himself for not wearing a heavier jacket. At least his military-grade sunglasses cut the midday sun's glare, for which he was grateful. In his line of business, even one moment of blindness could mean the difference between life and death.

He stopped before a man shading his eyes with one hand and holding the other outstretched.

"Jack Palmquist." The man shouted to be heard over the mechanical sound of the whirling engines. "I'll be your pilot today. It may be cold, but the weather's clear and we'll have a tailwind on the way. We should make good time."

Nate shook his hand. "Nate Reed. What does 'good time' mean?" He climbed aboard, the pilot following and securing the door before taking his seat.

Jack pulled out a navigation map. "Cooley Municipal Airport is about two hundred miles away as the crow flies. Best guess, we should arrive in about an hour, give or take."

"Sounds good."

"And since it's just you, feel free to sit up front if you like."

Nate hesitated, about to refuse. He had no desire to talk, but the waterways, wooded hills and limestone canyons of the Texas Hill Country would be spectacular. "Thanks. I will."

Turned out, Jack was a decent flying companion. Other than discussing a few logistics, he remained silent for the entire hour and ten minutes it took until they landed and taxied up to the terminal.

"I understand this is a round trip. We'll be returning to Victoria?"

"Yes. As soon as possible."

"All right. I'll go ahead and file my fight plan. Mr. Cain said I was at your disposal, so I'll be right here, ready and waiting, whenever you need to leave."

Again, Nate reached out and shook the man's hand. "Appreciate it. Um, Mr. Cain did mention to you that I would be picking up a passenger here, right?"

"Yes, sir, he did."

"Good. I don't anticipate this taking long. The man I'm meeting is supposed to be here already."

"As I said, ready and waiting."

Nate opened the door, stepped from the wing to the

ground and jogged several yards to the small but well-ap-
pointed terminal. Clean carpet, plush lounge chairs and
tables holding a spread of magazines.

Only one other person was there, a man sitting behind a
tall counter with a computer and phone to his right, a scale
to weigh luggage on his left. The man—Alan, according
to his name badge—was short, thin and maybe midfor-
ties. Definitely not the description Sara had given him of
her grandfather when the whole family had been arguing
about who should go get the retired judge.

Alan looked up from the magazine he'd been reading.
"Can I help you?"

"I'm looking for Archer Bennett. He was supposed to
meet me here."

"Judge Bennett called me, said he'd be fifteen minutes
late."

"How long ago did he call you?"

"About half an hour or so. But the judge lives a decent
stretch outside of town on the far side. And then there's the
train. Get stuck at one of the crossings, and it's anybody's
guess how long you could be sitting there." He shook his
head slowly. "'Specially if they start switching cars to a
sidetrack and disconnecting them."

Afraid he'd develop a tic in his eye if he listened to much
more, Nate wandered over to a wall of windows near the
front door.

Cassie had planned on calling in a favor for the police
escort, but Judge Bennett had told her not to bother, as he
and the chief were old friends. And exactly forty-six ex-
cruciating minutes later, a Cooley PD cruiser blazed into
the parking lot and a uniformed officer stepped out. He
rounded the car and opened the passenger door, holding

it for a man who fit the description of Sara's grandfather right down to the snakeskin boots.

Archer—wearing a pair of pressed blue jeans, a Western shirt with a black bolo tie secured with a silver Lone Star slide and a leather jacket—went to the trunk and pulled out a suitcase. Then he headed into the terminal.

"This man is waiting for you, Judge." Alan motioned toward Nate.

"Sorry I'm late," Bennett said. "Damn train. Nothing to do but wait the thing out."

"That's what I told him," Alan said. "Said it was probably a train."

"And you were right on the money." Bennett winked at him, then turned again to Nate. "I take it you're here for my protection, son."

He held out his hand. "Nate Reed."

Bennett gripped it tightly and shook with strength. "Judge Archer Bennett, but you can call me Archer. And son, I'm notifying you that I'm carrying."

Nate knew he was being sized up and shook the man's hand with equal force. "You're permitted to bring your weapon on board, sir, but it needs to be unloaded and safely stowed."

"I am well aware of the law. It's packed in a locked gun case in my luggage, unloaded."

They headed out the glass doors to the Beechcraft, where Jack was finishing his preflight checklist. Nate climbed onto the wing and held the door open for the judge, who crawled in with his suitcase.

Nate followed him in, and they buckled themselves into rear seats while Jack settled into the pilot's seat.

"Archer, this is our pilot, Jack Palmquist."

The two men exchanged greetings, then Jack started the

engines. Once the twin props sputtered to life, they taxied toward the runway. Ten minutes later they were airborne. The passenger area was comfortable, and it didn't take Archer long to locate the liquor bottles and glasses. He helped himself to three fingers of whiskey and offered to pour one for Nate, who refused.

He refused because he was working and needed to keep his wits about him. He was now responsible for keeping two people safe instead of one. And with no idea if the stalker was still in Cooley or back in Resolute, Nate had to be ready for anything.

"One of the nice things about being retired is that every hour is cocktail hour." The judge took a sip and released a happy sigh. "Now, son, my granddaughter filled me in on what's generally been happening, but I want to hear it from you."

Sara had told him her grandfather would pester everyone until he had all the details, so it was best to just get it all out there from the get-go. Nate spent the next twenty minutes going over everything that had happened to date. Well, everything stalker related.

"So, what does this bastard want from my granddaughter?"

"That's the frustrating thing. The text messages, the obit, even the threat to you have come with no demands, no motives. No 'do this or else.' My sister and her deputies are leaving no stone unturned in their search for the perp."

Archer sipped his drink. "Can you tell me if she's considered giving up the judgeship and going back to the Austin DA's office?"

"Wouldn't make a difference if she did. The texts started coming before she accepted the position in Resolute." Nate's voice filled with respect. "And I get the impression once she makes a commitment, she sticks to it. I'd be surprised if anything could drive her back to Austin before the election for a new judge in a few months."

"Pleased to hear that. Not about the texts—about the timing. I know full well that girl took this job to make me happy. Thinks that by becoming a judge, she'll be honoring me. Which is a big load of bullpucky. Hell, I'd be proud no matter what profession she chose. But she was always so enthusiastic about my work, and I didn't want to discourage any of her interests. Especially after what she endured."

In the bodyguard racket, Nate had learned early on not to pry. Detachment was key. But with Sara, he'd already crossed so many lines. So he urged Archer to continue. "Endured?"

"From my good-for-nothing son and his wife, the trust-fund baby. The two people who should have loved that girl the most. All she ever got from them was indifference or derision. Turned her into a timid mouse with their neglect." Archer's gaze seemed to shift inward, sadness pulling the corners of his mouth down. "Whatever spunk Sara has now was hard-won on her own behalf."

Nate saw regret on the old man's face, but he saw pride, too.

"I did what I could. Hell, I kept her almost every summer. She'd sit in court most days during the week. No life for a child, but she said she loved it." A gravelly chuckle came from deep within his chest. "When she got to be old enough to leave home alone, she wasn't having it. Still insisted on coming to the courthouse with me. Day in, day out, year after year." He looked Nate straight in the eye. "I love that girl like nobody's business, and I won't stand for someone tormenting her. You Reeds going to get this bastard?"

"Yes, sir, we are."

"That's exactly what I wanted to hear." Archer tossed back the rest of his drink, then watched the scenery below as they traveled back to Sara.

Chapter Twelve

"Pops texted that they just landed in Victoria," Sara announced to Cassie as she slid her phone back into her pocket and exhaled an afternoon's worth of anxiety. "They'll come straight here."

From the time Nate had left to get her grandfather, she'd been in either Cassie's or Adam's office, depending on which one was babysitting her at the time. Not that her friends used that term, but it was how she felt. Cassie even accompanied her to the sheriff's "private" restroom because it was actually a public one she'd commandeered with a sign and a lock.

Cassie, still researching possible stalker suspects, looked up from her computer. "I'm glad they made it back safely. Maybe now you can stop staring out my office window and sit down."

Taking one of the visitor chairs, Sara stretched out her legs and watched Cassie squint at one monitor, look at another one as if cross-checking information, then jot down notes. She'd only seen her friend a few times over the years—always when Cassie had come to Austin on business—but their friendship had been maintained through frequent phone calls. Catching up on work, agreeing that relationships were a time suck and more trouble than they were worth, sharing news about the people in their lives.

Although they'd definitely enjoyed themselves in college, they had both been serious students, working much harder than they'd played. It seemed the trend had continued as they pursued their careers. The two small frown lines between Cassie's brows never completely disappeared these days. Sara self-consciously smoothed the area at the top of her own nose with a finger, wondering if the same was true for her.

Even so, she had to give it to her friend—Cassie looked younger and happier now than the last time they'd seen each other. And Sara bet Bishop deserved the credit for that.

A knock sounded, and Cassie went to the door. "Who is it?"

"Adam."

"What's the password?"

"Very funny. Open the door."

"That's not the password. You can try again after twenty seconds."

Heavy footsteps faded away, and Cassie laughed. "His sense of humor is still a work in progress."

She'd just returned to her chair when a quick rap sounded before a key turned in the lock. Helen cracked open the door and peeked in, a stern look on her face. "Did you tell Adam I should give him *my* key to your office? You know I don't—"

"Allow anyone to touch your keys." Adam pushed the door in and stepped around Helen. "Yes, we know that. I apologize for lying, but thank you for getting me in here."

Cassie gasped. "You *lied* to Helen?"

The older woman straightened her back, pushed her glasses up on her nose and snorted. "I don't have time for this nonsense. And you're too old for these games, Adam Reed." She pulled the door shut behind her with more force than necessary.

Cassie and Adam stared at each before cracking up.

"I can't believe you did that." Cassie did a little snort-laugh that made Sara join in.

"Password?" Adam rolled his eyes as he took a seat.

Sara's phone chimed with a text, and as with the earlier one, her stomach clenched until she saw it was from her grandfather. "They're about ten minutes out, and he says Nate wants Adam downstairs by the time they park."

"*Who* says?" Adam glanced at her, brows raised.

"My grandfather. He texted me when they landed, and now they're almost here."

"Your grandfather texts?" Adam stood. "That's cool."

"What? You sound surprised that someone over seventy can text." Sara feigned outrage. "Why, Adam, is that age-ism I detect?"

Adam's posture stiffened and his jaw muscles flexed. "No, no. Nothing like that." He turned toward the door. "It's just, I was thinking about Judge Harmon, who refused to join the technical revolution. I guess what I'm trying to say is I'm impressed."

"Uh-huh."

"I'll be downstairs." He fled the office, but not before making sure they were locked in safely behind him.

"He didn't even say why he came in here in the first place. You really shouldn't tease my poor brother like that."

Rolling her eyes, Sara said, "Don't you start being a stick-in-the-mud, too." She hadn't realized how much she'd missed their good-natured bantering that had been com-monplace when they were college roommates.

Cassie's attempt at a steely expression dissolved into laughter. "Told you his sense of humor isn't fully developed."

"Well, if he's impressed my grandfather can text, Adam's in for a big surprise when he meets the man in person." Sara scoffed. "Pops only retired at seventy-five because it's the mandatory age for judges. But he's never slowed down."

"I only met him briefly at graduation, but you're right— he's going to redefine grandfathers for Adam." Cassie left her desk to look out her window. "And speaking of Pops..."

"They're here?" Sara crossed the room and stood next to Cassie.

With her heavy caseload at the DA's office, she hadn't visited Pops in months. To see him here, safe and sound, brightened what had been a long, fretful day. He appeared strong and imposing as he climbed out of the pickup, and she knew when he shook Adam's hand that Pops's firm grip had plenty of muscle behind it. *I bet you're impressed now, Chief Deputy Reed.*

As Adam had approached the passenger side of the truck, Nate rounded the back of it and stood behind her grandfather, the two brothers guarding him from all sides. The final threads of fear that had tied her in knots all day finally snapped.

It was one thing for her to feel secure in Nate's protection. But to watch him in action, his head on a swivel as he propelled her grandfather up the justice center's steps and to safety, filled her with admiration and gratitude and some other feeling she couldn't put a name to and didn't have time to figure out because her Pops was walking in the door.

"There's my girl." Her grandfather met her halfway across the office, his arms held wide to scoop her into a bear hug.

"Pops! I'm so glad you're here." Sara allowed the hug to

continue longer than normal because she knew he was as worried about her as she was him.

He finally released her and held her at arm's length. "Let me take a look at you, *Judge* Sara Bennett. These people taking good care of you?"

"Of course they are." She grabbed Cassie's hand and pulled her next to her. "You remember Cassie?"

"'Course I do." He tipped his head to the side and squinted. "But she's a mite more intimidating in that sheriff's uniform than she was in a graduation cap and gown."

Cassie smiled. "Nice to see you again, Judge Bennett. I hope your trip was uneventful."

"Gonna tell you all this one time and one time only. Call me Archer. I believe two Judge Bennetts in the same town will only confuse us all." He winked at Sara. "And yes, my trip was indeed uneventful. Would've been downright boring if I hadn't had Nate here to talk to the whole way."

Her grandfather gave her a stern look, and Sara shot a questioning glance at Nate as her cheeks began to heat. But his blank expression gave nothing away.

"I hear tell you blew up my gavel. That true?"

Although relieved he wasn't asking about Nate, Sara was heartbroken about destroying the gavel. "I'm sorry, Pops. If I'd had any idea—"

Her grandfather chuckled. "That chunk of wood's best days were in the rearview mirror long before I gave it to you. I'll get you a new one, inscribed with a special message. Best way for a judge to start their career."

Then he turned and looked each Reed in the eye. "So, what's the plan?"

AFTER A LOW-KEY law enforcement escort to the mansion, Sara stood in the foyer with her grandfather while Nate checked the house.

"Well, if this don't beat all." Pops meandered over to the staircase and grabbed the banister, trying to shake it. "The house may be old, but it's got good bones."

"And updated plumbing, thank God." Sara smiled. "It's taken some getting used to. But I still miss my condo."

Pops dismissed her words with a wave of his hand. "I never did think that hoity-toity penthouse was the right fit for you. Seemed more like someplace your mother would live."

Comparing Sara's choice of a home to her mother's lifestyle was an uncharacteristic comment for Pops to make, and the hurt she felt must have shown on her face.

"Sorry about that." He smoothed his bushy white mustache with his thumb and forefinger. "Guess the way they raised you has been on my mind lately."

Nate came down the stairs. "Everything's fine." His glance bounced from one Bennett to the other, maybe sensing the tension between them. "I'm going to scan the security footage while you two catch up."

Sara led her grandfather to a guest room on the second floor. "Do you need help settling in?"

"I travel light." Archer hoisted the bag in his hand, then set it by the bed. "But I could use a good cup of coffee."

Sara wrapped an arm around the old man's waist and leaned into him. "That I can get you."

With a mug of coffee in Pops's hand and an espresso in Sara's, they made themselves comfortable in the parlor. Well, as comfortable as one could be sitting on a stiff horsehair sofa. She would have preferred the upholstered chairs in the dining room, but she wanted to stay out of Nate's earshot. Pops's voice could carry, and she had no idea what direction the conversation might take.

Her grandfather looked like a lumberjack in a tea shop

as he searched for a place to set his mug. Sara saw a stack of glass coasters across the room and retrieved two for the side tables next to them.

Pops rested his hands on his knees. "I will say, you might want to see about some furniture more appropriate to this century."

Sara laughed. "I'm working on it. But I can't go overboard. I'll only be here a few months, just until Judge Harmon's term is up."

Pops's bushy brows headed for his hairline. "And then what?"

"Back home." She shrugged.

"Why are you so hell-bent to get back to Austin? I've never understood the attraction it holds for you." He sipped his coffee.

"It's where my life is." Smiling, she added, "And after I'm done here, maybe I'll have a better shot at becoming a district judge up there."

"Sara, I appreciate you wanting to follow in my footsteps. But you don't have to be a judge to make me proud of you." His blue eyes, almost as pale as hers, shined with tenderness. "I just want you to be happy doing whatever it is you love."

Folding one leg beneath her, Sara turned sideways on the couch to face her grandfather. "But I *am*. I love the judicial system." She took one of his hands, covered with prominent veins and age spots, in hers. "But I never wanted to become a judge *for* you. I want to be one *because* of you."

His brows pulled together like two caterpillars about to do battle. "Why don't you do an old man a favor and explain the difference."

"I've always wanted to make you proud of me, no matter what I did. And that's because I respect you so much—as a judge and as an honorable man. The summers I spent with you were my best childhood memories, and during those times I learned about ethics and morals and the difference a person can make when they live by their principles." She leaned forward and kissed his leathery cheek. *"That's* why I wanted to be a judge."

Pops ducked his head away from her and swiped at his eye. "You people ever dust in here? Something's making my eyes itch."

Sara kept a straight face. "I never dust in here. It gives my guests an excuse to cry without getting embarrassed."

At that, Pops straightened, scrubbed his hands across his face and chuckled. "I must be getting soft in my old age."

"You?" She shook her head. "Never."

"You mean the world to me, kiddo."

"The feeling's mutual." She took a sip of her cooling espresso. "So, you ready for dinner?"

"I just need to get one thing straight."

"Yes?" *Please don't let him ask if there's anything going on between Nate and me.*

"If you've always wanted to be a judge, regardless of the reason why, and you're now a judge, why give it up when the term's over? Why not run for the position?"

"Because I'm not a district judge, and this isn't Travis County." Sara sighed. "And like I said earlier, I enjoy living in Austin."

"Hmm. So being a rural county judge isn't good enough? You want to be more important than that?"

"That's not what I said."

"Sorry—I must have misunderstood." Pops stood, mug of coffee in hand. "Just do me one favor, okay? While you're here, take a good look around."

"At what?"

But instead of answering, he headed toward the kitchen, leaving her to wonder what pearl of wisdom she had just missed.

Chapter Thirteen

Despite Nate's suggestion that court be postponed for another day or more, he'd been overruled. Sara hadn't wanted the arraignments to get even more backed up than they were after the Thanksgiving-week holiday and the Pops Express trip yesterday.

And Pops had insisted on seeing her in action on the bench while he was here. The general consensus was that the Boone County judicial system would not be held hostage by Sara's stalker.

The last case of the day was the naked moon worshipper, and that one moved more quickly than expected since Sara refused to view the footage brought in by the neighbors. The woman agreed to wear clothes in the future or stick to her backyard. With that, Tuesday was a wrap.

While they waited in Sara's chambers for her to freshen up in her private bathroom, Nate turned to Archer. "What did you see outside the diner last night?"

The three of them had gone to the Busy B for dinner the previous evening, as Archer had been craving chicken-fried steak. Nate, sitting across from Sara and her grandfather, had noticed the old man sneaking furtive glances through the diner's front window.

"That obvious, huh?" Archer smoothed his mustache. "Just thought someone passing by looked familiar, but it was probably nothing."

"Brown jacket, ball cap pulled low on his forehead?"

Archer's eyes widened. "You don't miss a thing, do you?"

"Wouldn't be very good at my job if I did." Nate glanced at the closed powder-room door. "Where'd you recognize him from?"

"I didn't get a good look at his face, so I'm not sure." He shrugged. "It was more just a feeling, like I'd seen someone move the same way, walk with a similar gait."

Nate had spent enough time with Archer Bennett over the past two days to realize he was an intelligent man with good instincts. And the old man would never put his grand-daughter at risk. So Nate wouldn't push him just yet on who he thought he'd seen.

Sara stepped into the room. "I'm glad you were here for today's cases, Pops, and not the one I had a couple weeks ago. Live geese took over the courtroom."

"It was a joy to watch you dispensing justice, my girl." Archer's chest visibly swelled. "But I bet the geese were something to see."

"I can laugh about it now, but at the time…" She shook her head. "We ready to head home?"

"We've just been waiting for you." Nate finally pulled his gaze from her, no easy task when she was glowing with happiness. *Her grandfather brings that out in her.* A tiny prickle of envy toward the old man stung him.

They walked down the steps of the justice center, Nate looking around for possible threats.

Archer paused. "Nice little town you got here. That town square across the way is special. Gives the place a real down-home feeling. I'd like to get a picture or two while we're here."

Uncomfortable with them dawdling out in the open, Nate opened his mouth to urge them into his truck. But at the last second, he stopped himself. Something didn't ring true with this scenario. They'd already given Archer the fifty-cent tour of Resolute, and he hadn't stopped once for a picture.

Catching the sly look Archer aimed at him, Nate did another visual sweep of the area. Scanning the town square, he caught sight of the brown-jacketed man from outside the diner last night. Although his pulse jumped, Nate's eyes moved past the man as if he were nothing more than a light post.

The judge fished his phone from his jacket pocket and fiddled with it before aiming it past the corner of the town square toward some shops, as a tourist might do.

Nate's phone chirped, and he ignored it.

"Aren't you gonna get that, son? Might be something important."

Nate's siblings came down the front steps and joined them as he checked his messages.

Brown jacket park bench. Saw him outside my house in Cooley.

Nate forwarded the text to his siblings, then stepped closer to Archer. Pointing down the street as if at something of interest, he asked, "You sure?"

"As sure as cornbread goes with greens."

Sara stepped closer. "Will someone tell me what the hell is going on?" Her voice was low.

Archer put his arm around his granddaughter's shoulders. "Just look at my phone like I'm showing you pictures."

He pointed to the screen, and she nodded. "There's a guy in the park across the street who was outside my house a few days ago and outside the diner last night."

Sara's head jerked up, but before she could look toward the town square Archer whispered into her ear, and she focused on his phone again.

Nate pointed at the justice center's facade. "While you two pretend to take pictures of the building, make your way up the steps to the door."

Cassie nodded and laughed as if someone had made a joke, then spoke softly. "Nate, you go straight at him. Adam will circle around and come in from the north side of the square. I'll come from the east. Everyone watch for weapons." She glanced at Noah. "You stay with Sara and Archer, and as soon as we make our move, get them back inside." She walked toward her SUV, calling over her shoulder, "See you tomorrow."

Adam followed on her heels, heading for his vehicle.

Archer bellowed to Nate, "Son, I want a photo of my granddaughter and me at the top of the steps."

Noah followed them, standing just out of frame, as he would if they were really taking pictures. Nate backed up into the street, facing the justice center, pretending to do the old man's bidding. When the text popped up that Adam and Cassie were in position, Nate continued to hold up his phone as if snapping photos of Archer and Sara. But he'd flipped the camera around so he could watch the man in the brown jacket behind him.

No longer sitting on the bench, the man now leaned against a tree, splitting his attention between the picture-taking scene in front of him and his own phone.

While Archer and Sara changed poses, Nate waited until his siblings eased into his selfie screen. Then he shoved his phone into his jeans pocket, turned and ran toward the town square.

Startled like the proverbial deer, the man froze. Only for a second, but it was enough time for Nate to almost reach him. And when the stranger finally snapped out of it, he took off like a lightning flash, beelining directly for Cassie.

The head-on collision was avoided at the last moment when the man jerked sideways, pivoting into the landscaped areas and hotfooting it like his heels were ablaze.

Damn, he's fast.

Nate signaled Adam, each rounding on him from a different direction, but the guy ran like a world-class sprinter. Cassie circled back and joined in the chase as they left the square and tore down Main Street.

Nate saw the brown jacket whip around a corner a half block ahead. "Cut him off!" he yelled, waving his arms to indicate the direction.

Cassie angled left and headed for the next parallel street. As Nate started to round the corner, Cassie, running past the far end of the block, motioned for him to keep going on Main. At the next intersection, Adam peeled off onto the cross street while Nate continued east.

Passing the next alley, Nate saw a flash of movement and charged. The man was tiring. Nate gained precious inches on their person of interest. The man looked over his shoulder, slowing him down more. Nate surged forward, reached out his hand.

So close.

He leaped, yelling as the breeze sailed through his hair. For a second, he thought he'd come up empty. But at the last second, his arms wrapped around the man's torso, and he took him down.

As a painful expulsion of breath came from the man,

Nate silently thanked him for cushioning his own fall. Unable to struggle, the man gaped like a fish out of water, desperately seeking oxygen. Nate pulled the man's arm behind his back and slid his own through it, putting pressure on both the elbow and shoulder at once.

All the suspect could do was lie face down, groaning. Each time he tried to pull loose, Nate tweaked his grip, shutting all movement down.

Cassie and Adam converged on them from opposite ends of the alley.

Panting, Cassie pulled cuffs from her belt bag, then paused. "How are you keeping him pinned like that? It looks like you're barely holding him down."

Nate smiled up at her. Technique.

"I want to arrange for you to teach a class on that to my department." She cuffed the man's loose arm to the one Nate held, then sat him against the wall.

"Be happy to, sis."

"Want me to call for a car?" Adam asked.

Still out of breath, Cassie nodded. "I'm not taking any chances by walking this guy all the way back." While Adam radioed the office, she looked at Nate. "See how much fun you've been missing out on by not becoming a deputy? With four Reeds on the force, no criminal would dare set foot in Boone County."

"Nice try." Nate tipped his head toward the restrained man. "You got this?"

"Of course. Go on, check on your *client*."

He didn't need to be told twice. Getting a second wind, he jogged back toward the justice center. If this was their guy, Nate would finally be able to tell Sara that she was safe. The dark circles under her eyes would disappear and he'd once again see that dazzling smile of hers.

Then an ache in his chest slowed his pace, and he wondered what a heart attack felt like. But he knew this pain wasn't that.

If Sara was safe, she would no longer need a bodyguard. It would be time for him to leave for California.

LESS THAN AN hour later Nate stood in the small observation area, scowling at their runner through the thick one-way glass of the interrogation room. It appeared they had their guy. That should have set him at ease, but he couldn't shake the feeling that something wasn't right. It didn't help that his body confirmed his apprehension, remaining stiff, his muscles knotted with tension. "So, you're sure. You've never seen this guy before?"

Standing beside him, Sara crossed her arms over her chest, her hands holding her upper arms as if she were cold. Although physically safe at the moment, her cocooned stance told Nate fear still controlled her mind. And yet he couldn't bring himself to comfort her. He'd be leaving soon, and it was time to start separating business from pleasure. Go back to the way things should have been all along. Detached. Professional.

She shook her head. "Never."

Her brows furrowed as she watched Cassie and Noah enter the interrogation room. Harsh fluorescent lights illuminated four walls covered in gunmetal-gray paint, chipped and dingy. In the center of the room, two metal chairs sat on one side of a scarred metal table that was bolted to the floor. The runner sat on the opposite side, his hands free, but a handcuff bar attached to the table was ready in case the need arose. A camera was mounted on one wall, high in the corner.

Cassie stood back as Noah sat opposite the subject, handed him a plastic bottle of water and opened a folder.

Why let Noah have the lead?

This wasn't like Cassie at all, particularly on such a notable case. His sister was a take-charge kind of person, had been her whole life. Adam had been talking up Noah's performance of late, especially since he and Bree had cracked the meth-ring case. Still, it was hard for Nate to ignore years of memories concerning his twin's antics.

"This interview is being recorded. This is Deputy Sheriff Noah Reed. Also present is Sheriff Cassie Reed. Now then, sir, I need your name for our records."

A microphone carried Noah's voice into the observation area. His timbre was firm, the kind of tone that brooked no nonsense. Nate decided he would just have to trust Cassie to know what she was doing with regards to Noah.

The perp's dark, limp hair was plastered to his head with dried sweat. His stubbly chin hardened with hostility. "Am I under arrest?"

"Not yet." Noah rested his forearms on the table and leaned forward. Like a confidant or a friend. "Just want to ask you a few questions."

The man picked up the bottle of water and drained it.

"You know, I need some water, too. If you're done, I'll bring you another bottle." The man nodded, and Cassie picked up his empty by the bottom edge and left the room.

It was an old interrogation technique. Make the perp uncomfortable by adjusting the thermostat or creating a full bladder, then suddenly they were only too anxious to talk. As an added bonus, taking the bottle was a great way to grab a set of prints, if the subject continued refusing to talk.

Noah tried again. "So, your name?"

"If I ain't under arrest, how 'bout you tell me why you

dragged me in here. Otherwise I'm filing false-arrest charges." The man crossed his arms and tipped back in his chair.

"I need all four of those chair legs on the floor," Noah said.

"Or what?"

"Or I'll have to cuff you. For your own safety."

"This is some BS," the man muttered but dropped the front two legs to the floor.

Way to go, Noah. Another interrogation technique. Get a perp to comply in small ways before hitting them with the hard stuff. Nate reminded himself the man was only a person of interest, not officially a perp. Not yet anyway.

"We'd like to know why you've been following Judge Archer Bennett." Noah's voice remained neutral as Cassie returned with waters for everyone.

"Man, I don't even know who you're talking about."

After sipping some water, Cassie got that determined look. And that was the exact moment Nate understood her strategy. It was right out of the old trusty playbook—only Cassie was more subtle than most. Good cop, bad cop. Noah had gone in soft, and now Cassie…

She screwed the cap back on her bottle and in a deceptively calm voice said, "He's the man whose house you were seen outside of in Cooley. You were also spotted outside the Busy B Café, watching him through the window last night."

"You don't know what you're talking about. I ain't never been nowhere near Cooley in my whole life. Don't even know where it's at. And last I checked, it's not illegal to walk down a street outside of a diner."

"What's your purpose for being in Resolute?" Noah asked.

"None of your damn business. Got as much right to be here as you do."

Cassie twisted her lips to the side. "Hmm. All depends on what you're doing here." She took another sip of water. "So, why'd you run from us in the town square?"

And here it is. The bait and switch. Nate admired his sister's ingenuity. She was leading the man exactly where she wanted him, like a lamb to slaughter.

"Some strange guy comes charging me, damn right I'm gonna run." The man stretched his legs out beneath the table as if getting comfortable for a casual chat. "When the two uniforms joined in…" He shrugged. "I ran faster. What can I say? It was instinct."

Cassie gave her own shrug. "I totally get it. In your situation, who wouldn't run? But just so I have this straight, you were aware that my deputy and I were chasing you?"

Her trap was set. *Now, if only…*

The man snorted. "Kinda hard to miss when you and I almost collided."

The corner of Nate's mouth turned up in a wicked grin. He glanced at Noah, who wore a similar smirk.

Apparently Sara also knew the score because she whispered, "She's got him now."

Cassie nodded at Noah. "You're under arrest for eluding law enforcement officers. You have the right to remain silent…"

While Cassie went on Mirandizing him, Noah frisked the uncooperative stalker, pulling out the contents of his pockets and setting them on the table to be cataloged as part of the booking process—a set of keys, small pocketknife, lighter, wallet and some loose change. Then he cuffed him to the bar on the table as Cassie sat and picked up her pen. "I need your name, address and date of birth."

"The hell you say. I'm not telling you anything."

Noah tsked. "Sure you want to go that route? Refus-

ing to identify yourself when placed under arrest is another charge."

"Stubborn." Sara's face was a blank mask.

Nate wondered what she was thinking. Relieved the
nightmare was over and her life could return to normal?
If so, it didn't look like it.

As the interrogation room back-and-forth continued,
Nate took the opportunity to ask her again about the man.
"You're positive you don't know him from anywhere? The
Travis County courthouse or the DA's office? Maybe he
lives in your apartment building or delivered food to you?"

Sara shook her head. "I swear, I've never met this man.
If we did cross paths, I never even noticed him."

In the interview room, Cassie picked up the man's wallet
and tore open the Velcro tab. "Patrick Weaver of Austin,
Texas." Cassie stared at him. "Where do you know Sara
Bennett from?"

The man blew out a hard breath. "I already done told
you I don't know no Archer Bennett. Why would I know
his grandkid?"

"Never said they were related. Interesting that you knew
that."

Weaver sat straighter in his chair, concern radiating on
his face for the first time since he'd been brought in. "I
just guessed they were related. Same last name and all."

"Could have been his mother or his wife, and yet you
knew she was his granddaughter." Cassie shrugged. "You
can see why I'm having a hard time buying that you're
being straight with me."

"I am, I swear. It was just a guess. Like I said—just a
guess." Weaver continued to protest, but Cassie ignored
him.

Over his heated arguments, she pressed her shoulder

mic. "Chief Deputy Reed, please bring a tray and an inventory form for Mr. Weaver's possessions, then book him for eluding and failure to identify."

Weaver turned his head and glared at the one-way glass with hate-filled eyes. "She's back there, isn't she? I know you are!" he screamed. "You'll be sorry!"

SARA'S ARMS QUIVERED and her forehead felt clammy as the man's cold gaze seemed to study her through the mirrored glass. When a wave of light-headedness hit her, she recognized her body's reaction as the drop after an adrenaline rush. It wasn't every day she came face-to-face with a man bent on scaring the daylights out of her—or worse, his threat of violence.

"I guess we can add criminal retaliation to his list of charges." She tried to make light of the moment even while chilled to the bone by Weaver's last words. "He's not terribly bright, is he?"

Nate continued to stare into the interview room, seemingly oblivious to her discomfort, while Adam wrapped things up with Weaver. "Clearly he has a beef with you. His rant didn't jog your memory?"

No words of comfort. No reassurance that she was safe. That hurt. Far more than she imagined.

Patrick Weaver. Who are you? She ran his name over and over in her mind, trying to pick him out from among the millions of random memories jumbled in her head. There had to be a connection. From her work as an attorney, she knew stalkers were typically highly motivated individuals. Deluded, but motivated.

"Sorry, Nate, but I have no idea why this guy has so much hostility toward me. Is it too farfetched that a total stranger has been the one trying to upend my life?" Rubbing her arms in a futile attempt to vanquish the cold tingles, she leaned against Nate for support.

Hoping for the warm comfort of his arms, Sara was left feeling deprived when he chose to leave them hanging at his sides. She pulled away from his stiff and unyielding body, blinking back hot tears of fear, anxiety, a bit of relief and a whole mess of loneliness.

"At least we know who he is," Nate said. "The department can run background checks on him now."

Wow. Talk about your sterile, professional reply. Not at all the soft words of a lover, or even the compassionate comment of a friend. Okay, so their relationship wasn't slated for the long haul, but that didn't mean it had to be completely devoid of feelings. Did it?

The door to the observation space opened, and Nate stepped even farther away as Adam leaned into the room. "While we run him through our databases, you two want to join us in the bullpen? See what we find?"

"I would," Sara replied brusquely. "What about you, Nate? Or do you consider this assignment over?" If Nate wanted to play at cold detachment, it behooved her to follow suit. She didn't suffer fools lightly, even if that fool was her. Especially then.

Nate's eyes narrowed. "I don't care how good this guy looks as your stalker—I'm not leaving your side until we have proof."

Sara nodded and followed Adam down the hall, Nate right behind her. There was a part of her that acknowledged she should appreciate that he was still in bodyguard mode even with a suspect in custody. But another part of her wasn't quite ready to deal with the case being over and Nate going back to California for good.

One issue at a time. Sitting in a chair at an empty desk,

she focused on the activity in the room. Cassie and Adam had taken over bullpen computers instead of working in their offices—apparently for easier communication among the group. Sara could see a list of names on Noah's monitor as he scrolled through them.

While they ran a background check on Weaver and ran his name through criminal and fingerprint databases, Sara suddenly realized she hadn't seen her grandfather since she'd gone into the observation room. "Anyone know where Pops is?"

Noah chuckled. "Hanging out with Helen. Thick as thieves, those two. Fact is I'm pretty sure I heard Helen giggle, and that *never* happens."

Pops had been a widower for so long, Sara never considered him enjoying female companionship. She tucked the thought away for later.

Noah looked up from his monitor. "Got something. He works—or at least did—at the Travis County District Attorney's Office."

All eyes in the room swung toward Sara as her jaw dropped.

"In what capacity?" Cassie asked.

Noah's fingers flew across his keyboard. "According to this roster of employees they sent us at the start of our investigation, there's a Patrick Weaver listed as a mailroom clerk."

Nate pulled his chair closer to Sara. This time she didn't look at it as a gesture of comfort but as his eagerness to finish the job. The case against Patrick Weaver was stacking up, and Nate had just said he would leave once they had proof. "Sara? Ring any bells?"

She cursed her ability to focus intently on whatever she worked on. As an assistant DA, that had meant blocking out conversations, arguments, everything going on around her. "I think I've heard my administrative assistant address someone as Pat, but I never paid much attention. I suppose she could've been talking to the guy who delivered mail to our office."

"Maybe that's what this is all about." Adam swiveled his chair toward her. "Maybe he's been infatuated with you, and you never even knew he existed."

"Unrequited love." Noah nodded. "I've read plenty of case files about that. The person in love finally can't take being ignored anymore."

"I wasn't ignoring him." Sara's voice came out sharper than intended. "I was busy concentrating on my own work."

Cassie crossed the room and rested a hand on her friend's shoulder. "We're not saying you're to blame in any way. We're just trying to figure out a possible motive."

"What about his phone?" Nate asked. "How soon can you check its records?"

"I'll request a court order for its location data before we finish up tonight. If the data shows what I think it will, we'll have enough probable cause for a warrant to access his call and text history." She returned to her own seat and continued scanning the background check she'd been running.

"Since Sara's the judge, can't she—"

"Nope." Cassie interrupted Nate halfway through his question. "Conflict of interest. I'll have to ask the district court judge who serves Boone County."

By the time they were finished for the evening, they'd found no criminal records for Patrick Weaver. His fingerprints weren't a match for any in the databases. Cassie submitted the request for the court order, and everyone headed home to rest up and prepare for another busy day tomorrow.

Letting her grandfather sit up front with Nate, Sara relaxed in the back seat, trying to get a read on her own emotions. Relief warred with anxiety when she thought about her case. She was sure they'd caught her stalker, but the actual evidence was circumstantial.

Even if—*when*—they established his guilt, that didn't mean he'd stay locked up. As an assistant district attorney, she'd seen enough guilty people walk away on technicalities not to take conviction as a foregone conclusion. They needed more evidence because she had no intention of living the rest of her life looking over her shoulder.

Getting a read on her feelings for Nate was harder to pinpoint. Having her stalker behind bars was obviously the outcome she wanted, yet it left her relationship with Nate at a crossroads. She would no longer need a bodyguard. He would no longer need to stay in Texas.

They'd made no commitments to one another. No promises. And she realized from his behavior in the observation room that he was already putting distance between them. Physical *and* emotional distance. Not for some bodyguard code of conduct, but as a way to end things between them.

She and Nate had been sleeping together since Thanksgiving night, staying in separate rooms only since Pops had arrived. She'd known from the get-go that their relationship would be short-lived. But the thought that she'd already made love with Nate for the last time made her heart thump a sad, dull rhythm against her ribs.

Watching Resolute slide past the car window, Sara shook her head. *We didn't make love. We had sex. Love was never a factor in any of this.*

Chapter Fourteen

The next evening Sara stepped through the doorway of the Chute, reportedly the best restaurant and honky-tonk in the county. She'd heard about it when she was in town a decade ago and had wanted to check it out. She'd never made it inside then but was excited to finally see the county landmark.

As she and Pops walked ahead of Nate through the old cattle chute to the hostess stand, her head turned from side to side, taking in the busy bar on one side, pool tables and shuffleboards on the other.

"Will you look at that." Archer pointed toward the far end of the cavernous room ahead. "They have one of those mechanical bulls." He scoffed. "They've even got a line of durn fools waiting to break their necks."

Sara went up onto her toes to see the contraption she would have ridden without a second thought back in the day. Now she supposed flying through the air and landing in an undignified position wasn't the best look for the local judge.

"Howdy, Nate." The young, pretty hostess greeted him with a sparkly smile. "I hear you're quite the hometown hero."

Nate's eyebrows climbed toward his hairline. "What are you talking about, Crystal?"

She rolled her eyes. "You really think you can chase a bad guy through the streets of Resolute—and catch him, I might add—without everyone hearing about it?"

"Gotta love small towns." Pops chuckled, and Sara joined.

Nate crossed his arms and dropped his gaze. "I'm no hero. I was just doing my job."

"And there you go, trying to be all humble on top of it." Crystal finally pulled her flirtatious gaze from Nate and turned her attention to Sara and Pops. "Howdy, ma'am, sir. Welcome to the Chute."

"Please don't call me *ma'am*. Makes me feel ancient." Sara laughed. "I'm—"

"Oh, my goodness. You're Judge Bennett. The new judge." A blush crept up Crystal's neck. "I should have recognized you straight away."

"No reason you should have. I haven't really been out and about much since I arrived." Which hopefully would change soon. She smiled, hers a lot less flirtatious than the hostess's had been toward Nate.

Pops stuck his hand out. "And I'm the new judge's grandfather." His chest puffed out in obvious pride. "No reason you should've recognized me, either." He let out a hearty laugh that put the young woman at ease.

Crystal gathered menus and napkin-wrapped silverware. "Well then, howdy, Judge Bennett and Judge Bennett's grandfather. It's a pleasure to meet you both. I'm assuming you three are part of Sheriff Reed's party?" Nate nodded. "Y'all are the first ones here. If you'll follow me, I'll get you seated."

The hostess led them through the restaurant to a round table in a secluded alcove, away from prying ears and loud customers. She placed a menu at each place setting. "I'll send your waiter over for drink orders."

As Sara started to sit, Nate took hold of her elbow and directed her to one of the chairs against the wall. "Until further notice, we're still assuming you're in danger." He sat beside her while Pops settled in on her other side.

Her grandfather patted her knee. "I sure hope that's what this dinner is about. That they've got the right guy and can keep him locked up."

"Thanks, Pops. Me, too." She leaned her head against his shoulder for a moment before straightening, not wanting to give in to the mental exhaustion plaguing her. "Let's hope Cassie has discovered additional evidence."

Sara's curiosity about Weaver had made it hard to focus on the cases on her docket today. And then there'd been Nate. From the corner of her eye, she'd watched him standing to the side of the bench, stoically studying every face in the courtroom. He'd been civil last night and this morning. Friendly, even. But having observed the barrier he'd thrown up yesterday, she couldn't now unsee it.

A waiter, dressed in jeans and a cowboy shirt, approached the table. "Howdy, folks. My name's Justin, and I'm your server this evening. Can I get you started with drinks and an appetizer?"

"Howdy, Justin." Pops grinned at the young man. "I'll have a bourbon and branch."

"Very good, sir. And you, miss?"

Sara bit back a chuckle. Justin must've known calling a woman *miss* instead of *ma'am* made his female customers happy. "I'd like a glass of Riesling."

"Just water for now, Justin," Nate said. "Maybe something later with dinner."

"Of course, Nate. And by the way, great job yesterday.

Wish I could've seen you tackle that guy." Justin turned and headed for the bar.

"My, my." Sara chuckled. "Word certainly gets around fast in Resolute. Looks like we're having dinner with an honest-to-God hero, Pops."

"Must be why we've got this extra-special table with its own little cubbyhole."

Nate dragged his fingers through his hair. "Another reason I prefer Los Angeles. Nobody knows anybody out there."

"Ah, come on, son. Must feel pretty good to know people appreciate you so much." Pops met Nate's eyes. "And in case you didn't know, my granddaughter and I think you're a hero, too. Don't we, hon?"

Sara's smile, though genuine, tightened. "Of course we do." She unwrapped her silverware, not wanting to meet Nate's eyes. "Who wouldn't?"

Fortunately, Justin returned with their drinks. As he set a glass of ice water in front of Nate, he asked, "Sure I can't bring you something stronger?"

"No, thanks. I'm still on the clock."

"I thought the guy's locked up." Justin tucked his drink tray under his arm.

"Can't really talk about it." Nate kept his answer short. "You know, ongoing investigation."

Justin's eyes widened, and he glanced over his shoulder as if trouble was imminent before giving Nate a slow nod. "Gotcha."

Sara sipped her wine, staring blankly at her menu. Nate had just referred to dinner as still being on the clock. If she'd had any doubts that she was nothing more than a job, they were gone now. Made it difficult not to feel the fool, thinking the affection he'd shown her had been real. But nothing real could be shut off that quickly.

"Well, in case you change your mind, Sal said first round's on the house for the hero's table." Justin took off again, weaving his way through the tables in the main part of the dining room.

"Who's Sal?" Sara asked.

"The manager." Nate dropped his head back and closed his eyes. "I just hope he doesn't do something embarrassing, like make an announcement before the music and dancing starts later."

An attractive woman passing their table paused, then turned to stare at Nate. "I'm so sorry to intrude." An apologetic smile accompanied her heavy Texas accent. "But I couldn't help overhearing the waiter just now. Are you the one who arrested that strange man running through town yesterday?"

"No, ma'am." Nate managed a closed-mouth smile in return. "I'm not in law enforcement. The sheriff's department arrested him."

"But you caught him, right? That's what everyone's saying." She actually batted her lashes at him. "I just wanted to thank you for keeping our town safe. You really are a hero."

Nate studied the woman. "You were in court today, weren't you?"

"My goodness, how sweet of you to notice me, let alone remember." Her gaze floated from Nate to Sara, the woman's smile turning smug. "I was. Heard such great things about our new judge, I just had to come see her in action. A darn site more impressive than Judge Harmon." She nodded at Sara. "Well, I've taken up enough of your time. Y'all enjoy your dinner."

While the woman followed Justin's path toward the bar,

Sara arched a brow at Nate. In a Southern drawl as thick as the woman's, she said, "I do declare, you have admirers wherever you go, Nathaniel Reed." She nearly gave herself a seizure trying to imitate the lash flutter.

Her comment was half teasing—but only half. And it irritated her that the other half seemed to have jealousy behind it. Sara had never dealt with the green-eyed monster in her life. There was no logic in it showing up now.

Fortunately, Nate didn't react to her words at all. He was too busy reading something on his phone after it had chimed with a text.

"Cassie says they're just leaving the justice center. They'll be here in a few minutes."

Sara leaned toward him. "Did she say anything else?"

"Nope. We'll have to wait till they get here." Nate raised his water. "Here's to good news."

"Here's to sleeping in my own bed again." Pops chuckled as he held his glass up.

Sara clinked her glass against theirs. The only wish she had about *her* bed was that Nate would share it with her one last time. Then, annoyed at herself for being so weak willed, she said, "Here's to locking Weaver up and throwing away the key."

Pops turned his attention to Nate. "What about you, son? Sara mentioned you have a big meeting coming up. When do you leave for California?"

"As soon as possible. I'd originally planned on going back right after Thanksgiving."

Her grandfather frowned. "What if my granddaughter's safety isn't a done deal by the time you're ready to go?" He smoothed his mustache. "I understand you've got a business to run. But in my book, when a man takes a job, he doesn't quit until it's finished."

"Pops…" Sara rested a hand on his arm.

Nate nodded at the older man. "I feel the same way, sir. And I'll stay here as long as I possibly can." He met Sara's eyes for a moment, then looked away. "Worst-case scenario, I'll have two of my best bodyguards from California in place here before I leave."

Sara's eyes narrowed, and she swallowed back her growing fury. Nate had no right to think he could take off and leave two strangers in her home just because he had someplace else to be.

Realizing her soft touch on her grandfather's arm had turned into a biting clench, Sara removed it and with a deep breath, focused on smoothing the napkin on her lap. She felt Pops's stare and needlessly rubbed her hands across her thighs.

Turning to Nate, Pops asked, "You saying it takes two of your men to do what you do by yourself?" He tsked. "If that's the case, sounds like maybe they're not your best men."

Nate rubbed the spot between his brows with a finger as if warding off a headache. "No, sir, that's not what I'm saying. If it does become necessary, the only reason I'd double the protection is to give Sara more peace of mind."

Peace of mind, my sweet patootie. I'd like to give you a piece of my mind.

"Hmm." Pops sounded as unimpressed as Sara was annoyed.

Nate looked at her, and out of the corner of her eye she saw his forehead crease with curiosity or concern or confusion. She wasn't sure which, and she couldn't care less.

"You okay, Sara?" Pops asked her. "You've been quieter than a possum playing dead."

"I'm fine." She forced the words out with barely moving her lips. "I'm just peachy keen and hunky dory."

"Now, don't be upset with me for grilling Nate. My main concern is your safety." Pops put his arm around Sara's shoulders for a brief side hug. "But truth be told, I'll be happy when things are back to normal, too. As much as I love spending time with you, I miss my routine at home." He chuckled. "Never thought I'd become one of those old geezers set in their ways, but here we are."

That got a snort out of Sara. "You were always set in your ways, Pops. They just changed a little with the seasons. Remember when I was there during the summers? You basically kept your routine but adapted it to include me." Sara leaned her head against his shoulder. "Now they're changing with the seasons of your life."

Her grandfather planted a light kiss on Sara's cheek. "How'd you get to be so smart?"

"I must have inherited it." She smiled as they finished their well-worn joke together. "But it obviously skipped a generation."

Her own laughter filled Sara with a warmth that lifted her mood a little. Never one to get into personal arguments in public, she'd save her quarrel with Nate for later. Maybe it would be a moot point. Maybe Weaver was their guy, Nate could head home and she wouldn't need any more bodyguards disrupting her life.

Nate better hope that turns out to be the case. Because now she wanted to be done with him. And the sooner, the better.

"Sorry we're late."

Nate looked up to see Cassie slide into the chair next to Archer while Adam and Noah grabbed the other two empty seats. He watched them closely, looking for any hint about Weaver. Giving up, he asked, "Well?"

Cassie's mouth curled into a satisfied smile. "We got him."

Sara whispered, "Are you sure? How—" She cut herself off as Justin reappeared.

"Hey there, Cassie, Adam, Noah. How y'all doin'?"

"We'll be better after you bring us three margaritas on the rocks," Noah said. "Extra limes."

Adam glanced at Nate's glass of water. "You're not drinking?"

"Unless I'm told otherwise, I'm working." Nate shrugged.

Cassie leaned forward. "Nate, you're no longer working."

"In that case, why don't you go ahead and bring me one of those." He indicated Archer's bourbon and branch.

Justin nodded, then looked at Archer. "I'll go ahead and bring you a fresh one—" he glanced at Sara "—and another glass of wine." He stage-whispered to the newcomers, "First round is on Sal tonight."

"The court order came through." Noah's voice rose with excitement. "You won't believe what the location data showed."

Adam laid a hand on Noah's shoulder. "Let your sister tell them. The whole restaurant doesn't need to hear this."

Cassie picked up where Noah had left off. "The location data showed Weaver's phone had been in Austin until about a month ago." She met Sara's eyes. "It popped up here in Resolute the day before you arrived."

Sara's chin dropped. "He got here *before* me?"

"Probably saw that newspaper article and decided to get a head start." It was a plausible explanation, but the inferred planning involved made Nate edgy.

Cassie nodded and continued. "The phone's been in

Boone County most of the time since then." She held up a finger to emphasize her next words. "Except for a trip to Cooley, Texas, for the two days right before Nate flew up to get Archer."

"That's it. You really do have him." The relief in Sara's voice was palpable.

"But wait, there's more," Noah said in a middle-of-the-night commercial announcer's voice.

"The location data gave us enough to request a warrant for the phone's calls and texts, like we'd hoped." Cassie grinned. "It was issued this morning. The phone was wiped clean, but I sent it to the forensics lab. The tech said there's a good chance they'll be able to recover everything. And those texts he sent will tie him directly to you."

"Have you found out where he'd been staying?" Nate asked.

"Not yet." Adam paused while Justin returned with their drinks, took their food order and left again. "We checked with Doc, and he thinks Weaver might have checked into his motor court for his first couple days in town. But if it *was* him, he gave a fake name—Doc's eyesight isn't the best—and the room's been turned over at least twice since then."

"So we're working outward from Resolute, checking every possibility." Cassie took a sip of her drink. "But Weaver still isn't talking."

Sara's brows pulled together. "Then you still don't know why he did it?"

Noah shook his head. "Hasn't said a word since we put him in a cell. Hasn't even asked for a lawyer."

"We're still looking at possible motives. So far, the unrequited-love idea still makes the most sense." Cassie shrugged. "If he was obsessed with you and you weren't even aware of him, it's possible in his mind he convinced himself that you were rejecting him."

"And maybe something happened without you realizing it," Nate said. "Maybe a little thing, like he said hi to you and you didn't hear him."

Staring at nothing, Sara seemed to be rewinding her memory. "I suppose it's possible, but I don't recall anything like that happening."

"It sounds like all you've got is circumstantial evidence. Strong, but still circumstantial." Archer's expression reminded Nate of the man's long-term service in the judicial system. "At this point you can't even prove he was with his phone in Cooley."

"You're right." Cassie's tone was as grim as her expression. "But we've only had him in custody for one day. We'll get what we need to prove he's guilty." She visibly shook off her frustration and smiled at Sara. "In the meantime, we *know* he's our guy. So you don't have to live in fear anymore."

Sara returned the smile. "It sure would be nice to get on with my life."

As much as Nate had enjoyed his time in Resolute with his family, he was ready to get back to *his* life, too. Relaxing in his own place, rubbing elbows with celebrities, winning over new clients. *Trying to get over Sara* again.

When he asked about what else they'd done today on the case, Adam filled them in, from contacting the Travis County DA's office for Weaver's work history and human-resources file to trying to locate any relatives, friends or neighbors who could fill in blanks.

After their meals were served, Noah asked Nate, "So when do you blow this pop stand for Bikini Land?"

And there was the irreverent twin he knew and loved.

"As long as Sara's definitely safe—" Nate glanced at Cassie and got a reassuring nod "—either tomorrow or Friday. Depends how quickly I can get packed and book a flight."

Even as he spoke, Nate couldn't shake a vague uneasiness creeping through him. He'd like to just chalk it up to nerves about his upcoming meeting. But he wondered if it might be about leaving before he was one-hundred-percent satisfied Sara was safe, despite Cassie's assurance. He trusted his sister's confidence, and yet...

"Make it Friday," Cassie mumbled around a bite of steak, then swallowed. "We have to have a going-away dinner for you tomorrow."

"There's no need to make a big deal about this. We can consider this my dinner and—"

Cassie pointed her steak knife at him. "Nathaniel Reed, if you think you've got an ice cube's chance in hot tea of leaving town without a proper send-off, I must have dropped you on your head once too often when you were a baby."

Nate held up his hands in surrender. "Whatever you say."

"Damn straight." His sister turned to Sara. "I'll let you know the time and details tomorrow. You'll still be in town tomorrow night, Archer?"

"Of course. Maybe I can catch a ride with Nate to the airport on Friday, if our flights aren't too far apart time wise."

"I won't be able to make it," Sara said. "I promised Pops we'd spend his last night in town together, catching up."

Pops's brows angled upward in obvious surprise while her words hit Nate like a punch to his solar plexus. It seemed his attempt to put some distance between them in order to make his departure easier had backfired. He obviously hadn't handled the past couple of days well.

Amid protests from the others that Sara join them, he downed the rest of his bourbon and sighed. Just another example of him letting down people he cared about. Nate glanced at his watch and started counting the hours until he'd be back in California, where his only responsibility was his company—and there was no one to disappoint.

Chapter Fifteen

The next morning, exhausted from a sleepless night rehashing even the smallest details of the past forty-eight hours, Sara came down for breakfast to see Nate's duffel bag by the front door. At least he hadn't left for the Reed ranch, where he'd decided to stay until his flight to California tomorrow, without saying goodbye.

Low voices, as well as a dire need of caffeine, drew her to the kitchen. Pops and Nate were in the breakfast room, sitting in front of the security camera monitors.

Sara forced a cheerfulness she didn't feel into her voice. "Morning." Her mood had more to do with anxiety than insomnia, but that was her problem, not Pops's. Definitely not Nate's.

Pops turned in his chair and greeted her with a big grin. "Morning, kiddo. Nate's teaching me how this fancy security setup you've got here works."

"I'd like to show you, too, if you've got time this morning." Nate kept his attention on the screens. "It won't take long, and there's a manual in case you need to refresh your memory later."

He'd had a month to familiarize her with the cameras and alarms but had handled it all himself instead. And she'd let him. She'd allowed herself to become dependent on him for her safety instead of relying on him as an extra layer of security.

"Just let me get a cup of coffee, then I'm all yours." She kicked herself mentally as she walked into the kitchen. She *wasn't* his. She wasn't anyone's.

When she returned, Pops stood to give her his chair. "I'll let you two go over this while I make myself presentable for court."

"You plan on coming with me?" Sara could barely conceal her relief. Not that she needed anyone there. But a friendly face couldn't hurt. She'd just consider it a transition day. A bridge between having a round-the-clock bodyguard and flying completely solo.

"I wouldn't miss spending my last day in town with my favorite granddaughter if you paid me." Pops headed for the stairs.

"You do remember I'm your only granddaughter, right?" Sara called after him.

"Is that what you think? Remind me to tell you about my secret life sometime." His laughter floated back to them as he climbed to the second floor.

"He's quite the character." Nate chuckled. "Hell of a sense of humor."

"Yes, indeed." She sat in the now vacant chair and focused on Security and Safety 101. She didn't mind having the alarm system, but there was no way she would spend hours in front of these monitors, scanning the footage for a stray cat or an owl out hunting at night. Especially now, with Weaver behind bars.

Nate tapped the large, thick book. "Remember, you've got the manual if you forget any of this."

Good. Sara considered herself intelligent, but her eyes had started to glaze over by the time Nate finished the lesson.

"Well, guess I better get out of your hair." He carried his coffee mug into the kitchen and set it in the sink.

She followed him to the front door. While he picked up his duffel and computer bags, she crossed her arms over her chest. Mainly so she couldn't throw them around Nate and hug him, even if it was just a goodbye hug. "Thanks for...you know. Everything."

Nate nodded, staring at the floor as if he wanted to say something. Something important. Something that would erase the last few days and make everything between them good again. But that was just her wishing. In the end, he looked her in the eyes one last time and said, "See ya."

She was sitting at the dining room table when Pops came down a few minutes later.

He glanced at the front door. "Nate gone?"

"Yep." Like he couldn't see the bags were gone. Like he didn't know damn well Nate was gone.

Pops pulled out the chair across from her and sat. "How does that make you feel?"

She rolled her eyes. "Have you been watching TV psychiatrists lately?"

"Hey, better than TV judges."

Sara chuckled. "I don't know what I think, Pops. I thought maybe something was happening between us. But the second Weaver was arrested, it seemed like I was just a job to wrap up so he could leave town."

"There was definitely something happening between you. No doubt about it." He shrugged when she gave him a pointed look. "What can I say? Every time you two were in the same room it was hard to miss."

She planted her elbows on the table and dropped her head into her hands.

"You care a lot for him, don't you?"

Without lifting her head, Sara nodded.

"And it was obvious he cares for you."

This time she lifted her head and looked at Pops. "Could've fooled me."

"I'd guess Nate knew he had to get back to California and the way he was acting toward the end was just his way of protecting himself from getting hurt." He nodded as if approving his own idea. "Good old self-preservation."

Pops seemed to have it all figured out. But at this point, none of it really mattered. She sighed, chugged her coffee and stood. "Well, it's time to go to court."

Pops circled the table and gave her a hug. "You know you're going to be fine, don't you? However things turn out with Nate, you're tough enough to come out on top."

"Yeah, I know." But she didn't. Not really.

Chapter Sixteen

Late Friday afternoon, Nate unbuckled his seat belt as the plane taxied toward a terminal at LAX, expecting to embrace his old California attitude and lifestyle as soon as he stepped onto the jet bridge. At least, that's what he'd been telling himself he'd do for the past few hours in the air.

Despite enjoying his time at the family ranch with his siblings, much of the past year and a half had been dedicated to his father's time-consuming estate. There'd also been the grieving process for the old man, each Reed handling it in their own way.

But for the past several months, ever since the meeting with potential client Meryl Duncan had been scheduled, Nate had been champing at the bit to get back to the Golden State and once again live life on his own terms.

Unfortunately, he'd also spent his flight time telling himself to stop thinking about Sara Bennett. Not that it did any good. He hadn't been able to purge her from his thoughts since the moment he found out she was coming to Resolute.

Once the bodyguard gig started, she'd managed to upend his whole world just by being who she was. Intelligent, ethical, funny, hard-working, beautiful, kind... The list went on. And now, even though he tried not to, he missed her.

Disembarking, his steps through the terminal weren't nearly as light as he'd hoped. Once outside, Nate hailed a cab as he turned his face up to the pleasantly temperate California sun. But instead of enjoying it as he always had, now he found it lacking, a mere imposter of the blazing orb in Texas.

He directed the cab driver to Reed & Franklin, located in the financial district southeast of downtown. Thanks to their biggest investor, none other than singing sensation Byron Cain, the company occupied the top floor of a twelve-story historical building designed in 1922.

They made the drive up I-110 in record time, quite the feat in the always dense traffic. After unloading his bags and paying the fare, Nate entered the grand old building, passing under a towering arched entryway into a cool lobby of marble and brass, then headed for the elevator.

In contrast to the building's century-old ambiance, the reception area of Reed & Franklin was urban chic with pale hardwood flooring, exposed brick and bright splashes of color accenting the modern industrial furniture. Twenty-foot floor-to-ceiling windows offered a specular view of the downtown metro area and filled the open-concept area with a flood of natural light.

"Nate! You're back." His partner, Mathew Franklin, came out of his office and headed toward him. "Should have given me a heads-up."

Parking his bags near the elevator door, he met Matt halfway for a bro hug, slapping each other on the back.

"I didn't have a lot of notice." He shrugged as he dropped down onto a sofa, stretched both arms out along the top and crossed a leg over a knee.

Matt sat opposite him in a matching chair. "You *are* back for good this time, right?"

"Ah, you missed me." Nate laughed.

"Hell yeah, I missed you. I've spent so much time in the office, I'm starting to look like a vampire. And you know how well pasty white goes over at the beach."

"Don't even try to guilt me out. It's obvious from your perma tan that you've managed to get your minimum daily dose of surfing in."

"Ha. It wasn't easy." Matt dragged his hand through his sun-bleached blond hair. "Paperwork sucks, man."

"Don't lie—Sophia handled most of the extra work while I was gone." Nate was oversimplifying the situation, and they both knew it. True, Sophia had picked up a lot of the slack while he'd been in Resolute, but Matt had done the lion's share of the heavy lifting. "Speaking of our intrepid office manager, where is she?"

"Doctor's appointment."

Nate's pulse accelerated. "Everything okay?"

"Yeah, yeah." Matt waved his hand in the air. "Just her annual check-up. She should be back by two."

Three years ago, when they'd realized managing the workload and managing the company were two different things, Nate and Matt hired Sophia Rojas as their office manager. A tall, slender woman in her midfifties with no family, she never balked at working long hours. They'd come to depend on her to the point they'd be lost without her.

For the next hour and a half, Matt updated Nate on one of their upcoming jobs—coverage during the post-season college football match-up in Pasadena. Their job would entail keeping superfans away from celebrities and former big-name players who planned to enjoy the game from the exclusive Rose Bowl Stadium suites and private boxes.

"We're fully staffed?"

Matt nodded. "Copeland and Webber will take point. The venue exits have been mapped out, and we'll do our sweeps four hours before, then again two hours before game time. Sophia also has the timeline of activities and personal requests. So, we're all set on this one."

"Outstanding." Nate crossed the room to a mini fridge and grabbed a bottle of water. "Want one?"

"Nah, I'm good."

"Now, what about the Meryl Duncan meeting?" Nate retook his seat.

Matt grinned. "You mean our ticket to the big time?"

Reed & Franklin was in a solid financial position for a relatively small security company. Their clients paid them well, and they paid their employees well. But rent, overhead, employee benefits and all the insurance a bodyguard business needed kept them in constant search of even bigger, even higher-paying clients.

Meryl Duncan was as big as they came in Hollywood. With a word, she could make or break a company, and she wielded that power with a flippant eccentricity. She hired people on a whim and fired them with just as little thought.

Nate nodded. "Are we current on the holiday show she'll be starring in?"

"Sophia has researched all the details, prepared printouts and has them ready for us to study before we meet with her and her entourage." Matt pointed a finger at his partner. "Just remember, she specifically asked that you be at the meeting. Personally, I think she has a crush on you. Might be she's on the prowl for a new boy toy."

"*Nooo*, thank you." Nate cringed at the thought of spending personal time with the demanding diva.

Matt chuckled. "So you finally wrapped up your father's estate?"

"It's as done as it can be until Bishop finds my mother." Nate had been friends with Matt since working bodyguard jobs together for a company in Vegas. By now they both knew pretty much everything about each other's lives.

Matt's eyes bored into his. "And Sara?"

"What about her?"

His friend's easy smile returned. "Seriously, dude. When you first told me about her, I could tell you were crushing on her hard."

"So what?" Nate gave a nonchalant shrug. "She was a favor to my sister—a job. That job is over." His gut argued with him.

"You're saying the relationship is over?"

"There was never a relationship to begin with. We both knew that going in." Even as he spoke the words, they rang hollow.

"Okay, no relationship. All over. Great." Matt slapped his knees. "On your desk is a pair of tickets to the LA Comic Con that Nashira dropped off. She said you knew about it and you better be here for it."

Nate dropped his head into his hands with a growl. "I did know. And I guess I am here." Nashira was one of the women he saw on a casual basis.

Matt's ever-widening grin proved he was clearly enjoying himself at Nate's expense. "Didn't think that was your kind of scene."

"It isn't, but I promised Nashira I'd go with her."

"Didn't think that was her scene, either."

"Nashira's scene is anywhere that she thinks she'll meet someone to further her career. I can't really blame her. Her agent's pretty worthless, but he's her brother-in-law, so she's stuck with him." Nate was already regretting his promise. "She told me some important producer will be there because he's a fan of one of the headliners. I figured as long as I had to go, I might as well try to drum up some prospective clients for us."

"Good idea." Matt gave him a thumbs-up. "I'm in awe of your always-working mentality."

"And that's why my name comes first." Nate laughed as Matt flipped him off on his way back to his office.

His laughter faded away as Nate left the building and headed home to wash off the travel dirt. To relax. To reacclimate himself to the City of Angels, where for some reason, everything suddenly seemed slightly...off.

"SLOW DOWN, NATE. It's important that I'm seen."

Nashira Isa, an up-and-coming new face on the big screen, tugged his arm to slow his pace as they made their way through the Los Angeles Convention Center on Sunday, the final day of Comic Con.

Nate glanced at his watch. "I thought this shindig started at six." The *shindig* was an invitation-only gathering in the private suite of some big shot or another. He supposed he should pay attention to such things if he really wanted to find prospective clients, but tonight he found it hard to care.

Even at events that weren't necessarily his thing, as Matt would say, he usually enjoyed mingling. Instead, the lingering discontent that had cloaked him since his return to LA lingered. Even his craving to kick back in his own apartment had deflated after forty-eight hours alone with his thoughts.

"It *does* start at six." Nashira rolled her eyes.

"Well, it's only a few minutes till. Shouldn't we be speeding up instead of slowing down?"

Nashira tsked and shook her head but never once dropped

her million-dollar smile. "Fashionably late is preferred. Really, Nate. Don't you know how to make an entrance?"

Apparently he didn't and decided the best way to get through the evening was to shut up and let Nashira take the lead.

As they continued at their slower pace, Nate took in the booths and displays devoted to comics, gaming and pop culture. They strolled past celebrities, cosplayers in full costume and normally dressed attendees.

Plenty of people were checking out Nashira, too. At five-foot-ten, she was leggy and well-rounded and showing most of it off in a miniskirt and halter top. Her long, dark hair swayed as they ambled toward the escalator that would take them to the VIP room where she hoped to meet the producer.

Normally, Nate would have taken pride in keeping company with a beautiful woman like Nashira. But tonight he felt empty, devoid of emotion as they rode up the escalator.

The women he dated were like him, looking for no-strings-attached companionship. An enjoyable evening out, an even more enjoyable night in. No promises, no regrets.

But he hadn't anticipated how sleeping with Sara, a woman he admired and respected, a woman he actually cared about, could change things. And since Nate didn't like feeling muddled, he'd left Resolute with a vow not to dwell on Sara or the time he'd spent with her. But that hadn't stopped the lingering effect she had on him.

Feelings. He snorted. More trouble than they were worth.

By the end of Sunday evening Nashira had not only failed to find her producer but had also failed to find her way into Nate's bed. And if Nashira was in a foul mood because of it, he was doubly so. She should have been the one to excise all those irritating emotions he couldn't shake. But instead, Nate had dropped her off at her place without even a goodnight kiss. He couldn't make himself want a night of meaningless sex.

THE DAY OF the Meryl Duncan meeting, Nate was driving in the morning rush-hour traffic when his cell phone rang. Noah.

Nate pushed the control for Bluetooth. "What's up?"

"Where are you?" Noah's normally light tone was absent.

"Driving. Why?"

"Pull over."

"Not a chance. I'm already late for a career make-or-break meeting. Tell me why you called now or tell me later, but I'm not pulling over." Nate wasn't usually so sharp, especially with his twin, but ever since Comic Con three days earlier, he'd maintained a sour disposition. Even Sophia had called him out for it, not that it had made a difference.

He blamed his continued moodiness on stress overload. Once the details of protecting Meryl and her considerable entourage were finalized and Reed & Franklin had a signed contract in hand, everything would go back to normal.

"Pull over, now!"

"Son of a..." Nate jerked the steering wheel hard to the right and rolled to a stop on the freeway's shoulder. "Fine. I pulled over. Now tell me what's so all-fired important."

"Sara's gone missing."

Blood rushed from Nate's head as concern ripped through his gut. "What do you mean she's missing?"

"First of all, you need to know that everyone is working twenty-four seven to find her."

"Tell me what happened." Nate's steering wheel creaked under his grip. "*Now.*"

"Sara had dinner at Cassie's place last night. They decided to have a girls' night in because Bishop was out of town and Sara's been kind of moping around since you and her grandfather left."

Nate filed that info away for later consideration. "And then?"

"Cassie said Sara left around ten and texted that she'd made it home a few minutes later. But she didn't show up for work today, and nobody's seen her since."

Nate pressed his thumb into that spot between his eyes where headaches were born.

"The bailiff called Cassie this morning." Noah took a breath. "Cassie has a spare key to the mansion, so we went over there right away. She wasn't there. No signs of a struggle or anything."

"What about her car?"

"Parked in the driveway."

Unless Sara had stopped following their security protocols, her car should have been in the garage. Which meant if someone *had* kidnapped her, it happened last night before she drove it inside or this morning right after backing it out. Then again, maybe she'd gotten lax after they'd locked up Weaver. If she'd been taken outside, the house alarm wouldn't have gone off, but...

"What about her camera feeds? They would have captured anyone on the property."

"All the cameras caught was someone wearing all black, a ski mask and sunglasses and their gloved hand as they sprayed each camera lens with black paint. We checked in the neighborhood for witnesses of that and the kidnapping, but no one lives close enough to see much."

Damn it. That sounded like the same person he'd seen on camera when Sara's tires were slashed. "Listen, I'm not trying to tell you how to do your job, but take a careful look around the garage, okay? Especially the side away from the street. Look for footprints, cigarette butts, anything."

"Bree's doing that now."

"Okay, good." Nate paused, racking his brain. "Tell Cassie to take another go at Weaver. Hard."

"She already has been, but he's still refusing to talk. So far, anyway." Noah scoffed. "Little weasel."

"Did Forensics find anything on the phone?"

"Just got it this morning. A list of phone numbers. No texts to Sara, but he was texting someone. Adam's working that angle."

"I should be there."

"There's nothing you can do that we aren't already doing. We'll have her back safe and sound before you know it."

Will you, though? Nate recognized platitudes when he heard them but decided arguing was a waste of time. "Keep me updated. Like, every half hour. Got it?"

"You bet." Noah hung up.

Passing cars on the freeway zoomed by Nate as he sat there, processing. Sara had been missing for anywhere from two to twelve hours. Weaver was still locked up. If this was connected to the stalking—and it would be one hell of a co-incidence if it wasn't—that meant another player, one they knew nothing about. Thoughts of what might be happening to Sara pierced his heart like shards of broken glass.

Despite Noah's words of assurance, there was plenty he could do in Resolute. He could join the search. He could reexamine the security footage. And when Sara was found, he could be there for her.

He had spent the past month convincing her she was in danger, even if she hadn't wanted to believe it. But maybe he was the one who needed to quit lying to himself. Maybe it was time to admit his feelings for her.

He pulled up Matt's number.

"Nate. You almost here?"

"Sorry, Matt. Change of plans."

Chapter Seventeen

Sara's head lolled to the side. Trying to ignore the pounding beat of the bass drum inside her brain, she forced her eyes open. Before they slammed shut against the scorching sunlight, she caught a small crescent view of a room. A dirty, barely furnished room.

She wondered where she was but lost the thought halfway through it. Blinking away the blurriness in her vision, she realized the light was dim, not bright. Had she been blindfolded?

She went to massage her forehead with her fingers, but they weren't there. Panic gripped her—her fingers, hands, even her arms had disappeared. She twisted to peek at her shoulder, sending another blast of agony through her head. Her arms *were* there, she just couldn't feel them. They had been pulled behind her, apparently bound, completely numb. Glancing down, she noticed her ankles were tied to the chair legs.

Her tongue seemed to fill her mouth, and when she tried to swallow her throat refused to work. Alarmed she would choke to death, Sara fought against her bindings in a futile struggle. Shoving her tongue forward, it came up against a rough, nasty-tasting strip of cloth. A gag.

She forced herself to be still, taking a deep breath in

through her nose, then out. Looking around the room, she tried to get her bearings, searching for anything she could use to her advantage.

The space appeared to be a living room, maybe in an abandoned house. Trash littered the floor. Cobwebs filled the ceiling corners and hung from windows like lacy swag curtains.

Aside from two filthy upholstered chairs with ripped fabric and two sleeping bag–topped air mattresses on the floor, there was an overturned table with only three legs, a rusty metal TV tray and whatever she was sitting on.

Sara hadn't noticed the total silence surrounding her until heavy footfalls crossed the floor of another room. As the steps grew closer, Sara chose self-preservation over curiosity about her kidnapper—closing her eyes and letting her head hang forward.

Hard-soled shoes made their way toward her, grinding dirt into the hardwood floor. With each step, Sara's stomach tightened, and her mind tried to run away and hide. She cracked one eye open just enough to see Western boots pass by her.

Silence returned. Then in a flash, a hand wrapped itself in her hair and yanked her head up and back so far she thought her neck would snap.

"Nice try. You breathe differently when you're asleep."

The feminine drawl poked at Sara's memories.

Still holding Sara's hair in a painful grip, the woman circled around in front of the chair. "I won't punish you for this lie." She nodded. "It may have been nonvocal, but it was still a lie." She jerked Sara's head with each word. "However, I won't tolerate another one."

Her captor let go of Sara's hair with a shove and pulled the gag out of her mouth, leaving it to hang around her neck.

Sara recognized the woman as the one who'd approached their table in the Chute. The flirtatious one who Nate had seen in court. Blinking against the multiple drums now battling in her head, she opened her mouth, but her throat was parched, her tongue dry, her words broken. "Who... are...you?"

"Nobody you know. But you're about to." The woman pulled one of the upholstered chairs closer and plopped down on it. "Interesting how your boyfriend noticed me in court so quickly, yet I sat in a courtroom in Austin every day for a week while you prosecuted my brother and you never once looked around to see who was watching the trial, watching *you*."

"Your brother?" Sara had made it a practice to ignore the gallery of spectators when she was trying a case. Her focus had to be on the defendant and judge and jury, not weeping relatives of the victims or the defendant's furious family.

"Why don't we start with my name—see if you can figure out who he is all by yourself." She cocked a brow. "I'm Joan Dillon."

The last name was familiar, but Sara couldn't place it. As she mentally inventoried her cases, her still-fuzzy mind refused to cooperate. But the second she stopped trying, his face appeared. Not from the courtroom but from the files she and Nate had reviewed with Cassie and Adam. He'd been one of the many considered unlikely to be involved in this.

Boy, had they been wrong.

"David Dillon." Sara searched her memory. "DWI with a side order of drugs." Staring at Joan, she added, "Yeah, I can see the family resemblance now."

The woman barked a short laugh. "Well, well, well. Aren't you feisty in the face of danger."

Sara rolled her eyes. "So tell me, who's Patrick in all of this? From what I remember, you're David's only living relative."

Joan waved a hand in the air. "He's an incompetent man who's madly in love with me. A definite fly in the ointment when he was arrested, but at least he's loyal enough that he'll never give me up to the cops." She sighed, then brightened. "Obviously, the feeling's not mutual."

"Let me guess." Sara scoffed. "Because he worked in the DA's office, you arranged to meet him *after* your brother was sent to prison."

"Now don't go getting all high-and-mighty on me." Joan stood. "Seems you were doing the same thing with your bodyguard, playing kissy-face one day, then giving each other the cold shoulder the next." With a sneer, she left the room.

Even with all of Nate's security precautions, this woman knew so much about them while they knew nothing about her.

Nate. Sara took another deep breath, willing the tears to hold. She'd been missing him since before he left town, and not just because of the safety he had provided. But at this moment she'd give everything she owned to be rescued by her bodyguard. She silently cursed California and its appeal to him.

She had no idea what Joan Dillon planned to do to her, but allowing Sara to see Joan's face didn't bode well. Pops had always told her to live life without regrets. Yet right now she *definitely* had regrets. About how things had ended between her and Nate. Both times. About how she'd never get a third chance to change their future. It was agonizingly clear if Sara had a future, it wouldn't be a long one.

NATE WAITED IN the airport pickup zone, watching for No-ah's vehicle. He'd called the airlines while driving to LAX and managed to get a seat on the next nonstop flight to San Antonio. Between flight time and time-zone changes, it was already midafternoon in Resolute, and Nate had already spent too many hours imagining the worst.

He'd called his siblings several times throughout the day with the same question, always getting the same answer. Now, as he climbed into the passenger seat, he greeted his twin with a brusque hello and asked again. "Have you found her yet?"

"Not yet." Noah shook his head. "I'll catch you up on everything on the drive back."

Emotionally stretched to the breaking point, Nate buck-led his seat belt and stretched out his legs. "Go ahead."

"When we got Weaver's phone info from Forensics, there was one frequently called number. Adam cross-referenced it with the list of phone numbers we created from the in-mates' files."

"The ones we waded through in our first meeting?"

"Yep. He matched it to one of the numbers from those files." Noah glanced at Nate. "It belongs to a Joan Dillon. Her younger brother, David Dillon, was one of the men who threatened Sara after he was found guilty."

Nate searched his memory. "Was he the one put away for drugs?Something like that?"

"That's the one."

"So...what? He had his sister hire Weaver to harass Sara? Then who kidnapped her?" Nate pounded a fist on the dash-board. "This guy is going to pay—"

"Hold up, bro." Noah gave his brother a rap on the shoul-der. "First, the vehicle is government property, so watch it." He met Nate's glare with a wink. "Second, the prison unit warden okayed a video call between Cassie and Dillon, and he didn't know anything about this."

"Why would you believe anything he said?" Nate stared at his twin. "How could Cassie be taken in like that by a criminal?"

"I know you're upset, but we'll finish this faster if you calm down and just listen." Noah gave him the side-eye. "Can you do that?"

He blew out a frustrated breath. "Yeah."

"Okay. Cassie didn't tell David what was going on at first. She just asked him if he knew where Joan was, that we had some questions about an unrelated incident." Noah flipped on his turn signal and pulled out into heavy traffic, his brows crunched into a frown. "He said his sister has psychological problems. Schizophrenia, he thinks, but isn't sure. One minute she's fine, the next she's completely out of touch with reality, ranting about conspiracy theories and such."

Nate forced himself to remain silent until Noah finished.

"Seems she's very attached to her brother and was extremely upset when he was convicted. She visited him weekly at the beginning, but when she started coming up with ridiculous ideas about breaking him out, he told her not to come anymore." Noah shrugged. "Didn't want her messing with him getting a chance at probation down the road. Apparently she told her brother about some guy she was dating who she had wrapped around her little finger. According to David, she said the guy, who she referred to as Pat, would do anything for her to make her love him. But he said Joan doesn't have the capacity to love."

Nate waited a moment to make sure Noah was done talking. "Again, why are you all so sure he's telling the truth?"

"Because when Cassie explained what had happened

with Sara, Dillon seemed honestly shocked. He said if his sister was really involved in this, we needed to find her as soon as possible and get her the help she needs."

Nate looked out the side window, shaking his head in disbelief.

"*Also* because he reported all of this to the warden months ago. David informed him of Joan's bizarre ideas to break him out. Said he didn't want any trouble from her, so he wanted her removed from his approved visitors list." Noah glanced over his shoulder, changed lanes and hit the freeway on-ramp at full speed.

Frustrated with the whole situation, Nate leaned his seat back and crossed his arms.

"Dude, I understand your skepticism, but Cassie's gut feelings are almost always spot on. And I was there for the questioning, too. We all were. We stayed out of frame, but we could see Dillon's face while they talked. It sure seemed to me he was telling the truth."

"Whatever." Nate didn't have time for this. He needed to find Sara.

"You know, it doesn't matter right now if David was involved or not. He provided us with information. We can figure the rest out later."

"Can't you flip on your lights, make better time?" Nate knew he was in a bad mood and taking it out on his brother. But that was what twins were for.

"How 'bout I handle the driving and you take a look in that folder on the dash."

Nate opened the file. "What is this?"

"A printout of the texts between Weaver and David's sister. These link them together."

Nate skimmed through texts dating back to before Sara

had left Austin. The two had definitely been planning something. "What about the texts sent to Sara?"

Noah shrugged. "Could have been Weaver using a burner phone, but we think it was probably Joan using a burner or a VPN."

Nate let Noah drive in peace as he read through all the text messages. Besides the connection between Patrick and Joan, one other thing was evident—this woman definitely had the poor sucker wrapped around her finger.

By the time the twins strode into the justice center, it was almost 5:00 p.m.

"About time you boys made it back." Helen caught them before they headed to Cassie's office. "You're to go directly to the observation room. Your sister's about to put the screws to that awful man you caught."

"Tsk, tsk. That's not how we talk about our prisoners, Helen." Noah enjoyed tossing back one of her admonishments.

"Y'all just do whatever you have to do to find Sara, you hear?" She was still muttering to herself as the brothers rounded the corner and moved out of earshot.

Nate led the way into the small room, where Adam and Bree were already standing. They stepped aside enough for him to squeeze in at the glass.

"You're wasting your time." Weaver leaned back in his chair. "I already told ya I got nothing to say."

"I just want to update you on what we've learned." When Weaver only shrugged, Cassie folded her arms. "We've discovered that you and Joan Dillon are in a relationship and that she's David Dillon's sister."

Weaver's eyes widened, but he remained silent.

"Now, Patrick, here's the thing. We already have evidence tying you to the harassment and stalking of Judge

Sara Bennett." Cassie leaned forward. "And now we're going to have to charge you with her kidnapping."

"The hell you say!" Weaver jumped up, but his hands, cuffed to the table, kept him right where he was. "I got nothing to do with any kidnapping."

"But you knew Joan was planning on taking the judge. To what end? Hurting her? Killing her for proving her brother was guilty and helping to send him to prison?"

Nate understood why Cassie had asked that last question, but to hear his deepest fear voiced out loud made his head spin. He took a deep breath and refocused.

"I'm not saying another word."

"Have it your way. But Joan *did* kidnap the judge. And you'll be charged as an accomplice in anything she's done or is about to do." Cassie stood. "I was hoping you'd cooperate with us in return for reduced charges. Especially since Joan knows you're in jail and has hung you out to dry." She walked toward the door.

"Wait a minute." Weaver licked his lips. "Honest, I didn't know she planned on kidnapping the lady. All Joan told me was she wanted to scare her on account of her brother."

Cassie returned to the table and sat. "Where is Joan?"

He opened, then closed his mouth, his head tilted. "What'd you mean you could get my charges reduced?"

"Just that. I'll go the district attorney and ask that you not be charged with kidnapping." Cassie gave him a moment, then asked again, "Where is Joan staying?"

"Well, I don't know for sure. She was bouncing all over the place looking at houses, and—"

Cassie sighed and stood. "Good luck in prison, Patrick."

She hadn't even made it one step. "It's an abandoned house out in the country," Weaver said, his voice trembling. "I don't know how to get to it. I was only there once, and

Joan drove. It...it was white. Some of the windows were boarded up. There weren't any other houses close by."

"If you were only there once, where were you staying the rest of the time?" Cassie looked up from the notes she'd been scribbling.

"Joan got us a room in some lousy motel outside of town. We only moved to the house the day before y'all caught me."

"Which direction did you go to get to the house?"

"Well, our motel was west of town. Last thing I remember as a landmark was a big school, then we turned right, so we had to be going south." He looked up to the left, rubbing his chin. "Yeah, southeast of town."

Without glancing up, Cassie asked, "What's she driving?"

"A van. An old blue one, with patches of body filler. Joan's a lousy driver." When Cassie glared at him, he shrugged. "I don't know the make or model. All I know is it's ugly."

Cassie left the interview room to the sound of Weaver calling after her, "Hey, what about my deal? You gonna talk to the DA? We made a deal, right?"

Coming in to join the others, Cassie broke her glare with a wink at Nate. "Got 'em."

"A white house, southeast of town." Nate cursed under his breath. "Seventy-five percent of the houses in Boone County must be white."

"Adam's already sectioned a map into areas for each of us to search. If anyone finds a possible location, you radio for backup. Understand?" Cassie looked at each person in the room. "Here's yours." She handed Nate a copy of the map with his area outlined in yellow.

He headed for the door, but Cassie called him back.

"Here's a picture of Joan Dillon. Might help if you know who you're looking for."

Nate grabbed the photo, glanced at it and froze.

"What's wrong, bro?" Noah asked.

"Nothing." He didn't have the time to explain where he'd seen the woman before. And it didn't matter. All that mattered was finding Sara before it was too late.

As DUSK FELL, Nate drove south from town with the map app open on a tablet he'd borrowed from one of the deputies. He scanned it at stop signs, searching for houses without close neighbors. Even with that, he had to check out each house, searching for boarded-up windows and an old blue van.

Since he'd left his personal truck at the ranch when he flew to LA, Cassie had also loaned him an official sheriff's department vehicle, complete with a spotlight. He could use it when it got too dark to see, but it would also announce his presence. Maybe he'd be able to get by with the light from the almost full moon.

With both eyes peeled for the house and van and one ear listening to the occasional radio chatter between the other searchers, Nate's mind returned to Sara. If he was honest with himself, it had never left her.

He kicked himself mentally for skipping town while still uneasy about Sara's safety. But after being assured the right guy was locked up, Nate had chalked up his apprehension to the way things were being left between him and Sara.

"I might have something." Noah's voice came through the radio. After a moment of silence, he added, "Never mind. The house is light yellow."

Nate resumed the grid he was driving in his sector, about two miles south of town. The houses, farther apart now, sat back from the road. A lot of property between them seemed to be dedicated to crops. Some had barns. He agonized over the slower pace as darkness continued to fall, making it harder to make out details.

As he idled near a farmhouse surrounded by fallow land, the clouds pulled apart and the moon lit up the scene. Most of the paint had peeled off the structure, but what remained was white.

Rolling forward, Nate looked for signs of life. No movement. No vehicles. He continued down the street, but a glint in his side mirror caught his eye. It might have been nothing, but his gut told him to go back.

He turned at the next cross street and parked, making sure the vehicle remained out of sight from the house.

With no fences around the property, Nate made his way through the dormant field behind the house. He ran from tree to tree, changing his tune now and begging the clouds to block the bright moonlight so he wouldn't be seen coming.

A dilapidated barn sat behind the house. He sprinted inside and pressed himself against the doorframe, then peeked around it. The glint he'd seen was a reflection off a vehicle. A blue van, splotched with gray patches, practically touching the back door.

Relief from finding the house was short-lived as he wondered if he'd found it *in time*

He crept around the two-story house, making note of the windows—some boarded up, some missing, a few with broken or even intact panes of glass. Although the front door was clear, the van blocked access to the back door. When he tried to push through a holly bush to stand next to a window, its prickly leaves hooked into his jeans and scratched his hands, but he finally managed to peek through the filthy glass.

His shoulders sagged with relief. Luck must've been on his side, as the window he chose showed him Sara. She was sitting in a chair in the middle of the room, her ankles bound to the wooden legs, her arms cuffed behind her. Instead of fear or defeat distorting her features, she held her head high in defiance as she stared down the woman he now knew as Joan Dillon.

Nate wished he could call for backup, but he didn't have a shoulder mic and there wasn't time to go back and use the vehicle's radio. He pushed his ear closer to the thin glass.

"What did you expect? That I could just walk into a prison and demand an inmate be let go?" Sara scoffed.

"You put him in there, you can get him out." Joan walked into view. "Call the judge who was at my brother's trial and tell him you screwed up."

"It doesn't work that way."

"It should be even easier since you're a judge now, too. Tell him you'll owe him one."

Sara looked at the other woman as if she'd just landed from another planet. "Look, if you want your brother to get out, you should go back to Austin and hire a lawyer to file an appeal. You need to prove he's innocent before they'll let him go. And there's nothing I—or anyone else, for that matter—can do to circumvent the judicial process."

"So what you're telling me is you're no use to me." Joan crossed the room and picked up something from a table. "Is that right?" She sauntered back and stopped, facing Sara. Dim light from a camping lantern flickered off the shiny blade of a large knife in her hand.

Nate didn't wait to see Sara's reaction. Determined to

draw Joan's attention from Sara, he plowed through the thorny bushes and kicked in the front door.

Joan spun toward him and raised the knife in an overhead grasp. "Ah, it's the judge's boyfriend, come to save the day."

Holding his hands up, Nate showed her he had no weapon. "Nobody needs to get hurt here." He looked past Joan to Sara and saw a tiny smile of relief curling the corner of her mouth.

Joan followed his gaze, an ugly sneer transforming her face. "Stop talking to each other with your eyes. I know what you're trying to do. You think I can't tell what you're saying?"

If he could have told Sara anything with his eyes, it would have been how much he loved her, how scared he was to lose her. But he doubted his message would make it past a woman with a large knife amid a break from reality.

During her rant, Nate started moving slowly, trying to circle around her and get closer to Sara. Suddenly, Joan stopped speaking. She cocked her head, her gaze pingponging between Sara and him.

"Where do you think you're going?" She took a step toward Nate.

"Just checking to make sure Sara's all right." He shrugged and took a deep breath, knowing what he was about to say could make things better—or much worse. "David wants to know she's safe."

"Why would my brother want that? You don't even know my brother." She took another step.

"Yeah, I do. He's worried about *you*, too. He doesn't want you to get hurt, either." Nate stopped moving, worried if he got too close to Sara, she'd be within Joan's reach. "And I gotta say, he sounded pretty upset with you. Said if you hurt the judge, they're going to lock him up in solitary and he'll never get out."

"You weren't supposed to tell him!" she yelled. "This was going to be a surprise!" With a demonic shriek, she came at Nate with the knife.

Ducking to the side, he dodged the knife and grabbed her arms. They crashed into an armchair and flipped it backward, the knife flying from Joan's grasp. She twisted beneath Nate, trying to squirm out from under him, but he wasn't about to let her get to the knife. Wrapping his arms around her, he held her back to the floor, their legs still tangled together on the back of the chair. He just needed to get a grip on her arms and—

"Damn it!" The witch had chomped down on his bicep and wouldn't let go.

Nate gritted his teeth against the sound of tearing flesh, the scent of blood and its warmth as it flowed past his elbow. With his other arm, he grabbed her hair and tried to pull her head away from him.

Out of his clutch now, Joan seized the opportunity and scrambled out from beneath him. Nate grabbed for her ankle. Kicking back with her other foot, she rammed her boot heel into his face.

Dazed, Nate kept moving despite the pain. Despite the blood dripping from his fingers. Despite the grisly hole in his arm. He rose and went after the deranged woman as if Sara's life depended on it. Because it did.

Joan wrapped her fingers around the knife handle and struggled to her feet. Swinging the blade wildly toward Nate, she lost her grip on the knife, and it flew from her hand. Her momentum carried her forward at an odd angle, and she lost her balance, falling sideways. Clutching the small table to break her fall, she pulled it down with her as she went, along with the camping lantern.

Oil spilled across the wooden floor and ignited.

Grabbing the knife, Nate rushed to Sara and cut her bindings. "Are you all right?"

Sara nodded. "Just need to get the blood flowing again." She shook her arms out and cautiously tried to stand. Nate scooped her up into his arms and dashed outside to safety. But once Sara was free from danger, he ran back inside to save Joan.

The house was a tinderbox of dry and rotted lumber, and the blaze had already climbed the walls to the ceiling. Nate tried to reach Joan, but with each attempt he was driven back by heat and flames. Choking on smoke, unable to see anything, he gave up and made his way back to the front door.

Almost there, an ear-splitting crack sounded, and Nate looked up just as the second floor crashed down on top of him.

Chapter Eighteen

The rhythmic beeps of hospital machines monitoring Nate's vital signs almost lulled Sara to sleep. She fought the urge, watching a muted home-improvement show on the small television in the ICU room. The beeps were good signs. Signs that he was breathing, his heart was beating, he was alive.

Sara's tired gaze drifted to Nate. During the twelve hours since she'd pulled him from the burning house, the bruise on his face had started to darken. Almost like a tie-dyed superhero's mask. Which was what he was to her.

Cassie, Adam and Noah had filled her in on everything that had happened after she'd been kidnapped. The search, Weaver's information, Nate's return to Resolute the minute he'd learned she was missing. She'd even overheard Noah tell Cassie that Nate had been on the plane to Texas while his important meeting had started without him.

The guilt she felt for being the reason he'd missed that meeting was only a fraction of the amount of love she felt for him. She'd tried not to admit it to herself, and she would probably never tell him. She'd already messed up his life enough.

After pulling her chair closer to his bedside she touched

his cheek, the stubble stinging her fingertips. She jerked her fingers back when he stirred, his eyes drifted open and a small smile curled his dry, chapped lips.

"Hey, you." Sara's voice threatened to crack as her heart eased at the sight of Nate awake for the first time.

He croaked out what sounded like *Hey* in return, then reached for his throat. Sara picked up the cup of ice chips that the nurses had replenished each time they'd melted and held it for him until a few slipped into his mouth.

"That should help a little." She set the cup on the tray table, then brushed a lock of stray hair from his forehead.

Nate's eyes followed the movement, the lines between his brows deepening. "What happened?" he asked, his voice hoarse as he motioned toward her gauze-wrapped hands and arms.

"This?" She raised her arm and glanced at it. "This is nothing. Just a few blisters from the fire. No big deal."

He seemed to study her then, starting from the top. Her singed hair, the red streak across one cheek, the bandages on her arms and hands. "How did you get burned?"

"Well, I wasn't going to leave you in that house to die." She kicked up one side of her mouth in a smile. "Didn't seem right after you'd just finished saving me."

"The ceiling collapsed." Nate cocked his head. "You pulled me out?"

"Don't sound so surprised." She cleared her throat of tears, striving for levity. "I'm not as wimpy as you thought I was when you were my bodyguard." Sara raised one brow. "You just refused to let me be the strong, awesome woman I am."

He started to laugh, then stopped. "Ouch."

Sara's eyes widened, and she half stood from her chair. "Are you all right? What hurts?"

"Seriously?" Nate snorted. "Better to ask me what doesn't." His small smile calmed her. "But mainly my shoulder. And my face."

"If *you* think your face hurts you, you should see it from this side. It's painful." Sara laughed when his eyes widened in indignation. "Sorry—I couldn't pass up an opportunity like that."

"You've got a wicked sense of humor." Nate chuckled. "Looks like there's a lot more for me to learn about you."

Sara gave him an impish grin. "More than you can imagine."

"So what are all these tubes they've got stuck in me?" He eyed the machines and the drip bags hanging next to his bed.

"I'm not sure, but I know the most important one is pumping antibiotics into you. Apparently human bites are even more dangerous than they are painful. All kinds of nasty bacteria and stuff." Sara's lip curled in disgust. "The nurse said you'll be on this first round for at least another day, then they'll do surgery to repair the ripped muscle in your shoulder. That woman must have had extremely strong jaws."

"Speaking of Joan Dillon, they find her body?"

Sara nodded. "They haven't done an autopsy yet, not that there's much left for one. But the medical examiner told Cassie the spilled oil probably soaked into Joan's clothes right away, based on how I explained what happened." She looked down at her hand and fiddled with a loose string from the gauze. "You went back in to save her, didn't you?"

Nate was quiet for a while. Long enough that Sara wondered if he'd answer. Finally, his eyes focused on the side of the bed opposite where she sat, he spoke. "If there was any chance she was alive, I had to try."

Learning that he wouldn't let anyone, no matter how horrible they might be, die if he could prevent it, reinforced her opinion of him. "You're a good man, Nate. I admire your integrity."

"Just the way I was raised, I guess. I didn't always get along with my dad, but I learned a lot from him. He lived by his principles and ethics." He half shrugged, the movement of even his good shoulder making him wince. "I bet after all this, you can't wait to leave Resolute in your rearview mirror on your way back to Austin. Think you'll finish out Harmon's term or head out as soon as possible?"

Taken aback by his abrupt change of subject, Sara said, "I have no intention of skipping out on a commitment." It was her turn to get quiet, to put a voice to all the things she'd been considering since the abandoned house, when she hadn't known if she'd have a tomorrow. "Besides, all of this started when I lived in Austin and..." She smoothed the small section of blanket in front of her. "I've been doing a lot of thinking. I'm not so sure I want to go back."

Nate's forehead furrowed. "Where will you go, then?"

"Nowhere." At his look of confusion, she continued. "I'm going to stay right here in Resolute. When Harmon's term is up, I'll run and hope to win."

Nate closed his eyes for a long moment, then opened them again, catching hers. "And leave your luxury-condo living behind? The big city and all its attractions? I thought you wanted that top judge job in Travis County?"

Sara didn't flinch, in spite of the current of emotion she felt as they gazed into each other's eyes. "Somewhere along the way, I confused what I thought I *should* want for what I actually wanted," she admitted.

"I don't understand." Nate pressed the remote to raise the head of his hospital bed higher.

"In my mind, becoming a district judge in Travis County would be a way to be closer to Pops. More like him—because he was a district judge. And Travis County because it's where I was living and it wasn't all that far from him."

"So what's changed?"

"I have. My life has." Sara sighed, suddenly nervous. She hadn't planned on opening up about this to Nate. "I think I was always equating career with family. Aside from Pops, what I've never had, what I've always wanted is family. Family, friends and a simple life. And I have all that now. Here in Resolute." She laid her hand on his arm. "I'm treated like I'm one of the family when I'm at the ranch. I've met more people in the past month that I meet in a year in Austin, unless you count criminals," she said, laughing. "Between Cassie, Rachel, Bree, Marge, I'm well on my way to having lots of friends for the first time in my life. Even Helen tries to mother me, but in a good way."

Nate shifted in the bed, groaning when his sore shoulder moved. "Let me get this straight. You're planning on living in Resolute for the foreseeable future, continuing as the Boone County judge—"

"*If* the people elect me."

"Yeah, well, I have no doubt about that." He narrowed his eyes. "You honestly don't think you're going to get bored in our little Podunk town? Where you have to drive to Victoria to buy your fancy kitchen gadgets and coffees and such?"

"Oh, Nate. Living in California, I'm sure you know about online shopping and delivery. And besides, once I move all my stuff down here, there shouldn't be much else I'll need." Sobering, she added, "I never really loved living in Austin. I tried to. I convinced myself I did. But I never felt like I belonged. My entire existence revolved around work. I'm learning there's more to life than that."

Nate nodded. "I know what you mean."

He seemed thoughtful, and Sara worried that she'd over-stayed her visit. "I'm sorry—you must be exhausted. And it's probably time for more pain meds." She stood from the bed. "Thank you for saving my life."

He glanced up at her with a cryptic expression on his face. "Thanks for saving mine."

MOVEMENT IN NATE'S peripheral vision had him turning his head toward his hospital-room door. Three balloons, shaped like bananas, bobbed in midair.

"Come on in, Noah."

The door opened wider, and the balloons bounced into the room, followed by his twin.

"Recovered from your surgery?" Noah pulled a chair over to the bed, sat and let go of the balloons. Which, for some weird reason, stayed right next to him instead of floating up to the ceiling.

"I don't think so. They said I can go home Monday. What's today?"

"Whoa, you must be on some good drugs." Noah snick-ered. "Today's Saturday. You had your surgery yesterday. You know, Friday."

"Why are those balloons just sitting there?"

"They're not. They're standing." Noah pulled the bal-loons higher and showed Nate the cardboard feet connected to each string. "See?" He laughed.

Nate started to shake his head but stopped. Everything hurt. "Why bananas?"

"They were on sale." He gave one of the banana balloons a little push, and it waddled away. "Hours of amusement for the bedridden." Noah took a long look at his brother. "Seriously, how're you feeling?"

"Probably better than I look." He managed a small grin.

"Well, that's a good thing. 'Cause, boy howdy, you look like you were pulled through a knothole backward."

They laughed together, but when Nate winced, Noah sobered. "Sorry. I should have waited until you're better before I said anything funny. Even if it *is* true." He cleared his throat. "But at least now I can prove I'm the handsome one—instead of just claiming to be."

"Well, you better make the most of it while it lasts. Soon as this bruise drifts south of my chin and everything else heals up, you'll be back to runner-up Twin of the Year."

"I guess coming close to death like you did has an effect, huh?" Noah batted at one of the balloons.

Nate dragged his good hand through his hair. "It's not that."

"Then what?"

"Sara came to see me a few days ago." He ran his fingers across his blanket, remembering how she'd done the same thing when she was there. "She said she's not going back to Austin. Plans on staying right here in Resolute."

Noah folded his hands and rested his chin on his two forefingers. "Is this a good thing? Or a not-so-good thing?"

Nate shrugged. "Ow. I've got to stop doing that, damn it."

"Stop avoiding the question, bro."

"I guess it's a good thing for her, since it seems to be what she wants. It just surprised me. She had her life plan set in stone, and all of a sudden she changed it."

"Sometimes people change and their plans change with them. I think it's great that Sara realized she has a new definition of happiness and she's going for it." Noah kept eye contact with his brother. "What about you?"

"Me?" Nate frowned.

"Yeah. You." He raised his brows. "You ever think about changing your life plan?"

Nate shook his head. "No. At least not intentionally. But this last time I was in LA, things felt different. Off."

"How so?"

"I'm not sure." He blew out breath, searching for a way to explain it. "It was like the Golden State lost its shine. But now I'm wondering if it ever really had it." Nate scoffed. "You know what's weird? I never planned on going to California in the first place. I just wanted to get as far away from Dad as possible while I figured out how to make my own way." He felt foolish admitting this to Noah, but at the same time it was a relief. "I never really felt like I fit in out there. Even after living there all these years, I still felt like an imposter. A country bumpkin who put on an expensive suit to mingle with the beautiful people."

"Then why go back?"

This was a different Noah than Nate was used to. Asking hard, probing questions instead of the constant jokes.

Noah waved his hand. "Never mind. Let me ask you another question—why haven't you ever come back to Resolute?"

Nate didn't have to think long. "Because I never had anything to come back to. I mean, besides you guys, and you all have your own law enforcement thing going. I used to feel like the odd man out here, too."

"You feel that way this past year, year and a half?" Noah wasn't going to let up.

"No," Nate admitted.

"But still don't have anything to come back to?" His twin stretched his long legs out and crossed one boot over the other. "Nobody?"

Nate chewed on his lower lip for a while, an image of

Sara in his mind. He'd come back in time to save her life, but had he come back in time to win her heart? "Maybe."

"Was that so hard?" Noah laughed. "You both made the same decision. Sara's just smarter and braver than you, so she was willing to make it first."

"Look, Noah, I don't know if I have an snowball's chance in hell with Sara—"

"Trust me, you do. I know it, everyone knows it." He picked up one of the banana balloons and danced it around the room, singing, "My bro's finally in love."

"I KNOW, MATT. Yeah, I know."

Nate's first day home from the hospital wasn't going well. Pain pulsed in his shoulder. Even if it hadn't, that arm was in a sling, so he was basically one-handed. The bruise on his face had followed gravity's pull, so his mouth and chin were light purple while his eyes and nose had turned putrid shades of yellow and green. And he was talking to Matt for the first time since skipping out on the Meryl Duncan meeting.

"I'm sorry," he said. "I don't know what else to say."

"How soon will you be back on the West Coast?" Matt's usual levity had levitated up and out of the earth's atmosphere.

Nate propped his phone between his good shoulder and his ear as he lay on the couch. He was recuperating at the ranch with his siblings waiting on him, and he'd insisted on spending days in the living room so they wouldn't have to constantly run up and down stairs. "I'm not sure. They did surgery on my shoulder Friday, and this thing hurts like a son of a—"

"Sorry your shoulder hurts, Nate. But I can't keep things running on my own anymore."

An unfamiliar tone in his partner's voice alerted Nate that something was up, and he blew out his own frustrated breath. "We need to talk, Matt."

"Dude." Matt snorted. "I've heard that from enough women over the years to know exactly what it means."

"I'm sorry, but I've decided I want to move back to Texas." Like the release from a pressure valve, his stress dissipated in an instant.

"Wow. Well, this makes my news easier to break." He coughed out a nervous laugh. "Remember when I said I thought Meryl had a crush on you? Well, was I ever wrong."

"No. Don't tell me…"

"Yep. Meet Meryl Duncan's new bodyguard boy toy."

All Nate could think to say was "So she signed the contract?"

"Yes, she did. But, uh, she wants me to take point on the holiday celebration."

"That's fine. You were already pretty much in charge anyway." Nate couldn't understand why his partner sounded shaky.

Matt took a breath. "The thing is, starting with New Year's Eve, she wants me as her full-time bodyguard."

"Wow." Again, total loss for words.

"But she wants me as a direct hire instead of through the company. She said she'll use Reed & Franklin for big events and galas, but basically, she's buying me from you." Matt laughed. "But you're gonna love the price."

Nate wasn't sure if it was his meds or lack of sleep or nerve damage from the kick to his face, but his forehead suddenly felt numb. "Good for you. If this is what you want to do, go for it." He really was happy for his friend. He just didn't know how long Matt would survive in the clutches of Meryl.

Matt's voice smiled over the phone. "I'm happy for you, too. Does this have anything to do with Sara?"

"It might. Too soon to say."

"I hope it works out for you. It was pretty easy to tell when you came back this last time that you left part of yourself behind in Texas."

Apparently Noah was right—*everyone* had known before Nate realized it himself.

Matt broke into his thoughts. "But what about the company? If you're staying in Texas—"

"Don't worry about it." Nate's mind was racing, but at a snail's pace. "Can you and Sophia handle the event without my help?"

"Absolutely. Everything's planned out and ready to go. And I can deal with any other jobs we've got through the end of the year."

"Perfect. How 'bout you and I meet up after the holidays, figure the rest of it out." Nate was relieved, a little sad, but mostly he considered this another sign that he was making the right decision.

After ending the call, Nate almost didn't take his pill. But the nurse had stressed he should stay ahead of the pain, so he reached for the bottle just as Sara walked in from the kitchen. Cassie had insisted she stay in the guest room until her burns were healed.

"Here, let me get that for you." She hurried to the coffee table and picked up the bottle before remembering her fingers were too sore to open it. She handed it back to him. "We're quite the pair, aren't we? One hand between the two of us."

Nate chuckled. "At least we're on the mend." He washed his pill down.

Cassie had left a stack of blankets and pillows on the

leather armchair near the couch, so Nate turned onto his side and offered the empty space to Sara.

She perched on the very edge, stiff and proper. "I don't want to hurt your arm."

"Relax. My arm is fine." He shifted more against the couch back. "There's plenty of room."

She resettled herself, now leaning against his thighs. "Sorry, but I was in the kitchen and couldn't help but over-hear your phone call." She met his eyes. "Did I hear right? You've decided to stay in Texas?"

Nate nodded. "Yes. I think it's time."

"Your family will be happy to hear that." She pressed the edge of the quilt, just as she had the blanket in the hospital.

"What about you?"

Sara swallowed and looked away. "Me, too." She cleared her throat and forced out a small laugh. "It's just too bad you were such a thorough hero, you know? Now I don't need a bodyguard."

"How about a boyfriend?"

She blinked her wide, blue eyes. "I—"

"I love you, Sara. And I'm sorry as hell it took me so long to realize it. And even longer to admit it." He chuckled. "Cassie did say she dropped me on my head when I was little."

"They do say third time's the charm." Sara laughed as tears shimmered in her eyes. "And the thing is, I fell in love with you along the way, too." A small frown fought with her smile. "But are you sure you'll be satisfied in Resolute? You only ever wanted to get away from here."

"I never had a reason to stay before." He reached up and ran his hand through her new pixie haircut, necessary after the fire. It suited her, framing her face and showing off those big pale blue eyes. "Now I have the best reason of all."

Epilogue

Christmas, one year later

"Just a minute," Sara called out as she took one last look around her home, *their* home, before answering the doorbell. She'd had her first full-on family Christmas last year at the Reeds. But this year she'd asked if anyone minded her hosting the holiday, and the approval had been unanimous.

Nate had moved into the judge's mansion with her after they'd recuperated from their injuries almost a year ago, and life was everything she'd hoped it could be.

The bell rang again, and she rushed to open the door.

"Merry Christmas." Noah came in, carrying a pile of gifts. "Anyplace in particular for these?"

She pointed to the front living room. "Under the tree." Taking one of Bree's side dishes, Sara led her to the kitchen.

"Oh my gosh." Setting down her crudité platter, Bree inhaled until Sara worried she'd pass out. "It smells amazing in here."

"Thanks." Sara beamed. "I've never been much of a cook, but a judge's hours aren't quite as horrendous as an assistant DA's." She shrugged. "I've been having fun learning new things."

Bree glanced at the row of small pots on the window-sill, each sporting a different limp or dead herb. "Uh-huh."

Sara laughed. "Hopefully my cooking skills are better than my black thumb."

The doorbell rang again.

"I've got it!" Nate bellowed.

She returned to the foyer to find it filled. Nate took coats and jackets while she directed Adam and Rachel's mom, Martina, to the kitchen with their dinner contributions. Meanwhile, Rachel, approaching her due date with twins, herded Brad and Daisy into the front room.

The front door swung open again, and Marge and Doc pushed into the crowd, each carrying four boxed pies from the Busy B Café.

"Ha! You should've seen the look on Cassie's face when I told her *I* was bringing the pies." Marge barked out a laugh. "Don't worry, hon. I'll find the kitchen on my own. I've got a nose for it." Chuckling, she headed down the hall with Doc at her heels.

"The house is beautiful, Sara." Martina gave her a hug. "I hope it's okay that I just set everything on the counter."

"Thank you. And of course it's okay." She leaned in closer and asked in a low voice, "How's Rachel? She looks…uncomfortable." They both turned to watch Martina's daughter waddle over to the sofa near the tree.

Martina tsked. "That would be an understatement. But she's excited that it's two more girls because Daisy's been much easier to handle than Brad. I just don't think she realizes she's comparing a two-year-old girl to a six-year-old boy." She gave Sara a wink. "Doesn't matter—boys or girls, she's gonna have her hands full."

Sara turned and bumped into Adam.

"Merry Christmas. And well done in the kitchen." He gave her a bear hug.

"Thanks for all the secret lessons," she whispered.

Just like Bree, Adam inhaled deeply. "I think the student may be surpassing the master."

"Trust me," Sara said, glancing down at the small nicks on two of her fingers from today's kitchen activities, "that will never happen."

Adam joined the throng in the living room, and Daisy came toward him with her arms out. "Daddy!"

As he swung her up in his arms, Brad shot past him like a greased pig at the county fair, skidding to a stop in front of Sara. "Did you know my mom's having *two* more babies?" Sara nodded, and Brad added, "Two more *girls.*" He rolled his eyes, then took off running.

A blast of cold air hit Sara as Helen and Cassie came in.

"Here." Cassie handed Sara two packages of store-bought dinner rolls. "Instructions say you just have to warm 'em up in the oven." She yanked her jacket off and handed it to Nate as he walked past. "Best I could do since Marge stole my usual contribution."

"These will be great. I forgot all about rolls." Sara hugged her best friend. "Merry Christmas."

"Merry Christmas. Where's the wine?"

"You know where it is." She chuckled. "Help yourself."

Cassie turned when she was halfway down the hall. "Want me to bring you a glass?"

"We're eating in a few minutes. I'll have some then."

Nate came up behind her and snaked his arm around her waist. "I think everyone's here." Nuzzling her neck, he mumbled, "How soon can we get rid of them?"

Laughing, Sara swatted his arm. "All right, everyone,"

she said, raising her voice over the conversations. "We're going to have dinner first, then we'll open presents."

"Where's Archer?" Helen attempted to sound casual, but Sara had to bite her lip to keep from smiling. She and the Reeds had known for quite a while now that her grandfather and Helen had been enjoying each other's company. Pops said he visited often to see Sara, and while that might've been true, she knew that his recent look into local real estate probably had more to do with his new ladylove.

"He's setting up extra seating in the breakfast room."

Helen made a noncommittal sound and hurried down the hall.

Sara winked at Nate, then headed toward the kitchen.

"Here's a warm dish." Cassie stopped at the sideboard, looking around. "Is there an extra trivet anywhere?"

Bree moved one over. "Here you go. How many more do we need?"

"Beats me. I'm just bringing out what they hand me." Cassie returned to the kitchen.

Sara scooped stuffing from the turkey, Noah poured wine and everyone else except the kids and the older generation carried dishes of food into the dining room. When Adam handed Nate the carving knife, there was a brief look of confusion on Nate's face.

"Hey, man. Your house, your bird." Adam dropped into a chair, leaning back with a grin. "I'm just here to eat."

"Actually, it's Sara's house." Cassie pulled out a chair. "I mean, it *could* be Nate's house if he made an honest woman out of my best friend."

Nate's siblings all chuckled over the joke they'd kept up ever since Nate moved in last year.

Nate rolled his eyes and offered Sara the knife. "Would you like the honors?"

Sara raised both hands with a laugh. "Oh, no. I'm taking a page out of Adam's book." She quickly sat. "I'm just here to eat." Sara threw Cassie a look. "And as a judge of this here county, I take exception to you implying I am any less honest of a woman simply because I don't have a ring on my finger." She knew everyone was waiting for the last Reed to settle down—legally. But as Sara felt more loved and more secure in that love than she had in her entire life by simply having Nate by her side, she had no complaints about her bare ring finger.

"You do know how to carve a bird, don't you, son?" Pops, cheeky grin in place, raised an eyebrow at Nate.

Sara fought sudden tears when Pops gave her a wink. The Christmases they'd had together when she was a kid had been simple with just the two of them but happy.

Now, seeing the joy on his face and the glint in his eye, she knew she hadn't been the only one yearning for more. More family. More holiday spirit. More noise.

And they finally had it.

Nate squared up to the turkey like a man about to do battle. "Yes, sir."

And while the bird might have gotten a tad more chopped than carved, it was just as delicious.

HOURS LATER AND guests gone, Sara found Nate sitting on one of the sofas in the living room. He was gazing at the brightly lit Christmas tree as carols played softly in the background.

Sinking into the spot next to him, Sara leaned against him, exhausted, stuffed and spotting bits of ribbons and scraps of wrapping paper she and Cassie had missed during a quick cleanup. Nate's hand found her thigh, giving it a squeeze.

She'd never been happier.

After a minute, Sara's eyelids started to droop.

"What's that?" Nate's voice jolted her awake.

Pushing off his shoulder, she straightened. "What's what?"

"That." He pointed toward the fireplace. "Over there."

Squinting, Sara tried and failed to find anything out of place. "Where?"

"Your stocking." Arm still raised, his eyes cut to hers. "I think Santa came back."

Sara noted the lift at the corner of his lips. "He did, did he?"

Nate leaned back on the couch. "You better go see what he brought you."

Playing along, Sara pushed off the couch to stand and maneuvered around the coffee table toward the mantle. And when she lifted her red-and-green plaid stocking that she and Nate had picked out in a Christmas market in Victoria, it wasn't empty. "What did you do? You already gave me a gift this morning."

"That's not from me." Nate crossed one leg over the other. "Must be Santa."

"Uh-huh." Sara carried the stocking back to the couch with her, sliding out the gift once she sat down.

Sara's smile melted from shock when a small, black velvet box with a tiny bow on top toppled onto her lap.

"Oh." Nate plucked the box off her thighs, holding it up to the Christmas-tree light. "That *is* from me."

Sara opened her mouth, but nothing came out. She suddenly found it hard to breathe.

Dropping to his knee between the couch and coffee table, Nate opened the box. The single solitaire diamond glinted in the holiday lights.

"Not many people get more than one chance at true love with the person they're meant to be with. Somehow you and I got three, and we've managed to not let this third one slip away." He removed the ring and set the box down beside him. "I love you, Sara Bennett." He lifted her left hand. "Will you turn this chance into a lifetime by becoming my wife?"

"Ye—" Sara cleared her throat, tight with emotion. Despite claiming earlier that she didn't need a ring, she hadn't realized how much she wanted one. This one. Along with Nate's perfect proposal. "Yes, of course I will."

He slipped the ring on her finger, but before he could say another word, Sara stood and pulled him to his feet.

"I love you." She went up on her toes and kissed him, then whispered, "I think I may have left one more gift for *you* upstairs. Want to go open it?"

* * * * *

MURDER AT THE ALASKAN LODGE

KAREN WHIDDON

To my ultimate fishing buddy for life, Lonnie.
Catching those huge salmon was one of
my favorite things ever!

Chapter One

Today would be the day her spectacularly craptastic life took a turn for the better, Maddie Pierce thought as she waited impatiently for her luggage to show up on the rickety airline carousel. It had to because it certainly couldn't get any worse. Unless they lost her bags. Hopefully not, because even a hostile universe couldn't be that cruel.

Scowling, she reminded herself to keep a positive attitude. Which was extremely difficult since in the space of a few weeks she'd not only lost her awesome job working for the top commercial land developer in Dallas, but also, as she'd flailed about trying to figure out what to do next, her boyfriend of two years had dumped her for someone else.

She'd loved her job. The boyfriend, not so much. She suspected they'd each been placeholders for the other, filling in until something better came along. Sure, the timing had sucked, but Maddie couldn't really blame him.

As for the land developer, the company had sold to an even larger developer that was moving north from Houston. Massive restructuring had taken place, and entire departments were cut. Maddie's had been one of them.

Desperate to stay in the game, she immediately began the search to find something similar. Aware she might have

to relocate, she'd even branched from commercial real estate development and included residential. At her lowest
point, she'd sent out over two hundred and fifty résumés.
All to an alarmingly lackluster response.

Busy living in the fast-paced world of up-and-coming
young executives, Maddie hadn't managed to save much
money. She'd barely be able to make next month's rent, and
that would be if she didn't pay utilities or buy groceries.

She began looking at other jobs (bartending, office work,
waitressing) to tide her over. And then a certified letter had
arrived, informing her that she'd inherited half of an old,
remote fishing lodge up in Alaska. Which was about as
far as she could get from Dallas, Texas, and remain in the
United States. At this point, leaving and starting over actually suited her just fine. And even though the will inex-
plicably stipulated she'd need to live there one entire year
before owning her half outright, she figured she could use
that time to regroup and evaluate.

A new opportunity, she'd told herself, every time she'd
wondered about the cold or the ferocious wild animals she'd
heard were everywhere in the Last Frontier. Good luck, like
the stars had magically aligned or something to save her
butt. No job, no boyfriend, and her luxury apartment lease
had just ended. Since she'd never known the grandfather
who'd left her the lodge, both his passing and the certified
copy of his will had been an utter surprise. Especially since
he'd never made even the slightest attempt to contact her,
not once in her entire twenty-five years.

Serendipity or a random lightning bolt of fate, whatever. All signs were screaming that the time had come for
a major change. So, with no other choices, Maddie had
closed her eyes and taken the leap. Instead of placing her
belongings in storage for her eventual return, she'd sold or

given almost everything away. With the last of her funds, she'd booked a one-way ticket to Anchorage. As soon as she snagged her suitcase, she'd be meeting the man who'd inherited the other half of Grady's Lodge. She found his name intriguing. Dade Anson. She pictured a kindly older man, heavyset and wearing glasses, taking her under his wing and showing her the ropes. After all, not only had she never been to Alaska before, but she'd also never even set foot in a fishing lodge. Or really even gone fishing.

She had, however, done her research. Surprisingly, she'd learned fishing lodges, especially those catering to wealthy clientele, made a ton of money. This was where she knew her skills working for a land developer were likely to come in handy. She figured she'd modernize the place, do some advertising, and by the time her year had passed and she could sell, Grady's Lodge would be a completely different type of place. Trendy, popular and profitable.

Her life seemed to have done a rapid 360.

Until the text messages had started coming. If not for the weird, vaguely threatening texts, all from different, unlisted numbers, she'd be on cloud nine. The texts had started soon after she'd firmed up her decision to go. She'd since learned there was an app people could use to text and remain anonymous. Part of her wondered if Dade, was sending them. If he thought texts would scare her away, he was sorely mistaken. She'd decided to ignore them. So far, nothing had actually happened. And here in Alaska, she knew she'd be out of reach.

Finally, her suitcase dropped into the carousel and moved toward her. Once she'd grabbed it, she turned and took a deep breath.

Now to start the next phase of her new life. Part owner of Grady's Lodge.

This Dade guy had said he'd be waiting for her in a dark green Jeep Wrangler, parked right outside the baggage claim area. Pulling her luggage after her, she hurried toward the exit door, anticipation making her pulse race.

Outside, she inhaled, liking the crispness of the air, the way the light seemed different, making everything appear sharper, cleaner, somehow. Spotting the Jeep, she hurried over.

She shouldn't have been surprised when a man the size of a grizzly bear got out of the green Jeep. After all, this was Alaska. But still... This had to be Dade Anson. Not quite the kindly, older man she'd pictured.

The sight of him made every nerve in her body tingle. Astonished, she stopped dead in her tracks. Hot and dangerous, so much so that she thought this couldn't be real. For one thing, he was the largest man she'd ever met in person. As in, Jason Momoa's size, tall and massive with broad shoulders, a muscular body and the same kind of long, wavy, dark hair. He even had the same rugged face, compelling eyes and commanding presence.

Staring, she tried to collect herself. Men who looked like him didn't really exist in real life outside of Hollywood, did they? Clearly, they did. In the person of one Dade Anson, the man with whom she'd be spending the next year.

Taking a deep breath, she forced herself to move forward. "You must be Dade," she said in her best professional voice, holding out her hand. "I'm Maddie Pierce."

His huge hand completely engulfed hers. His fingers were calloused and rough. Though he could have crushed her hand, he simply shook it firmly before releasing her. With a quick flash of a smile, he reached for her bag, hefting it easily into the back seat.

"Welcome to Alaska," he said, apparently completely

unaware of his effect on her. "We've got a little over a two-hour drive before we get to Blake. Which means if you need anything before then, it's best to get it here in Anchorage."

Still a bit stunned, she tried to think. "I think I'm good, thank you."

He nodded. As his impersonal gaze swept over her, he opened the passenger-side door and stepped aside. "Great. Then let's get started."

Wondering how on earth this man had known her grandfather, she climbed up into the Jeep and fastened her seat belt. When he got in the driver's seat, his presence filled the interior of the vehicle. For one brief moment, she wondered if he'd fit. But despite his sheer size, he settled in easily behind the wheel.

He met her gaze, sending a jolt of attraction straight through her core. "Are you okay?" he asked, making her realize she might still be staring.

Flustered, she nodded. "I'm just a bit tired. It's been a long travel day."

"I can imagine." Starting the engine, he pulled away from the curb. Navigating traffic, he didn't speak again.

The urban environment of Anchorage surprised her. She'd read that Ted Stevens Anchorage International Airport sat five miles to the southeast of the city, but nothing could have prepared her for the sheer size and breathtaking beauty of the huge mountains that rose in the background. Where she'd come from, there was a saying that everything was bigger in Texas, but she guessed whoever had coined that phrase had never been to Alaska.

While she'd done her research on fishing lodges, she'd barely bothered with the state's most populated city.

Meanwhile, Dade Anson wasn't much of a conversationalist. In fact, he didn't talk at all once the initial introductions had occurred.

Twenty minutes passed. Then thirty. While Maddie had never been the kind of woman uncomfortable with silence, for whatever reason she felt the urge to fill the quiet with words. After all, she had a lot of questions.

"Did you know my grandfather very long?" she asked, turning to look at him.

"Almost my entire life," he replied, his voice clipped and his attention still on the road. The hustle and bustle of the city had given way to what she guessed might be the suburbs. Soon, she figured they'd leave even that little bit of civilization behind.

"You must have been very close." Of course, they had to have been. After all, Dade had been bequeathed the other half of the fishing lodge. Truth be told, Maddie had no idea why she'd been left anything. She'd never known her maternal grandfather. Growing up, this had brought her a lot of pain. She didn't understand why he never even attempted to contact her. Her mother had refused to talk about him, even though he was her own father.

"We were." Now Dade glanced at her, his gaze dark. "He was like a father to me."

Not sure what to make of that statement, Maddie nodded.

As she twisted her hands in her lap, she wondered why she felt nervous. Maybe because she was about to go off into the wilderness with a man she didn't know.

"Better get used to it," she muttered under her breath. Her life had been nothing but one change after another lately. She'd always considered her self-confidence one of her best strengths, but these days some of her nerve seemed to be slipping just a little.

Maybe more than a little. A lot. That was what she got for letting so much of her identity get tied up in a job.

"I'm sorry, did you say something?" he asked, his brows lowered. He glanced sideways at her.

"No," she lied, unwilling to admit that she'd been talking to herself. "Not really."

Though a muscle worked in his rugged jaw, he finally nodded. "Okay."

She waited for him to say something else, anything, but he didn't. Nope, definitely not a talker. Which actually was much better than someone who chattered on non-stop about nothing. She'd worked with a few clients like that. They'd been exhausting.

The long day of travel must have taken its toll on her. One moment, she'd closed her eyes to rest them, and the next, she was jolted awake when the Jeep hit a pothole or something hard. She let out a muffled scream, not entirely sure where she was for a second.

Glancing around, noting the giant man with muscular arms in the seat next to her, now staring, she remembered. Alaska. Alone in what now appeared to be the middle of nowhere, with a man she didn't truly know. Both of his hands gripped the steering wheel as he navigated an increasingly rutted road that wound through nothing but trees. If anyone lived out here, the houses weren't near the road.

"How long was I out?" she asked, covering a yawn with her hand. Her shoulders felt stiff, and she rolled her neck to try and help with that.

"No idea," he replied, his impersonal tone matching his expression. "Possibly an hour. Maybe longer."

She sat up, still trying to get the kinks out of her neck as she took in the landscape. A narrow slice of blue sky was visible through the forest. While it appeared they were still on pavement, she wondered if that would soon give way to gravel or dirt. "Are we getting anywhere close to Blake?"

"Not really." He waited a moment, and then he laughed. The richness of the sound washed over her, making her shiver. "Just kidding. We're almost there."

"I can't wait." Her first real Alaskan village. She'd done as much research as possible on the area and the fishing lodge she'd inherited. Research on real estate had been her specialty in her previous job. Blake was the only place even remotely close to the fishing lodge and where they'd get supplies. From the photos she'd seen online, it appeared to be a charming place. Like something out of a holiday card, except in need of some sprucing up.

Thinking of that brought something else to mind. "Does it snow a lot here?" she asked, even though she already knew it did.

"Define *a lot*," Dade replied. "I mean, it snows in the winter, of course. And in the fall. Sometimes in the spring. That's why the lodge is only open from May until September."

She knew all this. Again, she'd done her research. But she liked hearing him speak. The husky timbre of his voice did things to her. Pleasant things. Damn.

"Dallas doesn't get much snow," she commented. "I have to say, even though I checked out the stats online, I'm not sure how well equipped I am. I'm not a big fan of the cold."

The incredulous sideways look he gave her revealed his thoughts about that. "You've got some time to get ready," he said. "We're just about to open for the season. But yeah, there's going to be snow eventually. Definitely more than you're used to in Texas."

She nodded. "Tell me about the lodge. I tried to look it up online but couldn't find much. There are several larger fishing lodges in the general area, and they all have a major web presence. But not Grady's."

He snorted. "Grady wasn't big on the internet. We don't get it where we are, and he never wanted it brought in."

"What?" Now he'd managed to surprise her. "No internet?"

"Nope. No Wi-Fi. I think there might be dial-up or something, but who has the patience to deal with that?"

Not good. Considering her plans to set up a website and do some advertising, this wasn't good at all.

"What about in Blake?" she asked. "Do they have Wi-Fi there?"

"They do. But since it's a good thirty-minute drive or more, there doesn't seem to be a point. If people need to reach me, they can call on the land line. It's the most reliable."

Since she couldn't fathom this, she tried again. "You can get email on your phone, right? And use your cell to access websites?"

"We don't exactly get much cell phone service out there either," he told her, the glint in his eyes telling her he was clearly enjoying himself. "We use a satellite phone when outside for emergencies, but that's it. One of the reasons businessmen like to escape to our lodge. It truly is getting away from it all."

"Wow." She didn't know how else to respond to that. All of her research and she hadn't seen anything relating to modern conveniences.

"Trust me, it's better this way," he said. "You'll see."

While she had her doubts, she knew better than to voice them. "I guess I won't have much choice."

The dense forest began to give way to a house here and there. Some were actual log cabins, others more elaborate wood-frame homes. None of them were brick, like most of the homes back in Dallas. She guessed brick might be hard to get out here.

"We're getting close to town," he said. "If you don't mind, I'd like to stop. I need to fill up with gas and pick up a few supplies. Since we open in a week, I had to place the usual big order. We're pretty much booked up for the entire season."

Impressed, she nodded. "You don't do any advertising, do you?"

"No need. Most of our clients have been coming here for years. Before them, their families. The other clients are strictly word of mouth. We like it that way."

She knew better than, as the newbie partner, to immediately vocalize any plans she might have to change things. She'd need to take time to settle in, learn the ropes, see how things were run. Then and only then would she have enough knowledge to decide to make improvements.

As they crested a steep hill, he pointed. "Watch for it."

And then she saw Blake, Alaska, below them. A cluster of buildings along a single street, with a few side streets that appeared to be residential. One stop light, she saw.

Blake was much smaller than she'd imagined, and less picturesque without the snow, but still charming. They drove down Main, past several small businesses, and pulled up in front of a red wood building with a large sign proclaiming Murphy's General Store.

"Come on inside," Dade said, his voice slightly warmer than it had been. "You can meet some of the locals."

Since she'd been traveling for what felt like forever, she knew she didn't look her best. But aware she couldn't refuse and appear unfriendly, she unbuckled her seat belt and reached for the handle.

To her surprise, he opened the door for her, waited for her to get out and then closed it. "This way," he said.

Maddie had always considered herself a confident woman, but right now she felt like a small child about to walk into her first day of kindergarten.

He held the door open and gestured at her to precede him.

Stepping inside, her first impression was of a rustic kind of cozy warmth. There was, she saw, a little of everything. From handmade quilts to hunting supplies, food and medicine and everything in between. Including both men's and women's clothing.

"Hey, Dade!" A stocky man came out from around the counter and clapped Dade on the back. "And this must be your new partner."

PARTNER. DADE STRUGGLED not to wince. Watching as Maddie chatted with Kip, thoroughly charming the store owner, Dade clenched his hands into fists and told himself he couldn't just walk away and leave her there. He'd known before he'd even met her that he wouldn't like her much. How could he, when she hadn't even once bothered to try and have any kind of relationship, even a long-distance one, with her grandfather?

He'd been less than thrilled when Grady had told him he planned to leave the granddaughter he'd never gotten to know half of the fishing lodge. But Dade had loved Grady more than anyone else on this earth, and if doing that made the old man happy, who was Dade to argue?

When Grady died, Dade's entire world had shattered. Grady had been everything to him, and Dade felt his absence keenly. Nevertheless, he'd done what he'd been tasked to do and made sure Grady's last will and testament had been filed with the courts. Puttering around the lodge that Grady had built, Dade had still been struggling with the loss when he'd received the news that Maddie Pierce, estranged granddaughter and co-heir, had agreed to the terms of the will and was on her way to stay. For at least one full year.

Which Dade thought would feel like an eternity.

Though Grady had always talked wistfully about her, Dade had never gotten over the simple fact that she hadn't cared enough, not once, to even pick up the phone and call. Or send a single letter. Never mind visit. It had seemed as if she were trying to pretend that her grandfather didn't exist. That didn't sit right with Dade.

Anyone who could blow off a man as great as Grady Pierce wasn't worth Dade's time. Where the old man appeared able to forgive and forget, Dade couldn't. Not about something as important as this. Sure, Maddie might be far prettier than he'd expected, and sexy as hell, but he'd already made up his mind not to like her. Meeting her bright blue eyes, so reminiscent of Grady's, felt like a slap in the face every time.

Once the year stipulated in the will had passed, Dade planned to make her an offer, buy out her half of the lodge and send her packing. She could go right back to Texas, where she belonged.

For now though, they were stuck with each other. Which promised to be interesting.

Once Kip had rounded up all the items from the list Dade had given him and shown Maddie where to find the local baked goods and jams and jellies, Dade loaded everything into the back of his Jeep. He told Kip he'd see him soon and opened the passenger door for Maddie. Once again, his polite gesture appeared to surprise her. Maybe if she'd spent even a little bit of time with her grandfather, she'd have seen how Grady had been polite to a fault. He'd instilled the same manners in Dade.

Once they'd pulled away from the general store and were headed north on Main, Dade noticed that Maddie had again fallen silent. Good. Maybe she'd go back to sleep. He found making small talk with a total stranger exhausting.

"Eventually, we'll get used to each other," she said. Brushing her thick, dark hair away from her face, she sighed.

Startled, he glanced at her, wondering if she'd read his mind.

"Your expression gave you away," she told him, flashing a sly smile, her eyes sparkling.

What could he do but laugh? To his surprise, she laughed with him. The light, feminine sound brought both a sense of comfort and of uneasiness.

They both went quiet again as they left Blake behind.

"The road gets even rougher from here on out," he warned her. Since his description, at best, was an understatement, he wondered how she'd react once they started being bounced around. He had to give her props, though. Despite what had to have been a long day of traveling and now riding in the Jeep, she hadn't complained. Not once.

For the next few miles, the pavement got worse and worse, becoming almost nonexistent in places. Deep potholes and jagged ridges tested the Jeep's suspension. Eventually, they would reach a combination of dirt and gravel, which became treacherous in the rainy season and downright dangerous when it snowed.

Out of necessity, he slowed the Jeep down. Though she didn't comment, she glanced at him. For the first time, he noticed her death grip on the door handle.

"Are you all right?" he asked.

"I'm fine." Her clipped response told him otherwise.

"Soon, we'll be crossing the Neacola River," he offered. "It's pretty scenic."

And then they hit a deep rut. Because he'd allowed himself to be distracted, the Jeep front tire hit hard. This sent them both bouncing. Only the seat belts kept them from hitting their heads.

Maddie let out a muffled curse. Then, apparently embarrassed, she shook her head and looked away. "You weren't kidding about the bad roads," she said.

Worried about his undercarriage, Dade pulled over. "Wait here a second," he said. "I need to make sure that didn't damage anything. This Jeep is fairly new, and I want to take care of it. I'm usually paying better attention than that."

He got out, walked around the exterior of his vehicle, then crawled under. A brief inspection revealed everything appeared to be fine.

Relieved, he got back inside and buckled up.

"Do they ever fix the roads?" she asked. "I mean, I'm guessing our clients have to travel this way, too, don't they?"

Our clients? Though, at first, the words hit him wrong and he took exception, he realized she was right. As of now, they were both the hosts. The clients would be their clients.

"They do," he answered. "But most of them have been coming here for years, so they know to be careful. And as far as your question about repairs, if we want anything like that done around here, we have to do it ourselves. Every once in a while, Blake gets together a group of citizens and fills in the potholes. Snow and cold always come after and mess everything up again."

She frowned. "It's weird to me that there's no state or county maintenance for the roads."

"Oh, I'm sure there is in some places. For sure in Anchorage and Fairbanks and all the other heavily populated areas. Alaska is a huge state. There's a lot of wilderness and remote areas. Since they can't possibly get to them all, most of us Alaskans pitch in and do our part." He didn't even try to hide the pride in his voice.

"It's so beautiful here," she said, gazing out the passenger window. "I don't know if you've ever been to Dallas, but it's super flat. I love the hills and mountains and all the trees."

When he thought of Texas, he thought of heat. Lots of hundred degree summer days and winters with rain and no snow. Since he much preferred cold weather to hot, he didn't think he'd make it in Texas. He had to wonder how Maddie would fare here in Alaska.

The steadily inclining road began leveling out, which meant they were approaching the Neacola.

"Here's the bridge," he pointed out, unnecessarily. "And down below, there's the river."

As they reached the other side, he pulled over so she could take a look. "Lots of tourists stop here and take pictures to post to their social media. Just in case you wanted one."

"I'm not a tourist," she pointed out, making no moves to get out of the Jeep. He noted she didn't claim not to have any social media. "Though that is a stunning view."

"It is." He nodded. "There was an accident here not too long ago. A car went off the bridge and ended up in the river. One person was killed and another survived."

Turning to look at him, she tilted her head. "Was alcohol involved?"

"No. It's a long story, but the guy who made it stayed. He's now married to the new doctor in Blake."

"You'll have to tell it to me someday," she said, her blue eyes bright, her expression quizzical.

"Or better yet, you can hear it directly from them." Looking away, he cleared his throat. "I'm sure you'll meet them eventually. Especially since you're going to be here an entire year."

This made her wince. "You make it sound like I'm serving some sort of sentence."

"Aren't you?" he asked. "You might as well level with me. I suspect you wouldn't be staying that long if your grandfather's will didn't have that stipulation. Am I right?"

She met his gaze. "I don't know," she answered quietly, her expression thoughtful. "They always say when one door closes, another opens. That's kind of what happened to me. I'm ready for a new start."

Appreciating her honesty, he nodded. "All right then. Are you sure you don't want to take a look at the river?"

"I'm sure. Maybe another time."

He waited a moment longer before shifting into drive and pulling back onto the road. "We're lucky we have good weather today. With no rain or snow, we only have about twenty more minutes before we reach the lodge."

"I didn't realize you were that far away from Blake." She glanced back at the river. "And how is a fishing lodge located such a distance from the water?"

Her question made him grin. "The river curves," he said. "Grady built his place on the river bank several miles upstream. You'll see."

She stared at him, as if she wasn't sure whether he might be joking. "I see."

"Have you ever been fishing?" he asked.

Slowly, she shook her head. "Not really. When I was a teenager, one of my boyfriends took me out in his boat while he fished, but I never actually tried."

"Was it a lake?"

"Yes. He caught some largemouth bass and a catfish on a line he strung between two empty milk jugs." She grimaced. "He wanted me to cook them, too, but I'd rather eat my fish in a restaurant."

Not sure how to respond to that, he settled on a noncommittal nod. "Well, we have to cook our own fish up here. And our clients'. It's one of the services we provide to our guests."

For a second, she appeared taken aback. "I guess I can learn. Salmon, right?"

"Mostly, yes. Some people like to have it smoked, and there's a place in Blake that does that for them. They even ship it home if they want."

"That's a nice service," she said. "But I'm wondering why the lodge doesn't cut the middleman and offer this service instead. That way, we could get a cut as well."

Not sure how to respond, he considered not even bothering to dignify her statement by replying. But then again, she needed to understand where he stood on things.

"We're not out to gouge our guests," he told her firmly. "We offer a great experience for a fair price. People who book with us know what to expect. Most of them are repeat visitors, who know who does what and for what price. We're not going to suddenly tell them things have changed and will now cost more."

To his relief, she didn't have an answer for that. Yet. Somehow, he suspected she would eventually.

They drove along for several more minutes in silence. He'd just begun to feel comfortable when she spoke again.

"I'd like to examine the books."

"What books?" he asked.

"Your ledgers. I assume you do keep them. Where you log income and expenditures."

Somehow, he kept a straight face. "We don't keep records of any of that," he said, only half joking. "I mean, sure. We log income from guests. And we keep receipts from grocery bills. But it's a pretty straightforward operation. No frills. So not too much to examine."

She stared at him for a second too long. "Is it safe to assume you—we—do make a profit? Or is this your way of telling me that my grandfather operated this fishing lodge for fun?"

What could he do but laugh out loud? Even if having to explain all of this made him want to put his head down and curse the cruel twist of fate that meant he had to deal with her and her questions.

When he'd had his little forced chuckle, he kept driving. Jaw clenched, eyes on the road. Though she hadn't known about Grady's will. And since she hadn't met him, no way could she have understood a man like her grandfather and the joy he'd found in his small business.

At first, he could tell she was trying hard not to push him. But then, when he didn't elaborate or explain, she shook her head. "Why did you laugh?" she finally asked. "I wasn't trying to be funny. I simply asked an honest question."

"I know," he replied, shaking his head. Then, as he saw what looked like hurt flash across her beautiful face, he sighed and relented. "We make a profit, believe me. Even though Grady loved what he did, like everyone else, he had to make a living."

"Then why wouldn't you want to make more money?" She sounded genuinely puzzled.

"Money isn't everything," he said. Then, as her frown deepened, he decided to try to redirect the conversation. "Look, you just got here. You haven't seen how the place runs or gotten a feel for our clientele. Why don't you give it some time, learn everything you can about our operation, and then you can make suggestions about changes? Does that seem fair to you?"

Her gaze shadowed; she finally nodded. "You're right, of course. I'm sorry. I tend to be a little…over-enthusiastic."

"Better than apathy," he said, finally smiling a genuine smile. "You actually have a lot to learn."

Though she nodded, he knew she didn't have the faintest idea. Which was okay because he'd teach her. And he suspected she'd be ready to leave long before the designated period of one year had passed. Which wouldn't work out for him, as that would mean the lodge would never become his. The will stipulated both had to remain, and if one left, they willingly had to sign the lodge over to the other with nothing in return.

Since there was no way in hell Dade planned to go anywhere and he suspected she would never give him the lodge without some sort of payment, he'd do whatever he had to do in order to convince her to stay. Because after one year had passed, either party could sell. Then and only then, the lodge would be his.

Chapter Two

In the few weeks that she'd spent getting her affairs in order before she'd boarded a plane to Anchorage, Maddie had done extensive research on various Alaskan fishing lodges. She'd settled on two that she wanted to eventually emulate. Both of them were upscale and luxurious, providing accommodation and entertainment for both the anglers and their families.

At first, she'd found the idea of vacationing at a fishing lodge repellent, something that she'd never, ever be interested in doing. But as she'd delved into reading about them, she'd warmed up to the idea. Who wouldn't—with the opportunity to visit a spa or go on a wildlife tour, attend yoga classes and eat healthy, chef-prepared meals? Fishing, which might not be for everyone, appeared to be optional. With which she definitely could get on board.

While she understood her grandfather's lodge was rustic at best, she understood the potential. All she'd need to do was convince her new partner, Dade, of the opportunities ahead of them and then bring in investors for funding. Soon, they'd be operating one of the best Alaskan fishing destinations ever!

The future looked bright. And maybe it was due to the

spotty cell phone service, but the threatening text messages seemed to have stopped. She hadn't gotten one in two days.

Everything would finally work out. And yes, she did have a lot to learn. Though, no matter what her new partner thought, she wouldn't be catching or cooking fish. She had no interest in fishing, and cooking wasn't one of her life skills. The guests certainly wouldn't appreciate anything she fried up and tried to serve them. Once Dade sampled something she'd made, she knew he'd agree.

She'd more than make up for her lack of those skills with her others. She might not be a homebody, but she did excel in seeing overlooked potential. And she was a damn good decorator, skilled at hosting and making people feel welcome. All in all, she'd be a valuable asset to this entire operation. Dade would eventually learn that for himself. Right now though, she supposed she had absolutely everything to prove.

"Here we are," Dade said, gesturing to a faded wooden sign that read Grady's Lodge, 5 Miles, with a large arrow pointing down a rutted dirt track that disappeared into the trees. "Hang on," he told her, making the turn slowly. "It's a bit rough going from here on out."

For whatever reason, she suddenly felt nervous. While she'd done an exhaustive internet search for her grandfather's place, she hadn't been able to learn much. Of course, she hadn't even known of its existence until a few weeks ago. At least she'd been able to ascertain Grady's Lodge was real.

Her heart pounded. She sat up straight. Now she'd finally lay eyes on her inheritance.

Despite their slow speed, mostly a crawl, they bounced along the road, if one could even call it that. More like a path or trail. She made a mental note to make sure the way in was one of the first things repaired or improved. A nice couple of layers of asphalt or cement would go a long way to helping guests reach the lodge.

"People don't mind driving on this?" she asked, earning her an incredulous glance from Dade.

"You're in remote Alaska," he replied, as if that explained everything.

"I see." But she didn't. Gripping the door with one hand and the dash with the other, she tried to keep from hitting her head.

Since she'd studied numerous websites and photos of other fishing lodges, she had a pretty good idea of what to expect. Even if the only photos she'd located on the internet of Grady's were old and faded. As they pulled up to a medium-size frame home, she tried to see past the main dwelling to the rest of the property. She couldn't see anything, not even the water. There were just too many trees.

As soon as Dade shifted into Park, she opened her door and hopped out.

Dade exited a little more slowly, grabbing her luggage from the back. "Follow me," he said. "I'll show you to your room."

As he opened the door (unlocked, she noted) and flicked on the light, she eagerly stepped inside and took in the room. Small but neat, with older furnishings, it definitely had a masculine vibe. Every item in the room was functional. Nothing unnecessary or decorative. Even the artwork on the walls appeared to be photographs of various fishing expeditions.

Moving closer to one, she studied the picture of a grinning older man with his arm around the slender shoulders of a teenaged boy holding one of the biggest fish she'd ever seen. Glancing at Dade, she realized the kid had to be him.

Which meant the man must have been her grandfather. His craggy face appeared kind, and she saw traces of her mother in his lopsided smile.

"I regret not ever meeting him," she said sadly. Someday, she'd ask Dade if he knew why Grady hadn't ever reached out, but not today.

"He was one of a kind," Dade said from behind her, his voice husky with emotions. "I'm sorry that you never got the chance to meet him."

She shrugged, pretending his words didn't sting. Damned if she'd point out to her new partner that her own grandfather had never expressed the slightest interest in getting to know her. Which was why she'd found his bequest a complete and utter shock. None of this made sense.

Where Dade fit in, she wasn't yet sure. Judging from the photograph, he'd been around here for a long time. A sudden thought shocked her, making her turn. "Are we... related somehow?"

"What do you mean?" he asked, frowning.

"Are you Grady's son or grandson?" She pointed toward the photo.

For a moment, he simply stared at her and didn't answer. Finally, he lifted his chin and shook his head. "No. Not by blood, at least," he said. "He raised me like a father, and I consider myself his son. But there's no actual relation."

She felt a prickle of rancor hearing that, even without knowing the story. Her grandfather Grady had raised this man and loved him like a son. While Maddie had been forgotten and unwanted. Silly to feel like that now, since she couldn't miss what she'd never had. She guessed he'd left her half of this place as a way to make amends.

"I can give you a short tour," he added. "But it's really not a big house."

Nodding, she looked around. A small kitchen sat to the left of the living room, and a short hallway led to the bathroom and bedrooms.

"Is that where I'll be sleeping?" she asked.

"Yes. There are two bedrooms. Yours is on the right," Dade said, turning on the light and then depositing her bags on the double bed. "There's only one bathroom, which we'll have to share, but it's a solidly built house."

"Thank you," she told him, smiling slightly at his description.

Then, as she noted the cowboy hat hanging on the bed post, she took a second look.

"Was this…" She looked around, swallowing hard. "My grandfather's bedroom?"

"Yes. Mine is next door. This is the largest one."

She went slowly around the room, unable to resist touching some of the personal things on the oak dresser. A large stone, worn to smoothness by water. An old paperweight, gold shavings in a heavy glass globe. And a small clock, made of some kind of petrified wood. All occupied places of honor.

The bed appeared to be a queen rather than a full. A colorful, quilted comforter had been neatly folded at the end of the bed. It looked well-worn and homemade.

"There are clean sheets," he said, still standing in the doorway. "But I didn't empty the closet or the dresser. I wasn't sure if there might be something of his you wanted to keep."

Unsure how to respond to this, she swallowed. "What about you?" she asked. "You were close to him. Please, take anything you want."

He met her gaze. "Thank you. I appreciate that. But Grady already gave me everything I wanted."

Which meant she'd have to do what? Go through her grandfather's things? Toss them? "Is there a place where we can drop them off as donations? That way, someone else would be able to use them."

Expression thoughtful, he nodded. "Yes. We can take them to Kip at the general store. He'll be able to distribute them."

"Oh good." She didn't try to hide her relief. "I'll bag them up so the next time we're in town we can take them. That way, I'll have room for my own clothes."

He turned to go, his hand on the knob as if he meant to close the door behind him.

"Wait," she said, suddenly and absurdly afraid of being in this room alone. "When can you show me around the rest of the lodge?"

His gaze was steady as he studied her. Though she still found him a bit unnerving due to his sheer size, he'd been nothing but kind.

"I thought you might want to rest up first," he replied, his husky voice making her insides quiver. "Get unpacked, settle in. There's no rush, is there? It's not like you're going anywhere anytime soon, right?"

She knew he was right. In fact, earlier she had been looking forward to a short nap and then unpacking. But she hadn't expected the sudden swell of emotion at knowing she'd be going through the personal things of the grandfather she'd never known. She wished he'd left her a letter, something, anything to explain why he'd never once reached out to her.

Pushing the sudden longing aside, she grimaced. "You're right, of course. Thank you."

Without another word, he nodded and left, pulling the door closed behind him.

Alone in the small room, she went back to the dresser and pulled open the top right drawer. Inside, she found white, black and grey men's socks, all rolled up in pairs. She sighed, wondering why she felt so much like she was trespassing.

When Maddie had been a child, her mother had moved them around a lot. Maddie had gone to so many different schools she'd almost lost count. It seemed like just as she'd started fitting in and making friends they'd move again. And then once again, she'd become the new kid. The outsider.

She'd often longed for the kind of stability that came from deep roots, from family. The only thing she'd known about her grandfather was that her mother, Vanessa, refused to discuss him. This had led Maddie to believe Grady must have been some sort of monster. Her mother never attempted to dissuade her from that assumption. Right up until she died, she'd refused to say anything good about where she'd come from or the man who'd raised her.

Now, it appeared there were two sides to every story.

Water under the bridge, Maddie told herself. She opened another dresser drawer, saw the boxer shorts neatly folded inside and closed it. She'd do all her unpacking later. For now, her own things could remain inside the suitcase.

To reach the small bathroom that sat in the hall between the two sleeping areas, she had to leave her room. Hoping Dade wasn't in there, she gingerly opened the door and made her way out. To her relief, Dade had stacked clean towels and a washcloth on the counter for her.

After washing her face, scrubbing off the makeup, she went back to her room with the intention of at least trying to nap. But on the way there, she made a sudden detour to the kitchen. Underneath the sink, she found a box of white kitchen-size trash bags and took three. No time like the present. She had way too much nervous energy to even consider she'd have any luck at sleeping.

Putting a staunch lid on her emotions, she got to work.

It took much less time than she'd thought to empty the dresser. It helped that she worked fast, giving zero thought as to the man who'd owned these things. They filled up one trash bag.

Once she'd finished that, she moved on to the nightstand. Opening the small drawer, she found, instead of clothing, a silver medallion on a chain and several old, faded photographs. She almost slammed the thing shut, but curiosity got the better of her.

She took out the necklace first, studying the medallion. It appeared to be a Saint Christopher pendant. A large man with a child on his shoulders and a staff in one hand had been etched into the metal. Interesting. She remembered reading somewhere that many people wore them as a symbol of safe travels and protection.

For whatever reason, she found the medallion beautiful. Instead of dropping it into the bag with the clothes, she placed it back into the drawer for safekeeping.

Now the photographs.

She took them out carefully, afraid she might damage them. The first one was of her grandfather, though much younger, standing next to someone who had to be Maddie's mother. She appeared to be a teenager, maybe about fifteen or sixteen. Since Maddie had never seen pictures of her mother when she was young, she was taken aback at her innocent beauty.

And then she looked at her grandfather. The love in his expression as he gazed at his daughter came through as loudly as if someone had printed the words in red on the picture. Maddie studied it, noting the familiar stubborn look on her mother's face. Her crossed arms further attested to her mood.

The next photo was of her mother alone. Still young, but maybe a few years older than in the first one. In this one, she wore a denim jacket, and a rebellious glint shone in her eyes. If Maddie were to choose a word for this one, it would be *trouble*.

There were two more photographs. The next one seemed to be the oldest of all. Taken in black-and-white, it showed Grady Pierce as a young man, with his arm around the woman who must have been his wife. She'd died in childbirth, and Maddie's mom had never known her. Again, this picture embodied the word *love*.

Finally, the last shot was of an infant, lying alone in a pale pink onesie. Studying this, at first, Maddie thought it must have been her mother as a baby, but gradually she realized she'd seen the same picture in the baby book her mother had made. It was Maddie, a few months old. How her grandfather had gotten this, Maddie had no idea. As far as she knew, her mom and grandfather hadn't spoken after a pregnant and angry Vanessa had left Alaska for the lower forty-eight.

Though Maddie hadn't thought much about any of that since her mother had died, learning of the inheritance and her estranged grandfather's death had brought back a powerful curiosity about what had happened all those years ago to cause such a rift. Now, she'd likely never know.

After placing the pictures back in the nightstand next to the necklace, Maddie grabbed another trash bag and moved on toward the closet. The sight of all the men's clothes hanging neatly in there nearly stopped her short. But then she shook her head and began taking them off the hangers and shoving them into her bag.

She used the third bag for the shoes, coats and hats, feeling both guilty and accomplished once she'd cleared the space out. Now she had room for her own things, but a sudden wave of exhaustion had her rethinking the idea of a nap.

It had been a long day. Heck, it had been a long couple of months, if she were honest.

Kicking off her shoes, she gingerly climbed up onto the bed, closed her eyes and hoped she could sleep. Her scattered thoughts kept crowding her mind, but she forced herself to clear her head. She'd allow herself thirty minutes in an effort to try to sleep. If she wasn't out by then, she'd give up and finish organizing her new bedroom.

ALONE AGAIN IN the kitchen of the small house in which he'd lived for most of his life, Dade once again wondered what Grady had been thinking. He missed the man with a fierce ache, but damned if he understood him. Giving half of the lodge to that woman, an outsider from the lower forty-eight, could cause irreparable damage to everything Dade—and Grady himself—held dear.

She didn't belong. She'd never belong. One look at her perfectly done makeup and fashionable, impractical clothing revealed that. Maddie might be easy on the eyes, but everything about her screamed *big city*.

Hell, Grady himself had never even met her. Dade found it hard to respect someone who'd never made one single attempt to contact her grandfather. Not one letter or phone call or visit, even as the man grew older and frailer. Since his daughter Vanessa had passed away, Maddie was Grady's only remaining blood relative. He'd never stopped hoping to eventually connect with her. But his letters had gone unanswered, and he'd finally given up and stopped writing. His daughter Vanessa, Maddie's mother, had turned her against him, Grady had lamented. Since Dade knew all too well the story of Grady and Vanessa's estrangement, he'd simply nodded. Hell, Maddie hadn't even cared enough to notify Grady of Vanessa's passing a few years back.

And now, after Grady was dead and buried, she'd finally come. Several months too late. Even worse, in order for her to meet all the conditions of the will, Dade would be stuck with her for one entire year. And while he suspected she'd be more than happy to sell him her half of the place, he wouldn't be surprised if she attempted to gouge extra money from him. She'd never understand that deep connection he had to the lodge, to the wilderness and the water, the eagles and the fish. To the land.

Dade's roots ran deep, into the earth and sky. His ancestors had hunted and fished in these parts for hundreds of years. Somehow, Grady shared the same connection. The older man had taught a young Dade how to hunt and to fish, how to respect the sacrifice given by the deer and the elk and the salmon. How to honor the land.

Grady had been the only family Dade had ever known. He didn't remember much about his birth parents, only that they'd abandoned him when he'd been too young to take care of himself. Somehow, he'd ended up here at the lodge, a scared and half-frozen five-or six-year-old boy. Not knowing what else to do, the older man had taken him in.

At first, he'd thought he was only going to stay through the winter, while Grady quietly searched for his parents. Secretly, Dade loved being fed and warm and treated like he mattered. He'd hoped he never had to leave.

Despite Grady's attempts to locate his people, no one had ever come forward. Dade became part of Grady's family and part of Blake. He'd emulated everything the older man did, his honestly and honor, the way he became everyone's friend.

Dade owed Grady a debt he could never repay, not in this life or the next. He had raised him as his own and Dade had always felt that, for as long as he lived, Grady's Lodge would be his home. Dade wouldn't let anyone take that away from him. Especially not Maddie Pierce.

Right now, he found the woman a bit of an enigma. He'd been prepared to completely dislike her, and her willowy sort of beauty had come as a shock. He'd been alone too long, he thought, judging by his body's instant reaction to her. Since that would be the kind of complication they could both do without, he'd forced himself to try to study her impassively, without judgment. Truth be told, Maddie Pierce reminded Dade a little of himself, all those years ago. He'd spotted a certain kind of vulnerability in her gaze, when she didn't think anyone was looking.

Shaking off the foolish thoughts, Dade knew he had to be practical. After all, for the next year, they were going to be a team. They had less than a week to get to know each other before the first round of paying guests arrived. He'd need to get her up to speed on how the lodge was run, what the guests expected and her part in making all of this happen.

Honestly, he could use the help. He'd somehow managed to run it by himself last season, since Grady's illness had robbed him of his strength. Watching the man he thought of as a father grow weaker had just about killed Dade. Alone, he'd managed to keep his chin up and appear happy for their guests. He'd successfully finished off last season, but it hadn't been easy.

However, none of that compared to having to watch Grady die. All of Blake had attended the funeral, but

Grady's granddaughter had not. Dade had asked Grady's attorney to reach out to her, which he had. She hadn't replied back. In fact, none of them had heard a peep from her, until she'd learned she'd inherited part of the lodge.

To ward off his increasingly dark thoughts, Dade left the house and walked out to one of his favorite places, the boat docks. Here, several outboard, flat-bottom boats awaited the next group of fishermen. Dade had spent the past several weeks working on them, making sure the motors ran smoothly and had plenty of gas. He'd cleaned them up, too, polishing the sides and the seats until they shone.

He climbed into one and sat. Instead of starting it up and puttering out into the river, he simply glanced back at the lodge and tried to picture how this fishing season would go. There were six cabins, all facing the river and the boat slips. He'd already gotten a head start on readying them for guests, airing them out after the long winter, dusting and sweeping. The beds were not yet made up, but all the clean linens had been placed in each one. The small bathrooms still needed cleaning, as did the kitchens, but it wouldn't take long to do that. Especially now that he had some help.

Fishing season would be starting soon. The first group of guests had been staying here for years. Several of them had even come in for Grady's memorial service. This would be the first season open without him. Dade was determined to make certain it ran smoothly. Even with Maddie Pierce here. *Especially* with her here, he corrected himself. If she was going to be a partner for the first year, she'd be putting in the time and the work.

At least she appeared game. He had to hand it to her for that. He'd halfway been expecting her to sweep in here with a major attitude, full of entitlement and lofty expectations.

Luckily for them both, so far she didn't seem anything like that.

He'd let her get some rest and settle in, and then he'd show her around tomorrow before putting her to work. They had a lot to do to ensure everything would be perfect on opening day when the guests arrived. More than anything, he hoped she could help him out with the cooking. While they kept the menu simple, Grady had been a talented cook. His pan-seared salmon had been the most anticipated dish for every guest.

Speaking of work, as a matter of fact, he might as well get started. Heading toward the first cabin, he figured he had enough time to finish cleaning, plus make the bed up, before it would be time to head back to the main house and see about preparing the evening meal.

Since he'd done quite a bit of work on this unit already, he only had the bathroom left. Everything had been thoroughly cleaned after the close of last season, but dust accumulated over the winter months, and he wanted the shower, sinks and commode sparkling.

Once he'd finished with the small bathroom, he spritzed the mirror, wiped it and stepped back to look at everything with his best critical eye. He even checked the mini-fridge, now plugged in even while empty, which guests used to store their own beverages or snacks.

Pleased with the results, he grabbed the clean sheets and blanket and made up both beds. After he'd pulled the plaid comforters up and arranged the pillows, he exhaled. One down and five left to go. With two people per cabin, they could host up to twelve people at a time. Usually, their groups weren't quite that large, but as luck would have it, the bunch coming at the end of the week would have them operating at capacity.

Once he closed the cabin door behind him, he made his way home.

Back at the main house, he moved quietly, just in case Maddie might be asleep. Since she'd closed her bedroom door, he figured she likely decided to take a nap. He couldn't blame her. Dallas to Anchorage was a long flight.

With the ease of familiarity, he got out Grady's old cast-iron skillet, the rice maker and a bag of microwavable frozen green beans. Two large salmon fillets, some long-grain rice and steamed green beans would be their dinner tonight. He got started cooking, focusing on the familiar motions.

"That smells amazing," a soft voice behind him said. For whatever reason, his body sprang to instant attention.

"Thanks," he managed, keeping his back to her so she wouldn't notice his arousal. Cursing himself, he knew he had to get this under control before it became the kind of problem no one needed. Especially not him.

"It's salmon," he said. "We eat a lot of it around here."

"I love salmon." She came closer, until her slender hip bumped his. "Sorry," she said when he quickly stepped sideways.

A quick glance revealed she'd focused her attention on the stove.

"Are you frying that?" she asked. "I've never had fried salmon."

"It's blackened. Grady taught me to make it," he said, glancing at her to see her reaction. "Your grandfather was a really good cook. I hope you inherited that skill from him."

This made her laugh. The light, feminine sound was like the first chirp of a bird announcing spring. He couldn't help but stare, both enthralled and frightened.

"What?" she finally asked. "Why are you looking at me like that?"

Shrugging, he told her the truth. "It's been a long time since we had a woman around here."

"Women don't come here to fish?"

"Not often. Every once in a while, one or two accompany their husbands," he said. "But mostly, it's just men."

She studied him, her expression intent. "Do these women ever come back? After their one time, do they return the next season?"

He didn't even have to think about it. "Not often. I'd have to say there are only a few women who truly want to spend their vacation time fishing."

"You don't say." She cocked her head, the gleam in her eyes giving him a warning. "That must be why the other upscale fishing resorts have activities for women to enjoy while the men fish."

"We're not an upscale fishing resort," he said. "We never have been. Our guests come here for one reason only. To fish."

Instead of arguing, which he kind of expected, she simply stared at him. He could almost see the wheels turning inside her head. Yes, he knew about these other types of fishing resorts. They were luxurious, with amenities neither he nor Grady had ever wanted to have and prices more than double the cost of Grady's Lodge. Which was fine by him. Each type of lodge occupied their own niche. He and his guests preferred things the way they were.

He took the fish off the stove, made two plates and carried them to the table. "Come on," he said. "Let's eat. I'm guessing you have to be hungry."

Again, she flashed that smile. "Starving," she agreed, pulling out a chair and dropping into it. "This looks amazing."

Since he ate salmon so often he'd grown tired of it, he shrugged. "It'll do."

"Do you have any wine?" she asked. "A glass of pinot grigio would go great with this."

"I haven't picked up the beer and wine yet," he said. "I usually just keep that stocked for the guests. I can get you water or iced tea."

She frowned. "Water is fine. You don't drink?"

"Not anymore," he said, hoping she'd leave it at that. He grabbed a couple of glasses, filled them with cold water from the refrigerator and carried them over to the table. "I hope you like the fish."

Taking the hint, she picked up her fork and dug in. He did the same, trying not to watch her while she ate, but unable to help himself.

Concentrating on her meal, she didn't speak again until she'd cleaned her plate. "That was delicious," she said. "You're a really good cook."

Sitting back in his chair, he grinned. "Thanks. I can't wait to eat something that wasn't cooked by me."

Though she smiled back and nodded, he swore he caught a trace of worry in her expression. He really didn't know what he'd do if she claimed she didn't know how to cook. He wouldn't be surprised, but he needed a helpmate here, not another guest.

"I know you said you haven't really gone fishing, but you might like it," he told her, changing the subject. "After all, you're going to have to do a fair bit of it."

She laughed, as if she thought he was kidding. When he didn't laugh along with her, she stopped. "You're serious. But I don't understand. Why on earth would anyone want me to go fishing with them? I'm a complete novice, or worse. I'd have no idea what to do."

"We've got a few days to teach you a few things," he

said. "Sometimes, the guests want someone to drive the boat. That way they can concentrate on fishing."

"I'm thinking you're going to have to be the boat driver." Twisting her hands in front of her, she grimaced. "Honestly, I don't know how."

"I can teach you," he said, making his tone firm.

Her eyes widened. "I supposed you can," she replied. "But I doubt I'll be nearly as good as someone like you, who must have years of experience. Why would any fisherman want to deal with me when they could have a pro like you?"

"We have six boats. When we're full, they're all out at the same time. I can only pilot one."

"What about the other five?" she asked. "If they all need drivers, what do you do? Even if I were to drive one, that leaves four others. Are there other employees who could handle them?"

Slowly, he shook his head. "We have no employees. For years, it's been just me and Grady. Now it will be you and me. Most times, the fisherman handle their own boats. It's just every once in a while that they request one of us take them out. We just have to be prepared for when that happens."

"Maybe it won't."

While he hated to dash her hopes, he wanted to make sure she understood the reality. "Most likely, it will. We'll go out tomorrow so you can learn. It's actually pretty easy. They're all outboards."

She gave him a blank stare. "I don't know what that means."

"You'll learn. I promise. Now about the rest of it, we've got five cabins left to clean and get ready. We've also got to do a lot of meal prep right before the guests arrive. After that, we'll take turns on cooking duty."

"That's a lot," she commented. "Do you have a menu already made up?"

"We do." He smiled, hoping she could see his approval. He'd halfway expected her to claim she didn't know how to cook either. "We tend to stay pretty basic, nothing fancy. A lot of salmon, since it's so plentiful here. I'll show you a copy of it later."

Expression dazed, she nodded. "Thanks. I'm still a bit groggy from all the traveling. But I'd like to take a walk around the place, if that's okay. Maybe check out the cabins and the fishing pier."

Fishing pier? She meant boat docks. He decided to let that one pass. She'd figure out soon enough that around here, they fished by boat.

"Sure," he replied. "Are you ready to go now?"

"I am."

"Perfect." He grabbed a couple of cans of bear repellent and handed one to her. "Never go off without one of these."

Looking up from reading the label, she made a face. "You're joking, right?"

"Joking? I'm afraid not. You're in Alaska now. Bears are everywhere. Believe me when I say you don't want to get mauled by one."

Eyes wide, she nodded. "Just to be on the safe side, I'm sticking with you." She lifted up her can. "And I can assure you that this will always be in my hand."

"Good."

"I'm glad we ate," she said, her tone teasing. "At least I've had a good meal before my life flashes before me."

Despite himself, he smiled back. "I'm glad you think it was good. Let me get this cleaned up, and we'll go."

Chapter Three

"I'll do it." Maddie pushed to her feet, grabbed their plates and carried them over to the sink. She took a quick look around, hoping for a dishwasher, and when she spotted one, she let out an audible sigh of relief.

"I'm glad there's something I can do to contribute," she said, rinsing off their plates before stacking them inside. "I think I read that it doesn't get dark at this time of the year until late. Is that right?"

"It is," he replied. "The sun doesn't set until after ten in May."

"I think I like that." She finished stacking everything in the dishwasher. Eyeing the cast-iron skillet, she tried to figure out the best way to clean it. "Can this go in the dishwasher?" she asked, holding it up and turning toward him.

"No." He pushed up from the table and came over, taking the frying pan from her. "I'll take care of cleaning that later. And show you, so you can clean it when you use it."

Though she nodded, she couldn't help but wonder what he'd say if she told him she hadn't realized she'd be cooking for people other than herself. Honestly, she'd figured the lodge would have some kind of staff, even if it were minimal. Cooks and housekeepers at the very least.

Obviously not.

After washing her hands and drying them on a dish towel, she took a deep breath and pasted a smile on her face. While she hadn't been entirely sure what to expect, even her most basic expectations hadn't been met.

Which was okay, she told herself. Because change would be coming.

On the way out, she saw a huge stack of mail on the counter. There were magazines and envelopes, more mail than she personally got in a week.

"That's a lot." She gestured. "How often do you get mail out here?" she asked.

"It depends on the weather," he answered. "I try to pick it up once a week in town, though this time it was more like ten days. I grabbed it yesterday while we were there."

"In town? You don't have a mailbox?"

He glanced at her sideways. "This is remote Alaska," he said, as if that explained everything.

"And? What, do they bring the mail in by float plane?"

"Sometimes," he replied. "It all goes to Anchorage and is distributed from there. I take my outgoing stuff into Blake, and about once a week, they truck it to Anchorage."

Which gave an entirely legitimate meaning to the term *snail mail*, she thought.

"We might be accessible by road right now, but it's not that way always," he continued. "In winter, we're often cut off for weeks at a time. Or longer. Which means our mail service can be hit or miss."

"No mail and no Wi-Fi. How do you pay your bills?"

Unsmiling, he eyed her. "I have them set up on automatic payment. The ones that aren't, I know when they're due, and I can pay them by phone if necessary."

"But you said that Blake has Wi-Fi, right?" she asked.

"Yes."

"Okay." Before she even spoke, she knew he wasn't going to like her suggestion. But she didn't see any reason why they couldn't begin to move out of the dark ages and into modern times. "If Blake has it, and they're not that far away, it shouldn't be too difficult to get service out to the lodge. Have you ever looked into it?"

"No." He crossed his arms. "Sometimes it's a good thing to unplug from all that."

"I agree," she said. "For a while. But decent internet is an absolutely basic requirement for a normal life."

Shaking his head, he stared at her. "Slow down. You haven't even been here twenty-four hours, and you're already trying to change things."

"But for the better," she pointed out, her cheerful tone in direct contrast to his surly one.

"Come on." Clearly unpersuaded, he opened the door and gestured for her to precede him. "At least take a look at the place before you start thinking about what you want to change."

"Sorry," she said, though she wasn't. As she swept past him, she couldn't help but wonder why he had so much resistance to such a minor thing. Most people regarded internet as a convenience.

Outside the main house, all she could see were trees, which made her wonder why the home hadn't been built close to the water. He took her down a long, windy path through the forest. Bits of bright blue sky were visible through the leafy canopies. Despite herself, as they walked, she felt a sense of peace come over her.

Finally, they turned a corner and reached a clearing. Now, she could see parts of the river, a glittering blue thing shimmering not too far in the distance.

He stopped, and she noticed the small cabin, tucked within a strand of evergreens. Made of rough-hewn logs, it had a rustic feel. The covered front porch even had a couple of rocking chairs.

"Here's cabin one," he said. "They're all identical. This is the only one I've had time to get ready. We'll tackle as many of the others as we can tomorrow."

Climbing up onto the front porch, wood creaking under her feet, she barely heard him. She opened the front door, found the light switch and stepped inside.

The blue-and-green plaid comforter was the only spot of color in the room. Everything, from the log walls to the area rug on the floor, appeared to be in some shade of brown or tan. A small, white mini-fridge sat near the door.

She walked around the room before taking in the small but sparkling bathroom. Even the shower curtain continued the same monochrome color scheme, right down to the pictures of deer and moose on the beige fabric.

"Well?" he asked from behind her. "What do you think?"

That he'd even ask her opinion surprised her. "I love the comforter," she said truthfully. "It adds just the right pop of color to the room."

He nodded. "They're new. Grady ordered them right after last season ended. He died before I could show him how great they look in every cabin."

Though he kept his face expressionless, she could hear the sadness in his voice. "You miss him, don't you?" she asked softly.

"Yes." Turning away, he walked back outside, leaving her alone in the cabin.

Though she really wanted to get out her tablet and begin making notes of small tweaks she wanted to make, she knew now would not be the right time. Dade had already accused her of coming in and immediately wanting to make changes. While he wasn't wrong, she knew she needed to pick her battles. She'd check out the rest of the lodge, make her notes in private and maybe even speak with the first round of guests about their preferences. She suspected doing that would carry a lot more weight than if she simply came up with stuff on her own.

Outside, Dade waited for her on the balcony. He stood with his back to the door, leaning on the railing and staring off in the direction of the river. She noticed a large, stone fire pit with a circle of at least twelve oversized rustic wooden chairs.

"I like this," she mused. "I can see roasting marshmallows over the fire."

"More like beer and sausages," he said without turning around. "Let's move on. We've got a lot of ground to cover."

"Lead the way." If all the cabins were exactly the same, she hoped he wasn't going to show her the other five. Especially since he'd said they'd be cleaning them tomorrow.

To her relief, they walked past all the others, which were just like he'd said, carbon copies of each other.

They were headed toward the water, she realized. Due to the curvy path and all the trees, she only caught occasional glimpses of it shimmering bright and blue.

Another turn and a large, corrugated metal building came into view, with the path leading right up to its door.

"There's where we store the boats in the winter," Dade pointed out. "I started working on them a couple of weeks ago, one at a time. I made sure each was up and running before I put it in the river. We also have a couple of golf carts in there that we use to ferry guests from the main house to the cabins."

Though she smiled and nodded, she realized all her research had failed to prepare her for the actual reality of this place. Instead of managing various employees and fine-tuning the lodge's customer service, she'd be working in the trenches, doing the jobs she'd wrongly assumed would be performed by others.

She'd have no choice but to roll with the punches. She'd learned when she'd first entered the competitive field of commercial land development that she'd have to work hard and smart if she wanted to get ahead.

But then, look where that had gotten her.

More trees, another curve and then ahead, the river and the boat slips. There were ten, six of them filled by boats. The watercraft all appeared sturdy and serviceable to her inexperienced eye. They were all made of metal, with an outboard motor on the back end. While they didn't look very comfortable, she supposed they were perfect for fishing.

"They're jon boats," Dade said. "The most common boat in Alaska. They're cost-effective and tough, easy to navigate, and bouncing off the occasional rock doesn't hurt them."

"Bouncing off the..." She shook her head. "And you expect me to learn how to drive them? With so many boats, why don't you hire locals to come help out? It doesn't make sense to have only two people, one of whom has never done this before."

"It'll all work out." He sounded confident. Or delusional. She couldn't decide which. "Grady and I worked this way for years."

"Grady knew what he was doing," she pointed out, barely keeping the panic from her voice. "What is the reasoning behind not hiring a couple of guys from town?"

"If we actually have a need, we have some people we

can call. But like I told you earlier, most of our clients are regulars. They know their way around the river and prefer to take the boat out on their own. It's only occasionally that we get a group that wants someone to accompany them. Those tend to be first-timers."

Maybe there was hope. "Do you have any first-timers coming this year?"

"I'm not sure." He shrugged. "I'd have to check the reservation book. I know the first group is all return customers."

This startled her enough that she stopped walking. "Book? As in paper? You don't manage your reservations on a computer system?"

"Nope." Eyeing her, he grimaced. "That'd be kind of hard to do with no internet."

Which boggled the mind. "How do people make reservations anyway?"

He gave her a sideways glance, tinged with amusement. "They call or leave voicemails. We don't give out our cell numbers, just the landline, since that tends to be more reliable. I check the dates they're wanting in the book to make sure we have room. If we do, I write them down and confirm with them. Pretty simple."

"Like they used to do back in the days before people had internet." Dazed, she tried to understand. "Look, I get that Grady must have been old-fashioned. Sometimes, people can get stuck in the past and refuse to modernize."

"Maybe so," he agreed. "But everything has worked perfectly, so why fix something if it's not broken?"

Since she had a feeling she couldn't persuade him, at least not yet, she simply nodded. She had to wonder how much business the lodge lost each year due to the lack of convenience in making reservations.

"Would you like to go out in one of the boats?" he asked. "I really think you'll enjoy seeing the river."

Looking from him to the fast-moving water, she finally succeeded in staving off her fear and agreed. "Just promise me you'll take it easy. I'm not really comfortable off dry land."

"You can swim, right?"

Though sorely tempted to lie and say no, she reluctantly nodded. "I can."

"We'll be wearing life jackets anyway," he said. "No need to worry."

"I'm not." Which wasn't entirely true, but she didn't want to reveal all of her weaknesses up front. Water was supposed to be soothing, right?

They got onto one of the boats, and he retrieved a couple of life vests from under the seat. They put them on. She sat down and watched while he untied the boat, started the motor and pushed away from the dock.

At first, she clutched the sides of the bench seat, her heart pounding. But as they puttered along at a steady pace, she exhaled and began focusing on the beauty of their surroundings. The way the boat parted the water, the rich greenery on both sides of the river, the sheer majesty of the rock cliffs studded with occasional trees. All of this somehow soothed her. For the first time, she thought she might partially understand the lure of this remote and wild place.

Seated in the back of the boat near the motor, steering them, Dade seemed to blend with the wildness of the landscape. He belonged here, she realized, a sudden pang of longing making her catch her breath. He belonged here in a way she herself had never been able to anywhere she'd lived.

To chase away her sudden sadness, she did what she always did. Chitchat.

"This really is relaxing," she said brightly, pasting on a cheerful smile. "I'm so in the habit of constantly checking my social media feed that it feels weird not to."

"But kind of nice, too, right?"

She nodded. "Yes. You're right. There is something to be said about being unplugged."

The words had barely left her mouth when her phone pinged, announcing a text. Despite herself, she instantly tensed, resisting the urge to grab it and check it. It had to be her stalker. No one else would be texting her. All of her friends knew she'd gone to Alaska. "How am I getting text messages where there's no cell service?"

He shrugged. "It comes and goes. I told you, texts get through more than anything else. I really don't know how all that works. When we want to be sure to have a working phone, we carry a satellite phone with us."

"I see."

This would be the one time she wished her cell service wasn't working. On the plus side, at least she knew Dade wasn't the one sending them.

Though she tried her best to ignore her phone, when it sent the reminder ping, she pulled it out and glanced at it. The mystery person had messaged her again. Short and to the point.

You don't belong here. Go home. Or else.

DADE COULDN'T HELP but notice Maddie's strange reaction to getting a simple text message. She'd immediately tensed up, a flash of fear in her eyes. She'd immediately looked down, clearly trying to hide it. When her phone pinged again, she'd snatched it up, almost angrily. And then, the instant she read the message, her entire expression changed. Gone was the relaxed, awestruck woman enjoying the beauty of nature. She looked, he thought, miserable.

Dade didn't like it. He didn't like it one bit.

"Old boyfriend?" he drawled, before he could help himself.

"No," she replied, clearly distracted. "Ever since I got notified about Grady's death and my inheritance, I've been getting random texts." She met his gaze. "They're all from different numbers, none of them valid. I know because I've tried to call them back. Apparently, there's an app you can use to send texts anonymously."

He frowned. "These messages, are they threatening?"

"Only vaguely. In the beginning, whoever is sending them warned me not to come to Alaska. I haven't gotten one in three days, so I thought they'd given up." She showed him her phone and the words on the screen. "Now they want me to go home."

"Why?" he asked. "There has to be a reason."

"I have no idea." She shoved her cell into her back pocket. "To be honest, I kind of thought you might have been the one sending them."

At first startled, he realized he couldn't blame her. If their situations had been reversed, he would have suspected the same thing. "I'm not," he replied. "Truthfully, while I'm not entirely happy about the terms of the will, I admired and loved Grady. If this is what he wanted, then this is what he's going to get."

Their gazes locked and held. While clearly she hadn't cared for her grandfather, he mentally dared her to say anything derogatory about him.

To his relief, she didn't. Instead, she ducked her head,

appearing to withdraw into herself. Continuing to pilot the boat, he left her alone.

Finally, she lifted her chin and sighed.

"Where did you go to school?" she asked, out of the blue.

"What?" He stared at her, keeping his expression blank as he skillfully navigated around a fallen log. "Are you seriously changing the subject so you don't have to discuss those texts anymore?"

"Maybe. But I'm also curious."

"I went to school here, in Blake." He sighed. "And that's it. No education beyond high school, if that's what you're asking."

"It is." She smiled.

Not once in his life had he ever regretted staying at Grady's Lodge after finishing up high school. Grady had generously offered to pay his way through college, if he'd wanted to go, but Dade hadn't ever bothered to apply. He'd known for years what he wanted to do with his life, and he didn't see the point in spending time and money getting educated to do something else.

When he looked back at Maddie, she'd resumed studying the passing landscape. Slowing the boat, he pointed. "See those rocks over there? Just past them, the river gets really deep. We catch a lot of salmon there."

"Clearly, I didn't do enough research," she mused. "I focused on what I'd need to know to run a fishing resort from a management standpoint. I'm afraid I didn't take the time to learn the million small details that I need to know, like what kind of fish we catch the most, how they're caught and what the guests like to do in their off time."

Since she sounded more bemused than forlorn, he took pity on her. He even found himself smiling at her. "You'll learn. I'll help you. We're a team now, remember?"

Slowly, she nodded, her blue eyes locked on his. "Thank you."

"Keeping our guests happy is what matters," he continued, turning the boat around to head back to the dock. "Sometimes, after a day of fishing, after dinner, they like to sit around that fire pit you saw earlier. They drink beer, grill sausage and trade fishing stories until they turn in for the night. Once they go to bed, I make sure and check that the fire is out."

"Do you join them?" she asked.

"Sometimes Grady and I did." A pang of grief, sharp and deep, sliced through him. "In better days. Last season, he was too sick to do much."

She went quiet again. Part of him had hoped she might ask a few questions about her grandfather, at least pretend she cared. Instead, she averted her face and gazed out at the water.

He wished he knew why she despised Grady so badly. Maybe someday she'd tell him. He didn't know her well enough to press her.

Back at the slips, once he'd tied up the boat, he helped Maddie disembark. As they walked back toward the house, Maddie yawned several times, covering her mouth with her hand.

"I'm sorry," she said, noticing him watching. "It's been a really long day. Even though I napped earlier, I'm still pretty beat."

They reached the main house. Once inside, he turned on the TV.

"Satellite?" she asked, yawning again. "I mean since you don't get decent cell service, and I don't see any giant antennas, what else could it be?"

"Yes, satellite. It's spotty sometimes, but the only way

to get any channels at all." He noticed the way she kept glancing at her bedroom door. "If you're tired, we can talk again in the morning," he finally said.

"I'll keep that in mind," she replied, smiling through yet another yawn. "But I'm thinking, if you're able to have satellite TV, wouldn't it be possible to add an internet package?"

He nearly laughed out loud. She didn't give up, did she?

"Maybe." He shrugged, acting disinterested. "Actually, I have no idea. I've never checked. Grady was dead set against it."

"Well, since Grady is no longer here, maybe we can see?" she suggested gently. "Not only can internet access really help this business, but it'd be great for your guests and for personal use as well."

He had his doubts about that. Since he'd already voiced them at least once, he wouldn't again.

"If you want to check into it, then knock yourself out," he finally told her. "Bear in mind, we're going to be really busy the next few days before the first set of guests arrive."

"Hopefully, it won't take long to find out. I'll need information on your satellite TV provider, if you don't mind. Like the account number and their customer service phone number, that sort of thing."

Weary of the entire subject, he looked at her. So exhausted she swayed on her feet, she took advantage of his tiny concession and jumped in with both feet.

"Not tonight," he finally said. "Get some rest and we'll revisit the idea tomorrow."

"You promise?"

"I promise," he replied. "To be honest, unless the cost is ridiculous, I think having decent internet out here would be helpful."

Her smile lit up her entire face. Once again, his body went full-on DEFCON 1.

"Thank you," she said.

Temporarily unable to speak, he simply nodded.

"How much longer until the sun sets?" she asked, turning away to look out the window. "I want to go to bed, but it feels kind of weird to do it with the sun still so bright outside."

Composing himself, he checked his watch. "It's barely nine, so you've got another hour. The curtains in the bedroom are blackout, so with them closed, you'll barely be able to tell if it's light or dark."

Still, she hesitated.

"We'll be making an early start in the morning," he said, to nudge her along. "I figure we might as well get in practice. Fishermen like to get started as soon as possible."

"Early? How early?" she asked. "Will the sun be up?"

"I was thinking six," he replied. "And yes, sunrise is around five forty-five. We have long days this time of the year."

Despite her visible drooping, she still made no move to head to her room. Eyeing her, he thought about simply scooping her up and carrying her there, dropping her unceremoniously on the bed.

Except he wasn't that much of a Neanderthal.

Neither spoke. Silent battle of wills? Or maybe she was simply too exhausted to speak.

Finally, she dipped her chin in a nod. "Sounds good. I'll set my phone alarm."

After she excused herself, closing her bedroom door, he went back to the kitchen. He couldn't stop thinking about the text messages she'd mentioned getting. It really bothered him. He could see why she'd thought they might have come from him. Who else wouldn't want her here?

No one but Grady's attorney had known about the will. And Stuart Schmidt, the lawyer, had been one of Grady's oldest friends. Even if Stuart had downed a few too many beers in a bar one night, Dade still couldn't think of a single person in Blake who'd give a damn who Grady left the lodge to.

Whoever was sending Maddie the texts had to be someone from her previous life in Texas. If so, at least while she was here in Alaska, she'd be safe.

He knew he shouldn't care, but he did. Because he knew Grady would have wanted Dade to keep his granddaughter safe.

The next morning, after Maddie took her turn cooking and made them a simple breakfast of fried eggs and toast, they headed out and got busy readying the rest of the cabins. With both of them working, they were able to knock that particular chore out in a little under three hours.

"That was a bit of a workout," she said, smiling up at him as they walked back toward the main house. "But I like the sense of accomplishment."

Though he wanted to point out how great that was, since they'd be doing this after each set of guests left, he didn't. "What are we having for lunch?" he asked instead. "And I'm wondering if you'd had a chance to think about dinner, too."

Just like that, her smile vanished. "It's still my turn to cook? Even though I made breakfast?"

"Yep," he nodded. "We each take a day, remember? Today is yours. Tomorrow mine."

Her expressive sigh had him hiding his own smile. To his shock, he kind of liked her. If he could manage to ignore how she'd hurt Grady with her stubborn refusal to have anything to do with him.

"I forgot about the cooking rules," she finally said. "I don't know if you noticed or not, but I'm not really comfortable in the kitchen. I'll have to look through the cupboard and see what I can make with what we have."

He took pity on her. "For lunch, sandwiches are fine. Or soup. And I defrosted some ground beef, if you want to use that for dinner. We have a pressure cooker, too. Believe it or not, Grady kept a notebook with his favorite recipes. You're welcome to take a look at that if you like."

"Thank you." She glanced sideways at him. He noticed she kept her bear repellent clutched in one hand, always ready. "Is there anything you'd particularly recommend that's easy?"

"We have all the ingredients for you to make chili mac in the pressure cooker. It's quick and easy and generally lasts for a few days, when it's just two of us. It's also a guest favorite, though you have to double the recipe."

They'd reached the house. Inside, he went straight to the refrigerator, grabbed a can of diet cola and handed her another. "The first guests arrive on Friday," he said. "The rest of this week, we're going to plan out a menu, grab supplies and make sure we're as ready as possible."

After lunch, which consisted of a can of tomato soup warmed on the stove and grilled cheese sandwiches, he double-and triple-checked the list he'd compiled from all the times he and Grady had gotten ready for the start of fishing season.

Once he felt sure he hadn't missed anything, he showed her the list, explaining how many guests would be arriving and what they'd be served for meals. When she pointed out he'd left off paper towels and toilet tissue, he almost hugged her.

"Thanks," he said instead. "Every year, I forget something and have to go back. I'm thinking you just saved me having to do that this time."

"You're welcome." She beamed, his thanks seeming to energize her. "Are we going into town to pick up supplies now?"

"No, not until tomorrow. I thought we'd leave right after breakfast. This afternoon, I thought we could sit down and go over the menu for the first bunch. They'll be here Friday afternoon through Tuesday morning."

"Four nights?" She asked, appearing surprised.

"Yes, and three and a half fishing days."

"How many guests?"

He didn't even have to go check the log. "Eight. They'll be using four of the cabins. The Hilbarger family. Four generations of them. They've been coming here for years. They always want to be the first group of the season."

"What do they know about me?" she asked, leaning forward with both elbows on the table.

Surprised, he tried to figure out how to best answer. In the end, all he could give her was the truth. "Grady talked about you a lot. One of his biggest regrets was that he never got to meet you. But beyond that, no one knows anything else."

She recoiled at his words.

"Grady didn't want to meet me." Her flat voice and stony expression told him she believed every word. "He never made a single attempt to reach out. Not one. He didn't attend my high school graduation, or my college one either. He never sent one single Christmas card or birthday card or even a letter."

Dade stared at her, letting his disbelief show. "You're mistaken. I'm sure he did. I sat with him at that kitchen table many times while he wrote you. He tried to write you at least once a month when you were younger. I know for the last few months of his life, he wasn't able to write much, but he tried."

"What?" She shook her head. "If he did, he must not have mailed them. Because none of them ever made their way to me."

"I've no idea why you never got his letters or cards, but he sent them. I took them to the post office in Blake myself. Maybe he had the wrong address. I remember him saying it changed over the years."

Expression still shuttered, she shrugged. "We moved a lot, but I'm pretty sure we always had a change of address form in with the post office."

Unless someone had kept them from her, he thought, deciding not to say that out loud. Maddie would figure it out for herself. Or she wouldn't. Either way, he supposed it didn't really matter now. Any chance she and Grady might have had at forging a relationship had vanished with Grady's death.

Except this bit of knowledge changed things a little for Dade. Knowing she hadn't intentionally shut Grady out helped ease some of the bitterness that had festered inside Dade since he'd met her.

Though, realistically, he knew it shouldn't matter, it did. Maddie and he were partners, for at least a year, no matter what had happened in the past.

Chapter Four

The next morning, the soft ping of an incoming text message woke Maddie. Instinctively, she reached for her phone, rubbing the sleep from her eyes so she could see.

I see you haven't left Alaska yet. You'd better get going, and quickly, before something awful happens.

Her heart skipped a beat. Another veiled threat.

Until recently, she hadn't even suspected Dade might been the one sending them. But why wouldn't he? After all, if she left before her one year was up, he'd get the entire lodge as long as she signed it over to him.

Working in the cutthroat business world of commercial property management, she knew forcing her out would have been the modus operandi of many of the executives she'd worked with.

She couldn't say she would have blamed Dade either. It couldn't be easy to have devoted your life to something only to lose half of it to a complete outsider.

Except now she wasn't so sure it was him. Even if the app had some sort of scheduling capability, Dade had been nothing but pleasant to her. If he truly wanted to chase her

away, she would have expected him to be rude and con-
descending. Instead, he'd made it clear that they would be
a partnership. He wanted to honor her grandfather, a man
he'd clearly loved.

But her growing certainty that Dade wasn't texting her
begged the question—who was?

Some of her former work colleagues had been cutthroat.
And when she'd been laid off, they'd acted like she'd ceased
to exist. They wouldn't return her texts, never mind phone
calls. Not a single one of them even knew she'd inherited
property in Alaska. If they had, she suspected they wouldn't
have cared.

Theo, her ex, was now engaged to his side chick. From
what she'd been able to see on social media, the two of them
were expecting a baby and over-the-moon happy.

As for friends... With her demanding career, Maddie
hadn't made time for much of a social life. Between work
and Theo, she hadn't had the energy for anything else.

Which meant if no one from back home cared about her
move to Alaska, it had to be someone here.

She made a list of possible suspects in her mind while
in the shower. Maybe Dade had a girlfriend, someone who
was upset at the idea of another woman sharing his home
for twelve months. Or a really loyal guy pal who felt Dade
should have been given the entire fishing lodge.

A short list, she thought ruefully. And neither one
seemed all that plausible. After all, whoever it was had to
have gone to extraordinary lengths to get her personal cell
phone number.

In reality, she didn't have a clue. But she figured she'd
eventually find out. Because she definitely would stay here
the entire year in order to meet the stipulations in the will.
It would take more than a few vague texts to run her off.

Glad it wasn't her day to cook, she dried her hair and walked into the kitchen to find Dade already there, making pancakes.

"You're just in time," he said, smiling. She felt the warmth of that smile all the way to her toes.

"I like your cooking day best," she admitted, heading for the coffee maker. While her coffee brewed, she watched him as he poured the batter onto an electric griddle. He handled himself with ease, as if long used to knowing his way around a kitchen. There was definitely something sexy about a man like that. Especially one as ruggedly handsome as this one.

Nope. She shut that thought down. They were going to be working side by side for twelve months. Desire was the last thing they needed to bring into the picture.

As they ate breakfast—delicious, by the way—and talked, she found it interesting how she and Dade tiptoed around the subject of her grandfather. With every comment about Grady, Dade made it clear how much he admired the man. As for her, she couldn't seem to rid herself of the hard, cold nugget of resentment that sat like a festering lump inside. While Dade claimed Grady had been writing her letters, she had no proof of that.

He'd been kind enough to think of her in his will, but it was too little, too late. While she certainly appreciated the bequest, if she were honest, she would have liked to have known him. Growing up, she hadn't had much of a family. Just her mother, a woman who'd been more preoccupied with having a good time than spending time with her daughter.

All of that was in the past now, and Maddie believed in moving forward. She'd been given the opportunity to start a completely new life, and she'd seized on this with both hands. Dwelling on what might have been would only drag her down.

First thing she wanted to do was get them set up with the internet. And the whole cell phone thing perplexed her, so she'd also like to find out what, if anything, she could do to make it be more reliable.

"We'll deal with that later," Dade said, gathering up the dishes and carrying them over to the sink. For now, we've got to get ready for our guests. Lots of cleaning to be done."

Though back in Dallas she'd paid to have someone come clean her apartment, she managed to nod, hoping she appeared enthusiastic. Apparently, she didn't fool Dade.

"It shouldn't be too bad," he said, grinning. "With the both of us working, we should get those cabins done in no time. By the way, it's your turn to do dishes."

"I'd rather clean up than cook, any day," she retorted. "After we get all the cabins ready, can we sit down and go over the info I need to get internet?"

"We'll see." The non-committal answer had her shaking his head.

"Passive aggressive much?" she muttered.

His answering bark of laughter told her he'd heard.

Surprisingly, cleaning the cabins and setting up the beds wasn't as bad as she'd imagined. By the time they'd finished, she even felt a sense of accomplishment. Dade inspected the ones she'd done and gave her a thumbs up. "Good job!"

They went back to the house for lunch. While Dade made them a couple of BLTs, she pressed him for the satellite TV information. "I'd really like to get started making a few phone calls," she said.

"I know. But we still have a lot of work to do. I'll try and look for that tonight, once we're done for the day."

She knew better than to groan out loud. This was her job now. Until she learned the ropes and felt competent, she'd do what needed to be done.

True to his word, they spent the rest of the afternoon planning out the menu and making sure all the necessary supplies were on the shopping list. For once, she appreciated that all the meals were rustic and simple, since her culinary skills were, too.

By the time Dade announced they were finished, she knew the satellite TV customer-service line would be closed. Which meant she'd have to try again in the morning.

Once again overwhelmingly glad it was Dade's day to cook, she sat and watched TV while he grilled them some hamburgers. They ate dinner in what she thought felt like a companionable silence. Every time she looked at him, the sharp tug of attraction that zinged through her came as a surprise. Prior to coming here, she'd had a type. She'd tended to date well-dressed, blond men who worked in finance or real estate. Drop one of them on a deserted island, and she doubted they'd survive. With his shaggy dark hair and muscular build, Dade was about as opposite of that as a man could get.

If she were in his shoes, she might have been resentful that an intruder from Texas had swooped in and taken half of what he likely considered his. But instead, he'd been polite and considerate, accepting the situation with grace. Instead of trying to run her off, he'd taken the time to let her know what would be expected of her.

They worked well together and made a good team.

Even though the will had made it plain they both had to stay one long year, if either of them left, the lodge would go to the other. Dade could have decided to make her life miserable so she'd go back to where she'd come from. Then he would inherit it all and could go on running the fishing lodge the way he'd always done.

Except she didn't think one person could do this alone. Heck, she doubted two people would have an easy time of it. Once the first set of guests arrived, she'd have a better perspective on things.

For the first time in a long time, when she went to bed, she couldn't shake the feeling that things were all going to work out fine. There weren't any more text messages either. She could only hope that there wouldn't be.

That night, when she fell into bed, she knew she'd sleep well. It had been, she thought, a surprisingly good day.

IN THE MORNING, she woke up in a great mood. Though outside the sky had only begun to lighten, she got up first and grabbed a quick shower. A trip to town sounded like a lot more fun than she would have ever imagined. She'd always loved shopping, and even though they'd only be getting supplies for the lodge, she hoped to have time to purchase a few things to personalize her new bedroom. After all, it wasn't like she'd brought any decorative items with her.

By the time Dade woke, she'd already started breakfast. This time, she'd decided to keep it simple. She made scrambled eggs and toast, along with some sausage patties. Sipping her coffee, which for some reason tasted better than it ever had, she hummed under her breath as she prepared the meal.

Dade wandered into the kitchen just as she'd put the sausage patties in the frying pan. He made a beeline for the coffee maker, but halfway there he stopped and turned, eyeing her.

"You're up early," he commented.

"Breakfast is cooking," she chirped, hiding her smile at

his surprised expression. "Grab your coffee and sit. It'll be ready in a few minutes."

"That sausage smells great." Carrying his mug to the table, he never took his eyes off her. He sat, using his hand to brush a lock of his dark hair away from his craggy face. He looked unbelievably masculine and too freaking handsome for her peace of mind. She had to swallow hard and turn away. Time to force herself to focus on her cooking so she wouldn't burn anything and ruin their meal.

She could have stood and watched him eat, but instead made her own plate and sat down across from him. He ate fast, appreciation on his rugged face. Again, she caught herself sneaking looks at him, unable to shake the twinge of attraction.

"That was good," he finally said, after pushing his empty plate away. "Thank you."

"You sound surprised," she teased. "I don't think anyone could screw up scrambled eggs and toast."

This made him laugh. And, like everything else he did, he didn't do that halfheartedly either. He threw back his head and laughed, the deep, richness of the sound washing over her like waves on a tropical beach.

Flustered more than she should have been, since she suddenly found herself wondering how enthusiastically he made love, she busied herself collecting their plates and carrying them over to the sink.

If he noticed how she avoided looking at him, he didn't comment. Instead, he pushed to his feet and grabbed her arm.

"I've got those," he said. "It's my turn. Remember, whoever doesn't cook does the dishes."

"Not this time." Needing to keep busy, she waved him

away. "You go ahead and get your shower. I've already had mine."

Dropping her arm, he eyed her. "Okay, but you still have to make dinner."

"That's fine."

He didn't move. "Are you all right? You seem really motivated today."

All she wanted was for this buzz of desire to go away. It didn't bode well that she'd never felt anything like this, not in any of her other relationships, including the one with the man she'd believed she'd eventually marry. Until he'd dumped her.

Dade was still watching her, and she realized he'd asked her a question. Depositing the dishes in the sink, she took a deep breath and turned to face him. Annoyed that she had to actually brace herself for the butterflies in her stomach, she forced a smile. "I am. Both all right and motivated. For whatever reason, I'm really looking forward to going into town."

"Why?" he frowned. "You were just in town the other day, when you first arrived here."

"I enjoy shopping." The truth never hurt. She glanced over at their lengthy list. "Are you sure the general store will have all of that stuff in stock?"

His frown smoothed out. "Yep. We place a large order every year right before the start of the season. Kip knows it's coming, so he makes sure to have everything we'll need."

Damn. Part of her wished he were old and unattractive. The rest of her figured she might as well relax and enjoy the view.

Then, while she was still internally reeling from her visceral reaction to him, he pushed to his feet, flashed her a smile and disappeared into the bathroom.

A moment later, when she heard the shower start up, she allowed herself to sag against the kitchen counter. What was wrong with her? Sure, a month and a half had passed since she and Theo had broken up, but she definitely needed to get over this. The two of them were going to be stuck with each other for an entire year. She needed to keep reminding herself of that. And she might not know much about being a business owner, but she knew combining pleasure with work wasn't ever a good mix.

By the time Dade emerged from his shower, she'd finished cleaning up the kitchen. Out of habit, she'd tried scrolling social media on her phone. To her surprise, a few new posts had popped up in her feed before she lost the connection. She sighed as she dropped the phone into the new, cross-body designer purse she'd purchased at the Galleria right before leaving for this trip. Hopefully, she could take advantage of the internet access in town and see about getting something set up. She knew a guy back in Dallas who specialized in websites for businesses, so she'd get him to give her an estimate for one for the lodge.

The lodge. Better known as Grady's. Now hers and Dade's. She picked up some of the cookbooks and began leafing through them. Several were quite old and had some interesting recipes inside.

"What are you doing?" Dade asked, bringing her out of her thoughts. He strode into the kitchen, wearing a tight-fitting black T-shirt, jeans and boots. His hair had clearly been towel dried, giving it a tousled—and sexy—look. Staring at him, her mouth went dry. Dang, dang, dang.

"What?" she managed to ask, smiling. She babbled about finding what she wanted to make for dinner later and complimented him on the well-stocked kitchen.

If he noticed her scattered disposition he didn't comment. Instead, he seemed irritated as he turned around and went back to his room.

When he returned a few minutes later, he asked her if she was ready to go. When she said she was, he scooped the car keys off the counter, flashed another one of those smiles and headed toward the door.

Shaking off her daze, she followed after him, trying not to notice how good his backside looked in those faded jeans.

Once inside his Jeep, she buckled in, mentally giving herself a stern talking to. "Let's do this," she said, resisting the urge to give him a high five. Turning her face away, she concentrated on watching the landscape go past. Mile by mile, she began to relax. If she could manage to keep her mind out of the gutter, she could do this thing.

DADE STILL WASN'T sure what to make of Grady's granddaughter. Maddie wore impractical clothing, looked as if she'd be more at home in a metal-and-glass high-rise, but she didn't shy away from hard work. Sometimes, she seemed a bit bewildered, maybe even lost. Like earlier at breakfast. She'd kept sneaking looks at him as if he'd suddenly sprouted horns. When he'd gone in to take his shower, he'd actually checked himself out in the mirror to make sure he didn't have something on his face.

He didn't. Which meant he had no idea why she'd been staring.

By the time he emerged, she'd thoroughly cleaned the kitchen and was flipping through one of Grady's old cookbooks.

"I think I've found what I'm going to make for dinner later," she said, smiling slightly. "I've already checked and made sure we have all the ingredients."

"If we don't, you can get whatever else you need while we're in town."

Her smile widened, which made his body stir. "We do. You keep a well-stocked kitchen here."

"We do." His response came out slightly curt, since he had to regain control of his suddenly raging libido. To give himself a minute, he strode back into his room and pretended to be looking for something. Deep breaths and staring at the picture of him and Grady that he kept on his nightstand helped.

When he reemerged, she'd finished leafing through the cookbook and had taken a seat at the table.

"Are you ready to go?" he asked. To his relief, his voice sounded normal.

"I am." Again that devastating smile, sending a bolt of heat to his gut.

Asking himself what the hell was wrong with him, he pulled his keys out of his pocket. "After you," he said, gesturing toward the door.

Following her out to the Jeep, he couldn't help but admire her shape in those jeans. Which was perfectly normal, he thought.

Once he'd started the engine and they pulled away from the lodge, he enjoyed watching the way she studied the landscape with the enthusiasm of a tourist. He wondered how she, a Southerner, would adjust to the often brutal winters of his beloved state. He guessed he'd find out soon enough. First, they had to get through the fishing season.

"Any more of those texts?" he asked. Though he kept his gaze fixed on the road, he caught her quick intake of breath.

"Not since yesterday. It said they could see I haven't left Alaska yet. And then a vague threat if I didn't get going."

He didn't like that. Not one bit. No one had the right to threaten his partner. No one at all.

"Who all knows you're here?" he asked, drumming his fingers on the steering wheel."

She didn't miss a beat. "You. Only you."

This surprised him. "You didn't tell any of your friends? Or people you worked with? What about your family?" He also considered asking about a boyfriend, but for some reason that seemed too personal. If an ex was the person sending the texts, he guessed she'd have figured that out already.

"My mother passed away a year ago," she said, her voice level. "And the people I thought were my friends all vanished when I, uh, lost my job."

"Because you were coming here?" he asked, navigating his favorite hairpin curve easily.

Now, she hesitated a moment before answering. "No. Before that. My company reorganized, and my position was one of the ones that were let go."

Since she didn't sound angry or bitter or even sad, he nodded. "That all sounds like it worked out for the best. Otherwise, you might not have been able to come to Alaska."

"I guess so." She sighed. "Though, it didn't seem like it at the time. I had to process several life changes all at once."

He waited for her to elaborate, but she didn't. Though curious, he didn't want to press her. She'd tell him whenever she felt ready.

Once in town, he went directly to the general store and parked. "I called ahead," he said. "Kip is expecting us. That way we won't have to wait while he gathers everything up."

"Good thinking. But I'll still have time to look around a little, right? I'm hoping to buy a few personal things."

Surprised, he opened his door and went around to her side, doing the same for her.

"Thanks," she said, lightly placing her hand on his arm. "You have great manners."

Then, while he puzzled over the bolt of electricity that shot through him at her touch, she sailed on into the store, leaving him to follow along after her.

"Good morning," Kip said, beaming at them from behind the counter. "I'm glad you called, Dade. Though to be honest, I'd started putting the usual stuff together a few days ago. We're all looking forward to our small influx of tourists."

"Me, too," Dade replied. "We both are. Right, Maddie?"

Maddie had wandered over to the area where local artists' paintings, sculptures and other crafts were displayed. She looked up, clearly preoccupied, and nodded. "Of course."

Her response made Kip grin. "How's that working out?" he asked. "The whole partnership thing?"

"It's a work in progress. But we've already got the cabins ready for the first round of guests, the boats are running great, and all we need to do is stock up our supplies, and we should be good to go."

Kip's grin widened as he took the hint. "Well then, I guess I'd better start loading up your Jeep."

"I'll help you." Dade felt a pang. In better days, he and Grady had done most of the carrying and loading. It had only been the last few years that Grady's failing health had made him unable to lift much.

The entire time Kip and Dade made multiple trips from the storeroom to the Jeep, Maddie continued shopping, apparently oblivious. Dade considered asking her if she'd mind helping, but decided not to. After all, she'd be un-loading it along with him once they got back to the lodge.

Once everything was loaded, Kip tallied up the total, and Dade paid. He'd just finished tucking the receipt in his pocket when Maddie came up to the counter, carrying several paintings, a small sculpture and a couple of quilted pillows Mrs. Ashworth had made.

She deposited her haul on the counter and waited patiently while Kip rang her up. She used a credit card and signed her receipt. Accepting the plastic bags containing her purchases, she smiled brightly at Dade. "Ready?"

The irony of her question didn't escape him. "Yes. Let's go."

"Wait, I almost forgot," Kip interjected, after handing Maddie her receipt. "More mail came in for you. Let me go back and get it."

He hurried off to the back room.

"Did he mean me?" Maddie asked Dade, frowning. "I mean, I put in a change of address form at home, but I wouldn't think I'd be getting any mail yet."

"I think he meant the lodge," Dade replied. "Though I have to say, it's unusual to get mail more than once a week."

"You got quite a few things," Kip announced, carrying a cardboard box full of envelopes and things. "It looks like it's the usual fishing magazines that Grady always liked to subscribe to, catalogs and junk mail, plus several pieces of regular mail."

"Thanks," Dade said, accepting it. "I haven't even had time to go through the stack you gave me the other day."

Kip laughed. "Probably just bills anyway. I know how that goes."

Carrying the box outside, Dade placed it on the back seat of his Jeep. By the time he climbed in, Maddie had already buckled her seat belt. With the sun lighting up her dark hair, she looked more relaxed than he'd ever seen her.

She smiled when she saw him looking at her. "Everything I bought today will help personalize my bedroom. I'm happy to be putting my own touch on it."

That last sentence brought back memories. "Grady was on an HGTV kick for a while," he said. "It seemed like just about every couple on every single show wanted to put their own touch on something."

"Oh, I know." She laughed, the lighthearted sound like a breath of fresh air. "I used to watch those shows all the time, too." Then, sobering, she made a face. "It's funny, but I get it. Staying in Grady's former bedroom felt...odd. I'm hoping when I get it decorated, it might feel more like home."

The echo of loneliness behind her statement resonated with him. He considered himself lucky that he was driving. Otherwise, he might have done something foolish like pulled her close for a hug.

Back at the lodge, the two of them made several trips back and forth, carrying supplies from the Jeep to the house. Most of it went to the kitchen pantry, though Dade set aside all the various fishing and boating supplies to take out to the storage shed.

Once they'd gotten everything put away, she'd taken her new purchases into her bedroom. "I'll make lunch in just a little bit." And she closed her door behind her.

Her comment about lunch had him glancing at the clock. Surprised to see it was a few minutes after noon, he realized he'd worked up an appetite. He was curious to learn what she'd make for the midday meal, but he decided to go ahead and take the fishing and boating supplies down to the shed. He wanted to bring back up one of the golf carts, too, since they were getting close to the arrival of the first set of guests.

When he got back, he found her in the kitchen, stirring something in a mixing bowl. "I hope you like tuna salad," she said, smiling brightly. "I found a recipe in one of the old cookbooks, and since it looked easy, that's what I made."

"We had tuna?" he asked, since he didn't remember ever buying any.

"Well, no. But there's a lot of canned salmon, and I figured it would be close enough."

Salmon salad. He had mixed feelings about how that would taste. But seeing her bright expression, he'd choke it down and compliment it no matter what.

While she made their sandwiches, he couldn't make himself stop watching her. The largest city he'd ever visited was Anchorage, and he'd never seen a woman quite like her. Beautiful, sexy, yet also fearless, she carried herself with the kind of confidence most people her age could only aspire to. The interesting thing was he suspected some of that confidence was all for show. He'd seen how nervous she'd been about going out in the boat.

And despite her expensive clothing and perfect fingernails, she hadn't shied away from cleaning the cabins. She'd also tackled the chore of doing her share of the cooking without a single complaint.

To his surprise, the salmon salad tasted great. "You've just found another way to use the most plentiful fish in these parts," he told her. "I really enjoyed that."

Her cheeks colored. "Thanks. Finding new things to make is more interesting than I thought it would be."

While she took care of cleaning up, he carried the box of mail to the table and began sorting it. Bills went in one stack, junk mail in another and everything else in the middle.

One envelope in particular caught his eye. Handwritten, it was addressed to both Dade Anson and Maddie Pierce. "Weird," he said out loud, turning it over in his hands before grabbing the letter opener. Inside, a single piece of good quality paper had been folded in thirds.

Shaking it open, he saw it had been typed in a font designed to resemble handwriting. Which in itself was weird, considering the text of the letter was an offer to buy Grady's Lodge for a substantial amount of money, signed by a vice president of a large property investment company in Anchorage.

His first thought was that it had to be some sort of scam. He didn't think that offers of this sort were presented in such an unprofessional manner. Grady had used an attorney in Anchorage to make up his will and Dade figured anything related to the lodge would have been sent to him.

Did Maddie have something to do with this? Did she really think she could circumvent the terms of the will so easily? Eyeing her as she cheerfully puttered around the kitchen, he found that possibility hard to believe.

But then again, he really didn't know her that well.

Once again, he read the strange letter. Where had it come from? And how had they known about the fact that he and Maddie would be partners, at least for the next year? While most everyone in Blake had attended Grady's funeral, only a few people were even aware that Maddie would be coming to help out, which was how Dade had put it.

He'd told no one about Grady's will or that he and Maddie would be partners in running the lodge for the period of one entire year.

Which meant this offer had to have come from someone

Maddie knew. When he got to town again, he'd bring the paper with him. Once he had access to Wi-Fi, he planned to do some research on the internet. He needed to find out if this investment company even actually existed.

Maybe, he thought, Maddie's idea of getting internet at the lodge might be a good thing after all.

Right now, though, he needed to talk to her.

"Do you have a moment?" he asked, keeping his voice pleasant despite the anger swirling inside of him.

"Sure, what's up?" Carrying a dish towel as she dried her hands, she crossed the room.

He handed her the letter without saying a word. Reading it, she went absolutely still. "How did this person know about the ownership change?" she asked, turning the paper over in her hand.

"I was hoping you could tell me," he replied, arms crossed.

Immediately, she realized what he'd inferred. "You think I reached out to these people and asked them to present their best offer, don't you?"

"Did you?" he asked, letting some of his anger show in his voice.

"Of course not." Lifting her chin, she met his gaze. "Just like you, I'm well aware of the conditions of the will. If I don't keep my part of the agreement, the lodge goes to you. And vice versa."

Gaze steady, he nodded. "Since Grady knows I'd never sell, he didn't put any stipulations on if we jointly decided to sell it. So maybe you somehow think you can convince me to sell. Having someone send an offer arriving around the same time you do is a bold move."

"I just told you, I had nothing to do with it." Her eyes flashed as she dropped the letter onto the table. "You may not know me very well, but I don't lie. If I do something, I can promise that you'll know it."

Slowly, he nodded. He believed her. "I apologize," he finally said. "I just don't know what to think."

And then her phone pinged, announcing a text.

Chapter Five

The sound made Maddie's entire body tense. "Bad enough to be accused of something I didn't do," she said. "But now this. I don't even want to look at my phone."

"Would you like me to look at it for you?" he asked, his gentle tone completely different from the hard accusation of a moment before.

If she'd been at her old job, and he'd been a coworker, she'd have told him off with a scathing remark. But that life had ended. Without saying anything else, she nodded and handed over her phone.

"I need your passcode," Dade said. "Unless you'd rather key it in yourself."

"3535," she said.

After typing it in, he tapped on the text. Leave now or die, it said. He read it out loud. "Sounds like he or she is upping the ante."

"Yes. I've been trying to tell myself it's going to be okay as long as they didn't escalate to real threats. Saying *leave or else* is very different from saying *leave or die*."

"I agree." He glanced at the letter. "I wonder if the two things might be related."

"Interesting." The more she thought about it, the more

it made sense. "I worked in real estate development back in Dallas. People can get very cutthroat. If someone got it into their head that I'm standing in the way of them buying this lodge…"

"Except everyone around here knows I'd never sell," Dade said. "So why hasn't anyone been threatening me? Trying to push me out?" He hesitated before continuing. "Quite honestly, I think everyone in Blake believes Grady left the lodge entirely to me."

Blinking, she stared at him. In retrospect, she figured she should have been surprised, but she wasn't. Instead, she felt hurt. "Don't you think we should tell them? I mean, why else would I be here?"

"I don't know," he replied, holding her gaze. But she suspected he did.

"What happens here at the lodge is none of their business," he continued. "Because Blake is such a small town, people like to gossip. Our inheritance is private. They don't need to know anything about what Grady did."

Was that pain she heard threading through his gruff voice? For the first time, she realized having his beloved Grady leave half of his home to a granddaughter he'd never known might have hurt him.

"I'm sorry," she began, trying to find the right words to let him know she understood. But then the rest of what he'd said about Blake and small-town gossip penetrated. "Please tell me you haven't let them all think I'm your girlfriend or something."

"My partner," he clarified, a muscle working in his rugged jaw. "That's all I've said."

She groaned out loud. "Partner, girlfriend, they're all the same thing."

"Does it really matter?" he asked. "I don't like letting other people know anything about my personal business."

"*Our* personal business," she clarified. "And while I do understand your reasoning, at some point, I'd like everyone to understand who I actually am and why I'm here."

Expression bleak, he shook his head. "Why? You know as well as I do that after your year is up, you're going to sell your half of the lodge and go back to the lower forty-eight."

As she'd learned to do in her former career, she took a deep breath and mentally counted to ten before speaking. Burning bridges was rarely advantageous.

She could stand up for herself without doing that. Yet she didn't want to give away all of her plans for this place, not this soon. Dade would only be resistant, which would obstruct any forward progress.

"You don't know that," she finally said, her voice level. "This might turn out to be my calling."

At least he didn't scoff or roll his eyes, as some of the men she'd worked with over the years might have done. He simply studied her and finally inclined his chin in a quick nod of agreement. "Grady must have thought so."

"About that," she began, deciding it was time to try and get some answers. "Do you have any idea why? I never knew him at all. My mother raised me, and quite frankly, she hated him. She told me he killed her boyfriend, my father, and that she could never forgive him for that."

Quiet now, his expression thoughtful, he studied her. "Did you ever look into that story? There were various news reports published, I know."

"No," she admitted. "I heard that story for years from my mom. Ever since I was small. She passed away eighteen months ago." Swallowing, she pushed away that ache. "After my mom died, I never had a reason to look into anything about her past. To be honest, since I'd never heard from Grady, I didn't even tell him about his daughter's death."

"He knew," Dade said. "Believe me, he knew."

"What are you not telling me?" she asked. "Please. It was a long time ago, but I deserve to know the truth."

"I can only tell you what Grady told me. I believe him, since there was a full police investigation, and Grady was cleared of any wrongdoing. I'm sure you can look all of that up online next time we're in town."

"Or once we have internet." She crossed her arms. "But for now, let me hear what you know."

Nodding, he took a deep breath. "Your father—your mother's boyfriend—liked to drink. One night, when he was inebriated and your mother was pregnant with you, he attacked her. Grady intervened."

The version Maddie's mom had told her had been completely different. Fascinated, Maddie waited for him to continue. She hadn't known either her father or her grandfather, but she still felt emotionally connected.

"They fought," Dade continued. "He went after Grady with a broken beer bottle. Grady shoved him away, hard, and he hit his head on the cast-iron stove. He died instantly. Your mother wanted Grady charged with murder, though it was self-defense."

"You say Grady was cleared of all wrongdoing?" she asked.

"Yes. But your mother never forgave him. She stole all the money Grady had and ran away, moving to the lower forty-eight. Grady only ever heard from her when she needed money, which he sent. When he learned he had a granddaughter—you—he even traveled to Texas to try and meet you but was turned away. Over the years, he sent letters and cards with checks inside. The checks were cashed, so he knew they were received."

Maddie wasn't sure how to react. "I never knew," she said. "She didn't give me any of the letters or cards. I grew up thinking my own grandfather wanted nothing to do with me." Despite her best effort to remain emotionless, her voice broke and her eyes welled up with tears. "I never knew him." She let the tears stream down her face. "All those years wasted and for no reason."

With a muttered oath, he pulled her into his arms. "Don't cry. Please, don't cry."

She allowed herself a moment of weakness, taking comfort in his embrace. His strength, the sheer size of him, made her feel tiny and protected, even though she'd always considered herself a tall woman. She let herself sob, releasing all the emotions she'd kept locked up inside of her. Losing her mother, then her job and the man she'd thought she would marry. And now this, learning she'd lost something she hadn't ever had. A grandfather who'd actually cared about her.

Standing with her body pressed up close to his, she gradually became aware that something changed. The air around them, electrified. Conscious of every corded muscle, she heard the hitch in his breathing at the same time he shifted his body.

She tried to step back at the same moment he did. She looked up. She might have pulled his face down to hers, or he might have met her halfway. Either way, their mouths met and electricity sparked.

More than sparked. Blazed. She forgot her own name, where she was, everything but the delicious sensations of his lips moving over hers.

And then Dade abruptly lifted his head and stepped back.

Dazed, she stared at him. That had been a kiss unlike any she'd experienced in her twenty-six years. She suspected it would be all she could think about and dream about for quite some time. Already, she knew she wanted more.

Except Dade, with his shuttered expression and heaving chest, appeared the epitome of regret.

"That shouldn't have happened," he said.

Slowly, she nodded. "You're right." Because of course he was. They had to work together for the next twelve months. They couldn't chance complicating things with kisses. Or sex.

Which might turn out to be one of her deepest regrets. Because judging by the way her entire body wanted him, *craved* him, if they were ever to come together that way, it would be magical.

Her desire for him would be one more thing she'd have to throttle. Luckily, she'd always had a willpower as strong as steel. Heaven knew, she was going to need every ounce of it.

Because Dade was still staring at her as if she'd grown two heads or something, she managed to summon up a small smile. "Let's make a deal. How about we pretend that never happened and never, ever mention it again?"

The relief in his expression should have been amusing. Instead, she felt stung. Another bit of foolishness on her part.

"Deal," he agreed. "Now if you'll excuse me, I've got a lot to do. Tomorrow is a big day. I'll see you in the morning." And then, he turned and walked away.

True to his word, he made himself scarce the rest of the day. She wondered if he'd even show up for dinner, but then because she knew he had to eat, she went ahead and cooked.

To her surprise, she found she enjoyed using Grady's old cookbooks. The recipes were not only simple, but tasty.

Pan-seared pork chops, baked potatoes and green beans soon had the small house smelling amazing. With no idea where Dade might be, she went ahead and set the table for two. If she had to eat alone, so be it. She'd make him a covered plate and put it in the fridge for him to enjoy later.

But just as she put the finishing touches on everything, Dade strolled into the kitchen. "That smells great," he said.

She swallowed hard and pasted on her own friendly smile. "Thanks. It's ready, so you're just in time."

"Great." After helping her carry the food to the table, he took a seat.

As they ate, some of her tension dissipated.

"Another one of Grady's recipes?" he asked, after cleaning his plate. "I seem to remember that one. Very good. I enjoyed it."

"It was, and thanks." Pleased, she made no move to help when he began clearing off the table. Tonight, she planned to hole up in her room and read for a bit before going to bed early.

"Good thinking," he commented when she told him her plans. "Tomorrow's going to be a big day."

Though it felt like retreating, Maddie left him there doing dishes. She changed into her pajamas and climbed into bed with a thriller she'd started on the plane.

About an hour later, she heard the television come on in the living room. Judging this to be a good time to wash her face and brush her teeth, she headed to the bathroom.

Once she'd taken care of her evening ablutions, she went straight back to her room, even though she wanted a glass of water. She figured if she got thirsty later, she'd head to the kitchen after he'd turned in for the night.

Instead, she drifted off to sleep almost immediately. When she next opened her eyes, it was just before dawn. She sat up in bed and stretched. Nothing like starting the day with a sense of purpose and anticipation. Today the first set of clients would arrive. Surprisingly, she had butterflies in her stomach. The kind she used to get before a really big presentation at work.

She showered, put her hair in a neat French braid and then joined Dade in the kitchen.

As usual, her first sight of him caused an instant jolt to her equilibrium. How such a large man could move so gracefully, she'd never understand. It was his day to cook, which she counted as a good thing, since he'd be making the first dinner for their guests.

Guests. She'd trained herself to use this word, instead of *clients.*

Before she'd left Dallas, she'd purchased and downloaded several books on the hospitality industry on her Kindle. Most nights, before she went to sleep, she read them. She'd learned early on that most of the topics they dealt with didn't apply here. Except for the sections on making guests feel welcome. Those she devoured, figuring she could definitely put those principles to use.

"Are you okay?" Dade asked, eyeing her from the stove. "You look lost in thought."

She made herself a cup of coffee. "I'm a little bit nervous. But I'm really looking forward to meeting everyone."

Her comment made him smile. "They're good people," he said. "And I'm sure they'll be thrilled to finally meet Grady's granddaughter."

While she wasn't too certain about that, she held her tongue. She had no idea what her absentee grandfather might have told these people about her, but she'd prefer to let them judge her on her own merits.

After breakfast, Dade went down to the storage building. He came back driving a large golf cart that she hadn't even known they had. "It's for ferrying the guests to their cabins."

Shortly after ten, two large white passenger vans pulled into the drive. Maddie joined Dade on the front porch to greet them.

At the same time, doors opened and people began spilling from the vans. All men, varying in age from elderly to teen. They were in a jubilant mood, joking around with each other and hollering hellos to Dade.

Beaming, Dade greeted them, shaking hands and doing that back-clapping thing that men always did. She watched from a distance, unsure despite her voracious reading on how to be a good hostess.

A man with a shock of wavy white hair approached her. Smiling, he looked from Dade to her and back again. "I'm Elwood," he said, holding out his hand. "Who might you be?"

"I'm Maddie Pierce," she replied, trying for the right combination of friendly and professional. "Grady's granddaughter."

"Grady's granddaughter?" Elwood exclaimed, his voice booming. "Well, I'll be. Pleased to meet you."

Just like that, all conversation ceased. One by one, each man turned to stare.

Dade hurried over to join her. "My bad," he said. "I meant to do introductions. Hilbarger family, this is Maddie Pierce. And you heard right. She is Grady's kin. And she and I are partners here at Grady's Lodge."

Stunned to hear him finally say the words out loud, she smiled. "Yes, we are."

Now they all began talking at once as they rushed her, hands outstretched. A couple of the younger men had an appreciative glint in their eyes. But by and large, they all seemed friendly.

She shook hands, made small talk and finally began to relax. All the while, Dade stayed by her side. Which she appreciated more than she could express. She hadn't realized she'd be quite so nervous, but she thought she hid it well.

All in all, a perfect start to a new beginning. She'd even left her phone on her nightstand, just in case another one of the texts came through. She refused to allow anything to ruin this day.

DADE WATCHED WITH a sense of relief as his longtime customers absorbed Maddie into the fishing family. He'd wondered how they'd adapt to this change, especially this group since they'd been coming here the longest. He'd worried most about the older men, some of whom seemed set in their ways. The younger guys had taken one look at Maddie's beauty and had just about fallen all over themselves to get close to her.

This shouldn't have bothered him, but it did.

He kept his mouth shut and stayed back, letting them all greet her.

After a few moments, Dade announced that he was ready to take the first group of guests to their cabins. Since the single golf cart couldn't hold all of them at once, he'd have to make two trips. "You know the drill," he said. "I should have brought the other one up, but I forgot."

"We can walk down," one of the younger men volunteered, elbowing the teenager next to him. "We'll let Gramps and the uncles ride."

"If the other one is running, go get it, and I'll drive one," Maddie offered quietly.

Dade shook his head. "I appreciate that. We'll definitely do that next time. It's all good for now."

Then, before she could ask him what else she could do to help, he walked around to the back of the main house. A moment later, driving his white, four-seater golf cart, pulling a small trailer, he rolled up beside the group and beeped his horn. "Hop on in, gentlemen," he said, grinning.

While the oldest men in the group climbed in, Dade jumped out and began loading the trailer with the guests' bags.

"We'll carry our own," Jason, Elwood's oldest grandson, volunteered. "Come on, guys. A little workout won't hurt any of you."

Once Elwood, his two brothers and a couple of their sons had taken a seat, Dade started toward the cabins. None of them felt the need to fill the silence with small talk, which was one of the things Dade appreciated about the older men in this group.

As they pulled up to the first cabin, which Elwood and his brother Floyd always shared, Dade hopped out. Once they'd identified their bags, Dade carried them inside.

"We want to get in at least a couple hours of fishing before lunch," Elwood announced. "Are the boats all ready?"

Immediate fishing was another Hilbarger family tradition. Elwood asked this same question every year. "Yes, sir," Dade answered. "And I've set up bait boxes and tackle boxes in the same place they always are. So help yourself."

"Great. We will."

Since Elwood had to be in his early to mid-eighties, Dade asked if he wanted a ride down to the boat slips. Though in the past, Elwood had always refused, this time he nodded.

"That might be helpful," he admitted. "These old knees aren't what they used to be."

"Let's get everyone's luggage in their cabins, and then we'll head down. You know the drill. I can go out with you, or you can fish on your own like you usually do."

"No offense, Dade. But you know we like our private family bonding time." Elwood laughed.

Once he had everyone's luggage in the right cabins, he drove the older group to the boat slips. The younger men had beat them to it. Dade hung around long enough to make sure everyone's boat started and watched as they motored out into the river. They'd be gone a couple of hours, and someone would text or call when they were back so he could meet them there. He'd clean their fish for them and pack it on ice.

Then he turned around to head back to the main house. He'd have to fill Maddie in on what to expect next. While he knew it would be too much to expect her to help with the fish cleaning, he figured she could get the lunch ready and serve it when the clients returned. Past experience told him they'd all be starving and ready to celebrate their first catches of the season.

The one thing Dade had not allowed himself to do was think about that kiss. That amazing and electrifying kiss. While he wasn't one hundred percent sure she'd felt the same jolt as he had, allowing himself to continue to think the kind of steamy thoughts that would keep him up at night was foolish. Beyond foolish. Now that things had returned to a sort of awkward normalcy between them, he sure as hell didn't want to mess that up. If Grady's Lodge—*their* lodge—were to have a successful season, neither of them could afford to take any chances.

Back at the house, he found Maddie in the kitchen, chopping celery and mixing something up in a large bowl. She looked up when he walked in and smiled.

"Salmon salad," she said. "Since you seemed to like it, I thought I'd serve it on toasted brioche along with home-made potato chips for lunch."

"What about the menu we planned?"

She shrugged. "I'll mostly stick to it, but for some reason, this just sounded good."

Relieved, he nodded. "I think that would go over well. They'll likely fish for the next couple of hours, and when they get back, they'll definitely want to eat."

"And then what?" she asked. "Do they go back to their cabins until dinner? Or do they fish more? Please tell me that we're not supposed to entertain them."

He suppressed a chuckle, aware she likely wouldn't appreciate it. Judging by the edge in her voice, her earlier nerves had returned full force. "Other than making sure they have anything they need, they're on their own. You saw the mini fridges? Those are for them to store their own beer or soft drinks, anything they might have brought with them. They know the drill."

She exhaled and allowed her shoulders to sag. "Oh, good. I've been trying to come up with activities in case that was required."

Now a snort of laughter escaped him. Her eyes widened, but then one corner of her mouth curled up, and she smiled.

"I would have warned you," he said, grinning. "There's no way I would have sprung something like that on you unannounced."

"I appreciate that."

For a few seconds, they stood smiling at each other like fools. Then, realizing how dangerously close he was to kissing her again, he took a step back. "Did you get any more of those text messages?"

His question wiped the smile from her face. "Honestly, I don't know. I deliberately left my phone on my nightstand. I didn't want any distractions from our guests' first day."

"Good thinking." Now he regretted bringing the subject up at all.

"I guess I should go look," she continued, her expression grim. "Though I really wish whoever is sending them would take a break."

Though she kept her tone light, he could tell the subject bothered her.

As she turned to go past, he reached out and grabbed her arm. "Wait."

She froze.

"Don't look at your phone. You can check it later if you have to. I don't think you should let anything spoil this day. It's the first of many, but one you'll always remember."

Her gaze searched his face. He held his breath until she exhaled and nodded.

"You're right," she said. "My phone can wait. I've got to figure out how to make what we have on the menu for their dinner, too. I'm not used to cooking so much, never mind cooking in bulk."

"Let me help you," he offered. The look of gratitude on her pretty face made him regret not offering sooner.

"I'd appreciate that." Gesturing toward the rack of cookbooks, she sighed. "Any suggestions would be welcome. It's their first night here, and I want to make something special."

"I get that," he said. "Grady had the meals down to a science. He rotated them, but basically every group got the same dinner on their first night. Want to guess what it is?"

The way she wrinkled her nose was cute. "I don't know."

"Salmon. It's plentiful, easy to prepare and reminds them why they're here and what they're fishing for."

"I got that. What did you serve for sides?" she asked.

Walking over to the large stand-alone freezer, he showed her all the giant bags of frozen vegetables. "Grady always did a bunch of baked potatoes—those are stored in the pantry—and a variety of different vegetables along with them. We also have large bags of dry beans, though I'd advise soaking them overnight before you cook them."

"Broccoli!" she said, rummaging through the supplies. "Or green beans. Any of those will go great with salmon and baked potatoes."

"Sounds good. Give the potatoes slightly over an hour to bake since there are so many. You can always do them ahead of time and keep them warm. I can help you get them ready when it's time."

Lunch went without a hitch. The fishermen trooped into the kitchen, still talking about their catches. Dade had put all of them on ice in a special freezer in the boat shed. Toward the end of this group's stay, some of the salmon would be sent to the smokehouse to be smoked. Most of it would be packed on dry ice and sent home with them.

Everyone in the group appeared to enjoy the salmon-salad sandwiches and homemade chips. One of the teenagers acted as if he might refuse to eat it. He sat and stared at his plate for a few minutes, but then hunger apparently got the best of him, and he dug in.

"Now what?" Maddie sidled up next to Dade. "What do they do after they've eaten?"

Elwood, who apparently had pretty sharp hearing for a man his age, laughed. "Some of us take a nap. The younger ones like to go hiking. But once the food has settled, we take the boats out again and fish. That's why we're here after all."

Dade nodded. "So true. I'm going to clean up in here, and then I'll be down at the boat slips later if anyone needs anything."

"I'll help," Maddie offered, clearly deciding to ignore their earlier agreement. She caught his sharp look and shrugged. "What can I say? I like keeping busy."

After all the guests had left, Dade and Maddie worked side by side, in a rhythm that had begun to feel familiar. He realized he liked having her here, which surprised him as he'd been so certain he would hate it.

"Now what should I do?" she asked, drying her hands on a dish towel. Again, he found himself suppressing the completely inappropriate urge to kiss her.

"This is your little bit of downtime," he told her, turning away in case he revealed some of what he felt in his expression. "Take a nap, read a book, do whatever you want in the few hours before you have to start preparing dinner."

She nodded. "Okay. But I will say, I'm looking forward to you doing all the cooking tomorrow."

This made him laugh. He swore, he'd laughed more since she'd been here than he had in all the time Grady had been sick. There'd been days when Dade wondered if he'd ever laugh again.

"I'll be back to help you with dinner preparations," he said, heading toward the door. "But whatever you do, don't check your phone."

Now she laughed. The pleasant sound of it followed him out the door.

Passing the cabins, he waved at some of the guests who'd chosen to sit outside on their porches. Since it was a beautiful afternoon, he couldn't blame them. Even the mosquitos hadn't gotten that bad yet.

Down at the boat slips, he started up each one, checking to make sure they had enough fuel. Years ago, Grady had installed a gas pump with an underground tank near the water, and every year at the end of the season, he had a truck come out and fill it.

Since all of the boats currently had close to three-quarters of a tank, Dade left them alone.

"Hey, Dade!" Braden, one of Elwood's sons headed toward him. "Do you have a minute?"

"Of course, I do," Dade replied. He jumped out of the boat and waited on the wood dock while the older man walked over. "Is there a problem?"

"Not a problem exactly." Braden jammed his hands into his pockets. "I'm just wondering what's up with the guy lurking around the property? The kids are making jokes about him, but I've got to tell you, he's making some of us uncomfortable."

"Guy?" Dade asked, searching the other man's face to ascertain whether or not he was serious. "What are you talking about?"

Now Braden stared. "Some guy has been watching us from up in the woods. Several of us saw him when we first took out the boats. And, again, he was there when we got back from fishing. I figured he must be a new neighbor or something because we've never noticed him before this trip."

"I had no idea. I've never seen him." Frowning, Dade glanced around. "I haven't heard of any new neighbors. But even if someone had bought some property nearby, all of the land around here belongs to the lodge."

"That's what I thought." Braden nodded. "I figured he might be trespassing. You really need to check it out."

Dade definitely agreed. He couldn't help but wonder if this stranger had something to do with the texts Maddie had received. "I wish I could hang around in case he shows up again, but I'd better go check on Maddie."

Chapter Six

When Dade finally came back from the boat area, he seemed preoccupied. He went directly to his room, barely nodding at her as he passed by the couch where she'd been sitting with a book. She briefly considered calling after him to ask if something was wrong, but then decided he'd tell her if he wanted to. She'd started reading a thriller that everyone at her firm had been reading when she'd left, and she could see why the book was so popular. She could barely put it down.

Engrossed in the story, she'd barely read another chapter when Dade returned. He dropped down onto the armchair opposite of her and sat silently waiting until she looked up from her book.

"Are you all right?" she asked, beginning to feel a little concerned. Something in his expression seemed...off.

"I just heard something weird," he said, dragging his hand through his longish hair. "It may be nothing, but I think you need to know."

"Weird?" she asked, wondering if she'd inadvertently done something wrong. "Is all okay with the guests?"

"The guests are fine. I stayed to double check everything before they headed out on their last fishing expedition of the day," he said. "That's when one of Elwood's sons told me they'd noticed a strange man lurking around the woods watching them. I hung around awhile trying to catch a glimpse of him but didn't see anyone. I'll try again in the morning."

"Strange man?" she asked slowly. "Someone trespassing? Because my understanding is Grady's property extends a good bit in all directions."

"Yes, it does. Anyone lurking around the boat slips is definitely not supposed to be there."

Closing her book, she set it aside. "But why? Has he said anything to any of the guests?"

"No. My first thought is that someone might have gotten lost while hiking and stopped to watch them take the boat out. It's the most likely."

"Except you said it happened more than once," she said.

"Right. He was there when they left and again when they returned several hours later."

Now, she sat up straight. "That's weird."

"I know. I'm definitely going to try and confront him if he's there again in the morning. But I wanted to make you aware, just in case he has something to do with those texts you've been getting."

Startled, she instinctively reached for her phone, only to realize she'd never retrieved it from her nightstand. "I guess I'd better go see if he's messaged me again. While it's actually been really nice not dealing with it, I can't pretend it's not happening and hope he goes away."

His gaze never left hers. "I agree. Though it doesn't hurt to take a break once in a while."

Which meant she needed to go check for any new texts. "I'll be right back."

All the way to her bedroom, she found herself hoping

her stalker had decided to take the day off. Honestly, she dreaded checking her phone. Which was ironic, considering how attached she'd been to the device when she'd been living in Dallas. She'd always been one of the first in line to buy the latest version of her particular model. Now, she could barely stand to look at it.

Having limited access to social media didn't help, she had to admit. But the texts, the awful, anonymous texts, needed to stop. Heck, if the stranger in the woods had anything to do with sending them, she'd march up there and confront him herself.

Her phone sat right where she'd left it, on her nightstand. Bracing herself, she picked it up. Once facial recognition had logged her in, she saw she had twenty-three text messages. Twenty-three. "This can't be good," she said out loud, walking back into the living room without looking any further.

"Another text?" Dade asked, pushing to his feet.

"Yes." She tried to keep the dejection from her voice but failed. "More than one actually."

"Do you want to look at them together?" he asked.

Not bothering to try and hide her relief, she nodded. "Yes, I do."

He sat again, and she dropped down in the spot next to him. Sitting so close their hips touched felt comforting. She took a deep breath and opened her phone.

All of the text messages came from a single number. They started out innocuous enough, short and to the point. They followed the same pattern they had before, ordering her to leave and making threats about what would happen if she didn't.

But instead of sending one or two in a short time span, her stalker had seemed to grow more and more agitated.

"All caps," Dade mused. "I don't get why he's so angry. Do you usually reply? Is that why, because you didn't?"

"No, I never reply," she said, wondering if he too felt the heat generated where their bodies touched. "I usually delete the text and then block the number. Which doesn't matter because I'm guessing they just choose another one from the app."

She got to the very last text and sucked in her breath.

I'M WATCHING YOU! PREPARE TO PAY FOR WHAT YOU'VE DONE!

"What have I done?" she asked, swallowing hard. "I don't understand why this person hates me so much."

"I think you should try texting back and ask him."

At this point, she would have tried just about anything. "What should I say?"

"Just ask him why he's texting you and explain you have no idea why. Maybe you can get him to explain what the hell he wants," he said.

Figuring she had nothing to lose, she did exactly that.

Who are you and why are you saying all these things? I don't know what you think I've done to you, but you clearly have the wrong person.

Then she and Dade both sat staring at the screen, waiting to see if there would be a response.

When a reply finally came, it wasn't at all an answer, or even close to what she'd expected.

You're a liar as well as a thief. I wouldn't sleep too soundly if I were you. Because soon, you'll pay.

"Wow," she said, shaking her head. "Still no answers, just more vague threats."

"But the name calling, isn't that new?" Dade asked.

Distracted, she read the text again. "I think so. Obviously, he believes I know what the heck he means. But I honestly don't have any idea."

"Liar as well as a thief." Dade read the words out loud. "I wonder what he thinks you stole."

"Or she," she corrected. "This person could be male or female."

"True."

"And as far as me stealing anything, I haven't. I've never stolen a single thing in my entire life. Not even as a teenager." She shrugged. "I don't get the point of sending these texts. If you have something bad to say about me, say it to my face. Don't dance around the subject with random accusations."

"I agree," he said, surprising her. "I'm a fan of being direct, especially if you want to accomplish anything. And I guarantee you, if I see that guy who's been lurking around in the woods, I'll be very direct."

"I'd like to go with you," she said, putting her phone face down on the coffee table. "I'd like to ask him to his face if he's the one sending these texts."

Dade slowly shook his head. "Not this time. I don't want to risk it, in case he's armed or something."

Horrified, she stared. "You think he might *shoot* at you?"

Expression neutral, he stared right back. "There's always that possibility. I'm hoping he won't, since he didn't take any pot shots at the guests. But you never know."

She didn't like that. Not one bit. "I'm assuming you'll be armed, too?"

"Yes. I always am." He raised his shirt, letting her see his holstered pistol. "Around here, it pays to be careful."

"Of what?"

"Let's see." Letting his shirt fall back into place, he grimaced. "We're in a remote part of Alaska. Out here we have snakes, bears, wolves and various other dangerous animals. Not to mention the occasional drifter who finds his way to our neck of the woods. One thing Grady taught me as a young kid was to always be prepared."

He made sense. She might have lived all her life in the city, but she knew plenty of women who carried a small handgun inside their purses.

"Will you teach me?" she asked, surprising herself. "How to shoot, I mean? Since I'm going to be here for a while, I'd like to protect myself, too."

"Sure. We'll make time for that," he said. "But right now, we need to start getting dinner prepped. They'll be back and hungry before you know it."

"Let me put this phone back in the bedroom." She picked it up from the coffee table and turned the sound off. "It's easier if I don't have it around. I don't want to be jumping at every text message. Too distracting."

"I think that's a good idea," he agreed, holding her gaze a moment too long.

After she shoved the phone into the nightstand drawer, she returned to find him already gathering ingredients on the kitchen counter.

They worked side by side in the kitchen, Dade with a graceful ease that seemed astonishing in such a large man. Though it was her turn to cook, she ended up letting him take over and simply imitating what he did. After all, he'd done this sort of thing numerous times before.

By the time the group trooped back into the dining room,

everything was almost ready. Though Maddie had never cooked a meal on this large of a scale, Dade made it surprisingly easy.

Once everyone was seated, they began serving the food. The salmon had turned out perfectly, same with the baked potatoes. Dade had made a condiment tray with butter, bacon bits, sour cream, shredded cheese and green onions. And he'd shown her how to take a couple of large bags of frozen broccoli and turn them into a cheesy casserole. For dessert, they'd put a large, premade frozen peach cobbler into the oven, which they'd serve along with vanilla ice cream.

They also served a basket of still warm yeast rolls.

Only once every guest had been served did they retreat to the kitchen to scarf down their own meals.

"That was really good," Maddie marveled, pushing away her empty plate.

"It was." He smiled approvingly. "Now, we need to clear the table and serve dessert."

Everyone tucked into the cobbler, clearly appreciative. Once again, Maddie and Dade stepped back, staying in the background. They'd left just enough cobbler in the pan for themselves.

"Nice how that worked out," she told Dade, making him laugh.

"And it always will," he promised.

After everyone had eaten and wandered back to their cabins, Maddie and Dade cleaned up, side by side. Since he'd helped her cook, she pitched in on the cleanup. "We make a pretty good partnership," she said, keeping her tone light.

"Yes, we do," he agreed. The warmth in his voice made her tingle all over.

Once the last dish had been put in the dishwasher and the machine turned on, she dried her hands on the dish towel and turned to look at him. "Now what?"

"We're done for the day, unless someone needs something. From now until breakfast, they'll amuse themselves. Even though it doesn't get dark until late, they won't be fishing anymore today."

She nodded. "Now that I'm off the clock, I'm going to get back to that book I was reading. What about you?"

"I'm going to do a brief patrol of the area," he said, his carefully blank expression not fooling her. "I want to make sure that guy isn't camping out somewhere nearby."

With that, he quietly let himself out the back door.

She went to get her book, but found she couldn't really concentrate. So she carried the book outside and dropped into one of the chairs there.

In the distance, she could hear the sound of laughter. Despite everything, she found herself on the path, headed down toward the cabins.

As she drew closer, the sight of flames leaping into the darkening sky stopped her in her tracks, an unfamiliar ache in her chest.

The guests had ended up seated around the bonfire in the pit, exactly as Dade had predicted. They'd broken out the beer, at least for the older ones, while the teenagers had moved to the open meadow to toss around a football.

Her first instinct was to reach into her pocket for her phone so she could snap a picture. Then she remembered she'd left it in her nightstand. Maybe another night she'd capture an image on her phone. Tonight, she'd have to keep this inside her heart.

And she missed Dade. Way more than she should have.

As she stood on the path staring, she wondered what

it would be like to join them sitting around the fire pit. To be part of such a thing. Naturally, she wouldn't. Hosts didn't crowd their guests. Even Dade, who'd known them for years, gave them plenty of space.

Still, the idea of sitting around a fire as the night air cooled sounded inviting. She wondered if there would be any time between when this group left and the next arrived. If so, maybe she and Dade could do that. If he ever came back.

Her worry grew as the shadows lengthened and Dade didn't reappear. Several scenarios played out in her head. What if the intruder had taken Dade by surprise and captured him?

Turning around, she trudged back to the front porch. If he didn't show up soon, she'd have to go look for him.

DADE KNEW EVERY inch of these woods like the back of his hand. After all, he'd been roaming them since he'd been a child. He searched every hollow log, downed tree and hidden grotto that he knew of, finding nothing. If that guy was camping on these lands, Dade saw no sign of it.

Circling the ridge above the boat slips, he also looked for clues that someone else had been here. While he didn't think the intruder would be foolish enough to try and build a fire, he had to have left traces of his presence.

From this vantage point, he could see the cabins and the group beginning to gather around the fire pit. Soon there'd be orange flames reaching into the night sky. As a youngster, this had always been his favorite time of the day. More than once, Grady had caught him hiding in the shadows watching the adults' merriment around the campfire.

These days, he knew they'd likely invite him to join them, welcoming him with the easy camaraderie of long acquaintance. But Grady had drummed into him the importance of keeping himself separate from the guests. They visited, sure. And during Grady's long drawn-out illness, some of the guests had wanted to spend time with Grady in the main house instead of fishing.

Grady, being himself, shooed them away. He'd told them they'd paid to fish, not shoot the breeze with an old man. Grady had never realized how much his guests loved him or that they'd considered themselves family.

He pushed aside the melancholy memories before turning and making his way back to the house. He knew a path that would skirt the group at the fire pit and would bring him to the main house from the south side.

When he made his way out of the woods, the sight of Maddie's slender figure standing on the front porch made his breath catch in his throat.

She turned toward him as he approached. With her face in shadow, he couldn't read her expression. "Any luck?" she asked.

The husky timbre of her voice sent a shiver up his spine.

"Nope," he replied, taking the steps up two at a time. By tacit agreement, they both dropped into the side-by-side rocking chairs.

He began slowly rocking back and forth, willing his heart rate to return to normal. Next to him, she sat motionless, staring out at the plume of smoke still visible below them.

"They seem to be having a good time," she mused.

"Yes. It's a nice close to a good first day."

Still, she didn't turn to look at him. "Did they catch a lot of fish?"

"Enough to keep them happy," he replied. "We have a large freezer down at the boat shed where we keep them on ice. Some of them will go to the cannery to be canned or smoked. Most will be packed on dry ice and taken home with them."

She nodded and began rocking.

They sat out on the front porch while the sky darkened. The crickets began to sing, warring with the sounds of merriment from the guests below.

"Sometime in between guests, could you and I sit around that fire?" she asked, her low voice wistful.

The yearning in her tone made his throat ache. He knew that feeling all too well.

"We will,' he replied, deliberately keeping his voice light. "That's tradition around here, too."

"It is?" Now she half turned, facing him. Then, without waiting for an answer, she sighed. "I've never experienced anything like this before. Sometimes I feel like a little kid who's been sent away to camp for the first time."

"I thought all you city kids went to summer camp," he teased. "You really never went?"

"No. We moved around a lot. My mother didn't like to stay too long in one place. I think she skipped out on rent most times. And we definitely couldn't afford summer camp."

Again, he felt that twinge of sympathy, of kinship. He'd never known his people or where he came from. If not for Grady stepping in and filling the void, he suspected he would have crashed and burned long ago.

It took every ounce of willpower he possessed not to pull her into his arms and offer comfort.

They sat outside for a long while, the darkness complete and absolute long before he finally stood and stretched. "I'm going to go in and start getting everything ready for the morning. The day will start early."

"Really?" She stood, too. "Even though they sound like they'll be up drinking until dawn?"

"Yep. Sure, some of them will have hangovers, but I guarantee not a single one of them will stay in bed. They're grown men."

She followed him inside the house. "I know that's true. What can I help with?"

Once again, he was working side by side with her. As partners went, Maddie wasn't half bad. He certainly hadn't been expecting this.

By the time they'd finished prepping for tomorrow, Maddie was swaying on her feet. Taking pity on her, he told her he'd see her at sunrise, reminding her they'd be starting early.

He went to bed shortly after. Instead of tossing and turning the way he'd been lately, he fell into a deep and dreamless sleep.

The next morning, he worked quickly, glad they'd done all the meal prep the night before. Maddie's bedroom door remained closed, but he imagined she'd be out shortly. She emerged just as he'd finished making a large sack of breakfast sandwiches for the group to take out on the water with them and a large thermos of black coffee. This had been a long-standing tradition for the second day for as long as Dade could remember.

"Good morning," Maddie said, stumbling over to the coffee maker. While her cup brewed, she apologized for not helping him assemble the sandwiches.

Once again he found himself resisting the urge to touch her. "You helped plenty last night. This didn't take me long at all."

He'd dug out an old coffee maker so he could make a large pot rather than the individual brewer they normally used. Maddie watched him fill up a thermos and offered to make a second thermos, but he told her they didn't need it. "The younger ones drink cola instead of coffee, so they'll have packed an ice chest."

"Oh." She brushed back a wayward lock of hair from her face. "Do you want me to go with you?"

"No. Just wait here," he said. "I'll be back once they're all out in the water."

She nodded sleepily and sipped her coffee. Looking at her, with her tousled dark hair and kissable lips, he once again battled that sharp stab of desire. He supposed he ought to be used to it by now, but the sheer intensity of his need for her never failed to surprise him. It only seemed to get worse day by day.

"I'll be looking for that intruder, too," he reminded her. "So it might be a bit before I get back."

"What are you going to do if you manage to catch the guy?" she wanted to know. "Does Blake even have a police department?"

"No, we don't," he answered. "We tend to call for the state police, who get here when they can. We do have a place we can hold criminals, if necessary. But as far as this intruder goes, it really depends on his intentions. He could be some harmless wanderer who strayed too far off the beaten path."

"True." She yawned, covering her mouth with her hand. "Or he could be the person who's been sending me those awful text messages."

Forcing himself to drag his gaze away from her, he slowly nodded. "That's what I'm hoping to find out. He likely has already moved on."

Except Dade wasn't sure he truly believed that. Grady's Lodge sat far off the beaten path. No one ever accidentally wandered out this way. Well, no one except Dade himself when he'd been a small child. And even then, despite the fact that he'd been far too young to have been left on his own, he suspected someone had dropped him off.

He shook his head, wondering why losing Grady had made him think so much about the past. Nothing he could do would change what had happened to him then. And Grady had been the one to change that for the better. Dade missed him so damn much.

And wanted Grady's granddaughter way more than he should. For an instant, he wondered if the old man had planned and hoped for this.

"Are you okay?" Maddie asked, her soft voice almost as appealing as her kissable mouth.

"Sure," he lied. "Just a little tired." With that, he turned to go.

The lights were on in all the cabins, but no one had yet emerged. Though the sun hadn't yet cleared the horizon, the sky had started to lighten enough to bathe everything in an early morning glow. He loved this time of the day the best. It had always felt borderline magical, which was something coming from a man who didn't believe in magic.

Pushing aside his fanciful thoughts, Dade saw nothing out of the ordinary, at least not around the cabins or the fire pit, with its still smoldering ashes.

On his way down to the boat slips, he scanned the tree line, keeping an eye out for any signs of an intruder. Nothing, not even any wildlife, which was unusual. Normally, he expected to see a bear or two fishing for their breakfast in the water.

As he tinkered around with the boats, making sure they all had enough gasoline, the guests started to make their way down from their cabins.

After greeting him, they immediately went for their breakfast sandwiches. Some devoured them right then and there, while others tucked them into pockets or backpacks to eat later.

Elwood's son Braden strode over to Dade. "Any sign of him?" he asked quietly.

"No," Dade answered. "Maybe that means he's moved on."

"I hope so." Exhaling a sigh of relief, Braden watched the youngest group of fishermen. "My wife would kill me if I let anything happen to our grandsons."

"I got you, man." Dade clapped the older man on the back. "I'm sure that guy was just some drifter who wound up in the wrong place. I walked the woods yesterday and didn't find anything indicating he might be camping out here. And no one has seen him this morning."

"You're probably right." Expression relieved, Braden turned a complete circle, checking out the woods around them. "I appreciate you checking on this."

"No problem," Dade replied. "And if by any chance you happen to see him again, please let me know immediately. I'm going to hang around here until you all are out on the water."

Going from boat to boat as each group climbed aboard, Dade made sure no one needed anything. He untied each from the dock, helped push them out into the water, and watched as motors were started and the fishermen moved away. All the while, he kept watch but saw nothing unusual.

As the last boat turned the bend on the river and vanished from sight, a brown bear emerged from the woods slightly upstream. Dade eyed the familiar sight and wondered if the intruder had truly gone or had simply gone into hiding, waiting for a better moment to strike.

Then, chiding himself for his fanciful and uncharacteristic thoughts, he made his way back toward the main house. About halfway between the boat slips and the cabins, he caught a glimpse of movement. Was that a man watching from behind a large pine tree?

Heart rate in overdrive, Dade took off running. Not directly toward his target, but more to intercept him. If this intruder intended to make his way toward the main house, that meant Maddie could be in danger. Not if he could help it. No way would he let that happen. He needed to take this guy down once and for all and find out what he wanted.

Chapter Seven

After Dade had left, Maddie had drifted around the small house, wondering how simply sharing space with him put her into a heightened state of awareness.

She'd never met anyone like him, and she suspected she never would again. Men like him didn't exist in the fast-paced life of the city. His large size wasn't the only reason he filled up a room. He'd been kind and patient as well, but to be honest, she hadn't been able to stop thinking about that kiss.

Though clearly, she hadn't had the same impact on him.

All for the best, she supposed. Because that knowledge, and the common sense that had always served her well, had been what kept her from going to his bedroom in the middle of the night to slake her constant yearning. Talk about a disaster waiting to happen. Just the thought made her want to hyperventilate. But then again, she'd never dealt with rejection well. And having to face a man who'd from that moment on look at her with nothing but pity... Her skin crawled at the thought.

That didn't mean she stopped wanting him. Ever present, desire simmered just under her skin. Hopefully, after they'd spent a few months together, that would go away. But for now, she had to figure out a way to deal with it.

And keeping herself in check didn't keep her from dreaming about him. Oh, she did, with achingly sensual detail. She might be able to turn her craving off during the daylight hours, but at night her subconscious got free reign.

Think of something else, she told herself, slugging back the rest of her coffee. Out of habit, she reached for her phone so she could scroll social media.

But then, she remembered. Last night, when she'd returned to her room, too exhausted to think clearly, she'd switched her phone off without even checking for text messages. She'd shoved it in her nightstand drawer.

Which was where it might have to stay. It had been ages since she'd been this unplugged, and while at first she'd found it uncomfortable, now she'd started to think she could easily begin to like it. There wasn't much that interested her on social media these days anyway, and without reliable internet, those feeds had trouble refreshing.

Not having to worry about some unknown person constantly threatening her turned out to be an additional bonus. Sometimes she thought she might never turn her phone on again.

After finishing her coffee, she made a second cup and then assembled herself a breakfast sandwich. She ate at the small kitchen table and tried to think about what she could do to help out. Though he hadn't mentioned gathering up towels or anything, she needed to ask if she should be swapping them out or doing loads of laundry.

For now, since she was alone and the camp was emptied, she planned on staying put. She'd even taken the extra precaution of locking the front and back doors to the main house, something that she'd never seen Dade do. Just in case.

A loud bang from outside made her jump. She was too afraid to open the door, so instead she hurried around from window to window, peering outside to see if she could see what had made the noise.

Finally, she spotted the culprit. A large raccoon had knocked over one of the metal garbage cans and was now rummaging through the spilled contents. Smiling, she watched for a moment, the intensity of her relief making her sway.

She hated feeling so paranoid. But learning about the intruder spotted on the property had been jarring, to say the least. The possibility that her phone stalker might have gone from text messages to showing up in person absolutely terrified her. Discovering that Dade at least carried a weapon helped some, but she'd never been one to rely on others for something she could do herself. As soon as possible, she wanted to learn how to handle a firearm and get one of her own.

The backdoor knob rattled, and she jumped. Someone started pounding on the wood. It startled her to the point where she froze. But then she heard Dade's voice calling her name.

After she hurried to let him in, her apology stuck in her throat when she took in his disheveled appearance. His color high, breathing ragged, with his mane of hair wild around his face, he looked as if he'd just taken on fighting a bear in one-on-one combat.

He also looked hot as hell. She tried not to stare.

"Good thinking," he growled, brushing past her. "From now on, always lock the door when you're here alone."

She nodded. "I will. But, Dade, are you all right?"

Slowly, he turned to face her. His eyes still were wild. "I'm fine. I thought I saw someone on the way back from the boat slips, but I couldn't catch him. And I'm not even sure it was a person, rather than a trick of light."

She managed to nod. "Did any of the guests see anything?"

"No. In fact, Braden appeared relieved. He's going to text me when they're on their way back in, so I can meet them down there. Until we clear this up, I don't want to take any chances with anyone's safety."

Knowing she needed to get her raging libido under control, she turned away and made a show out of looking out the kitchen window. "I get it, believe me. A few minutes ago, a raccoon got into one of the trash cans. The noise scared the heck out of me until I realized what it was."

"That must have been Clyde." He said that so matter-of-factly that she stared.

"Who must have been Clyde?" she asked, confused.

He gave her a sheepish smile. "The raccoon. He's been around here for years. Grady used to put out food for him. I've been meaning to do that, but I forgot. That's probably why he got into the trash. He's hungry."

Since he said this as if it was the most ordinary thing in the world, she decided to go along with it. "I see. What do raccoons eat?"

His smile widened. "A little bit of everything. They'll snack on fruit, veggies, nuts, fish, insects, frogs, even small rodents. We mostly feed them spoiled fruit and vegetables. And some of the leftover parts of fish. They really enjoy that."

"Really?" She started to make a face and then thought better of it. "Aren't raccoons considered a nuisance?"

"Sometimes. But Clyde's been around since he was a

young, sickly one. We think his mother was killed. Grady was always one for taking in orphaned things. Clyde would have died if not for us."

She noticed the way he included himself. A sudden image of a younger Dade, nursing a tiny raccoon back to health, made her feel all warm and fuzzy inside. Who knew a man so big and tough could also be so soft and caring.

Nope. Thinking like that would be dangerous. She gave herself a mental slap and nodded. "I see. Well, I guess you'd better go back to feeding him. I suspect he made quite a mess out there when he knocked over that trash can."

"I'll clean it up." He checked his watch. "I'll need to start getting lunch put together soon. Since they had breakfast sandwiches, I wanted to do something a bit more filling for lunch."

"Like what?" she asked. "I'd be happy to help."

"I appreciate that. While we're still keeping meals simple except for dinner, in the past, they've really enjoyed hamburgers and hot dogs cooked on the grill. I made sure the propane tank is full, so I'm good to go. We'll just need to prep all the condiments. Onion, lettuce and tomato for the burgers, and chopped onion and pickle relish for the hot dogs."

While he was outside straightening up the trash cans, she located several packages of hamburger and hot-dog buns. Dade had also stocked up on industrial-size cans of baked beans, so she used the electric can opener and dumped them into the Crock-Pot, which she turned on high. That way, she wouldn't have to worry about them burning.

"That's exactly what we always serve as a side," Dade said, gesturing toward the beans. "Now we just need to get busy chopping."

Working side by side, him chopping onions, her slicing tomatoes, she felt content. In fact, she'd begun to realize this might not be a bad life after all.

They'd just finished up when Dade's phone buzzed, indicating a text. "They're heading back in," he said. "Apparently, they had quite a catch. I'm going to head down there to meet them."

"I'm going with you," she declared, hurrying to wash her hands in the sink. "I need to get out of the house."

Though he glanced at her sideways, he didn't argue. "Let me make sure the front door is locked. From now on, until we figure this out, we're locking up any time we leave the house."

Once outside, she waited while he dug out his key and locked the back door. "I take it this isn't something you normally do?"

"Locking up? No. We've never had a need." He glanced at her, and the hard edge to his gaze softened. "We will get this figured out."

Though she wanted to melt right there on the spot, she managed to nod instead. "I hope so. It's been a lot. Not only did I uproot myself and move thousands of miles away, totally changing my life, but then some random person decides to start stalking me. I still don't know why."

"Stay by my side," he ordered as they started off down the path. "I take it you got more text messages?"

Busy scanning the woods for anything out of the ordinary, it took her a moment to answer. "Honestly, I don't know. I haven't looked at my phone."

They continued on in silence for a few seconds. The cabins had just come into view when he spoke again. "I understand not wanting to deal with all of that. But I don't think ignoring the texts is the safest thing to do."

Startled, she stumbled and nearly fell. Dade reached out and grabbed her arm, keeping her upright. It took a moment for her heart rate and breathing to return to normal.

"Sorry," she finally said, shaking his hand off and moving forward again. "I'm not usually clumsy."

Instead, he grabbed her again. "Wait. Don't move."

His low, urgent tone got her attention. Instantly on alert, she moved closer to him. "Did you see something?"

"I don't know. Maybe." Though he stood still, he constantly scanned the woods around them. "We need to keep moving. Act casual, as if we're completely unaware anyone could be out there."

Could? Heart once again racing, she somehow managed to move forward.

"Keep looking straight ahead," he said. "I'm checking the woods. If someone is out there, they're likely watching you."

She wanted to ask him if he still had his pistol, but didn't. Instead, she reminded herself that they didn't truly know if anyone actually *was* watching them. And also, even if someone was, they might not be the same person who'd been sending those texts.

As she kept moving forward, every nerve ending on edge, she understood why she shouldn't have tried to ignore those texts. What if the sender had made more specific threats, in effect giving her a warning? What if he'd specifically mentioned he'd be out in the woods today waiting for her?

"It's going to be okay," Dade muttered, clearly understanding her nervousness. "We still don't know what this person wants. It might not even be related to the texts."

Though she nodded, she wanted to tell him her gut told

her it was. But then again, she'd always had a vibrant imagination. The possibility did exist that she might be making too much out of nothing.

Riiiight.

She wanted this person caught, and she wanted him caught now. She needed to look him in the eye and ask him what she'd ever done to deserve all the hateful text messages. Because while Maddie knew she wasn't even close to being a saint, she'd always tried to treat other people the way she herself wanted to be treated.

Somehow, she and Dade continued to move forward. Though she worked hard to appear oblivious, she could no more keep herself from constantly scanning the woods around them than she could keep herself from breathing.

"There," Dade growled. "Keep moving and stay right next to me. I think I spotted him, near the meadow where we store our boat trailers."

Only the force of his arm linked through hers, propelling her forward, kept her going.

Was this it? Were they finally about to confront the faceless and nameless person who'd been stalking her?

"Hey! Good morning!" Two of the teenaged members of Elwood's party came running up. "We slept in, so we missed the fishing. Are you on your way to meet them at the boat docks when they come in?"

"Yes." Disengaging his arm from hers, Dade turned to face them. "Will you two keep Maddie here company for a minute? I need to check on something up in the meadow."

"Sure," they replied, jostling each other for a chance to stand close to her.

Relieved and resigned, she smiled at them. They ended up on either side, flanking her.

"Good," Dade said, already making his way up the hill. "I'll see you in just a few minutes."

And then he disappeared into the trees.

TAKING A BACK way to make it appear he'd doubled back toward the house, Dade made his way toward the meadow and the small group of trees where he swore he'd seen someone standing. Enough was enough.

The boats with their guests would be back soon. Hopefully, all that activity would be enough of a distraction that the intruder wouldn't realize Dade had circled around behind him until it was too late.

When he reached the meadow, he didn't see anyone. No footprints or crushed grass. Nothing but all the boat trailers, lined up in neat rows. Dade skirted around the edges, sticking close to the trees. If he continued on in this direction, he'd come out on top of the cliffs overlooking the river and the boat docks. That would be the best place for a trespasser to observe while remaining as invisible as possible.

But as the trees thinned and the soft earth gave way to rock, he still saw no sign of anyone else. From up here, he could see the boats coming in from a bit down the river. Below, Maddie and her two teenaged escorts had just reached the docks. Dade saw no signs of anyone else in the immediate vicinity.

Maybe, just maybe, the intruder had moved on. It now seemed entirely possible that, instead of being tied in with Maddie's threatening texts and the letter asking them to sell the lodge, this had been some hiker who'd taken a wrong turn.

Relieved, he turned to make his way down to the boat slips to join Maddie in greeting the returning guests. Half-way down the path, something exploded.

The force of the blast nearly knocked him off his feet, sending him staggering. It took him a few seconds to figure out what had just happened. A second blast, and then a third, shook the earth. Dade cursed, his heart pounding. And then he started to run, pressing 911 on his phone as he went. Luckily, the call went through. He managed to tell the operator his location and what had happened. "Send help," he pleaded, before ending the call.

By the time he reached Maddie, he realized the explosion had been behind them. The plume of black smoke and accompanying fire carried their own kind of danger. Though he hoped the foliage had remained damp enough from all the recent rain, a forest fire would be devastating.

"What was that?" Maddie gasped, when he reached her. She pointed to the smoke. "Did something blow up?"

"Judging by the area, I'm going to guess it was near the boat storage shed. We do keep extra gasoline there. Plus some propane tanks."

Both teenagers seemed nervous. Dade studied them. Had they done something to cause this? "Is there anything you two need to tell me?"

Immediately, they both shook their heads. "No, sir. We're just hoping that wasn't our cabin."

Dade nodded. "You two wait here for your family. When they get here, tell them to hurry. I'll need everyone's help to make sure this fire doesn't spread." He glanced at Maddie. "Come with me. Let's get started."

Leaving the two boys behind, they raced back along the path. As they rounded the corner, the boat storage shed came into view. One side of the metal building had been blown out, and an inferno raged inside. Flames licked at the air, but hadn't spread beyond the building yet.

"Is anything else going to blow?" Maddie asked.

"Good question. But judging by the force of the first blast, and the fact that there were a couple smaller explosions after, I'm going to guess everything that could blow up, did."

Wide-eyed, she nodded. "Shouldn't we call someone?" Maddie bent over, trying to catch her breath. "I'm guessing Blake has some sort of volunteer fire department."

"We do, and I did." Satisfied that, for now, the fire appeared to be contained, he started for the tractor. "Just in case they don't get here in time, I want to be ready. If I have to, I'll knock the rest of the building down to keep the flames contained."

She went with him, clearly wanting to stay close. "How will they get the fire truck out here?" she wanted to know.

"We don't have a fire truck. They call it Project Code Red. Lots of small villages utilize it. We have a fire department in a box. It's two metal trailers with thirty-gallon solution tanks, a water pump and one-hundred-foot hose reels. It uses compressed air to produce firefighting foam with a small amount of water. They can be hooked up to pickup trucks, all-terrain vehicles, heck even snowmobiles in the winter. Works really well."

Inside the shed, something else popped. The flames briefly reached higher. Dade was grateful for Grady's foresight in clearing the immediate area of trees and foliage and spreading gravel on all sides of the metal building. If left alone, there was a very real chance the fire would simply burn itself out.

When Maddie slipped her hand into his, he froze. But he didn't pull away, figuring all of this had terrified her, and she most likely needed comfort.

Plus, if he were honest with himself, he liked being the one to offer that to her.

"What could have caused this?" Maddie asked.

"That, I don't know. But it definitely wasn't an accident."

The group of returning fisherman all arrived, the younger ones first with their elders bringing up the rear. In the days before Blake had gotten the Fire Department in a Box, as it was called, Dade would have organized everyone into a bucket brigade, which wouldn't have been too useful at putting out a fire of this size.

The fire volunteers arrived a few minutes later, which meant they'd broken every speed limit to get there. Dade motioned his guests back while the firefighters got set up. Maddie, appearing remarkably calm, helped herd everyone out of the way.

Though Dade had seen the fire system work before, he still found it fascinating. He knew the crew had attended three days of training to learn how to use it, and their expertise showed. Working quickly, they began the process of spraying the foam. It didn't take too long to knock the flames down to a manageable size. They continued until the entire fire was covered in foam and extinguished.

The guests cheered. Grinning, the firefighters high-fived each other. "This never gets old," one said.

Another came over to Dade. "Any idea what caused this?" he asked. He stuck out his hand. "Mike McKenzie."

"Nope." Dade shook Mike's hand and kept smiling, aware he didn't want to alarm any of the guests. "We had propane tanks in there, which exploded. Beyond that, I don't have any idea."

"If you're planning on filing an insurance claim, they're going to want to know," Mike advised. "They'll probably want to send their own investigator out, but I can tell you up front, if he waits too long to get here, any evidence that's buried under all that foam will have disappeared."

Since Dade wasn't sure if Grady had insured any of the outbuildings beside the main house and the cabins, he simply nodded. "I'll keep that in mind," he said.

Mike went back to his crew and helped them finish packing everything up. "We're going to take off now," he said with a friendly wave

After a chorus of thank yous, Dade, Maddie and the entire group of guests watched as the firefighters loaded up and drove off. Once they'd gone, Dade turned and noticed the ice chests the guests had used to bring their catches up in. He realized he no longer had the huge stand-alone freezer in which to store the fish. That had been destroyed in the fire.

And though he had another large one at the main house, he'd packed that full since he'd be feeding various groups of guests for the next several months. For now, he'd see how much of the day's catches could be stored in there, even if he had to toss some frozen vegetables. Beyond that, dry ice might be an option. Taking the salmon to the cannery to be smoked or canned was another one.

Right now, he supposed he had to break it to the guests that anything they'd caught yesterday had been lost. He'd opened his mouth to do exactly that when Elwood shook his head and hobbled on over to him.

"They'll figure it out," he said quietly. "And if they don't, I'll tell them later tonight when we're sitting around the campfire. You've lost a lot more than some salmon."

Before Dade could reply, Elwood walked off, heading in the direction of the cabins. Noticing, Braden and the others immediately followed. Even the teenagers went, though they straggled behind the adults.

Dade turned to Maddie, who stood staring at what remained of the boat shed. Clearly lost in thought, she didn't appear to notice him watching her. Finally, he cleared his throat.

"Let's head back to the house," he said. "We've got to feed this crew lunch. I'm sure all of this made them work up an appetite."

"Really?" She shook her head. "I've completely lost mine."

"You'll get it back, once the shock fades."

Side by side, they made their way toward the main house. He fired up the grill, glad they'd done all the prep work earlier. The beans were still simmering in the Crock-Pot, so she stirred that and began setting out the meat for him to cook.

Soon the mouthwatering aroma of grilled burgers and hot dogs filled the air. Maddie put out all the buns and the vegetables they'd sliced, along with mustard, mayo, ketchup and relish.

The smell pulled the guests from their cabins. As Dade had predicted, they declared themselves to be starving. For the next thirty minutes, Dade manned the grill. By the time everyone had eaten, Dade's stomach had begun rumbling.

"Maddie?" he asked. "Do you want a burger or a hot dog?"

Despite her earlier declaration that she had no appetite, she chose a burger. He made himself one, too, and they scooped up the last of the baked beans.

Instead of joining the boisterous group at the main dining table inside, they sat down in two rickety outdoor chairs near the grill and balanced their plates in their laps.

Neither talked. Instead, they ate with a single-minded intensity.

When he'd finished his burger, Dade went and got another. Maddie grabbed a hot dog. He tried not to watch her eat, but failed miserably. Somehow, she managed to make eating look sexy.

Finally, with their bellies full, they sat back and groaned. "At least with paper plates, there won't be as much cleanup," she mused.

Right on cue, the back door opened, and the teenaged members of the Hilbarger family came barreling out. Acknowledging Dade and Maddie with a quick wave, they raced on past.

A moment later, the rest of the group emerged.

"That was really good," Elwood commented. "We've all decided to take a couple hours and nap before we do our afternoon fishing."

"Sound good," Dade replied. "Just let us know if there's anything you need."

Once the entire family was gone, Dade began cleaning the grill while Maddie put away everything else. They finished around the same time. He walked back inside to find she'd taken a seat at the smaller kitchen table and had gotten them both a tall glass of iced tea.

"What a weird day," she mused. "I certainly hope that explosion and fire was an accident."

"I doubt it was."

Eyeing him, she slowly nodded. "You're probably right."

"I think you need to get your phone and check the texts," he said. "Your stalker may have actually given us a heads up about his plans for today."

Eyes huge, she stared. "I thought of that. If he did text a warning, all of this might have been averted." The recrimination in her expression and voice tore at his heart.

Without thinking, he took her hand, marveling at the softness of her skin. "Maddie, I didn't mean for you to blame yourself. You have zero control over what this guy does."

"True. But if I'd kept up with the text messages, that might have given us a clue." She clung to his fingers as if they were a lifeline.

He wanted to kiss her. Instead, he gave her hand a squeeze and made himself let go. "How about you go get your phone, and we'll check? You might be bashing yourself for nothing."

With a nod, she hurried off into her bedroom. A moment later, she returned, cell phone in hand. "I'd turned it off. It'll take a minute to come back on."

"Okay," he responded.

"I'm dreading looking." Expression grim, she waited a moment, then tapped on the screen and waited for the facial recognition.

"There are thirty-three text messages," she said, her voice faint. "All from the same person. And it's a different number than the one before. That's how that app works."

"Thirty-three?" Astounded, he waited for her to tell him what they said. Instead, she passed him her phone.

"You read them. Only tell me if there's something I need to know. If it's just more of that useless nonsense, then I really don't care."

He nodded and opened the message thread. The texts started out short and succinct. Scared yet? You should be. They continued on in a similar fashion for a bit. There were ten texts essentially saying the same thing.

And then the tone of the messages changed.

You think you're better than me, don't you? Both of you do, I can tell. But you're not. You're nothing better than thieves. The time has come to make you pay.

And this gem—Death would be too easy. You need to suffer.

Disgusted and worried, Dade shook his head. "Still vague. More threatening, but nothing specific."

"So, he didn't threaten to set something on fire or shoot at anyone?" she asked.

"No. Read it yourself." Passing the phone back to her, he waited while she scrolled through the thread.

"You're right," she said, once she'd finished reading. "But he seems to be coming more and more unhinged. I have to wonder what he thinks I stole."

"We," he corrected. "He's referencing both of us."

Glancing back at her phone, she read it again. "You're right. He is. Then why aren't you getting texts? Why just me?"

"I'm guessing because he somehow got your number. I barely use my cell phone, and all the calls to the lodge come on the landline. It's more reliable than cellular and is tied to an answering machine."

"I remember you telling me that. It seemed archaic then and still does. Somehow getting my number doesn't make sense," she said. "If he could obtain mine, then why not yours?"

Dade winced. "The last time you and your mother disappeared, Grady paid a private investigator a small fortune to find out everything he could about you. I'm guessing your cell phone number was one of the things he learned."

Appearing dazed, she dropped into a chair. "Wait. You're saying Grady had my phone number for *years*? Then why did he never call me?"

"Actually, he did." He kept his voice gentle. "Several times. You never answered, I'm guessing because you didn't recognize the number. He said he didn't feel comfortable leaving voicemails." He took a deep breath, wondering if she'd been aware of the rest. Somehow, he doubted it.

"Is there more?" Regarding him steadily, she waited. "I can tell there's something else. What are you not telling me?"

"Your mother answered the last time he tried. Apparently, she recognized Grady's number. She told him that he was dead to her and to never bother you again. That damn near broke him."

"What? You're saying my mother knew he was trying to reach me? That's not possible." But something in her expression revealed she thought it might be.

Since he hadn't known her mother, he kept quiet to let her sort things out inside her mind. Who knew, but her stalker might be tied to something or someone in her past.

Chapter Eight

Her grandfather had made numerous attempts to contact her, and her mother had turned him away. Learning this hurt. More than she'd have believed possible after all this time. Maddie shouldn't have been surprised. What was one more betrayal in a lifetime of them? But this one cut deep. Ever since she could remember, Maddie had expressed her longing for more family. Her classmates had siblings, plus aunts and uncles and cousins, while Maddie had only a mother who'd seemed disinterested at best.

When younger, Maddie had pressed for more information, aching with a childish longing for the joyous holidays, summer outings, that her friends enjoyed. Maddie's mother had scoffed at her questions. Instead, she'd reiterated that they were on their own. No one cared about them at all. Not even the endless string of men her mother constantly brought home.

In time, Maddie had given up and stopped asking. She'd managed to avoid the brittle bitterness that was her mom and accepted gratefully any of her friends' invitations to join them, whether at the holiday table or on short vacations. She'd managed to keep her home life secret, hiding her mother's increasing spiral and doing her best to live her own life.

Maddie had worked hard, graduating high school at the top of her class, and earned several scholarships to help pay for college. Instead of being proud, her mother had mocked her, claiming Maddie was too serious and had no idea how to enjoy life. Through all her adolescence, Maddie had steadfastly refused her mother's attempts to show her how to party. She'd said a hard no to the drugs, the alcohol, all of the things her mother felt made life bearable or fun. Early on, Maddie had determined that she would not be like her mother.

When her mother had died, too young, Maddie had mourned, but truthfully, she hadn't felt any more alone than she had before. She had her friends and her boyfriend and, as she had in school, focused on building her career.

Then, her life had been upended, and she'd wound up here.

Dade cleared his throat, making her realize she'd retreated into her thoughts. She blinked and met his gaze, surprised to realize he still had his hand on her shoulder.

"Are you all right?" he asked, expression concerned.

"I'm not sure," she answered truthfully. "It's shocking to have heard one thing all my life, only to find out it had been a lie. Learning my grandfather had cared, had even reached out more than once, is a hard truth to learn too late."

"I'm sorry." Dade placed his large hand on her shoulder. "Grady often wondered if he should have tried harder. He'd never stopped hoping to reconcile with his only daughter and to get to know you. Even though he never got the chance, please know he loved you from a distance."

Love. Her mother had scoffed at that word, claiming such a thing didn't exist. She'd actually forbidden Maddie from saying she loved her, which broke now-adult Maddie's heart.

Fighting the urge to lean into his touch, instead she shrugged and took a step away. Even so, she could still feel the lingering warmth where his fingers had been.

"Thanks for telling me all that," she said, trying for breezy. "But I think we need to focus on figuring out what this person who keeps texting me wants. Clearly, if he set that fire, he's getting more and more dangerous."

Gaze locked on hers, he slowly nodded. "You're right. I think the time has come to challenge him. I know you've asked and he hasn't responded, but maybe there's a way to do it to get him to say what he wants."

"Challenge him? But that goes against everything I've ever heard or read about how to react to a stalker. Wouldn't that make him angry.? You're supposed to ignore them, block them, and eventually they'll go away."

"Since that hasn't worked, I think you need to change up the plan," he pointed out. "Engage him. Find out what he thinks you—we—stole. Maybe we can get some insight. Or even better, help him realize he's bothering the wrong people."

The more she thought about it, the more the idea made sense. She took a deep breath and opened up the text thread. I think you have the wrong person, she wrote. I don't know what you want or what you think I've done.

"There," she said, hitting send. "We'll see how he responds."

Dade nodded and moved to take the chair across from her. Refusing to sit and stare at her phone while awaiting an answer, she placed it on the table. "What are you making for dinner?" she asked.

If her quick change of subject surprised him, he didn't

show it. "Since we had such a big lunch, I'm going a bit lighter for the evening meal."

"More fish?"

Her question made him laugh. "Yes, but this time we're serving it as part of a big salad. Do you want to help me prep?"

"Sure." She glanced at her phone and decided to leave it face down on the table. If her stalker responded, she'd get the alert, though she already hated how jumpy she now felt. "I still wonder if engaging him was the right thing to do."

Dade grimaced. "Well, ignoring him only seemed to make him angrier. I guess it depends on if he responds or not. Maybe this will encourage some sort of a dialogue rather than a bunch of threats."

She could only hope. Except the phrase that kept going through her mind was something along the lines of *never negotiate with terrorists.*

The rest of the day passed uneventfully. To Maddie's surprise, dinner was a huge success. Everyone raved about the salad bar they'd set up in the kitchen and several of the younger members of the Hilbarger family went back for seconds and even thirds.

As they had the night before, while Dade and Maddie cleaned up, the group made their way back to their cabins.

"Will they have another bonfire tonight?" Maddie asked, a little wistful.

"Most likely. They've already picked up ingredients to make s'mores." He shook his head. "I figured maybe they'd have had enough fire for one day after what happened, but clearly not."

Unable to help herself, she glanced at her phone, still face down on the smaller kitchen table. "He hasn't responded," she said, picking up her phone to double check that she hadn't missed an alert. "But then, I'm not sure if that app he uses has already changed his number. If so, he might no longer be able to receive texts at that one."

"I didn't think about that." Dade shook his head. "Let me try sending a text from my phone."

"I don't think you should," she cautioned. "He doesn't have your number right now. If you text him, he will."

"I don't mind. Let's see if he's brave enough to threaten me." He picked up his phone. "What's the number?"

She read it off and watched as he typed it into his phone. "I'm creating a contact, too," he said. "Makes it easier."

"You know that number will change if it hasn't already." She opened the messages tab and scrolled. "So far he's used several different numbers to send me texts."

"I guess we'll see," Dade said. "I just texted him and asked him if he had anything to do with the fire."

"Bold move." She exhaled as she finished wiping off the counter. "Now we're good until breakfast."

"Yep. And it's your turn to cook tomorrow."

The teasing note in his voice made her smile. "I'm well aware. I've already been revamping my menus. Those old cookbooks of Grady's have been a lifesaver."

"Do you need any help with prep work?" he asked.

"Not tonight. I'm just making a traditional breakfast for tomorrow. Eggs, bacon, toast. Nothing fancy. But after that, I might need your help."

"You've got it," he promised.

They ended up outside again, sitting side by side in the two chairs on the front porch. Dusk hadn't quite fallen, so their guests hadn't yet started gathering around the fire pit.

"It won't be long now," Dade mused. "When I was a little kid, I used to hide in the woods and watch them. That's why Grady bought these chairs. We'd sit here instead, listening to the guests laugh and party. Grady taught me how to whittle, and the two of us would compete to see who could make the most detailed carving."

The affection in his voice made her heart ache. Dade had clearly loved Grady, and this made her wish she'd had the chance to know her grandfather. Even just a little.

"Do you still have any of them?" she asked. "The carvings? I'd really like to see."

Dade went really still. "I still have every single one," he told her. "The ones Grady carved are important to me."

She waited, realizing this might not be something he wanted to share. After a moment, he got up and went inside. Though she wasn't sure if he'd be back, she stayed in her chair.

A moment later, he returned, carrying a large, brown wooden box. Sitting, he kept this on his lap. Slowly, almost reverently, he opened the lid.

Curious, Maddie leaned over to see what was inside.

Dade lifted out something small, wrapped in cloth. Gently unwrapping it, he held it up and studied it. "This was the first piece Grady made for me. I've had it since I was really small."

"May I see it?"

For a moment, she thought he might refuse.

"Sure." He handed it over. "It's not fragile or anything, but I've been careful to make sure it doesn't get scratched."

Accepting it, she turned it over in her hand. The small piece of carved wood had been polished to a high sheen.

"It's a bear," she said, amazed at the details.

"Not just any bear. Grady carved Old Smokey, the black bear that used to live near the boat shed."

"It's beautiful," she said, handing it back. "Will you let me see the others?"

One by one, he removed carved figurines from the box. Most of them were various animals and birds. One incredibly detailed bald eagle made her catch her breath. "This one looks so real," she said. "I think it's my favorite."

Dade ducked his head. "Thanks. I carved that one."

Sensing further praise would embarrass him, she simply nodded and passed it back to him. "I've been hoping to see a real bald eagle soon," she said. "I know they're all over the place out here in Alaska."

"They are." He finished wrapping all the carvings back up and put them back into the box. "Would you like something to drink?" he asked, pushing to his feet.

Though she wished they had wine, she asked for water.

With the box tucked close to his chest, he went inside. A moment later, he returned, carrying two tall glasses of ice water.

The light had begun to change, dusk finally settling over the sky. Below, they could hear the sounds of their guests, likely getting ready to light their bonfire. Someone turned on music, a wireless speaker, no doubt, streaming from their phone.

The music drifted through the quiet evening. Sultry, slow, it wasn't the music of the younger boys but that of the elders, men Elwood's age. The rawness of the singer's voice started an ache inside Maddie's chest.

"Grady used to love her," Dade said, his voice quiet.

Throat tight, Maddie nodded. "I've never heard her before. Who is that?"

"Etta James. Old-school stuff."

"I think it's beautiful." Realizing that, for whatever reason, she was perilously close to tears, Maddie stood, placing her water glass on the deck near her chair. With her back to him, she wrapped her arms around herself and swayed, drawn to both the music and the complicated swell of emotions it brought to life.

Behind her, she heard Dade stand up. "Would you like to dance?" he asked, his low voice matching the notes in the song.

Instead of answering, she turned and walked into his arms.

They fit together as if they'd always been a couple. Despite the difference between her frame and his height and breadth, she nestled herself against him. When he started to move, she followed his lead. Her pulse settled into a slow and steady beat, echoing the rhythm of the music. As the light faded, so did everything else except for the scent of this man and the feel of his muscular arms wrapped around her.

Then all at once, the music cut off, replaced by the sounds of laughter and good-natured shouting back and forth.

Dazed, Maddie moved away, wondering what the hell she'd been thinking.

"They're lighting the bonfire now," Dade said. He'd already turned away, looking out in the direction of the cabins and the fire pit. The steadiness to his voice told her she'd made too much of their dance. The intimacy she'd experienced had clearly been one-sided.

All for the better, she supposed. Still, needing some time to get her composure back, she excused herself and went inside.

AFTER THE DOOR closed behind Maddie, Dade exhaled. It had taken every ounce of self-control he possessed to keep from kissing her. Worse, she appeared to have no idea of how she affected him. If he kept on like this, he'd be taking ice-cold showers every single day for the next year.

Watching as the sky turned dark, he dropped back into his chair. The scent of the smoke from the bonfire drifted his way. He had to figure something out. The more he got to know Maddie, the more he liked her. What had happened between her and Grady hadn't been her fault, as he'd earlier supposed. And while he suspected she might have her own plans for the lodge that he wouldn't agree with, he couldn't fault her work ethic or determination to help the place succeed.

He actually liked her. And not because of her smoking hot body or the way the corners of her eyes crinkled when she smiled. She'd come to a remote location in a state she'd never been, far from her home in Texas, and deserved so much more than a guy who found himself aroused every time they were in the same room.

Which meant Dade needed to simply...stop. He had to rid himself of his desire for her and make himself think of her as his partner, which she was.

And never, ever again ask her to dance.

The door opened, and Maddie emerged. She appeared subdued, as if she'd also had second thoughts about their impromptu dance.

After sitting, she sighed. "I got a response to my text."

It took a moment for her words to register. Whatever he'd expected her to say, it wasn't that. He blinked. "Can I see?"

"Sure." She passed her phone over. "Basically, he seems to think we stole something from him, but when I asked what, he wouldn't say."

You're thieves of the worst kind, and you don't even care.

But you still can make this right, Dade read out loud. "Make what right? He doesn't ever come out and say?"

"I know." Sounding miserable, she made a face. "I think I'm going to ask him. All this vague nonsense and the fact that he's escalated his threats to cause an actual fire make me think it's likely all inside his own mind."

Slowly, he nodded. "I was about to ask what he's getting out of all this, but it's entirely possible that he's living with his own, made-up and distorted reality."

"Let's see." She held out her hand. Once he'd given back her phone, she began typing. "There," she said once she'd finished. "I asked him to tell me specifically what we've stolen and how. I told him up front that I have no idea what he's talking about."

"Good." He settled back into his chair, listening to the sounds of partying coming from the guests. "Other than the fire at the boat shed, I think it's safe to say they're having a great time."

"Have they caught a lot of fish?" she asked.

He appreciated the way she honed in on what would be most important to them. "Yes. Some of it was lost in the fire, but I think by the time their stay is over, they will have caught more than enough to make up for it."

"That's good. I assume you're going to make sure we have a place to store it since that freezer was destroyed?"

"I am. I've already put in an order with Kip for a new freezer, but in the meantime, I've reorganized the one we have here at the house. I'm also going to talk to them about taking some in to be canned or smoked, or getting started on shipping it home."

Her phone pinged, making her start. "I'm almost scared to look," she said, wincing. "But here goes nothing. I'll read it out loud."

Leaning forward, he waited.

You have stolen my birthright. My identity. All that I am and all that I should have been. For that, you will have to pay.

She put her phone down. "A different number. And more nonsense."

"Well, you tried. If he wants something, he's going to need to spell it out. Otherwise, neither of us have any idea."

Slowly, she nodded. "When he talks about birthright, I wonder if he's someone who knew my mother. Or my father."

Since this was the first time she'd mentioned her father, he waited to see if she'd elaborate.

"Though I never knew my father's name," she finally said. "My mother always refused to even talk about him. After she died, I went through her things, but she must have destroyed anything related to him. Because I learned nothing."

Again, he felt that twinge of kinship. He kept his mouth shut, though, because the only person who'd ever known about his past had been Grady. The last thing he wanted from Maddie was her pity.

"This is surprisingly pleasant," Maddie mused, leaning back in her chair and closing her eyes.

"Surprisingly?"

"Yes." She didn't even move. "You have to understand, I've always been a Dallas girl. I've never lived anywhere like this before." She waved her hand vaguely. "Look at all the stars in the sky. At home, you can see only half of them."

They sat together in companionable silence. He appreciated once again the way she didn't feel the need to fill the silence with aimless chatter. His awareness of her, the prickling of his skin, his consciousness of her breathing, felt both amazing and scary as hell.

Until Maddie had arrived, Dade hadn't realized how badly his life had been lacking. Grady had teased him, especially toward the end, telling him man wasn't meant to live his life alone. Honestly, Dade hadn't thought the idea sounded that bad.

Now, with this woman who often seemed his complete opposite, Dade had to wonder if Grady had planned this all along.

That night, he tossed and turned, burning with desire for the last person he should crave.

With the sunrise, the final morning of the Hilbarger family's visit dawned. After breakfast, the unusually quiet group thanked Dade and Maddie before trooping back to their cabins to pack up. Though the posted checkout time was noon, neither Grady nor Dade had ever been particularly picky about enforcing that. After all, since they were a small operation, they'd always given themselves a couple of days in between fishing parties to get everything cleaned up and ready.

Nevertheless, the Hilbargers had everything loaded up in their vehicles by eleven.

On their way out, Elwood and Braden stopped off at the main house to say goodbye. Braden helped his father get out of the SUV, and the two of them came up to the porch where Dade and Maddie waited.

"We enjoyed it," Elwood said, his weathered face creased in a smile. "And our wives will soon be enjoying trying to figure out new ways to cook salmon."

"You say the same thing every year," Braden chided. "We just wanted to give you both a personal thank you. We'll see you again about this time next year."

"Make sure and reserve the dates," Dade responded, smiling. "I know how you all like to be the first group here once the season starts."

"We do and we will." Elwood moved forward, shaking first Dade's hand and then Maddie's. Braden did the same. And then both men got into their vehicles, and the caravan drove away.

"Whew." Exhaling, Maddie sat down. "How long do we have before the next group of guests arrives?"

He pulled out his phone to check the calendar. "The next group arrives on Friday. We get to take the rest of the day off if we want. That gives us Wednesday and Thursday to get everything cleaned and ready."

"That seems like a lot of lost revenue," she said, frowning. "Do you always have groups arrive on Friday and leave on Tuesday?"

"Pretty much. Sometimes, they might want to stay an extra day, which is fine. They have to book that up front, so we know. Since we're a small operation, we need at least a couple days to clean and restock."

"Hmmm." Finally, she nodded. "I guess that makes sense. I know I'll definitely appreciate time to recharge."

He managed to keep from laughing, just barely. "I don't know how much of that you'll be doing. We've got to clean the cabins, wash the bedding and towels, and after taking a quick inventory, make another run into town for supplies."

Though only their second time working together, they got busy and had all the cabins cleaned and the bedding stripped and washed in record time.

While the washer and dryer were going, they raided the backup stash of linens and remade the beds. Once that task had been completed, all the cabins were ready for the next occupants.

"Half a day," he mused. "That just might be some sort of record."

His comment made her laugh. "I'm guessing I move a bit faster than Grady did."

Though his first instinct was to be defensive, he realized she meant no offense. And she was absolutely correct. Even before his illness, Grady had been getting up there in years. As a result, he'd moved quite a bit more slowly.

Since they'd gotten so much done, he was able to spend the rest of the day taking inventory of their supplies. Together, he and Maddie made a menu for their respective cooking days and compiled a grocery list. They needed to keep as much of the house freezer empty as possible, so any fish the guests caught could be stored there. Fresh ingredients would mean a little more work, but would also provide a better dining experience. Since the next group were all businessmen who traveled quite a lot, he knew they'd definitely appreciate that.

"We'll head into town tomorrow after breakfast," he said.

Smiling, she nodded. "I'm looking forward to it. Now, I just need to figure out what we're going to eat for dinner tonight. Originally, I'd thought something light, but with all the work we've done today, I'm thinking maybe something heartier."

With her long hair up in a messy bun and her eyes glowing, she looked beautiful. More than her outward appearance, she appeared comfortable, as if she finally felt she belonged here. Eyeing her, he realized he could no longer imagine running this lodge without her.

"Sounds good." Grateful she couldn't read his thoughts since he ached to kiss her again, he managed to smile back. Turning away to distract himself, he went into his bedroom and closed the door.

What the hell? Chastising himself silently, he paced the confines of his room. Maddie hadn't even been here very long. Certainly not nearly enough time for him to like her so much.

However awful Dade's life might have been in the years before Grady took him in, after then he'd had a normal life. Better than average, as Grady made sure he was warm and fed, attended school, and most importantly, felt loved. Grady had thrown him his first ever birthday party for his eighth birthday, with a cake he'd made himself.

Growing up, Dade had dated a few girls from Blake. One of them had even been semiserious, until she'd broken up with him to go away to the University of Alaska. Since then, he'd kept things extremely casual, going on a few dates here and there in the off-season. Since there were more men than women out here, these had become few and far between.

Clearly, it had been too long since he'd indulged in being physical with a woman. That had to be why being around Maddie had him in a near constant state of arousal.

He considered taking a cold shower, but ultimately decided to go for a walk. As he strode through the house for the back door, Maddie must have sensed his mood as she simply looked up and waved without asking a single question.

Outside, he breathed deeply of the fresh air and set off to patrol the grounds. He couldn't risk the intruder deciding to set something else on fire, so he planned to stay alert and watch for any signs of that man back on the property.

He found nothing, which was a relief. And all the walking and focusing on something other than his simmering desire had helped. When he returned to the house, he felt back to normal.

"You're just in time," Maddie said. "Dinner will be ready in just a few minutes."

"Let me wash up, and then I can help you," he said.

"No need. I've got it all handled." Her sweet smile made him catch his breath. When he headed to the bathroom to wash his hands, he splashed a little water on his face and tried to think about fishing.

She surprised him with dinner. Though she'd clearly gotten the idea from one of Grady's old cookbooks, the mini meatloaves had long been one of Dade's favorites. Grady had even made them, at Dade's request, for birthday dinners.

Watching him expectantly, Maddie placed everything on the table. She had no way of knowing what memories this particular meal held for him. Or that Grady had cooked with a special touch. Dade didn't think Maddie's could possibly taste as good.

But they did. Surprisingly, even better. "Did you tweak the recipe?" he asked as he went back for seconds.

"Yes. Do you like it?"

"I love it," he replied, meaning it. "This is really great." And then he told her about the memories the simple meal brought him.

She listened, her expression rapt. "I love when you tell stories about my grandfather. It makes me feel as if I'm finally getting to know him."

Luckily, they sat across from each other at the table. Otherwise, he might not have been able to keep himself from kissing her.

"I'll clean up," he said, his tone firm. "You go ahead and relax now. We'll be heading to town in the morning."

"Sounds good," she replied, and headed into the other room to turn on the TV. "By the way, I'm planning to talk to

Kip tomorrow about the internet service provider. I'm hoping I can get everything set up within the next few weeks."

Since she'd used the same no-nonsense tone he had, he decided to simply nod and get busy doing the dishes.

He managed to make it through the rest of the night without problems, though he turned in early, claiming exhaustion.

The next morning, he rose before dawn and, after making coffee, got busy fixing them breakfast. Since she'd made such an effort the night before, he decided to make the most Southern thing he could think of, biscuits with sausage gravy. By the time she emerged from her room, he had the first batch ready.

She exclaimed over the meal, which had him grinning like a fool. They ate heartily, and when they'd finished, she shooed him out of the kitchen so she could clean up.

After they'd both showered—separately, though he'd been unable to keep from imagining them under the spray together—they piled into his Jeep and drove into town.

"As a bonus, no new texts," she said, showing him her phone.

At the general store, they shopped, sticking closely to their list. When they were done, Dade marveled at how smoothly everything had gone. His mood light, he found himself wishing he could treat Maddie to something special. Maybe a meal in town, even if Mikki's donut shop, restaurant and bar might not be up to her city-dweller standards. Since only a few hours had passed since they'd had breakfast, the timing wouldn't work today. Next time, he vowed, after this upcoming round of guests left.

On the drive back home, he turned the radio on to a classic rock station. To his amusement, Maddie sang along to a couple of songs. She had a pretty decent voice, he thought, smiling.

Even the trip from Blake to the lodge went quickly. He turned onto the driveway, happier than he'd been in a while.

But the instant he pulled up to the house, he knew something was wrong. "Maddie," he warned, shifting into Park. "Stay in the Jeep."

"Why?" She sat up straight. "What's going on?"

"The front door is open. And I locked it when we left. Whoever broke in might still be inside."

Chapter Nine

Maddie swallowed. "I refuse to stay by myself. I'd rather take my chances with you."

For a second, Dade's grim expression made her think he was going to refuse. Instead, he nodded and then lightly touched her arm. "Fine. Just stay right behind me."

She jumped out and did exactly that, staying close enough that she could reach out her hand and touch him.

When he pulled out his pistol, her breath caught. She wanted to ask him if that was really necessary, but realized in a place where they couldn't call the police, they only had themselves.

"It's likely the stalker," she whispered. "Right?"

Instead of answering, he shrugged. He didn't need to actually respond because who else would it be?

Keeping his weapon aimed in front of him, like she'd seen FBI agents do on numerous TV shows, they moved through the front door. Though absolutely terrified, she stayed right on his heels.

They went from living room, which appeared undisturbed, to kitchen. Again, everything seemed to be exactly as they'd left it. Still, Dade didn't lower his pistol.

"Our bedroom doors are closed," he pointed out, his voice low. "They were open when we left."

She bit back a curse word, suddenly terrified of what they might find when they opened the doors. Clearly, she'd watched too many horror movies.

"Mine first," he decided. "Get back behind me."

Realizing she'd moved too far away, she hurried to get closer. She marveled at how safe the sheer size of him made her feel.

Dade turned the knob and shoved open his bedroom door.

"Empty," he said. "But look."

She peered around him and gasped.

The room looked like a tornado had torn through it. Dresser drawers had been emptied, their contents thrown around the room. The bed linens appeared to have been slashed with a knife, tattered and shredded. She wondered if the mattress had also been destroyed.

Even the mirror above the dresser was shattered, glass shards all over the floor.

A muscle jumped in Dade's jaw, but he didn't speak. Instead, he turned and went next door to her room.

As he opened the door, she braced herself. Dade moved to block her view. "Maybe you shouldn't see this," he said.

Having none of that, she pushed herself past him. And gasped. "This is even worse than what they did to your room. I wouldn't have believed that was possible."

"At least you don't have a broken mirror," he drawled.

Which was true. Instead of shattering her mirror, the intruder had used Maddie's best red lipstick to write across the glass.

*Go back to Texas! And take that fake son with you.
Or you both will die.*

She had to read it twice. "Fake son? What do you think that means? I don't have any children."

Dade's expression was somewhere between fierce and anguished. "I think he means me. Grady always told everyone that he loved me like a son." Despite his stony demeanor, his voice cracked a little at the end, which broke her heart.

Not sure how to respond, she focused again on surveying the damage. Like in Dade's room, all of the contents of her dresser drawers had been strewn around the room. Since she had fewer belongings than he did, her cleanup would be slightly easier.

Her bed had also been stripped, the sheets cut up into ribbons of tattered material. And her nightstand had been turned over, the antique lamp broken into three pieces.

The nightstand. Heart in her throat, she hurried to set it right side up. Then she realized all the little mementos she'd kept that had been Grady's were gone.

This bothered her more than anything else. She barely managed to bite back a cry.

Yet somehow, Dade appeared to know. "What's wrong?" he asked. "I mean, other than the obvious?"

When she told him what had been taken, he blanched. "How'd they know?" Then, without waiting for an answer, he spun around and headed back to his room. She followed right behind him.

He went directly to his own nightstand, which still stood upright with the drawers slightly open. When he looked inside, he cursed. "Son of a... He got everything Grady left for me, too."

A horrible thought occurred to her. "What about the wood carvings?"

Rushing to his closet, he reached into the back and pulled out the large brown box. Even from several feet away, she could tell his hands were shaking as he opened it. "They're still here," he said. "He didn't find them."

The relief in his deep voice brought tears to her eyes. "That's good," she managed. "The bastard didn't take everything."

"Right." Jaw tight, he placed the box back inside his closet. "I can't believe I'm saying this, but I'm going to call Kip and see how long it would take him to get in some kind of camera system."

"You'll likely need internet for that," she pointed out.

He glared at her. "Then we'll get internet. Right now, we'd better get started cleaning this mess up. And once we're done, I want to file a police report mentioning the specific threat. We might as well get everything on record. There's no telling what this guy might do next."

Back in her room, she began refolding her clothing inside the dresser drawers. Since she didn't have a whole lot, putting her things away didn't take long.

Next, she snapped several pictures with her phone. She hoped Dade did the same thing to document what had been done in his room. What worried her was that she didn't know how long before things escalated again. First the boat shed, then the main house. What would be next? Unfortunately, she suspected it would be physical attacks upon them.

When she started shaking, she dropped down onto the edge of her bed. Wrapping her arms around herself, as if for comfort, she struggled with the urge to cry. Finally, she gave in, letting the tears roll down her cheek and stifling her sobs so Dade wouldn't hear.

Dade appeared in her bedroom doorway anyway, his large body making the space seem much smaller. She glanced up, bit back a cry and swiped her hands across her face. "Sorry," she mumbled. "It's all just a bit much for me. I'll be fine in a minute."

Instead of leaving, he sat down next to her and pulled her into his arms. "Let it out," he told her, smoothing the hair away from her face.

So she did. All her life, she'd never been much of a crier. As a child, her mother hadn't allowed it. She'd learned to keep her emotions inside, which she knew wasn't healthy.

But now, with this big man holding her, his large body making her feel safe and wanted, she wept. Her body shook with the force of her sobs.

And through it all, he sat unmoving, a rock. As her tears dried, something shifted inside her. Anguish became... need. Her breath hitched as she turned in his arms. She buried her mouth at the base of his neck and inhaled his scent, that unique mixture of pine and outdoors.

When she raised her face to his, she saw her desire reflecting back at her, darkening his eyes. Without hesitation, she pressed her body against him. "I want you," she said. She'd never meant anything more.

"Are you sure?" he rasped, his gaze glittering, his mouth mere inches from hers.

"Positive."

Claiming her lips, he kissed her with a raw hunger, his tongue mating with hers. His hands hot upon her skin, he pushed her clothing away, lifting her shirt over her head. She helped, stepping out of her shorts and standing before him in her bra and panties.

When he reached for her bra, she chuckled and pushed his hand away. "You next," she said, tugging at his T-shirt. While he removed that, she fumbled with his belt, aching to touch his swollen body. Once the belt had been undone, she helped him ease his jeans down, unable to suppress a gasp as she freed his massive arousal.

He reached for her. Meeting him halfway, she arched toward him, a moan escaping her. One hand tangled in her hair, he caressed her. She allowed herself to explore his skin, his muscles, him. Hard everywhere she was soft, passion roared through her, firing her blood.

To her amazed shock, he had a condom in hand. He managed to get it on before returning to kiss her again. They fell back onto her bed, locked together. Gasping with need, she welcomed him inside her with a kind of desperation she'd never experienced before.

He began to move, slowly at first. Craving more, she used her body to urge him faster. When he did, she bit down to muffle a shout of triumph. *This*, she thought, giving in to sensation. This was what a thousand books had been written in futile attempts to describe. Nothing she'd read or watched or heard about had prepared her for anything even close to this.

Dade cried out, seconds before she did. Waves of pleasure, pure and explosive, rocked her, making her entire body shudder with ecstasy. Deep inside of her, he did the same, before collapsing.

After, they held on to each other, waiting for both their heart rate and breathing to slow. While she lay there, secure in his arms, Maddie marveled at how perfect their lovemaking had been.

She also realized that they'd both made a huge, irrevocable mistake.

It would be best to clear the air. She didn't want the two of them slinking around, trying to avoid each other for the next year.

Pushing herself up on one elbow, she rolled over to face him. His amazing brown eyes were open, and she once again felt a jolt as he met her gaze.

"This doesn't have to change things," she said, keeping her voice soft.

"Doesn't it?"

Since she couldn't tell from his tone if he was teasing or serious, she lifted one bare shoulder in a shrug. "Wouldn't things be easier that way?"

"Maybe," he conceded, his expression inscrutable. "But I've never been one to take the easy way out."

She didn't know how to respond to this, so she didn't. She knew for certain that the only thing she didn't want him to say was that they should never do this again.

If he said that, she thought she might shrivel up and die.

Dramatic, yes. But they were going to be sharing the same space for a year. Why deprive each other of the pleasure of this? They were both adults. They could handle it.

"Can we?" he asked, making her realize she'd spoken her thoughts out loud.

"Yes," she responded, her voice firm. To prove her point, she pressed a quick kiss on his lips. "Otherwise, we're going to spend the next twelve months tiptoeing around this thing between us. As long as we both agree there won't be any emotional entanglements, I don't see any reason why we can't continue to, um, enjoy each other."

He laughed out loud at this, the sound a combination of amusement and possibly an underlying thread of anger. "Damn, you're innocent."

Wondering if she'd imagined the anger, she decided not

to allow herself to feel insulted. Instead, she smiled. "Possibly so. But sometimes that's a good thing."

"Maybe it is." He kissed her again, nothing casual about the way he slanted his mouth across hers. He continued to kiss her until she couldn't think, couldn't breathe, until she'd melted into a puddle of desire.

When he lifted his head, she nearly begged him to make love to her again.

"Still think you're right?" he asked, the glint in his eyes telling her that, this time, he was teasing.

"I know I am," she replied.

"Good." With that, he pushed himself up off her bed. "I'm going to take a quick shower, and then you can if you want. After that, we'll eat. I don't know about you, but I've worked up quite an appetite."

Grinning, he turned around and left, giving her a great view of his naked backside.

Sated and comfortable, she dozed until she heard the shower cut off. A few minutes later, he returned, his hair damp and a towel wrapped around his waist. "Your turn."

"Great." She made a conscious choice to try and be as comfortable with her nakedness as he'd been. Pushing back the sheet, she swung her legs over and stood. Shoulders back, chin up, she strode from the room as if she felt perfectly normal parading around without any clothes.

In the bathroom, she closed the door and finally exhaled. While she'd had a couple of relationships since college, the only even remotely serious one had been her last boyfriend, the guy who'd dumped her after two years together. Everything about that relationship had been mundane, and once she'd gotten past the sting of rejection, she'd been glad to be free of it.

After showering, she felt fabulous. Energized and ready

to tackle any problem that might come her way. As if on cue, her phone buzzed, indicating a text.

She really, really didn't want to check it. But as Dade had said, she couldn't simply ignore this person and hope he'd go away. He'd already proved that wasn't going to happen.

Like my handiwork? If you don't, it doesn't matter. Unless you leave Alaska and go back to Texas, things are only going to get worse.

Sighing, she left her hair damp and joined Dade in the kitchen, where he'd started preparing them large salads for lunch.

"He messaged me again," she said, handing over the phone.

Dade frowned as he read the text. "Again, he's wanting you to leave. Like he's refocused on you once more."

"What does this person hope to gain from all of this?" she asked. "Let's say I did listen to him and packed up and high-tailed it back to Texas. You'd get the lodge. It wouldn't be sold. How would that benefit him?"

"I don't know." Expression grave, Dade grimaced. "Unfortunately, I suspect he's mentally ill. Which means you can't expect to apply logic to any of his actions."

"Maybe not," she conceded. "However, there has to be a motive. What made him decide to target us? I take it no one bothered you before, right?"

"Right." Gaze steady, he regarded her for a moment. "The next question would be, what changed? You came here, true. But did anyone send you weird texts before you learned that Grady had died?"

"No. And since he referred to you as a fake son, does

he believe we took something that should have been his? Like the lodge?"

Dade shrugged. "It seems likely."

"Then I have to ask, so please don't take offense. Did Grady father any other children that you know of?"

"None taken," he replied. "I don't believe so. Grady took me in as a young boy, out of the kindness of his heart. If he had any other kids, he definitely would have made sure they were part of his life."

She believed him. "I truly wish I'd known him. He sounds like he was a wonderful man."

"That's what really bothers me. It seems like if this stalker would just sit down and have an honest conversation with me, we could clear things up."

Getting out her phone, she pulled up the text thread, took a deep breath and hit the button to call the number. As she'd expected, a recording came on saying it wasn't a working number.

"What did you just do?" Dade asked.

"Tried to call him. I agree with you. It's high time we all just had a conversation. This harassment has got to stop. But he's not using that number any more. Like usual, the next text will come from a completely different one. And it won't allow calls either."

"Then we'll have to send a text right away," he said. "As soon as we get his. That's the only chance we have of reaching him."

THAT NIGHT, IT took every ounce of willpower Dade possessed to remain in his own bed, in his own room. He would have thought that the amazing sex they'd had would be enough to satisfy him for a while. But instead, he craved more.

He tossed and turned, so aroused that he considered taking an icy shower or taking matters into his own hands. But somehow, he managed to drift off to sleep.

It rained during the night, the kind of heavy rain that left the air heavy and always created a lot of sticky mud. When Dade stepped out onto the front porch, the first thing he noticed were the paw prints a few feet away from the house.

Maddie, right behind him, almost crashed into him when he stopped short. Her coffee sloshed a little onto her hand.

"Look." He pointed.

Stepping past him to see, she frowned. "What the heck caused those?" she asked.

"Wolves. More than one. What's unusual is they came so close to the house. Bears will do that, but wolves usually keep their distance." Though he didn't say it out loud, he couldn't shake the feeling that something was wrong.

"That's not good, is it? My first thought is the cabins," she said. "Good thing we don't have the next batch of guests yet. I'd be worried about teenagers and wolves."

"The next group is a bunch of older businessmen," he said absently. "Mid-forties. They come every year. Luckily, we have one more day before they arrive." He started off the porch, feet slipping a little in the mud. Two steps and he turned back to look at her. "Wait here."

Naturally, she ignored that. Coffee cup in hand, she followed him. "Where are you going?"

"To see where the tracks lead. With so many wolves, they must have a fresh kill somewhere around."

That finally made her stop. "Like a dead animal?"

Somehow, he reined in his so far unfounded worry. "Yes. Probably something big. Maybe a deer, I don't know."

Eyes huge, she took a step backward. "I think I will wait here. I'll let you figure it out."

Which was probably for the best. She took a seat in her

usual chair and sipped her coffee. Satisfied that he didn't have to worry about her, he began following the tracks into the woods.

In a few places, he lost them. Leaves and brush obscured their path. But he managed to pick them up again. They led to a small clearing off the beaten path, where at one point Grady had contemplating building another storage shed. Though he'd kept the area cleared of trees and brush, he never utilized it.

In the middle of the grassy area, Dade saw a fresh mound of dirt, as if wild animals had been digging for buried bones. Since other wildlife didn't bury their dead, this couldn't be a good thing.

With a sickening feeling in the pit of his gut, Dade moved closer. This was no deer. Though scattered around what appeared to be a fresh grave, the bones, with most of the flesh removed from them, were clearly human. The wolves had been feasting on human remains. Someone had been recently buried here. Had they been murdered here as well? And if so, by whom?

Suddenly, the unknown man who'd been lurking around the lodge became much more dangerous.

Knowing better than to disturb anything further, Dade backed away and hurried toward the house. Maddie stood when she saw him coming, as if some of his urgency had conveyed itself to her.

"What was it?" she asked.

Though he hated to destroy the peace of one of their last private mornings before more guests arrived, he had no choice.

"A body," he replied. "Human, from the looks of it. I've got to call the state police and report this. Then I've got to figure out how to protect the site until someone can get here."

She followed him inside, silent while he made the necessary phone calls. In addition to reporting what he'd found just now, he also relayed information about the explosion and resulting fire, plus the numerous sightings of a stranger lurking around in the woods.

The person he spoke with at the state police office took down everything, remarked that they'd just called about a break-in the day before, and promised to send someone out as soon as possible. From past experience, Dade knew this could be anywhere from a few days to longer. Hopefully, since there'd been a murder, it would be much quicker.

Once he'd ended the call, he turned to find Maddie staring at him. "You think my stalker killed someone?"

Since he didn't believe in sugarcoating the truth, he nodded. "If that man is the same person who's been texting you, it's a very real possibility. I imagine once the state police get here, they'll send for someone with a search-and-rescue cadaver dog. Just to make sure there aren't more unmarked graves out there."

She blanched. "If there are, that would mean he's what? A serial killer?"

Unable to help himself, he reached out and gently squeezed her shoulder. "Let's not go there yet. Until we find out for sure what else is out there, okay?"

Slowly, she nodded. "Either way, whether there's one body or five, he's a murderer. And since he has a major grudge against both of us and has broken into the house, I'd say we're in danger."

He couldn't fault her logic. "Yes. Which means we need to take precautions."

Briefly, she leaned into his touch before appearing to

collect herself and moving away. Clearly restless, she went to the window and looked out. "Like what? I know you're armed, but I'm not. I don't have the faintest idea how to handle a gun. I need you to teach me."

Though with the next group of guests about to arrive, he had no idea when they'd find time to do such a thing, he nodded. Briefly, he wondered if they should consider cancelling, but not only did they have their reputation to uphold, they needed the money. "We'll try. But it's more than me simply showing you how to load and shoot," he said. "There's safety issues, target practice and learning how to clean the weapon. And since I don't want to do any of that around our guests, we'll have to work it in between groups."

Turning, she met his gaze. "I get it," she said. "I don't like it, but I totally understand how having daily target practice might be bad for business."

He shrugged. "Maybe we can time it for while they're all out fishing. Sound carries around here, but if they go far enough out..."

Her smile started a warmth inside his blood. "I'd like that," she said. "And thank you."

Aware he needed to focus on something else to keep himself from getting any more aroused, he swallowed and kept the conversation on track. "Also, I heard back from Kip about the security cameras. He's ordered them, and while he can't say for sure when they'll be in, he's hoping it won't be more than a couple of weeks."

"I don't like being this worried about our safety," she told him, her voice soft, her expression vulnerable. "It was bad enough getting all those weird texts, and then the explosion and fire, but this? A body buried nearby? Maybe more? And there's a strong possibility we—or more specifically, I—might be next."

"Come here," he said gruffly, tugging her into his arms. He'd simply hold her, he told himself, nothing more. Offering comfort seemed like the least he could do.

Except his body clearly had other ideas. The instant their skin made contact, he went on red alert. And when she turned her face up to his, he could no more keep himself from kissing her than he could keep his heart from beating.

She kissed him back, making sweet little guttural sounds in the back of her throat. He tried like hell to maintain some semblance of control, but when she pressed her body up against his, he went wild.

They undressed quickly, managing not to tear their clothes off. He again managed to get a condom on. Then they fell upon each other, just like before. Hot, passionate and uniquely Maddie.

This time, instead of leaving her bed after, he fell asleep with her in his arms.

When he opened them again to sun streaming through the window, he realized Maddie had already gotten up. He found her in the kitchen, humming under her breath while she mixed something up.

"Good morning," she said, smiling.

He liked that she never acted awkward around him. Going up to her, he kissed the back of her neck. She shivered, which made him consider taking things a step further. But coffee beckoned. He made himself a cup, using the opportunity to get his act together before turning to face her again.

"What are you making?" he asked.

"Something else I found in one of Grady's cookbooks." Her eyes sparkled. "Have you ever had a baked Dutch baby pancake? It sounds amazing. I even found some lemon juice to put on it along with the confectionary sugar. I'm about to put it in the oven."

While the pancakes baked, they sat at the kitchen table drinking coffee. "I hope the police take my call seriously," he said. "Finding an actual dead body ramps all of the other stuff up to the next level."

"Surely, they will." She sounded certain. He didn't have the heart to tell her it all depended on who got assigned to the case and how much time that officer felt like spending on investigating it.

The baked pancake turned out amazing. Bursting with pride, Maddie commented that it turned out she enjoyed cooking far more than she'd ever thought she would.

"And you're really good at it, too," Dade told her, meaning it.

Between the two of them, they polished off the entire thing. "I think we should consider adding this to the breakfast menu for the guests," Dade suggested. "You'd have to make several, but unless they're labor intensive, I think they'd be a big hit."

Beaming, Maddie nodded. "I'll consider it."

Watching as she bustled around the kitchen, Dade realized they'd begun to feel like a true partnership, though it felt as if it had the potential to become something deeper and possibly more enduring than just business.

Because thoughts like that could be dangerous, Dade pushed them away. He got up, helped her clean up and then headed for the bathroom to shower. Again, he thought about asking her to join him, but decided against it.

When he'd finished and she'd gone in to take her own shower, he once again went over the guest list for the next group. Since they'd been to the lodge the year before, Dade checked his notes from that visit. Grady had taught him to always make notes, that way guests who returned could be taken care of in ways that enhanced their experience.

The Alaska State Trooper arrived shortly after Maddie finished showering, which was faster than Dade had ever known them to be. Dade had just gone outside, planning to head down and fuel up the boats, when the police car pulled up.

Dade stopped and waited. The police officer got out, his uniform freshly pressed, and smiled.

"I was in the area," he said, answering the question before Dade even had a chance to ask it. "I'm Officer Taggert."

"Dade Anson."

They shook hands, the other man sizing Dade up. While Taggert was tall, Dade still towered over him by at least half a foot.

When Maddie walked out onto the front porch, looking stunning, the police officer grinned. "Good morning, ma'am. You must be Mrs. Anson. I'm Officer Taggert, with the Alaska State Troopers."

"Maddie Pierce." She stayed on the porch. "I hope you can figure out what's going on. Honestly, I just want this man caught so Dade and I can get on with running this fishing lodge."

"Yes, ma'am," Taggert replied, smiling. He never took his eyes off her as he moved on up to the porch. "Do you mind if we take a seat so you can tell me what's been happening?"

Maddie blinked. "Didn't Dade tell you already?"

"Yes, ma'am, he did. But I'd like to also hear it from you."

Dade nearly snorted out loud at the obvious flirting. For her part, Maddie seemed oblivious. Instead of commenting, he lifted his hand in a wave. "I'll be down at the boat docks. Officer Taggert, when you're finished, let me know. I'll take you up to where I found the shallow grave."

Taggert barely looked up. "Will do," he said, getting out a notepad and a pen. "Now, Maddie, why don't you start at the beginning."

Shaking his head, Dade took off. His flash of anger and—to be honest—jealousy, surprised him. Maddie wasn't his, she was her own person and could make her own choices. If she wanted to flirt with Taggert, that was none of Dade's business.

As long as the man did his job. Maybe that was why Dade felt so irritated. Finding a body in a shallow grave after having the house broken into and the boat shed set on fire seemed a pretty damn important reason to investigate.

Dade got to work refueling the boats, one by one. When Taggert strolled up less than fifteen minutes later, Dade motioned that he'd be right with him. Pleasantly surprised, since barely fifteen minutes had passed, Dade topped of the gas tank and drove the boat back to its slip.

Once he'd tied it up and killed the motor, he stepped out. "Follow me," he said, and took off for the meadow. "Wolves dug the body up, and I'm afraid they did a number on it."

"We've got a really good forensics team," Taggert replied. "I've already given them a call, and they're on their way to collect the remains."

Dade nodded. It looked like the state police were taking this case seriously after all.

Chapter Ten

Though she'd been glad to send the flirtatious policeman away to do his job, now that she found herself alone in the house, Maddie felt more nervous than she'd expected. Which made sense because she had no idea what else her stalker might be capable of. Finding a body in a shallow grave on the property sent her anxiety into an entirely different realm. Though an official determination hadn't been made yet, she just knew the body had been a woman.

In the beginning, she'd treated the random texts like some kind of tasteless joke. They were annoying, but she hadn't truly viewed them as any kind of real threat. She'd even briefly considered the possibility that they were being sent to the wrong person.

The fire, then the break-in and the note on her mirror had stripped away any of her previous delusions. Whoever this man was, he seemed to enjoy the process of tormenting them. He hadn't made any demands, other than ordering her to leave. Since that was the one thing she couldn't and wouldn't do, and he refused to allow her to communicate with him, they were stuck in a weird limbo of his making.

Even living in downtown Dallas, she'd never felt as if her life might be in danger. These days, she did.

She briefly considered walking out to find Dade and Officer Taggert, but since doing that would make her more vulnerable, she decided to remain inside. As a precaution, she locked all the doors.

She kept busy putting together all the ingredients for dinner. She'd decided to make a pork roast, and she'd been able to find one small enough that two people could share it for a couple of days. Following one of Grady's recipes, she peeled potatoes and carrots, cut up onions and put everything in the Crock-Pot. After adding the seasonings, she closed the lid.

In the past, she'd never been much for cooking. She'd had a lot of food delivered and had rarely cooked anything more than instant oatmeal or frozen pizza.

Now look at her. She'd practically become a domestic goddess.

What next? She wanted to keep busy. Should she make some bread? Why not? She'd seen an older bread machine with the recipe book tucked inside. Smiling at her sudden culinary longings, she located the machine, found all the necessary ingredients and started a loaf of basic white bread.

Keeping busy worked. At least, provided a necessary distraction. Yet the entire time she bustled around the kitchen, she kept a lookout for any movement outside the windows and listened for any sound that might be out of the ordinary.

Finally, she caught a glimpse of Dade and Officer Taggert walking up toward the house. They appeared to be deep in conversation.

More relieved than she cared to admit, she unlocked the front door and stepped out onto the porch. Neither man looked up as they went over to the police cruiser.

Opening the driver-side door, Taggert reached inside

and then handed Dade what looked like a business card. After pocketing it, Dade stood and watched as the other man drove off before making his way back to the porch.

"What did he have to say?" she asked.

"He's got a forensic team on the way, so he wanted to know if there was any kind of motel in town. I told him he could stay in one of the cabins if he wanted, though not for long since we have guests due to arrive soon." He shrugged. "He told me he'd let me know, but for now, he wanted to check out the lodgings in Blake."

"That's weird. Is there a place to stay in town?"

"Sure. Kip's always got a room or two for rent. That's where I sent Taggert. If it doesn't work out, I'm sure he'll be back."

Dade lowered himself into a chair, his expression troubled. "What I'm worried about is the effect this police investigation will have on our guests."

"That's understandable. But since that meadow is off the beaten path, hopefully the two won't intersect. Especially since there won't be teenagers in this next group."

He looked up. "True. They're all middle-aged businessmen. All they're interested in is fishing. They tend to drink a lot around the bonfire at night, but beyond shoveling down whatever we serve them and sleeping, they want to be out on the water."

Placing her hand on his arm, she smiled. "It sounds like it will all work out."

"Will it?" He met her gaze, expressionless. "We still have to worry about the stalker. What will he try to do next? I don't want any of the guests hurt while they're on vacation here."

"Do you think he'll still hang around, once he realizes there's a police presence?"

"Who knows. I haven't yet figured out what this guy even wants." Dade grimaced. "And now we don't know if he's some sort of serial killer or if we're dealing with two different people."

Since *that* thought had never occurred to her, she took a moment to process it. "You don't really think that, do you?"

"No," Dade admitted. "I'll admit I'm struggling with this. It's difficult not to be angry. First, I lost Grady. Then…"

"You had me foisted on you," she supplied. "It's okay. I get it."

"Fine. I'll just say running the lodge for the next year with a total stranger wasn't something I'd planned on. But so far, I have to admit, we've been able to work it out. We are well on our way toward making a good team."

Touched, she nodded and waited to see what else he'd have to say.

"Then this guy inserts himself into our lives. This is our business, our home. He's got to be stopped, before anyone else gets hurt."

"I agree."

The landline rang, the sound carrying outside. Startled, they both looked at each other. Then Dade jumped to his feet and hurried inside to answer.

Maddie stayed where she was, trying to relax on the front porch. She could hear the occasional word from Dade's end of the conversation, but not enough to understand the entire call.

A moment later, Dade returned. If he'd looked serious before, now he appeared positively grim.

"That was our next group. They've had to cancel and are aware they'll be forfeiting their deposit."

Stunned, she stared at him. "Why? Did they hear about everything that's been going on here?"

He dragged his hand through his hair. "All he said was that something came up. He did apologize, for all it's worth. I can't believe this."

"Are we going to be okay without that booking?"

Dade sighed, dropping into the chair next to her. "I don't know. I'll have to run the numbers. They were a good-sized group and repeat guests. It's going to hurt us, for sure. Especially since we don't have another group coming for ten days."

"Does this happen very often?" she asked. "People cancelling their reservations at the last moment?"

"No. In fact, it's never happened as long as I've been here."

The bewilderment in his voice made her long to comfort him. But then she realized an awful possibility. "Dade, what if all these things are tied together? Do you think there's any chance that this stalker has somehow gained access to our guest reservations and is doing his best to turn them away?"

Instead of rejecting the idea outright, Dade considered her words. "If we did everything on the internet, I'd definitely think that might have happened. But since we still do everything the old-fashioned way with pen and paper, I don't see how."

About to remind him that the house had been broken in to, she saw the moment he came to the same realization.

"Damn it." Shoving himself up from the chair, he stormed into the house.

She hurried along right behind him, hoping she might be wrong.

The table that housed the landline phone sat next to a

small, simple wooden desk. He opened the middle drawer and cursed. "It's gone," he said, his bleak voice matching his expression. "Our reservation book is gone."

Though she wanted to ask him if they had some sort of backup, she knew better. It would be too much like rubbing salt into an open wound.

"Damn it." He began rummaging through the desk, as if he thought it might merely have been moved or misplaced. "It has to be here somewhere. How would he even know where to look?"

"You have a point," she said. "Because even though you told me you have everything written down, I had no idea where you kept it. I should have asked."

"Help me look." Continuing his frantic search, he glanced at her. "Please. I'm trying to remember the last time I looked at it. I'm hoping I just forgot to put it back."

"I'll check the kitchen," she said. "I seem to remember you looking at something when we were planning our supply run for the upcoming visit."

"That's right!" His expression cleared, relief shining in his brown eyes. "I bet that's where it is."

But though they both searched every inch of the kitchen, they found no sign of the missing notebook.

"I'm going to check my bedroom. Would you mind checking yours?" he asked.

Even though she'd never handled the dang thing and had no idea what it looked like, she agreed. After all, when the break-in had happened, the house had been in such disarray that anything could have ended up in the wrong place.

She went through her dresser first, checking underneath all her clothes. She looked in her closet and on top of her bed, moving aside the pillows and even the sheets. As she'd expected, she found no notebook.

Right before leaving her room, she dropped down to check under her bed. That was when she saw it. A red spiral notebook, on the floor, right in the middle.

On her hands and knees, she couldn't quite reach it. She had to wiggle herself under the bed, arm outstretched, until she connected and dragged the notebook toward her.

Once back out, she called for Dade. "I think I found it!"

"Seriously?" He appeared in her doorway.

When she held out the notebook, he took it and began flipping through it. "This is it," he said. "I'm so relieved. Where was it?"

"Under the bed. I think it was shoved under there."

"Nothing appears to be missing." The relief in his voice made her smile. "Though he might have taken pics with his phone, at least he didn't destroy this. While I have a good memory, without these records, I'd really struggle remembering who was coming when."

"We need to make some sort of backup," she suggested. "Since you don't have anything set up online, how about we use our phones? We could simply take photos, just like you think he might have. That way we have something to refer back to."

"We'll do that." He pulled her to him and hugged her, fierce but quick. "How about I take you out to dinner tonight to celebrate?"

"Out to dinner?" Puzzled, she frowned. "I don't remember seeing any restaurants in Blake."

"There's only one. Mikki's."

"The donut shop?" She didn't even try to hide her disbelief. "You want to go out to eat donuts for dinner?"

"Mikki sells donuts in the morning," he said. "After that, she runs a restaurant and bar in the adjoining space. It's a great place to go have a drink and a bite to eat. In fact, it's the only place." He thought for a minute. "One of our newer residents, Brett Denyon, is a renowned chef from Anchorage. He married our doctor, Dr. Taylor. He's in the process of opening up another restaurant, but it's not ready yet. I think it's supposed to open Memorial Day weekend. So it's Mikki's, right now."

"That sounds...interesting." She thought for a moment. "Actually, I'd like that a lot. It'll be fun."

The slow smile that spread across his handsome face started a fire low in her belly. Flustered, she looked around her room. "Do I need to dress up or anything?"

"Not really. It's Blake," he replied, as if that explained everything. "Just be comfortable. It'll be nice to eat something that someone else prepared."

"Yes," she agreed. "It will."

"Let me know when you want to go. We can do lunch or go later, for dinner, if you'd rather."

She didn't even have to think about that one. "Dinner, please. I like the idea of relaxing out somewhere else at the end of the day."

He smiled, once again making her entire body tingle. "Sounds good. We'll leave here around seven."

Suddenly, absurdly tongue-tied, she settled on a nod.

WHILE DOING SMALL chores around the property, Dade found himself really looking forward to their dinner out that evening. While he wouldn't go so far as to call it a date, in truth, it felt like one. Either way, both he and Maddie needed a break from all the drama that had been occurring lately.

Though he hadn't said as much to Maddie, until they'd found the body in the field, he'd truly believed the stalker had followed her here from Texas. He'd suspected it was someone who'd had a grudge against her. Maybe an old boyfriend or someone from her former job.

Now, with the possibility that someone had been murdered around here recently, he had to admit he might be wrong.

But a *local*? Dade had grown up here, at least since Grady had taken him in as a small child. He knew these people, loved them (or at least most of them), and knew he could depend on them if he ever needed help. The same way they knew they could depend on him.

Dade could not think of a single one of them who'd set his boat shed on fire or break into his house. Hell, he and Grady had never even locked the doors. There'd been no need.

And he still didn't know if the guests' unusual cancellation had something to do with the stalker or some other valid reason. Though he didn't want to appear too pushy, he decided to call the man who'd originally made the booking and find out. He'd been so stunned at the call cancelling everything, he'd forgotten to get the guy's name.

He flipped through the notebook and retrieved the guest's contact info. Using the landline, he called. When after several rings, he went to voicemail; he left his name and number, asking for a call back.

Satisfied with that, he took a peek ahead to the set of guests due to arrive the week after the ones who'd cancelled. This time, a smallish company had booked an employee retreat as a team-building exercise. There would be two women executives and four men. Maddie would definitely be an asset with that group.

Hell, so far, Maddie had been a great partner. And more, though the instant he thought about their sensual activities between the bedsheets, his body stirred.

Shaking his head at himself, he got busy power washing the boat docks. Usually, they kept this machine in the boat shed, but luckily Dade had moved it to the garage to tinker with it. Otherwise, they'd have lost that, too.

Thinking of all the fire damage made him scowl. Hopefully, this Officer Taggert would be on the ball. If they could just get the stalker and potential killer caught, he really thought he and Maddie could have a successful season.

Grady, he thought fondly, had truly known what he was doing. Dade's earlier anger and sense of betrayal when he'd learned what Grady had done had been misplaced.

He finished up power washing, and after he put the washer away, his phone pinged, indicating a text.

Officer Taggert had texted that he'd rented a room from Kip and would be staying in town. The forensics team was scheduled to arrive tomorrow and would be transporting the body back to the lab in Anchorage.

Dade texted back, offering the policeman one of the cabins since there'd be no guests. Having law enforcement on the premises could benefit them all, he thought.

Thanks, but I'd rather stay in town, Taggert replied quickly. It's interesting the nuggets of information I can pick up when I hang around with the locals. You never know when I might hear something that could help me with this case.

Since Dade couldn't argue with that, he let it go.

The unusual afternoon heat hadn't even started to lift around the time they were supposed to leave for Blake. Dade decided to remote start his Jeep right before they were ready to go in order to give the air conditioning time to cool off the interior. Even though he'd left the windows cracked open, he knew from experience it would still be hot.

He went inside to get his keys. Stepping into the house, he got distracted by Maddie puttering around the kitchen.

"What are you doing?" he asked. "You're not cooking, are you?"

"I am, but not dinner." Her bright smile had him aching again. "I decided to test out a recipe for banana bread since we had a few going bad. I thought we could have it later when we got back or even in the morning with breakfast."

Words briefly stuck in his throat. Though she had no way of knowing, Grady had always made Dade banana bread to celebrate special occasions. Birthdays, he'd made it the day before, calling it a pre-birthday cake since he always made a real one on Dade's special day.

"Thanks," he managed. "That sounds great."

Something in his voice must have revealed a hint of his inner turmoil. Eyeing him, she tilted her head. "Are you all right? Don't tell me you don't like banana bread?"

"I do," he assured her. "Grady used to make it a lot. It just brings back a lot of memories." Not wanting to discuss it any further, he checked his sports watch. "Are you still wanting to leave at seven? I want to let my Jeep run a few minutes so it will cool off."

"I will be. The bread will be done in about five minutes. I just need to brush my hair and change, and then I'll be good to go."

"Sounds good." Turning to go to his room, he knew later he'd have to eat that bread, so he needed to get a grip on his emotions. He didn't like the way things that had always been happy memories made him miss Grady so badly he ached.

Like he always did, he shoved his emotions back inside and grabbed his wallet. It had been a while since he'd had dinner at Mikki's. He checked out his appearance in the mirror and decided to change his T-shirt to a clean one. While he was at it, he changed out of his work boots into a better pair.

When he walked back into the living room, the freshly baked loaf of banana bread was cooling on the stove top. Maddie's bedroom door was closed, so he guessed she'd gone to get herself ready.

A moment later, the door opened, and she emerged. Instead of her usual jeans, T-shirt and sneakers, she'd changed into a bright red sundress with white polka dots. She wore sandals, and he saw that she'd painted her toenails the same color as her dress. She'd also put on lipstick and long, dangly earrings that showcased her beautiful neck.

He stopped in his tracks, his mouth dry. She looked... different. Stunning as usual, but in a big-city rather than rustic-fishing-lodge kind of way.

In that instant, he understood she'd likely never stay here. She didn't belong, and he chastised himself for ever thinking she would. Despite all that, he kept wanting her, the sharp fierceness of his desire roaring to life inside him.

Standing there staring at her, fully aroused, he wondered how he'd managed to let her get so far inside his heart.

Again, another thought he needed to shut down.

"What's wrong?" she asked, her hand going to her hair. "Is this dress too much? I just thought it would be fun to wear something different."

"No," he managed. "You look amazing."

"I'm glad you think so," she replied, lifting her chin. "Because I wasn't planning on changing. It's a hot day, and I like getting dressed up once in a while. Are you ready to go?"

Holding out his arm, he couldn't help but grin. Just like

that, she'd managed to put things back to normal. "Let's do this."

When they reached the Jeep, he hurried over to open her door and help her up. The brief flash of leg as she climbed inside made his gut tighten. Mentally shaking his head at himself, he went around to the driver's side. As he'd hoped, the Jeep had cooled down comfortably.

"This is really nice," she said, buckling herself in.

"Remote start for the win. And I just started it a few minutes ago."

By the time they arrived in Blake, Dade felt like himself. Relaxed and happy to be sharing an evening out with Maddie. His business partner.

Mikki's seemed busy, the small parking lot behind the building at least three-quarters full. He found a spot and, after killing the ignition, jumped out and hurried over to help Maddie.

"Thanks," she said, taking his arm. "You're really a gentleman underneath all that wilderness-man exterior."

Again, he found himself grinning at her. With her arm in his, they walked into the bar and restaurant.

The first thing that struck him was the noise level. He hadn't been here during the evening rush in forever. Every seat at the long bar was occupied, and most of the tables were, too.

He found them a table close to the small dance floor, across from the makeshift raised stage. "They have live music sometimes," he said, pulling out a chair so Maddie could sit. "It's usually someone fairly local."

A waitress hurried over and gave them menus. "I'd love to take your drink order," she said. "The bar is a little backed up, so it might take a couple of minutes."

"I'd like to try a King Street hefeweizen," she said,

surprising him. "Or a Glacier hefeweizen, whichever one you have."

He ordered a club soda with lime. After the waitress left, he leaned forward and looked at Maddie. "How'd you know about our local beers?"

"Like I said, when I knew I'd be helping run Grady's Lodge, I did a lot of research. I wanted to learn all I could about local brewing companies. Hefeweizen is my absolute favorite beer, so I memorized the two most popular ones that are brewed in this state."

Impressed, he nodded. "Once again, I see I underestimated you," he said.

"People tend to do that," she replied, smiling. "It's okay because I have a lot of confidence in my own abilities."

Once more, she made him laugh. "I like you, Maddie Pierce."

"I like you, too, Dade Anson."

They sat there grinning at each other like a pair of fools until the waitress arrived with their drinks.

"Here you are," she said. "Are you ready to order?"

Since neither of them had even taken a look at the menu, they shook their heads. "Give us just a few minutes, please," Dade requested.

After taking a sip of her beer, she made a hum of pleasure. The sound made his body tighten.

"This is good," she said. She picked up the menu and began scanning the offerings. "I assume you must have eaten here before. What's good?"

Since he figured she, like him, would be heartily sick of eating salmon by now, he told her to try one of the burgers. "They have several to choose from. I always get the blue cheese burger and fries."

"Interesting," she replied, taking another drink of her

beer. "I've always been partial to a decent Swiss and mushroom burger myself."

Stunned, he stared. "That's what Grady always ordered," he told her, his throat aching. "With onion rings."

"That sounds perfect," she said cheerfully, putting the menu down. "Seems like Grady had great taste. Maybe I inherited it from him."

The waitress appeared to take their order, which gave Dade a moment to get his act together. Once she'd written down their burger choices, she hurried off toward the kitchen.

The ebb and flow of the conversations going on felt completely different than the peaceful nature sounds he'd grown accustomed to.

"This is nice," Maddie said, sipping her beer and looking around. "And it's actually the first time since I arrived that I've felt like part of a community."

Genuinely curious, he studied her. "What do you mean? You've been an integral part of Grady's Lodge."

"Thank you." Beaming, she gestured vaguely at the packed bar. "But this is different. We're in town, in Blake. And no one is staring at me, wondering what I'm doing here. This may sound silly, but I actually feel accepted."

He could have said several things, like point out that she'd been to town with him on supply runs on numerous occasions. Or point out that she was with him, and by now everyone in town knew that Grady's granddaughter had arrived to help run the lodge. But Dade could relate. He had never forgotten the feeling of being on the outside looking in and wanting so desperately to belong.

"You *are* accepted," he said gently, taking a long drink of soda to cover any emotion.

"Hey, Dade!" Samuel Quinton, a burly man with a bushy beard walked over. "And you must be Maddie."

After the introductions, Samuel pulled out a chair without asking. "Did you hear? Amy White is missing."

"What?" Immediately thinking about the shallow grave in the meadow, Dade frowned. "Since when?"

"Yesterday," Samuel replied. "She went out hiking on her own and didn't return home in time for dinner."

Dade exhaled. If she'd just gone missing the day before, that meant it wasn't her body they'd found torn up by wolves.

"On her own?" Maddie asked, looking from one man to the other. "Why would she do that? I'd think it wouldn't be safe."

"She grew up here," Samuel answered. "Most of the kids who live in the area around Blake know these woods like the back of their hands. She's an amateur photographer, so she was always going off on her own and taking pictures. They found her car parked near that bridge by the river. Her phone and camera were inside. It's not like her to not check in. Her parents are really worried."

"I imagine they are," Dade glanced around the room. "I'm assuming they contacted the state police?"

"Yep. Did you know there's an officer staying in one of Kip's rooms above the general store?" Without waiting for an answer, Samuel continued. "Having him in town turned out to be handy. He's sent for a search and rescue team out of Anchorage. Meanwhile, the rest of us are meeting up in the morning to fan out and help look. Do you want to join us?"

"Definitely," Maddie said. "Where are we meeting?"

"The general store. Kip is helping organize the whole

thing." Smiling with approval, Samuel clapped Dade on the back.

Their food arrived just then, so Samuel pushed to his feet and took his leave.

As usual, the burgers were large and meaty. They'd been cut in half to make them easier to manage. Maddie regarded hers. "Wow."

Though the mouthwatering aroma made his stomach growl, he found more pleasure watching her experience her first bite than chowing down himself.

She bit in, chewed, and her eyes went huge. "That's amazing," she said, going in for a second bite.

"Yes, they are," he agreed, finally picking up his and beginning to eat. He hadn't traveled outside of the state, but he could honestly say he believed Mikki's had the best burgers anywhere. Including his own home-grilled ones.

Only once she'd devoured the first half did she slow down long enough to try one of the large, perfectly crispy onion rings.

"I wonder what happened to the missing girl," she mused. "Do you know her?"

"Not really." He dipped one of his fries in ketchup and popped it into his mouth. "I went to school with one of her older brothers. She's pretty young. I think she might have just graduated high school."

"I have to say, when Samuel first mentioned someone was missing, I immediately thought of what you found in the field."

He appreciated the way she chose her words with care. Though none of the nearby tables appeared to be paying attention to them, he didn't want anyone to overhear. Spreading half-baked rumors could get out of control in a town as small as Blake.

"Me, too," he admitted. "That's why I asked when she went missing."

Maddie eyed the other half of her burger, making him wonder if she planned to get a to-go box. Instead, she picked it up and took a huge bite. Making a sound of pleasure that made his mind go elsewhere, she rolled her eyes and proceeded to demolish the rest of her food.

Since he'd already finished most of his, he ate his fries and watched her.

When she'd finished, she blotted her mouth with a napkin and drank the last of her beer. "That was amazing."

As if on cue, the waitress appeared. "Does anyone want dessert?"

Both Maddie and Dade shook their heads. The waitress dropped off the bill, told them she'd be their cashier and left.

"My treat," Dade said, grabbing it before Maddie could.

She thanked him, leaning back and patting her stomach. "I'm stuffed."

Once he'd paid, they walked outside.

"We'll have to do this again," he told her, taking his key fob out of his pocket and hitting the remote start button.

Instead, his truck exploded, the force of the blast knocking them both to the ground.

Chapter Eleven

Dazed, ears ringing, Maddie struggled to get up from the pavement. Knees and elbows bleeding, dress torn, it took her a few seconds to process what on earth had just happened.

"Maddie?" Dade's voice, raspy and interrupted by a bout of coughing, reached her through her stunned fog. "Maddie, are you all right?"

Somehow, she managed to stagger to her feet, still not able to see clearly. "I...think so. What about you?"

"I'm okay."

Since his voice seemed to be right beside her, she slowly turned, hand outstretched, trying to connect with him. She swayed, unsteady on her feet as she waited for her vision to clear. Smoke, there was so much smoke. She, too, began to cough.

Dade, still coughing, took her hand and pulled her close. "I'm right here. Lean on me."

She did. Supporting her with his arm, they moved away from the fire.

Dimly, she realized that people had spilled out of Mikki's when the Jeep had exploded.

"The volunteer fire department is on the way," someone said.

"Dade, Maddie. Are either of you injured?" Officer Taggert appeared, shepherding them both toward the bar.

"I don't think so," Maddie replied. "A few minor scrapes, that's all. Nothing serious, at least for me." She glanced at Dade, finally able to see him, and gasped. "Dade. Your face. It's all bloody."

Eyes narrow slits, he stared at her. "Head wounds bleed like a mother. I'm good."

Then his legs appeared to buckle, and he went down.

Taggert barely managed to get under Dade before he hit the ground. While Taggert was a large man, Dade was even bigger.

Slowly, Taggert eased Dade onto the pavement. "Can someone send for the doctor?" he shouted. "I know you have one. I saw the sign for the medical clinic."

"She's on her way," someone called back.

Uncaring of her bloody knees, Maddie knelt next to Dade. His eyes, while open, appeared dazed, the pupils dilated. She took his hand and squeezed. "Stay still," she murmured. "A doctor is on the way."

A moment later, a woman with long, red hair in a ponytail came running up. "I'm here," she gasped, slightly winded.

Maddie looked up, realized the doctor appeared to be pregnant, and then also saw another man hovering nearby who must be her significant other.

Meanwhile, the Jeep continued burning. Vehicles on both sides of it had now caught on fire.

"Everyone move away," Officer Taggert shouted. "Any of the others could blow at any moment, once that fire hits the gas tank."

"We need to move you to safety. I'm Dr. McKenzie Taylor," the doctor said. "Dade? Can you hear me?"

Dade blinked, clearly struggling to focus. "Yes. But it's like you're really far away." He swallowed hard. "No idea why."

"You hit your head," Dr. Taylor said. "Brett, can you help me lift him?"

The other man came over. Letting go of Dade's hand, Maddie stood. Watching the quickly spreading fire, she tried not to panic.

With Officer Taggert on one side and Brett on the other, they managed to get Dade back on his feet. Though he swayed slightly, the color slowly returned to his face.

"Let's get him into my car and take him to the clinic," the doctor ordered. "I need to take a good, thorough look at him."

As the two men walked Dade away, Maddie got a good look at the back of his head and gasped. "He's got a bad cut," she told the doctor. "He must have hit it when we were knocked to the ground."

Once Dade had been placed safely inside the doctor's vehicle, Taggert returned to the scene to do crowd control and clear the area. Maddie looked back. "Oh, thank goodness. The volunteer fire department is here."

"Come on," Dr. Taylor said. "If you're coming with us, we need to go."

Immediately, Maddie got into the back seat and closed the door, and they were off.

"What the heck happened back there?" Brett asked, turning around from the passenger seat to meet Maddie's gaze. "How'd those cars catch on fire?"

"We don't know." Maddie sighed, briefly closing her eyes. "We'd had dinner at Mikki's and were leaving. Dade hit his remote start, and his Jeep blew up. Which means someone deliberately set some sort of bomb."

Brett narrowed his eyes. "Why would anyone want to do that?"

"It's a long story," Dade murmured. "For another time."

Understanding, Maddie took Dade's hand. Brett, too, appeared to get the hint, as he turned back around to face the front and didn't press the issue.

They reached the medical clinic. Maddie wondered how, if he still couldn't walk, they would get Dade inside. But Brett helped him out. After taking a moment to get his bearings, Dade waved the other man off and moved toward the entrance on his own. Maddie kept close to his side.

Dr. Taylor rushed past them and opened the door. While Brett held it open so Dade could enter, she began turning on the lights. "The exam room is this way," she said. "Brett, would you take Maddie to the break room and help her get those knees and elbows cleaned up? I've got some wipes on the counter back there."

Maddie didn't budge. "I want to go with Dade."

"I understand," the doctor said calmly. "But right now, I need to do a full examination and clean up his head wound. I'll call you as soon as you can come in."

"It's going to be all right," Brett told her. "McKenzie is an excellent physician. She'll take care of your boyfriend. Let's go get you fixed up."

Capitulating, Maddie didn't bother to correct his misconception. There was no need to explain she and Dade were partners. She followed him back to the kitchen, while the doctor took Dade into the exam room and closed the door.

"Have a seat." Brett gestured at a table with four wooden chairs. "Do you mind if I get some wipes and help you get cleaned up?"

She liked that he asked, at least. "I can do it myself," she replied. "They're just scrapes."

"No problem." Fetching the wipes, he handed them to her and took a seat. "I'm sorry this happened to you. Any idea who placed that bomb?"

Looking up from wiping the blood off her knees, she debated how much she should say. He had kind eyes, she thought, and the way he'd looked at Dr. Taylor had been like something out of a romance novel. "Someone has been threatening me, ever since I arrived here," she said. "A little before that, even."

As she told him the details, leaving nothing out, his pleasant expression darkened. By the time she'd finished, he looked absolutely furious.

"You know, when I came here, I had something similar happen to me. I was in an accident and had some temporary memory loss. There were some bad guys after me, too, and I had no idea why."

"That's why Officer Taggert is here," she said. "He actually came to investigate the body the wolves dug up. Now that he's heard about everything else, including the missing girl from town, he's likely going to have a lot more to look into."

"It sounds like he might be staying here awhile," Brett agreed. "Can I get you anything to drink? We have soft drinks or bottled water here in the break room fridge."

Before she could answer, the exam room door opened, and Dr. Taylor stepped out. She smiled at Brett before turning her attention to Maddie. "He has a pretty nasty gash on the back of his head," she said, walking over. "I've cleaned it and put some stitches in. He also has a concussion, so when you take him home, you'll need to keep an eye on him. Keep him hydrated and moving every couple of hours. If you see any swelling or anything unusual, that could indicate something more serious. If that happens, give me a call."

More serious? Like a cracked skull? Maddie pushed back a sudden wave of fear. "Maybe we should take him to the hospital and have a CT scan or an MRI done, just in case," she said.

Both Dr. Taylor and Brett stared. Finally, the doctor's expression cleared, and she shook her head. "I forgot, you're new here. The nearest hospital is in Anchorage, over two hours away if you're lucky. For life-or-death urgent situations, they'll send a plane or a chopper. For everything else, we treat it ourselves."

Slowly, Maddie nodded. "Sorry, I'm still getting used to things out here."

Dr. Taylor smiled. "It's okay. When I arrived, I found I had to make a lot of adjustments. Practicing rural medicine is certainly a lot different."

"Will Dade be okay?" Maddie asked. "That's what really matters."

"Yes." Dr. Taylor's firm tone felt reassuring. "Just keep an eye on him. Dade's a strong man and—"

"I have a thick skull," Dade said, emerging from the exam room. Seeing the cuts and bruises on his handsome face, Maddie winced. His walk seemed a bit wobbly, and he had a large bandage on the back of his head. "Come on, Maddie. Let's get back to the lodge."

Relieved to see him, Maddie took a deep breath. "I'd love to, but how? We no longer have transportation."

Dade cursed and took a step forward. Apparently, he moved too fast. He had to grab a hold of the doorframe to steady himself. Blinking, he took a moment to collect himself. "You're right," he said. "My Jeep is gone. We have to be able to get into town and back."

He took a deep breath and dragged his hand across his battered face. "Grady has an old truck that I haven't started up in a while. I'll need to work on getting that running. We can use that. At least, until the insurance comes through, and I can buy another Jeep."

"In the meantime, we can take you both back to the lodge," Dr. Taylor offered. Brett nodded, agreeing.

"We'd appreciate that," Dade replied. "I can call Officer Taggert on the way and find out if he's learned anything." He took a deep breath. "Let me settle up with you, and then we'll go."

"I'll just send you a bill," the doctor said. "My assistant handles all of that sort of thing, and obviously, she's not here this late at night."

"Sounds good." Moving with clear difficulty, Dade turned toward the exit.

Maddie jumped up, aware he'd need some assistance. But Brett beat her to it, sliding his shoulder under Dade's arm. "I got you, big guy," Brett said.

Since Brett could clearly handle Dade better, Maddie turned and rushed to open the door instead.

When they were all outside, Dr. Taylor locked up. Blake helped Dade into the back seat, and Maddie climbed in next to him. Brett took the passenger seat, and the doctor got in behind the wheel.

Once they were all buckled in, Brett turned to look at Dade. "You'll need to direct us. While I've heard of your fishing lodge, I've never been out there."

"Me, neither," Dr. Taylor chimed in. "I have no idea how to get there."

Dade was leaning back in the seat with his eyes closed, but opened them long enough to give a few directions. "Beyond that, Maddie should be able to point out the way," he said. "She's been to town and back a few times."

Brett looked at Maddie. Slowly, she nodded. "Sure. I can do that."

To leave town, they had to drive down Main Street and right past Mikki's. From what Maddie could see as they went past, the fire appeared to have been extinguished and most of the crowd had dispersed. She couldn't see Officer Taggert, so she figured they'd have to wait until tomorrow to hear what he had to say about all of this.

Which likely was a good thing, since Maddie would have her hands full tonight taking care of Dade.

SITTING IN THE back seat next to Maddie, Dade kept fading in and out. He couldn't shake the strange lethargy that made him incapable of moving much. And his head felt like it had been split open with an axe, even if that sounded a bit dramatic.

Still, he'd a thousand times rather be the one who'd been hurt. As long as Maddie was all right, he'd be fine.

Maddie. Even with his inability to focus, he knew one thing. In the short period of time he'd spent with her, Maddie had come to mean more to him than she should. In fact, he'd begun to think he couldn't imagine life without her.

He shook his head at his inner thoughts but then winced. All this had to be due to his head injury. He'd never been a man given to fanciful thinking.

Somewhere between Blake and the lodge, he must have dozed off. Luckily, Maddie had apparently remembered how to get back to the lodge because when he opened his eyes again, they'd just pulled up to the house.

"Do you need help getting out?" Brett asked, turning around from the front seat.

Since Dade wasn't sure how to answer, he shrugged. Even that small movement sent jagged shards of pain shooting through his skull.

Briefly closing his eyes, when the door opened and Brett reached in, Dade grunted. "Give me a sec," he said. He managed to push himself up and grab hold of the other man's arm. Once out, he waited a moment to get his bearings. Then, shaking off Brett's attempt to help, he managed to make his way up the front steps and to the door.

Turning the knob, he cursed again. He'd forgotten that they'd locked it when they left. And the keys had been in his hand when the Jeep exploded. He had no idea what had happened to them.

"Let me unlock the door, please," Maddie requested, right behind him. "I picked up your keys after you fell."

Conscious of the doctor and Brett watching them, Dade shuffled aside. Once Maddie had opened the door and turned to help him inside, he tried to turn and wave to Dr. Taylor, but couldn't find the coordination or the energy. He settled for stepping over the threshold without stumbling.

"I hate this," he said, teeth clenched.

After she closed and locked the door, Maddie came over and kissed his cheek. "I imagine you do. How about we get you settled on the couch with a pillow and a blanket?"

Any other time, Dade might have retorted that he didn't need to be coddled, but right now, having someone take care of him felt nice. He started to nod, but remembering the pain that came with sudden head movements, settled on a faint smile instead.

He lowered himself onto the couch, and she went to his bedroom, brought out his pillow and put it at one end of the couch. He managed to get his shoes off, and she helped him lie back.

"Would you like out of those jeans?" she asked. "They're pretty torn up."

"Sure." Though he really didn't care. All he wanted to do right now was get some sleep.

Any other time, the feeling of her small hands unfastening his belt and tugging down his zipper might have been arousing. Instead, he sighed with relief as she helped pull the jeans off, freeing each leg. Clad only in his boxers, he settled back onto the couch.

"I'll be right back," she said.

A moment later, she returned with an old throw blanket that she'd found somewhere.

"Here you go," she said, covering him as if he were a young child. "Let me get you a glass of water."

While he liked having her fuss over him, he'd much rather their positions were reversed. He'd always been the caregiver, never the vulnerable one in need of help. He'd taken care of Grady when the older man had fallen ill, and he'd done a damn good job of it. Dade simply needed to regain his strength, and he'd be back to his old self in no time.

He dozed off while waiting for her to return with the water.

When he next opened his eyes, all the lights had been turned off, and the house was dark. Gingerly, he raised himself up on his elbows and realized the pain in his head had subsided.

Swinging his legs off the sofa, he sat all the way up, holding himself still for a moment. He would get up, he thought, and go to his bed. But he wanted to wait until his eyes adjusted to the darkness. And a brief spurt of dizziness gave him pause.

"Are you okay?" Maddie's soft voice, from the chair on the other side of the couch.

Stunned, he attempted a nod. This time, the head movement didn't hurt nearly as much as before. "I'm better, I think," he replied. "Have you been there all night?"

"You've only been asleep for a couple of hours."

Sitting with her in the complete darkness felt like another kind of intimacy. His body stirred. It surprised him that he could want her so damn much, even while bruised and battered. "Go on to bed," he told her. "You don't need to sit with me. I'm fine."

"You're not fine. And the doctor told me to keep an eye on you due to your concussion. I was just about to wake you when you sat up on your own."

Since he couldn't dispute that logic, he sighed. "I never thought I'd say this, but I'm actually glad the next group cancelled. They would have been here the day after tomorrow."

"Me, too," she agreed. "Though I hate the lost revenue, at least this way you can heal up."

"True." Deciding he'd had enough of being disabled, he tried to push himself up to his feet. He made it, but just barely. And he felt glad for the darkness because he felt more unsteady than he liked.

"Let me help you." Somehow, Maddie got right beside him. "Are you needing to go to the bathroom?"

"I'm not a child," he said crossly. Immediately, he felt bad. "Sorry. I'm not used to being hurt."

"I get that." Despite everything, she sounded cheerful. "But we're partners, remember? I'm here to help you. I know you'd do the same for me if our situations were reversed."

Partners. With a grunt, he acknowledged her point. "Thank you," he said. "I think I can walk on my own now."

"Great. I'm just going to stay close to you just in case."

And she did. He made it to the bathroom without incident and closed the door.

When he emerged, she was standing in the hall. "Do you want to go back to the couch or would you rather spend the rest of the night in your bed?" she asked.

In the dim lighting, he could see that at some point she'd changed into a large T-shirt that ended at her thigh. The soft, thin material did little to conceal the lush outline of her curves underneath.

Again, desire blazed to life. "My bed," he managed. Then, since walking would be even more of a challenge, he used the wall for balance.

Luckily, it wasn't far. Once they reached his room, Maddie turned on the lamp. Standing in front of it had the effect of turning her T-shirt translucent. He'd thought his arousal couldn't be any fiercer. Turned out, he was wrong.

Her eyes widened as she noticed. "You need to rest," she said, her voice firm.

Though he hated to admit it, he knew she was right. "Maybe in the morning," he said.

She turned back the sheets and gestured. "In bed you go."

Despite his still raging arousal, he managed to crawl between the sheets. "Will you lie here with me?" he asked. "Nothing else. Just hold me until I fall asleep?"

"I will." She got into bed with him, pushing him gently onto his side so that his back was to her. "But only if you face that way."

Then she wrapped her arms around him and held him until he fell asleep.

When he opened his eyes next, the sunlight streaming in through his window announcing the morning, to his astonishment, Maddie was still asleep next to him.

Instant desire slammed into him. He forced himself to keep still, trying to be content with watching her sleep.

Finally, when he had his body under control, he slipped from the bed and headed to take a shower. Once the next group of guests arrived, neither he nor Maddie would be able to sleep past sunrise, so Dade decided he wouldn't wake her. She'd worked hard and deserved her rest. Thanks to the last-minute cancellation, they'd have a lot more time in between groups of people. He'd figure out a way to make up for the lost revenue.

After showering, he headed to the kitchen. He made his usual cup of strong coffee and got to work preparing a hearty breakfast. Today would be a busy one, since he had to deal with the insurance, see if he could get Grady's old truck running and stop by Dr. Taylor's office so she could check him out again.

Now, he actually felt relieved that the next group had cancelled. If they hadn't, it would have been difficult to get ready without a working vehicle. Though the cabins had already been cleaned and made ready, they still would have needed to shop and meal prep before the guests arrived.

Now, he could work on Grady's truck, and then they could simply focus on figuring out who was doing this to them and why.

Turning the bacon, he shook his head. This, the off days in between guests, had always been fun. In years past, he and Grady had thoroughly enjoyed themselves, making bets on who could do what the fastest. Grady had a way of making everything, even the most menial of chores, seem fun.

Dade missed him more than he could ever explain.

"Mornin'." Maddie appeared, her hair tousled, her eyes still sleepy. "That bacon smells delicious."

"Breakfast is just about done," he said, working to control his body's wham-slam reaction to her. "Grab yourself some coffee."

"Coffee," she breathed, moving toward the pot. "That's exactly what I need."

Unable to help himself, he watched while she got herself a mug and poured. She carried that over to the table and sat. "I take it you're feeling better this morning?"

"I am." He couldn't help but smile. Seeing that, she blushed, which made him want to kiss her. And more.

He set a plate down in front of her. "Here you go. Eat up."

Momentarily distracted, she eyed the meal he'd made. Fluffy scrambled eggs, thick pieces of toasted bread and perfectly cooked bacon.

He went back, got his own plate and took the seat across from her. "Is something wrong?" he asked.

"Not really," she said, picking up her fork. She took a bite, made a sound of pleasure and continued eating. After a moment, he grabbed his own fork and did the same.

Once she'd finished her breakfast, she sat back in her chair and looked at him. "Something is wrong," she admitted. "A lot is wrong, and you know it. Not only is someone stalking us, but I'm worried about the missing girl from town. What if the guy who killed and buried that woman on our land has her?"

He nodded. "I've thought the same thing. I'm hoping that's not the case, and she shows up home soon. And since they've organized a search for her, if our stalker does have her, he'll be running out of places to hide."

"Maybe so." She drained the last of her coffee and got up to get another cup. When she returned to her chair, she met his gaze. "I think it's time to go on the offensive."

"How so?"

Leaning forward, she grimaced. "It's just weird that this

guy is texting, breaking into our home, setting things on fire, and we don't have any idea why. He's made no demand, other than insisting I go back to Texas. What does he actually want? Is there a way we can confront him and find out?"

"That might be dangerous, don't you think?" he pointed out. "Sometimes, unstable people with unresolved mental health issues don't have a valid reason. Since it seems like he's started ramping things up, I don't know."

"I want to talk to Officer Taggert and see what he thinks." She lifted her chin. "If this guy turns out to be a killer, then we're already in danger. I came out here ready to start a new life. I'm working hard and learning from you. I have plans. Big ones."

Swallowing, she took a long drink of her coffee while she visibly gathered her composure. "In the last several months, I've had a lot of losses. I'm not willing to endure any more. Inheriting half of this fishing lodge became a second chance for me. I moved far away from familiar places and people, and I refuse to let this person drive me off."

"I admire that," he said, meaning every word. "And you're doing great. We make a good team. As far as the stalker, I'd also like to know what he wants and why he's doing this to us. I have to think he has some sort of grudge against the lodge. Maybe he was a past guest or something. But he seems to be doing everything he can to shut us down."

"I hadn't thought of that." She sat back in her chair, expression dazed. "Until you just said that, I'd assumed his attacks were personal, directed at me, and you just got caught up in it due to proximity. I mean, he started texting me right after I learned of my inheritance, before I even left Texas."

"True. I honestly don't know. If he'd give us an opportunity to have an actual conversation, maybe we could finally find out what he wants."

The sound of multiple vehicles on gravel outside had him and Maddie looking at each other.

"What the...?" Dade asked, getting to his feet. "Stay put and let me check this out."

Eyes wide, Maddie nodded.

Before he went out, he grabbed his pistol, checked to make sure it was loaded and put on his holster.

Then he took a deep breath, opened the front door and stepped out onto the front porch.

Three large SUVs had parked in front of the house. As Dade stared, the doors opened and several men emerged.

"Dade, my man." A tall man with a trendy haircut and mirrored aviator sunglasses stepped forward, hand outstretched. "Bradley Hartfield. We're really looking forward to another few days of fishing here. We can't wait to get started."

It took a second before Dade realized who these people were. The guests who'd called and cancelled. Except obviously they hadn't. It appeared that their stalker had struck yet again.

Chapter Twelve

Heart pounding in her chest, Maddie waited. Once again, she felt frustration at her lack of control and inability to help Dade protect the lodge.

A moment later, he came barging back into the house, looking flustered and slightly out of breath. "The guests are here. You know, the ones who we thought called and cancelled."

Horrified, she stared. "But they didn't?"

"Obviously not. Which means someone else pretended to be them just to mess with us."

She didn't have to ask who. "Okay. We can deal with this. The cabins are all ready, and I'm sure we have enough food to cobble together some meals. How long are they staying?"

To her surprise, he hugged her. "Thank you. These guys have four nights and three days. It's our standard package."

She nodded. "What would you like me to do?"

"Come on outside and let me introduce you. Then we'll get them settled in their cabins, and we'll figure out a menu for their stay."

She took a deep breath and followed him outside.

A group of forty-something men, dressed in expensive casual wear, stood around three large, late-model SUVs, all black. It looked like a presidential motorcade or something.

Exchanging a quick glance with Dade, Maddie pasted a bright smile on her face. "Your cabins are all ready for you," she said. Since this group seemed comprised of relatively fit men, she doubted she'd need to get out the golf cart. "If you all will follow me, I can take you there."

"We're doing the same ones as last time," one of the men said, a tall, lanky guy who wore mirrored sunglasses and had an air of inflated self-importance.

Maddie recognized the type. She'd certainly dealt with a lot of them at her old job back in Dallas. "Since I wasn't here last year, I'll just let you all pick and choose the cabins," she said. "Follow me, please."

No one moved.

"Last year, the guys got out a golf cart so we didn't have to carry our luggage," another man said. "We'd like that same service this time."

Several of the other guests agreed.

"I'll get it." Dade's smile came off as more fierce than welcoming.

Though Maddie's first impulse was to rush to help Dade, she didn't. Instead, she attempted to make small talk while they waited, asking about their flight or drive and where they were from.

Naturally, the guy with the sunglasses took over the conversation, talking about his important job in banking and how he'd wanted to vacation at a golf resort, but his buddies here had insisted on Grady's Lodge. "Which means I'd better catch a lot of fish," he concluded, managing to sound vaguely threatening. "I've never been much for wilderness type things. I get enough of that living in Anchorage."

A couple of the other guys laughed. "You live in a condo downtown," one said. "And you've been here before. Last year, you said you had a great time."

Grinning back at them, he shrugged. "Maybe I did. We drank so much last time, I can't really remember if we did or not."

This comment was greeted by cheers and more laughter.

Dade and the golf cart came around the corner, and the guests began piling their luggage inside. Once everything had been loaded, leaving barely enough room for Dade to drive, he pulled away. "Follow me, gentlemen," he ordered.

Immediately, all the men trooped after the golf cart, without a second look at Maddie.

Relieved, she watched them go. After they'd left, she realized that she actually felt apprehensive. This group of guests brought a completely different vibe than the last one. But she could handle them. After all, she'd worked around men like them before.

She went back inside and started cleaning up from breakfast. At least it was still early, which would give her enough time to figure out what to serve for lunch. She grabbed a notepad and pen and started taking inventory. If she could get a menu planned out based on what they actually had, all would work out fine.

By the time Dade returned, she had the week's menu all planned. She handed him the notebook. "I'd like your thoughts. I checked on our supplies, and I can make all of these meals. Do you think this would work for this group?"

Accepting the book, he looked it over. "This is amazing," he said. "Good job."

She smiled. "I'll do all the meal prep and the cooking. Why don't you concentrate on seeing if you can get that old truck running?"

To her surprise, he grabbed her, hauled her up against him and kissed her. When they finally broke apart, their breathing was ragged. "You're something else, Maddie

Pierce," he said. "I wish Grady could have gotten to know you. He would have been so proud."

Swallowing hard, she turned away so he wouldn't see the sudden tears that sprung to her eyes.

A moment later, Dade cursed, which made her turn around. "All my tools were in the boat shed. Which means they're gone. I don't know how I'll be able to work on that truck now."

"Did Grady have a toolbox in his truck?" she asked, taking a guess. Working in property development, she'd been around more than one construction foreman with a pickup and one of those long, metal toolboxes bolted into the bed.

Dade nodded with relief. "He did." Grabbing her, he kissed her again, this time a quick press of his lips on hers. "I bet I can find what I need there." Glancing at his watch, he grimaced. "But first, I need to make sure these guys all get safely out on the water."

Once Dade raced off again, she got busy doing prep work in the kitchen. She'd make a simple but filling lunch. Shaved beef sandwiches with melted cheese and potato chips, which should go over well with this type of crowd.

For dinner, she got busy thawing several packages of bratwurst. She figured Dade could throw them on the grill, and she'd make a huge bowl of potato salad. While she got the water boiling for the potatoes, she opened an industrial-size can of beans and put them in the Crock-Pot, along with barbeque sauce, chopped onions and some green pepper. If she had to guess, she'd say this group would be hungry. Since she'd rather have too much food than not enough, she'd make a lot.

Several hours passed. Dade texted, letting her know the boats were coming back in, and they'd all be up there for lunch. Since she'd already gotten everything ready, she heated up the shaved beef, loaded the brioche buns and sprinkled shredded mozzarella cheese on top.

By the time the group trooped into the main dining area, she had everything ready.

As she'd expected, they fell upon the food like starving jackals. She watched from the doorway, not liking the way that Bradley guy stared at her. She couldn't tell what he was thinking.

Deciding it didn't matter, she retreated to the kitchen, where she'd kept back a couple sandwiches for herself and Dade. They ate together at the smaller kitchen table, listening to the good-natured joking and conversation from the other room.

"Did they catch a lot of fish?" she asked quietly.

"A few," Dade answered. "But that hotshot guy Bradley is mad that he didn't get any. Hopefully, he will when they go back out later."

After the guests finished their lunch, several of them declared they wanted to go back to their cabins and nap before the next fishing outing. Maddie waited for them to go, managing to hide her impatience.

Finally, only one man remained. Bradley. He remained sitting, watching as Maddie and Dade gathered up the paper plates and plastic utensils. Anyone else might have offered to help or, at the very least, left and gotten out of the way.

"Do you make a large profit here?" he asked, his dismissive tone indicating he felt he already knew the answer.

Maddie glanced at Dade. He'd stopped what he'd been doing to turn and look at Bradley. "I'm sorry, but we are not in the habit of discussing our operation with our guests."

"Why not?" Bradley challenged. "That answer makes it sound like you have something to hide."

Ignoring him, Dade carried the condiments back into the kitchen.

"What about you?" Bradley asked, directing his attention to Maddie. "I'm assuming even though you're new, you must know something about this business. Is it profitable?"

"Why?" Facing him, Maddie stared. "Are you thinking of investing?"

"Of course not," Bradley huffed. "I'm just curious how a dump like this stays in business."

"If you think the lodge is so terrible, why don't you leave?" Hands on hips, Maddie challenged him. "We have plenty of guests who truly enjoy their stay here."

His mocking laugh made her see red. "I don't know why you and your boyfriend are so defensive. I just asked a simple question. Does this place turn a profit?"

Exasperated, Maddie bit back what she really wanted to say. "None of your business. Now if you wouldn't mind vacating the dining room, we've got some cleaning up to do."

He finally stood, making a show of stretching lazily. Looking her up and down as if he could see through her clothes, he smiled. "I meant no offense," he said.

If he considered that an apology, he was wrong. She nodded, said nothing more and continued clearing the table. When she joined Dade in the kitchen, she heard the sound of the door opening and closing.

Depositing her tray of paper plates and plastic utensils in the trash, she went back to make sure the dining room had finally emptied.

"I don't like that Bradley guy," she said. "He's rude and entitled."

Dade looked up from the sink, where he'd been cleaning pans. "He was like that last year, if I remember. Just try not to let him bother you. He'll be gone soon enough."

Once he'd washed everything she'd used and stacked it in the dishwasher, he dried his hands on a dish towel. "I'm going to go down and refuel the boats. They'll be going back out in a couple of hours."

"I'll start doing prep work for dinner," she said. "That way, all I'll have to do is cook."

The rest of the afternoon passed uneventfully. Once the group of guests had left for the afternoon fishing trip, Dade went out to work some more on Grady's truck.

When dinner time arrived, the sunburned group filed in, exchanging jokes and teasing each other happily. Dade grilled bratwurst and once he'd delivered a heaping platter to the kitchen, he murmured to Maddie that he'd be back shortly. Nodding, Maddie served their guests without incident, and then, since Dade hadn't reappeared, she made two extra plates and set them aside. She'd wait to eat until Dade could.

Once they'd finished, everyone thanked her and filed out of the room. Judging from the conversations she'd overheard, they were eager to get the campfire going and break out the beer.

About thirty minutes after the house cleared out, Dade appeared. While he washed up, she warmed their food.

Thanking her, he ate quickly. "I'm going back out there," he said. "I think I've found the problem. It's the carburetor. I'm hoping I can get it fixed tonight."

She nodded, careful to hide her disappointment. "I'm planning on parking myself in front of the TV for a while. Unless there's something I can do to help you?"

To her surprise, he kissed her cheek. "No, but thank you for offering. I'll be back as soon as it gets dark or I get the truck started, whichever comes first."

And then he was gone.

She stared at the door for a few seconds after he left. Odd how she, a woman who'd lived alone her entire adult life, could feel his absence so strongly.

After settling down in front of the TV, she must have dozed off. The next thing she knew, Dade came bursting into the house. "I did it!" he exclaimed. "I got the truck running!"

Sitting up, she blinked at him, trying to emerge from the fog of sleep. "That's awesome."

"It is." He came over and kissed the top of her head. "Go back to sleep if you want. I'm going to jump in the shower. I need to wash off all this sweat and grime." He held out his dirty hands and laughed. "I'll show you the truck in the morning. It's almost dark outside, but at least we have transportation again."

After he left, she checked the time on her phone. Almost nine thirty. She got up, stretched and padded into the kitchen to get a glass of water.

The house phone rang. Startled since it was kind of late, Maddie glanced at the thing, debated whether or not to answer and then snatched the receiver out of the cradle.

"Hello?"

"This is Bradley Hartfield, from cabin 2. We are in need of more clean towels. Right away."

Before she could even reply, he hung up the phone. She noticed he didn't even try to be polite.

Since Dade had jumped in the shower, if their guests were going to get clean towels, she'd have to bring them. She wondered what had happened, because each cabin had been fully stocked with all the necessities, including towels. And judging by the sounds occasionally drifting up from below, most of the other men were still sitting around the campfire, drinking and telling fish stories.

Unsure what to do, she considered poking her head in the shower and getting Dade's thoughts. They'd both worked hard all day, her cooking and cleaning up after serving their guests both lunch and dinner, and him popping in to help before going back to trying to get the old pickup truck running.

The last group of guests—her first—had seemed to understand unspoken boundaries regarding requests. Maddie really didn't understand how anyone could phone after nine thirty at night and expect towels. Or anything, honestly. It wasn't as if she considered that an emergency.

Maybe the towels could wait until morning.

Except she didn't want to give any guest, especially one with an entitled attitude, a single reason to complain. This was a simple, straightforward request. She went into the laundry room, grabbed a couple of fresh, folded towels from the basket and headed toward the door. On the way, she grabbed one of the flashlights they kept on the counter and scribbled Dade a quick note, just in case.

Outside, darkness had settled over the sky. Glancing up, she still marveled at the vast star-scape visible out here, so far away from city lights. The scent of smoke from the campfire below drifted on the air, and she could still hear the sound of men's laughter. Which meant they were still enjoying their evening. And why shouldn't they be? They were on vacation, and though fishermen were early risers, it wasn't that late yet.

Cabin number two had lights shining from the window, which meant at least one of the guests must be inside. Maybe Bradley had decided to turn in early and take a shower. She stepped up onto the small front porch and knocked.

"I have your towels," she said.

A moment later, the door opened. A man she didn't recognize stood in the doorway, clad only in a wet towel. "I'm Bradley," he said. Another man holding a bottle of whiskey stood behind him, leering drunkenly.

"Here," Maddie said, shoving the towels at Bradley. "Breakfast will be at six in the morning."

Instead of reaching for the towels, he grabbed her arm and yanked her inside, kicking the door shut behind her.

ENJOYING THE SPRAY of hot water on his sore muscles, Dade wished he'd invited Maddie to join him in the shower. But he knew she'd been working hard to feed their unexpected guests. No doubt when he came out, she'd be sitting on the couch watching television and trying to relax.

He definitely could use some of that, too. In fact, he planned to join her in just a minute. Hopefully, he could convince her to join him in his bed later.

Wandering out into the living room, he looked around. Baffled to find the room empty, he took a quick peek into her bedroom. Not there.

In the kitchen, he found her note on the counter.

Taking towels to cabin 2. That Bradley guy wanted them right now.

Dade frowned. While he wasn't sure how long it'd been since she'd left, he didn't like this scenario at all.

He considered texting her, but decided he'd go down there and help her. After grabbing a flashlight, he made an abrupt turn and went back for his pistol.

Just as he opened the back door and stepped outside, a scream cut through the night air.

"Maddie!" he bellowed, taking off at a run.

By the time he reached cabin 2, all of the other guests had gotten there. The cabin door stood open and lopsided, telling Dade someone had likely kicked it in.

He sprinted up onto the small porch, pushed through the men and saw Maddie standing in the corner. Her eyes were wild, her clothing torn, and she clutched one of his flashlights like a weapon. The towels she'd brought were scattered around her feet.

Bradley sat on the floor, nursing a cut to his head. Another man sat on the edge of the bed, drinking from an open bottle of whiskey and clearly too drunk to register what was going on.

Though Dade wasn't sure what had happened, he had a pretty good idea.

He went to Maddie first. "Are you all right?"

It took a moment for her gaze to focus on his face. "I am now," she replied, her mouth tight. Her gaze flashed past him to Bradley. "That fool tried to mess with the wrong woman."

Tamping down his fury, Dade slowly turned to look at Bradley. "Are you sober?"

Slowly, the other man shook his head. "Not really."

By now, the rest of the group had crowded inside.

"How many of you are sober enough to drive?" Dade asked. "Or have all of you been drinking heavily?"

The group fell silent, shuffling their feet and looking at each other.

"Since I don't want to send impaired drivers out onto the road, you can pack up tonight and leave in the morning." Dade let his voice reflect his disgust. "Your time here at the lodge is over. And you are not welcome back."

Now all of them started talking at once. Most of them

protested, a few of them openly chastising Bradley and his roommate.

Ignoring all of this, Dade took Maddie's arm. "Let's go," he said, leading her through the crowd and back toward the path to the main house.

No one followed.

Maddie held on to his arm with a death grip the entire way. Once they'd reached the house, he held open the door. She finally let go of him and stumbled inside.

He stayed close to her all the way into the living room, where the TV was still on. Grabbing the remote, he turned it off. "Do you want to sit down?" he asked.

With a nod, she dropped onto the sofa.

Sitting down right beside her, he took her hand. "Do you want to tell me what happened?"

"Sure." Her mouth tightened. "I got a call demanding fresh towels right now. I took them, and when I knocked on the door, that drunk idiot yanked me inside and tried to assault me."

"How were you able to fight him off?" he asked.

"Luckily, since I worked with so many construction workers at the job I had in Dallas, I took a couple of self-defense classes. Just as a precaution. To be honest, I never had to use any of what I learned until tonight. That fool never saw it coming."

He squeezed her hand. "Do you want to press charges?"

"Charges?" Slowly, she shook her head. "I'm not sure. Right now, I just want him out of here." With a loud sigh, she made a visible attempt to relax, rolling her neck. "Thank you for telling them they have to leave."

"He's lucky I didn't beat him to a pulp," Dade said, meaning it. "But since you already did that, I didn't see a need."

For the first time since he'd found her, she cracked a smile. "True." She thought for a moment. "For a minute there, I even considered the idea that Bradley might be my stalker."

Since he had no idea where she might be going with this, he waited.

"But then I realized, no. He isn't. He's just an entitled jerk from Anchorage."

He put his arm around her and pulled her close. She rested her head on his shoulder, taking long, deep breaths until some of the tension seemed to leave her.

They slept in the same bed that night, though they didn't make love. He simply held her, offering comfort and nothing more. She'd been through a lot, and he counted his blessings that it hadn't been worse.

Though his body needed sleep, he couldn't turn his mind off. Thank goodness she knew self-defense. He shuddered to think what might have happened to her if she hadn't.

With Maddie sleeping soundly, snuggled close, he finally dozed off. He knew she'd let him know if she wanted anything more than comfort.

When he woke in the morning before dawn fully aroused, he slipped from the bed while she still slept. Careful not to wake her, he took a quick shower. By the time he went into the kitchen and made himself his first cup of coffee, he felt relatively normal.

Meanwhile, Maddie continued to sleep. Dade stood there a moment in the doorway to the bedroom and watched her. He hoped when she did wake, she'd feel at least refreshed. Having the guests, especially Bradley, gone would no doubt help, too. He knew it would be better for him since if he saw that Bradley guy again, he'd have to fight to keep from punching him in the face.

Pushing away a surge of anger, Dade sipped his coffee and took several deep breaths. As he often did these days, he thought of Grady. Picturing the older man's reaction to someone laying hands on his granddaughter made Dade realize Bradley better consider himself lucky that he'd only been asked to leave. Maddie could press charges. Even though she'd said she wasn't sure, she might still change her mind and decide to. Dade hoped she would.

When he walked outside shortly after sunrise, he saw the three black SUVs were still there. Fine, since he figured the guests likely weren't even awake yet. He'd simply walk around the place, do what needed to be done and basically stick around to make sure they left as soon as possible.

Right now, he wanted to check on the boats and make sure they were all tied up properly. More than once, he'd had to go out and retrieve a boat that hadn't been secured.

As he walked past the fire pit, the embers from last night's blaze still glowed. Beer cans and bottles littered the ground all around it, along with pieces of trash from snacks. Since he figured the boats would likely be in a similar state, he went back to the house and got several large trash bags. Maddie still slept, so he took care to be extra quiet.

Then he began cleaning everything up.

Just as he'd filled the first trash bag, the door to cabin one opened. One of the guests, a short, quiet man named Robert, emerged. When he caught sight of Dade, he walked over, his expression apologetic.

"I just wanted to let you know that the rest of us don't condone Bradley's actions," he said, shoving his hands into his jeans pockets. "I barely even know him, but in the short time I've spent with him, I dislike him immensely."

Dade nodded, pretty sure he knew what the man was going to say.

"That said, I'd like you to reconsider making the rest of us leave. Bradley and his buddy, yes. What he did was wrong. Beyond wrong. But most of us were simply enjoying ourselves around the fire. We had no idea what he planned to do. And as soon as we found out, we tried to stop him."

Since his anger from the night before still simmered deep inside him, Dade had to force himself to consider Robert's words. The other man had a point. Except for the mess they'd left, the rest of the group hadn't done anything wrong.

"Fine. The rest of you can finish out your stay. Only the two guys in cabin 2 need to go. Can I trust you to make sure that happens?"

"Of course." Robert nodded. "We're all pretty pissed off about it, so it will be our pleasure."

Robert's unusually formal way of talking made Dade smile. "One more thing," he said. "Can I ask you to talk to everyone about not littering? I've been picking up trash from this entire area."

"My apologies." Robert looked down. "I will definitely speak to them about that."

"Great." Dade picked up the last two beer bottles and straightened. "I'd appreciate it."

Robert nodded. "Consider it done. And thank you so much. I have to say, I'm really glad you agreed. I haven't caught my big fish yet. That's the entire reason I came on this trip." He took a deep breath. "It's my first time here. I never expected anything to happen like this."

Hearing this, Dade felt a little better about his decision to let the rest of the group stay. "I hope you catch that fish," he said, clapping Robert on the back. "Just make sure Bradley and his buddy get in their SUV and leave, okay?"

"Will do. I'll tell the others once they wake up. I thought

I'd go for a hike and try to clear some of the cobwebs from my head." Robert gave a sheepish smile. "I'm not used to drinking that much beer."

"You got your bear spray?" Dade asked.

"Yep." Robert pulled it from his shirt pocket. "I wouldn't go out into the woods without it."

"Good deal," Dade turned away. "Be careful out there, man."

Once the other man had walked away, Dade made his way down to the boat slips. As he'd expected, while the boats had all been securely tied, the guests left a mess inside them. He went from one to another, picking up litter. By the time he reached the last boat, his trash bags were full. Now he'd just need to haul them back to the house. By the time he did that, he hoped everyone would be awake. He couldn't wait to evict Bradley and his friend.

As he made his way back up the path, Robert came charging from the woods. "Dade," he shouted, his complexion red. "You've got to come quickly. I found a body in the woods!"

Chapter Thirteen

Snuggling down deep into her pillow, Maddie took her time opening her eyes. When she did and realized Dade had already risen, she sighed. Disappointed but not surprised, she glanced at the clock. Nearly seven, which meant she'd overslept a little. But since the guests would be going home, she planned to enjoy as much of the day as possible.

The sounds of someone shouting outside had her jumping to her feet. She dressed hurriedly and rushed to the back door.

Halfway down the path to the cabins, Dade stood talking to one of the guests. The man was gesturing wildly, clearly upset. Other guests were emerging from their cabins, likely because of the noise.

Maddie hurried down, glancing quickly over at cabin 2 as she didn't want to see either of those men's faces again. That door remained closed.

"What's going on?" she asked as she reached Dade and the guest.

Expression grim, Dade shook his head. "I've got a call in to Officer Taggert. Robert here found a woman's body in the woods. I went up there with him to take a look, and I'm afraid it's the missing girl from town."

For a quick second, Maddie couldn't catch her breath. "Is she dead?"

"Unfortunately, yes." Dade took her arm. "From the looks of it, she was murdered. It's not anything you need to see."

Straightening, she pulled herself free. "I appreciate you wanting to protect me," she said, choosing her words with care. "But if I'm going to survive whatever this is, I have to be able to know exactly what's going on."

Gaze locked on hers, Dade slowly nodded. "When Officer Taggert gets here, you're definitely welcome to accompany us to the body, if that's what you want."

Robert looked from one to the other. "I really would prefer to stay and catch my big fish. But this scenario changes things. I find I need your assurances that it will be safe."

"I don't know what to tell you," Dade replied. "Both victims, if they were killed by the same person, were women. Since you're not…"

"My gender gives me better odds," Robert finished. "Though, I will say that finding a dead body while out for a morning stroll is disconcerting, to say the least."

Just then, something caught Robert's eye, and he grimaced. "It looks like the occupants of the second cabin are emerging. Let me go on over there and make sure they leave right away."

Both she and Dade watched as Robert hurried away. Since Maddie didn't want to see Bradley's face ever again, she kept her attention on Dade. "What did he mean by saying he wanted to stay? I thought they were all leaving this morning."

"He pointed out that he and the others had nothing to do with Bradley's actions and that they all rushed over as soon as they figured out what was going on to try and stop it. So I agreed the rest of them could stay as long as Bradley and his roommate leave."

"That makes sense." She touched Dade's arm. "Does it look like they're leaving? I'm sorry, but I really don't want to look."

"Right now, they appear to be in discussion. I'm keeping an eye on things."

"Robert has an interesting way of talking," she commented, desperately needing a distraction. "Very formal. Like an older person. I kind of like it."

"He seems like a nice guy." Dade kept his attention fixed on whatever was going on over at cabin 2. "I'm hoping those other two don't give him any trouble."

"Me, too."

"Wait here," Dade ordered. "It looks like they're arguing. I'll be right back."

Suddenly, Maddie realized she hated allowing herself to feel as if she'd done something wrong. She spun around and marched herself back to where both Dade and Robert were arguing with a clearly furious Bradley.

"Is there a problem?" she asked, her voice icy. "Because if there is, since Officer Taggert with the Alaska State Troopers is already on his way, I'm thinking I might just go ahead and press charges."

"For what?" Bradley asked, sneering. "Nothing happened."

She kept her head up and held his gaze. "For assault, to begin with. You put your hands on me, which definitely wasn't welcomed."

Bradley opened his mouth, likely to argue, but his friend grabbed his arm and steered him back toward the cabin.

"We're going to pack," the friend said, glancing back

over his shoulder at Maddie. "We'll be out of here in just a few minutes."

As promised, they'd vacated the cabin, loaded up their black SUV with their luggage and driven away all before Officer Taggert pulled up.

Lucky for them, Maddie thought darkly. But she had to admit, just having them gone made her feel lighter.

"Good morning," the police officer greeted them. He got out a pad of paper and a pen and looked at them expectantly. "Why don't you tell me what's happened. Start at the beginning."

"There's been a lot going on," Dade said slowly. "Starting with Maddie getting a bunch of vaguely threatening text messages."

"Threatening how?" Taggert asked.

Maddie shook her head. "That's just it, they're intentionally vague. He's using an app to disguise his actual phone number. He clearly wants me to go back to Texas, but hasn't actually said why. We don't know why he feels this would be to his benefit."

"The last group of guests spotted a stranger trespassing on lodge property," Dade said. "He was watching them. I went looking, but other than finding the remains of a small campfire, I never was able to catch him. The guests didn't like having him lurking."

"I didn't appreciate that either," Maddie added.

"And then he set the fire at the boat shed and blew up my Jeep," Dade continued, his large arms crossed. "He's escalating and is now an actual danger, but we still have no idea what he wants."

"But no actual proof he did any of that." Taggert looked from one to the other. "Do you feel this is the same individual who murdered the two women?"

"We don't know," Maddie answered. "But it seems likely."

"I see." Grim-faced, the police office considered everything for a moment. "I think you should try to get him to tell you what he wants." He took a deep breath. "My forensic team is expected to arrive this afternoon. Now they have two bodies to examine. We need to try and keep wildlife away from this new one. But first, I've asked the parents of the missing girl to come out here. If it's her, they can give us a positive ID."

Maddie closed her eyes. Her heart ached for the family. She couldn't imagine the anguish of having to identify the body of a beloved child.

"I'd better get back up to the house and make these guests some breakfast," she said. "It'll be something simple, like pancakes with bacon and sausage."

After the group had eaten, Dade went down to the boat slips with them to see them off. When he returned, he helped her do some meal prep for the lunch and dinner. "I promise I'll be cooking tonight," he said. "Steaks on the grill along with baked potatoes. It'll be a welcome break from salmon all the time."

This made her smile. He had a point.

The family of the missing girl arrived right after they'd finished getting the food ready. Office Taggert pulled up right behind them.

Dade went out to meet them, with Maddie following right behind. "I'm so sorry," she murmured, meaning it.

The woman nodded, her eyes red and swollen from crying. Her husband kept his arm around her, supporting her even though he appeared on the verge of collapse himself.

"This way, folks." Taggert gestured that they should follow him. Silently, they all trooped after him, on a hiking path that any other time might have sparked exclamations of beauty.

Though she'd insisted on going, Maddie hung back. She realized she had no desire to see the body, and she didn't feel right being a witness to these people's private grief.

Noticing, Dade slowed his steps and then backed up to her. "Are you all right?" he asked.

"I'm fine," she replied, even though she wasn't certain she was. "I'm worried about those folks." She gestured, even though the others were no longer in sight.

"Me, too." He took her hand, just as the dead girl's mother let out an awful, anguished cry.

Tears in her eyes, Maddie stood and bowed her head. When she raised it again, she met Dade's gaze. "We have to stop this," she said. "Before anyone else gets killed or hurt."

Later, while Officer Taggert spoke with the family, Maddie and Dade returned to the house. They had lunch to prepare because soon the remaining guests would be looking for a meal to carry them through their afternoon fishing session.

Once everyone had been fed and they returned to their cabins, Dade and Maddie cleaned up. They'd barely finished when the police forensics van arrived. Officer Taggert, having finished with the family, had joined the guests for lunch. He ate with a quiet, determined air and didn't interact with anyone else.

After the meal, when all the guests had drifted back to their cabins, Taggert took his leave. "I'll be back later to meet the forensics team," he promised. "Thanks for the grub."

Since Dade had already started washing the dishes, he didn't respond. Maddie walked the officer to the door and thanked him for coming. Then she went back to the kitchen and helped Dade finish cleaning up.

"What do you think about Taggert?" Dade asked.

"I like him," she replied. "He seems focused on doing his job."

"I agree." Dade put the last pan into the dishwasher, added soap and turned the machine on. "Is it just me, or is today dragging?"

"It's been a long day," she said and sighed. One of the remaining guests had gifted her a bottle of white wine as a gesture of good will. She'd stuck it in the refrigerator, and now that it had gotten cold, she poured herself a glass. "Would you like some?" she asked Dade.

"No thanks." He lifted up his glass of iced tea. "I'm good."

"Sorry." She sat. "I forgot you told me you didn't drink." She glanced at her wine glass and frowned. "Is it okay if I do around you?"

"It's fine," he replied. "I used to have a problem, so I quit. Being around alcohol doesn't bother me."

"Okay, good. I'm going to go sit outside, if you want to join me." Taking a sip of her wine, she exhaled. "I really just need to try and relax and clear my head."

He followed her out to the front porch. The fishermen were still in their cabins, no doubt resting up before another night sitting around the bonfire.

"You know, Taggert made sense," Dade said, sitting down in the rocking chair next to her. "We need to figure out a way to get this guy to tell us what the hell he wants."

"Maybe." She shrugged, taking another sip of her wine.

"Though, at this point," Dade continued, "I think it'd be better if we could just trick him into letting us capture him."

"Us? Wouldn't that be something the police need to handle? This guy is guilty of several crimes."

"If we could prove he's the one who did all of this." Dade's expression echoed the frustration in his voice. "Right now, we have nothing to go on other than some texts and spotting a stranger trespassing. None of that would hold up in a court of law."

"Unless the forensic people find DNA on the murder victims. That would clinch it, right?" she asked.

"It would be enough to charge him, once they figure out who he actually is."

She sighed. "I hate to seem like I'm avoiding reality, but I really need to decompress. Do you mind if we change the subject?"

Just then, in some kind of ironic twist, her phone pinged. Immediately, she tensed.

Dade sat up straighter. "It's been a while since we've heard from him."

"True." Instead of looking at her screen, she passed the phone over to him. "Here. You deal with it."

You should be dead, he read out loud. Immediately, he typed something and sent it. "I asked him how that would benefit him, if he killed us both."

No response. In fact, her phone sat silent for so long she figured the stalker would do like he always did and ghost them until his next text from yet a different number.

Then, as Dade appeared ready to hand it back to her, it pinged again. "Vengeance, he says. He feels we stole something from him and should pay with our lives."

"Ask him what," she prompted. "What did we steal?"

But before Dade could text it, another ping sounded.

Grady's Lodge should have been mine. Grady owed me that much.

Looking up from the phone, Dade frowned. "Who is this guy?"

"I don't know," she replied. "Since you've lived here for years, I wonder if you know him."

Shrugging, Dade sent another text. "I asked him if he's willing to meet in person to discuss this."

Her heart skipped a beat. "I'm not sure how I feel about that."

"I doubt he'll agree, but I have to try. We need to end this, once and for all."

Though they both waited, the stalker didn't text again.

THE NEXT MORNING, Dade woke up alone in his bed and reached for Maddie. It took him a few seconds before he remembered they'd each slept in their own rooms. The guests would be here until tomorrow, so they had one more day of fishing left. Thus far, Robert's big fish had eluded him, though he remained ever hopeful.

Padding into the kitchen for a much-needed cup of coffee, he noticed Maddie's bedroom door remained closed. Since the sun had just started to rise, he tried to be as quiet as possible.

Nevertheless, he'd just taken his first sip of coffee when Maddie emerged, looking tousled and sleepy and absolutely gorgeous.

For a heartbeat or two, he froze, simply staring. Luckily, she didn't appear to notice.

Only once she'd made her coffee and taken a drink did she look at him. "What's on the agenda for today?" she asked.

"Once the guests go fishing, I'm going to go look up one

of Grady's oldest friends," Dade announced. "I'm hoping she might know who this person is claiming he should have inherited Grady's Lodge."

"She? Did Grady have a girlfriend?"

Dade smiled. "You might call her that. They had an arrangement. Interesting woman. I always liked her."

"I'd like to go with you," Maddie said. "I'm willing to try anything that gets us a step closer to identifying this person."

First, they needed to make breakfast. Since Dade hadn't cooked in a few days, it would be his turn. He decided to make a bunch of scrambled eggs, hash brown patties, toast and bacon. While he cooked, Maddie poured several glasses of orange and tomato juice and set the table.

Right on time, the guests trooped in. Since today would be their last day, they were ready to get out onto the water.

As soon as they finished eating, they headed to their cabins to grab their things.

"I'll meet you down at the boat slips," Dade said. He helped Maddie clear the table.

"Go ahead and go," she told him. "I'll clean up."

Grateful, he kissed her cheek. She froze, before turning to smile at him. "Come here, you," she said, pulling him close and pressing her mouth against his. "If you're going to kiss me, you might as well do it right."

Laughing, he kissed her one more time, lingering a little longer. Then he took off, mood jubilant despite all that they had going on. Maddie brought out the best in him, somehow. He couldn't help but wonder if he affected her the same way.

When he reached the boat slips, Robert and one other guest were already there, stowing their supplies.

"Today's the day," Robert exclaimed, smiling broadly. "I'm going to catch the big one. I can feel it in my bones."

"I hope you do," Dade replied, meaning it.

Over the next fifteen minutes, the rest of the group showed up, chose their boats and headed out. Dade waited until every last one had gone around the bend in the river before returning to the main house.

When he arrived, he found Maddie sitting on the front porch, reading. She looked up as he approached and smiled. The warmth in her eyes made his breath catch.

"Hey," she greeted him. "What's up?"

"We've got a few hours to look up one of Grady's old friends. Are you still in?"

"Yes." She put down her book and jumped up. "Let's go."

Taking her arm, he led the way to Grady's old truck. Proud of the work he'd done to get it running, he helped her up. Then he climbed in the driver's side and turned the key. Instantly, the engine rumbled to life.

"First try," Maddie said. "I'm impressed."

"Thanks." He waited until she'd fastened her seat belt before shifting into Drive. "Brace yourself. This thing rides rough."

Which turned out to be the understatement of the year. And the ancient truck didn't even have power steering, so turning became more of a chore than usual.

"Grady didn't have any other relatives in the area?" she asked.

"Not that I know of," Dade answered. "Grady and I did just about everything together. He mentioned one distant cousin, but that guy lived in California."

"So you're thinking this stalker might be a friend?"

Dade shrugged. "Anything is possible. I know Grady

kept his relationships low-key and quiet, but I'm also wondering if this is related to his former girlfriend."

Turning her head, she stared. "You mean it might be possible that the person who's been texting me and doing all of these horrible things might be female?"

"Doubtful. Angela wouldn't do anything like that. I know her too well. As far as any other woman, it's unlikely, but you never know. Officer Taggert says females are rarely, if ever, serial killers. And with two dead bodies, he's inclined to think the murderer is a male."

Maddie went quiet, clearly considering his words. "What about a team? One man, one woman. Like maybe the woman has a brother or a boyfriend who's helping her get what she feels she should have."

"That's another strong possibility. The only thing is, Grady was pretty old, and all of his friends are, too."

"And whoever killed those two women had to be stronger than them," she added. "Which would rule out most seventy-five-to-eighty-year-olds."

"Right. That's what I'm thinking, too. But we won't know until we have a few conversations. The first place we're going is Angela Bishop's house. That's the woman I told you about. She and Grady had an arrangement for years. I think she might have even known your mother. She was always kind to me. I want to get her take on all of this and see if she can think of anyone."

Maddie nodded. With the sun shining in her long black hair and her blue eyes glowing, she looked stunningly beautiful. And he swore he could see some of Grady in her features.

Pushing the thought and the feelings that accompanied it away, he drove from memory to the little frame house where Angela Bishop lived. He'd been there many times growing up, though he hadn't gone back after Grady had gotten so sick. Angela had visited once or twice in the beginning, but he hadn't seen her again until she'd attended the funeral.

Parking in front, he killed the engine and turned to Maddie. "I hate to show up here unannounced, but I don't have her phone number."

Maddie eyed the overgrown lawn and out-of-control shrubs. "It almost looks like the house is empty."

"It does," he agreed. "But Blake is a small town. If anything happened to Angela, I would have heard about it."

He led the way up the front porch, noting the rickety condition of the wood. "I need to come back out here and make some repairs," he said. "I feel bad. I got so caught up in taking care of Grady and then keeping the lodge going that I never checked in on her. Clearly, she could have used some help."

"She doesn't have any family that live close?" Maddie asked.

"Not that I know of." Dade pressed the doorbell, waited and then tried it again. Nothing. Glancing at Maddie, he tried knocking. Three sharp raps on the wooden door. Loud enough even for an elderly woman with poor hearing.

But the door never opened, and as far as he could tell, there were no signs of movement inside of the house. Just in case, Dade tried the handle, but the door was locked.

"I guess she's not home," he finally said, looking around. "I'm not sure if she's still driving, but there's no car here."

"Unless it's in the garage." Maddie pointed to a rickety frame building with a single garage door. There were no windows, so he had no way of knowing if there might be a vehicle inside.

"I'll ask around in town," Dade decided. "Before he got

sick, Grady used to meet up with a couple of guys at the donut shop once a week. They'd sit around, drink coffee and shoot the breeze."

"I guess we'd better go." Maddie turned to make her way back toward the truck. As she did, a beat-up four-door Toyota careened around the corner and pulled into the driveway.

Dade grabbed Maddie's arm. "That looks like Angela's car."

But instead of a petite woman with long, wavy white hair, a slender man with wire-rimmed glasses and a goatee got out. "Can I help you folks?" he asked, his tone friendly.

"We're looking for Angela Bishop," Dade said, keeping Maddie's arm tucked into his. "Do you happen to know where we might find her?"

"She's in a memory care facility in Anchorage," the man said, smiling easily as he made his way toward them. "I'm Chet Bishop, her nephew. I'm about the only family she has left."

Introducing himself and Maddie, Dade shook his hand. Then Maddie did the same. Chet had a firm, steady grip, which made Dade inclined to like him.

"I can get you the address if you'd like," Chet offered. "I'm sure she'd love to have visitors, even if she can't always recognize people she knows."

"That'd be great, thank you."

Chet pulled out his phone. "What's your number? I'll text it to you."

Since Dade had expected the man to jot something down, he hesitated. Then, with Chet eyeing him expectantly, Dade rattled off the number.

Typing quickly, Chet looked up from his phone, still smiling. "There you go."

Dade's phone pinged. There was Chet's text, with the name of the memory care facility and the address. "Thanks," Dade said. "Have you been in town long?"

Chet looked from Dade to Maddie and back again. "Not really. Why do you ask?"

The last thing Dade wanted to do was make the other man aware of his suspicions. "No reason. Blake is a small town, and people talk. Since I haven't heard anything at all about you or about Angela, I was just curious."

"I keep to myself," Chet responded, the flatness of his tone no doubt meant to discourage any further questions.

Nevertheless, Dade continued to press. "Are you staying here at Angela's house or are you selling it?"

"I'm just visiting for now," Chet answered, his narrow gaze revealing his annoyance. "And yes, I'm staying here and getting a few things taken care of for my aunt. She hasn't decided yet if she wants to sell the place or hang on to it."

With a patently bored expression, he glanced at his watch. "Well, it was awfully nice meeting you. I'm sure I'll see you around."

"I'm sure you will," Dade replied. "Nice to meet you, too."

Maddie murmured something similar as they turned away.

Chet stood on the porch watching as they got in their truck.

Once they were out of sight of the house, Dade shook his head. "I'm really sorry to hear about Angela. But I'm glad she has family looking out for her."

"Me, too." Maddie half turned in her seat, looking back toward the house even though they couldn't see it. "Was it just me or did that guy seem a little defensive?"

Dade considered. "He did," he conceded. "Maybe because placing a relative in a facility is a difficult decision. If Anchorage wasn't so far, I'd definitely make the trip and pay her a visit. Right now, I plan to call and check on her."

She nodded. "This might sound like a weird question, but do you think there's a chance that Chet might be the stalker?"

"There's always a chance," Dade answered bluntly. "And since he's the only new person around here, I plan to pass his name on to Officer Taggert. It can't hurt to have him run an investigation on Chet."

"I agree. Do we have time to stop in town?"

"Not now. We'd better get back to the lodge in case that group comes back with a boatload of fish. Plus, those old men that Grady used to hang out with only meet up in the mornings. We'll have to try and catch them another time, after our guests leave."

She nodded. "This sounds odd, but I'm glad we at least have a suspect. Even if he's the only one, it's better than nothing."

"True. I'd really just like this to be over so we can get on with our lives." He glanced at her, struck by a thought. "You haven't even gone fishing yet, and we're on our second set of guests."

"That's fine." Her quick response made him smile. "I don't really need to actually fish, do I? So far, everything has worked out just fine."

He decided to take pity on her. "You don't have to if you don't want to. But someday, I think you and I should go just for fun. It's relaxing."

"For everyone except the fish," she quipped. "Seriously, I'm good. Also, don't ever expect me to hunt either. It's just not my thing."

If he hadn't been driving, he would have pulled her in for a thorough kiss. Instead, he laughed and told himself he'd kiss her later, once they were back home. Together.

When they pulled back into the driveway, they saw the state police forensics van had gone. Officer Taggert's cruiser sat in front of the house, and he'd apparently been waiting for them, since he got out as soon as they pulled up.

"We've got everything we need," he said. "The body is on the way to the lab so they can determine cause of death. We were able to pull some DNA samples, so hopefully we can get a match."

Dade nodded. "There's someone I'd like you to look into," he said. "He says he's Angela Bishop's nephew and is staying at her place. His name is Chet, and here's his phone number and the address."

Taggert scribbled down the information. "I'll check him out. Meanwhile, you two watch your backs. If you see anything out of the ordinary, call me. I'll be hanging around town until after Memorial Day."

Startled, Dade checked the date on his phone. "I hadn't realized it's this close to the end of the month," he said. "There's always a cookout and a parade, though on a smaller scale than the Fourth of July."

Taggert grinned. "Yes, I've heard. I'll see you there."

With that, he got into his car and drove away.

Dade watched him go, unable to shake a sense of foreboding. He didn't know why, but he felt like all this would be coming to a head soon. He'd have to make sure to keep Maddie safe if it did. No matter what it cost him.

Chapter Fourteen

The guests came back an hour later, which gave Maddie enough time to help Dade with dinner prep and to make a quick dessert. Robert had caught his big fish, and his jubilant mood had everyone smiling. Since it was their last night, Dade grilled brats. They served them up with sauerkraut, a giant pot of barbequed beans and buns.

Declaring themselves ravenous, the guests ate and laughed and ate some more, until they said they were stuffed. That was when Maddie brought out the strawberry shortcake she'd whipped together. Everyone oohed and awed, and then they fell upon the dessert like a pack of starving wolves. She barely managed to rescue a couple of small slices for her and Dade. They ate them quickly in the kitchen before returning to the big dining table and starting to clear it.

As the group began to make their way back to their cabins, Robert lingered. "I wanted to thank you both," he said, looking from Dade to Maddie and back again. "I wasn't even in the original group slated to come, but one of the others dropped out, so I was able to step into their place. I really enjoyed this vacation, and I can't wait to show off my fish."

"I'm glad you had fun," Dade replied, slipping his arm around Maddie's shoulders and pulling her close. "And I've got everyone's fish packed in dry ice, ready to take with you. I'll see you again in the morning."

"Roger that." For a second, Robert's smile slipped. But then Maddie told herself she must have imagined it because when she looked again, it was back in place.

After he left, she looked at Dade. "I have to say, I'll be glad when we have the place to ourselves again. How long do we have before the next bunch arrives?"

"The usual three days. Memorial Day is Monday, and a lot of people take advantage of the long weekend. The next group arrives on Friday. We have enough time to clean up and get everything ready."

"Then that will have to do," she replied. "Want to join me out on the front porch? It'll be nice to just sit and relax for a little bit."

"Sure." He poured two glasses of iced tea and handed one to her. "Let's go."

Outside, the afternoon's heat lingered in the air. As they settled into the rocking chairs, Maddie sighed. "This is my favorite part of the day."

His answering smile started a warmth deep inside her. "Me, too."

When her cell phone rang, she actually jumped. It had been so long since she'd received an actual call. Picking it up, she stared at the name displayed on her screen.

Mighty DFW Property Management Company

Her old job. For a heartbeat or two, she considered whether or not to answer. The parting had been less than amicable, and she couldn't imagine any conversation after the fact improving on that.

Dade looked at her, frowning. "Are you going to take that?"

She sighed and pressed the button to decline the call. "No. It's my former employer. I have nothing to say to them."

"Are you okay?" he asked, his gentle tone reflecting his concern.

"You know what?" she replied. "I definitely am okay."

When he reached for her hand, she slipped hers into his willingly. She liked touching him. The contact always made her feel as if she could draw upon his gentle strength. She'd never known anyone like him.

In fact, she thought she might love him. No, she corrected herself. She did love him. With all of her heart. She could only hope that someday he might feel the same way.

At any other point in her life, a thought like that would have shocked and dismayed her. Now though, it only felt right. She'd come to this place, to this new life, for a reason. And since she suspected her grandfather had done a bit of matchmaking with his bequest, she wished she could thank him. He'd given her a new life.

As she took a long drink of her iced tea, her phone chimed, letting her know she had a voicemail.

Curious, she played it back on speaker.

"We'd like to apologize for how the events leading up to your termination played out. We've always regarded you as one of our best employees. In fact, we'd like to offer you your old position back, with a twenty-five percent raise in salary and a new title to go with it. Please contact me immediately to discuss. My name is Grant Resinor, the new director of human resources. I'm at extension 5567."

Stunned, she stared at her phone. "Wow," she said, glancing up at Dade. "I definitely didn't expect that. Especially since I was told my position had been discontinued, and I was no longer needed."

Expressionless, he nodded. "What do you want to do?"

What did she want to do? Odd question, but she liked that he bothered to ask. Even though, judging by his shuttered gaze, he thought he already knew the answer.

She sighed. "None of that matters anyway. By the terms of the will, I have to stay here for one entire year."

Instead of agreeing, he turned in his seat to stare at her. "True. But the attorney seemed to think there's a way to circumvent that clause, if we both agree. So what do you actually want, Maddie Pierce? If you want your old life, there's got to be a way you can have it. That way we both get what we want."

What the…? Was he trying to get rid of her? She shook her head and looked away. "I'm turning it down," she said flatly. "I made a decision to honor Grady's wishes, and that's what I plan to do."

Finally, he looked away. "Up to you." His dismissive tone grated on her.

"You know what?" she shot back. "I do have plans, though. For the lodge. There's a reason my old employer wanted me back. I'm really good at what I do. I've done a ton of research, checking out the other, really profitable fishing lodges in this part of Alaska."

At first, he didn't respond. Since she figured he'd shoot down her ideas without even listening, she simply stopped talking.

"And?" he finally asked, when the silence had stretched into minutes. "I know some of the larger ones have amenities we don't. They have more staff and other facilities to entertain the guests. And they attract a completely different sort of clientele than we do."

Impressed despite herself, she nodded.

"I've done the same research," he admitted. "When Grady first made me a partner, and I thought I had things to prove. I pitched those same ideas to him several years ago."

"And what happened? Was he receptive or totally unwilling to consider any changes?"

"He agreed to let me implement a few things," he said, his expression rueful.

Surprised, she stared. "And?"

"But first, I had to come up with the money. Those kinds of changes—additions, more employees, upgrades—all cost money. While we do make a profit now, there's not enough to make any kind of meaningful changes. And we have to live on the excess once the tourist fishing season is over. Running out of funds during the winter months would be disastrous."

She shrugged, thinking of how things were done in the world she'd recently left. "Then take out a loan. Once your profits increase, you can pay it back quickly."

"Grady's number one rule is no debt. And I do agree with that," he said. "We own everything outright. As long as we pay our taxes, no one can take anything away from us."

"I can't disagree with you there," she admitted. "But sometimes you have to take risks."

"Not with this," he said firmly. "This lodge is my entire life. Yours now, too. And I have to say, I now see the beauty of Grady's vision. The simplicity and rustic experience is what brings our guests back year after year. People wanting a more luxurious vacation can go to one of the other lodges. It all works out."

"But there's so much money being left on the table," she protested. "It takes money to make money."

"Truth." He looked at her, and the warmth she saw in his gaze took her breath away. "You haven't been here very long, Maddie. Give it a bit longer. You've been fitting in really well, I think. You might be surprised at how fulfilling this life can be."

She thought about his words for a few minutes. To her surprise, she realized he might be right. She'd been so focused on her vision of how things should be that she hadn't allowed herself to appreciate how awesome they actually were. Changing things might ruin the charm.

Finally, Dade cleared his throat. "Are you going to call them back?" he asked. "Because if you really want your old job back, maybe we can reach some sort of agreement."

Hearing him say that hurt more than she could believe possible. Lifting her chin, she looked him right in the face and smiled. "We already have an agreement, remember? That's the only one I'm willing to concentrate on. You're not getting rid of me so easily, Dade Anson."

She pushed up from her chair and headed back into the house. Whether or not she called Grant Resinor back didn't matter. The only thing she cared about at this moment was Grady. Had she imagined their growing closeness, the partnership that seemed so amazing? Was he actually secretly wanting to get rid of her, so he could have the lodge to himself?

Once inside the house, she felt restless in a way she hadn't since arriving here. Before, receiving a job offer and an apology from what she'd considered her dream employer would have sent her over the moon. Now, she realized she had absolutely zero desire to ever go back to that environment. She wanted to stay here, with Dade, and run the fishing lodge she'd inherited.

Even if he really hoped she wouldn't.

The rest of the evening, she managed to avoid Dade. Though she really wanted to take a long walk, with a potential serial killer still on the loose, she couldn't risk it. Luckily for her, Dade made himself scarce, claiming he needed to check on the boats and make sure the guests didn't need anything before they left in the morning.

While he was gone, Maddie shut herself up in her room with a good book and read. She'd definitely be sleeping alone tonight.

The next morning, she rose early and headed to the kitchen, hoping to get her coffee before Dade woke. Instead, she found him already there, sitting at the kitchen table as if he'd been waiting for her.

"Good morning," he said.

She managed to mumble something back. Busying herself making her coffee, she knew she couldn't tiptoe around the subject forever. But she thought if she gave herself more time to process everything, maybe it wouldn't hurt so much. Only then did she think she could go back to acting relatively normal.

For now, polite and distant would have to do.

DADE WAS ABOUT to ask Maddie if she was okay when a loud banging from outside sent him up out of his chair and out the back door.

He skidded to a stop as soon as he realized what was causing the noise. A large black bear had gotten into the metal trash cans, knocked them over and was vigorously searching for food.

Glad the guests were still in their cabins, Dade went and

grabbed the air horn that Grady had kept handy for such occasions. If anyone was still sleeping, they'd be wide-awake soon.

He blew the horn, and the bear took off. When he returned to the kitchen, Maddie had taken her coffee and disappeared into the bathroom. A moment later, he heard the shower start up. He knew she was avoiding him, and he couldn't really blame her. She thought he wanted her gone so he could have the lodge to himself.

But the truth of the matter was more complicated. He liked the way their arrangement had been working. Over the course of a few weeks, he realized he didn't want to even consider running the lodge alone. He wanted Maddie, his friend, his lover, his partner, by his side. But only if she wanted that, too. That was the reason he'd tried to give her a way out. If she wanted to go, he'd move heaven and earth to help her. He preferred to remain debt free. But if Maddie decided this wasn't the life for her, then he'd take out a loan if he had to so he could buy her out.

And though he knew he needed to explain why he'd said what he'd said, he wouldn't do that yet. She needed to make up her mind without any prompting from him.

Later that morning, the usual flurry of getting the guests checked out to go home kept them both busy. Dade hated the way Maddie would barely look at him, and he fought the urge to offer up the reasons for what he'd said.

As the group finally drove off, Robert beaming since he'd texted all of his friends photos of him finally catching his big fish, Maddie and Dade stood side by side and waved until the SUVs disappeared from sight. Then she dropped into one of the porch rocking chairs. Dade sighed and did the same. He didn't know how long he could take her giving him the cold shoulder.

"Do you want to talk?" he finally offered. "I can explain—"

"No need." She cut him off, her breezy smile not reaching her eyes. "I understand more than you know. It's all good. We have to work together and get along. But you should know that I have no plans to go anywhere. I chose this life, and I'm going to see my decision through."

He took a moment to let her words sink in. Then, his heart lighter than it had been in ages, he nodded. "I'm glad to hear that," he said, meaning it. "I just wanted to make sure."

Then, while she stared at him, her expression confused, he grinned. "I kind of like having you around."

She started to shake her head and then sighed. "That's good, because we're stuck with each other for a year. You're going to have to get used to it."

Changing the subject, he told her about Blake's annual Memorial Day festivities in a few days. "We might be a small town, but we do it up right. This isn't as big of a celebration as the Fourth of July, but it's a lot of fun. The guests like to attend, but not always. Would you like to go?"

"With you?"

Slowly, he nodded. "Yes. With me."

"I'd like that."

Her soft answer brought his grin back. He'd make sure she had a great time.

Getting the cabins ready for the next set of guests, they fell into an easy routine. It didn't take long before the rooms were done, with clean sheets and towels. They'd settled on a simple menu and did the prep work quickly. By the time the new group arrived, they were ready.

"We make a good team," Dade said, complimenting her. Chin up, she nodded. "We definitely do."

MEMORIAL DAY MORNING, Dade woke up feeling as excited as a little kid. Until Grady's illness turned severe, the two of them had always gone into town for the various holiday celebrations. Blake might be small, but they enjoyed a strong sense of community. Parades, cookouts, the ice cream social on the Fourth of July. Everyone knew everyone else, and Dade looked forward to sharing all of that with Maddie. Not for the first time, he felt grateful that Grady had stipulated she had to stay an entire year. And the fact that she actually wanted to, well, that was the icing on the cake.

They drove into town right after breakfast, arriving early enough to stake out a great spot along Main Street.

"The parade starts at nine," he told her. "And after that, they do a cookout with hot dogs and hamburgers in the empty lot across from Mikki's. There's a big, open, grassy area near the medical clinic, and people set up booths, selling their wares. Everyone walks around and catches up. It's a lot of fun."

His enthusiasm made her smile. When she reached for his hand, he thought his heart might just explode out of his chest.

By the time the parade started, people lined both sides of Main Street. The mood felt celebratory, as most considered this holiday the unofficial start to an all-too-short Alaskan summer.

"Here they come," he told Maddie. And sure enough, the bright yellow 1955 Cadillac Eldorado convertible carrying Mayor Gregory Norman and his wife, Jane, led the procession. With his white hair and beard, Greg resembled Santa Claus, and he enjoyed that role in the winter months.

Today, however, he wore a bright Hawaiian shirt decorated with palm trees and pineapples. Next to him, Jane donned huge red sunglasses. Together, they smiled and waved to the citizens of their town.

Various floats, some having seen better days, followed. The Blake 4-H club kids rode their horses and mules, beaming as they pranced past.

A couple more classic cars, the small high-school marching band, one more float, and the parade was over. Laughing and joking, everyone made their way to the cookout area. Most people had brought their own coolers, with drinks and snacks and maybe even an occasional adult beverage.

Long rows of picnic tables had been set out. The four older guys who made up a Beatles tribute band had set up on a makeshift stage and were warming up. Kip had propped the door open to the general store, and a quick glance showed Mikki's had done the same.

"Where'd you say the outdoor market is?" Maddie asked. "I love that kind of thing."

"They'll be setting up after we eat."

"You didn't tell me it's a potluck." She pointed to where several people were setting out dishes and desserts on a banquet table. "I should have brought something."

"It's not. Those were sides donated by Mikki's and Chef Brett Denyon, Dr. Taylor's husband. I heard he's wanting everyone to sample some of the offerings at his new restaurant."

"Which opens this week," Dr. Taylor said, grinning. "Can you tell I'm a little bit proud of my man?"

Maddie laughed. "I can't blame you. We'll be sure to try it, once our current set of guests leave."

Mayor Norman stepped up on the stage with the band

and tapped the microphone. "Thank you all for coming," he said. "Now let's eat, shop and mingle. And never forget the reason for this holiday—remembering those who gave their lives in service to our great country."

Everyone clapped and cheered. Hamburgers and hot dogs were thrown on the grills, and people grabbed plates and lined up for food. Several people stopped to talk to Dade and meet Maddie.

"Everyone is so friendly," she mused, and then stuffed the last bit of her hot dog and bun into her mouth.

After the meal, hand in hand, they meandered over to the outdoor market, along with most everyone else. Maddie bought a necklace and a jar of homemade blackberry preserves. Dade couldn't remember the last time he'd had such a perfect day.

They ended up back at the picnic area, where several other couples were dancing to the music. Dade sat down on one of the benches and pulled Maddie into his lap.

"It was a good day." Head on his shoulder, Maddie leaned back into him. They shared a leisurely kiss, neither caring who might see.

"I like having you around," Dade murmured, tightening his arms around her.

For a second, she stiffened, making him wonder if he should have kept quiet. No doubt, she was remembering him asking her if she wanted to leave. He considered explaining but decided such a serious discussion would be for another day and time.

Finally, Maddie sighed and relaxed again. "I like being here. This town, these people, are amazing. At least today we got a bit of a break from everything."

All around them, groups of people were drifting away.

Some returned to their vehicles to drive off. Others went inside Mikki's to have a few drinks and prolong the fun.

"Are you ready to head home?" he asked, catching her covering her mouth to hide a yawn.

"Sure."

He helped her get up, and then, keeping his arm around her waist, they headed toward where he'd parked the old truck.

The lot had mostly emptied, though there were still a couple of small groups standing around talking. When they reached the truck, Dade stopped short and swore.

Someone had slashed all four of the tires.

Maddie sagged against him. "Looks like I spoke too soon. Even on a holiday, our stalker won't leave us alone."

Tamping down his anger, Dade made his way toward the closest cluster of people. "Did any of you happen to notice anyone suspicious?" he asked. "All my tires have been slashed."

But no one had. And Dade had no idea how they were going to get back home.

"Let's go into Mikki's and see if we can talk someone into taking us home," he said.

"This is the one time I wish we had Uber or Lyft," Maddie joked, her smile looking forced. He hated to see that look of worry on her pretty face.

"True." He took her hand. "But Blake is full of good people. Someone will help us out. I'll have to get one of the guys from Eddie's to replace all of the tires tomorrow. Luckily, he carries recaps, so it won't be as expensive."

She nodded. "I have no idea what that means, but as long as you can get it fixed, I'm glad."

As they stepped into the crowded bar, Dade led her over to an empty table. "You might as well sit while I see if I can find someone willing to drive all the way to the lodge," he said. "Would you like a beer?"

Her gaze searched his face. "Is that okay? I know you don't drink."

"They know me here," he told her. "Club soda on the rocks with a twist of lime. What would you like?"

"I'll have a beer," she decided. "A hefeweizen, I don't care what brand."

Dade went up to the bar to place their order. A few minutes later, he returned with their drinks. He took a seat across from her, scanning the room while he sipped his drink.

The door opened, and Chet walked in. He smiled when he spotted Dade and Maddie and headed over toward their table.

"Nice to see you two again," he said. "You don't happen to know who drives an older model Chevy pickup, dark green, do you? Someone slashed all four of their tires. I figured I'd let them know."

"That's my truck." Grimacing, Dade took a sip of his club soda. "No way we're going to be able to drive it home tonight. That's why we came in here. To see if we could find someone willing to give us a ride."

"I can do that," Chet offered. "I was just going to have a beer and head home anyway. Where exactly do you live?"

"That's just it." Dade told him the location. "It's a fair way out of town and pretty much the opposite direction from your aunt's house."

"Oh." Chet shrugged and dropped into a chair. "It's all good. I seriously don't mind. It's not like I have anything else planned, anyway. How about you buy me a beer, and then after that, we can get going?"

Before Dade could reply, Maddie spoke up. "I'll get it. You two talk. I'll be right back."

Watching her walk through the crowded room to the bar, Dade sighed.

"She's something else," Chet commented. "Are you two a couple or...?"

Tearing his gaze away from Maddie to focus on the other man, Dade smiled. "It's complicated," he said. He took another drink and changed the subject. "What about you? Did you enjoy the Memorial Day celebrations here in Blake?"

"Sure. I like this town. I used to come here all the time as a kid and visit my aunt."

Which seemed odd. Because Dade didn't remember Angela Bishop ever even mentioning a nephew, never mind having one hanging around. While Dade might be a few years older, he would have thought Angela would have wanted the two to play as young boys.

"When was this?" he asked. "My grandfather took me to visit Angela a lot when I was a kid. I'm surprised we haven't met."

A weird, wary expression crossed Chet's face. "Yeah, I don't know. Maybe the timing just wasn't right."

Maddie returned just then with the beer, which she placed in front of Chet. She slid back into her seat, looking from one man to the other. "What's up?" she asked, picking up her own glass and taking a sip.

Chet took a long drink of his beer and smiled. "We were just talking about how strange it is that we never ran into each other as kids."

Something in Chet's smile didn't sit right with Dade. Right then and there, he decided there was no way he would allow this man to take them home. He'd find somebody else.

A large, boisterous table of guys caught his attention. He'd gone to school with most of them. Surely, one of them would be willing to drive, especially if Dade offered gas money.

He caught Maddie's eye. "Excuse me," he said, picking up his drink to take with him. "I'll be right back."

All his old friends greeted him loudly. Dade chatted for a few minutes, discussing the parade and next year's high-school reunion. Once, Dade glanced back over at Maddie and Chet, saw they appeared to be in deep conversation, and returned his attention to his old friends.

One of the guys noticed. "Is that your girlfriend?" he asked.

At this point, Dade decided he wasn't taking any chances. "She's my everything," he replied, meaning every word. He braced himself, certain they'd all tease him. Instead, they mostly appeared envious.

"She's beautiful," Tim Ragan said. "You're a lucky man."

Dade thanked him, before telling the group about his tires getting slashed and him and Maddie being stuck here in Blake. Immediately, a couple of them vied for the opportunity to give Dade a ride home. "A great chance to catch up," Johnny Everitt said. "And to meet your lady." Since he and Tim had ridden to town together, Tim agreed.

Relieved, Dade told them he'd be right back.

When he turned, ready to tell Chet he wouldn't need a ride after all, the table was empty. Both Chet and Maddie were gone.

What the hell? Both drinks remained, Chet's beer virtually untouched, Maddie's almost empty. Dade scanned the bar, thinking maybe Maddie had gone to the restroom or something, and maybe Chet had spotted a friend he wanted to catch up with.

But he didn't see either of them, anywhere.

"What's wrong?" Tim asked.

"Did you happen to see where they went?" Dade asked, gesturing toward the empty table. "Since you're facing that way?" He refused to panic. Not yet.

"The skinny dude?" Johnny asked. "I think your girl-friend mustn't have been feeling well because she looked like she could barely stand. He helped her outside. Check there. They likely went out for some air."

No longer caring what anyone thought, Dade rushed outside.

Johnny had said Maddie had trouble standing. But she'd been fine a few minutes ago. Had Chet dropped something into her drink? How quickly does a roofie work?

Two women had been murdered. If he didn't find her soon, Dade had a feeling Maddie would be next. Which meant Chet had to be the stalker, the one who'd been send-ing all the text messages, started fires, blown up the Jeep and broken into the house. And now, slashed the truck's tires.

Johnny and Tim appeared, having followed Dade out-side.

"Any sign of her?"

"No." Dade took a deep breath and told them a rushed, abbreviated version of what had been going on. "We've got to find her."

"Call her cell phone," Tim suggested. "If she has it on her, and she's anywhere nearby, we could hear it ringing."

Since at this point, Dade would try anything, he pulled out his phone to do exactly that. As he went to call her, his phone rang.

"It's her," he said, relief flooding him. But when he an-swered, no one was there.

"Look!" Johnny pointed. "Something's going on in that part of the parking lot. Those people are circling something. And they're hollering."

Seeing the commotion, Dade took off running. Johnny and Tim were right behind him. When they reached the group, which had grown to several people deep, Dade pushed his way through. He spotted Chet crouching protectively over a woman sprawled unconscious on the pavement.

"Maddie!" Dade shouted. Then, when Chet made to block him from reaching her, Dade swung. His fist connected squarely with Chet's jaw, sending the smaller man flying backward.

Dade paid him no mind. All of his attention on Maddie, he dropped to the pavement and lifted her in his arms. For one awful second, he couldn't tell if she was alive, but then she moaned and shifted in his arms.

Holding her close, he looked up to find Tim and Johnny restraining Chet. "What did you give her?" Dade demanded.

Chet looked away without answering.

"A state trooper named Taggert is staying above the general store," Dade said. "Can someone please go get him? This man needs to be arrested."

"I've called Dr. Taylor," someone else said. "She's on her way."

Chet turned and glared at Dade. "I have as much right to the lodge as you do. More, even."

"How so?" Dade asked, keeping his voice level.

"I'm Grady's son."

Stunned, Dade wasn't sure how to respond. "If you are, then Grady didn't know. He wasn't the type of man to abandon his responsibilities."

Chet spat. "Looks like he did. That's why I wanted to take what should have been mine."

Later, after Taggert had arrived and taken Chet into custody, Dade helped get a still unconscious Maddie into a vehicle so they could transport her to the Medical Clinic.

"We'll get some fluids into her," the doctor said. "And we'll take some blood so we can find out what she was given. Most importantly, we'll need to monitor her."

"I can do that," Dade said, settling into the seat next to Maddie. Unwilling to let go of her, he took her limp hand and held it in his. "Is she going to be all right?"

Though Dr. Taylor looked grim, she met his gaze. "It depends what she ingested and how much. Do you know what she was drinking?"

"She just had one beer," he replied. "But I have no idea what Chet might have put into it when she wasn't looking."

"We'll get her fixed up," the doctor promised.

At the clinic, Dade stayed by Maddie's side. Her eyelids fluttered, and she moved her head restlessly from side to side. She appeared to be trying to wake up.

Watching her, Dade tried to bottle up the simmering fury he felt. It was a good thing Officer Taggert had taken Chet into custody because if Dade were to get his hands on him right now, it wouldn't be good.

As if Dade's thoughts had summoned him, Taggert called. "This guy wants to talk to you," he said. "He's admitted to drugging Maddie. Also to sending the texts, the fire and explosion and the murders, but he keeps saying you owe him."

"He's going to have to wait," Dade replied. "I'm at the medical clinic with Maddie. I'm not leaving her until the drugs are out of her system. Please keep him locked up, and I'll let you know when she's better."

After ending the call, Dade watched while Dr. Taylor took Maddie's vitals. She started an IV and took some blood, saying she hoped to run a few preliminary tests on it. "Though we don't have as fancy of a lab as an emergency department, we make do."

"Thank you," he said. "I'm staying with her."

Since it wasn't a question, she nodded. "I'm staying, too. I'll be checking in periodically."

Sometime in the middle of the night, Maddie groaned and cried out. She began gagging and retching. Instantly awake, Dade barely got a plastic bedpan under her before she threw up.

Dade looked up to see the doctor standing in the doorway. "Vomiting will clear out her system. Why don't you go home and get some rest? I'll keep an eye on her and call you if anything changes."

"I'm not leaving her."

Something in his voice, perhaps, or possibly the way he looked at Maddie made the doctor smile softly. "I know that feeling," she murmured. "I'm glad she has you."

With that, she left the room, closing what must have been her office door behind her.

"Dade?" Maddie's voice, raspy and dry. "What happened to me?"

Then, before he could answer, she began to cry. "Chet drugged me. He was going to kill me."

Pulling her into his arms, he smoothed the hair away from her face. "Shhh, it's all right. I've got you. You're safe here with me. Officer Taggert took Chet into custody."

Wiping away her tears, she sighed. "It's over? It's finally over?"

"Yes, it's finally over. Chet believes he's Grady's son.

I have my doubts. But a simple DNA test should tell the truth."

"His son?" Maddie frowned. "That explains why he felt entitled to the lodge."

"It does. And if he hadn't done all the horrible things that he did, if the DNA test says he is, I would have made sure he got part of the lodge. Now, no matter what the results, I want him to go to prison."

"Me too."

He held her close, feeling as if he never wanted to let her go. That part of her life might be over, but something else, something better, had just begun.

"Why are you smiling?" she asked, looking up at him. Then, before he could answer, she took a deep breath and continued. "What you said the other day, about taking my old employer up on their offer. Do you really want me to leave?"

There were several things he could have said. Excuses, explanations, and none of them real. "I do not." Heart in his throat, he met her gaze. "I want nothing more than to have you stay. But it has to be your choice. Not because of some terms in a will. But because this—our life, our partnership—is what you want."

Slowly, she nodded. "It is. But what about you, Dade? What do you want?"

"You," he answered, his voice raw. "I like what we're making together. I think we have a real chance at a future."

Then, thinking about how he'd felt when he thought he'd lost her, he realized he was still holding a bit of himself back. Going all in, he decided. "Maddie, I think I might love you."

Her beautiful blue eyes filled with tears. Still holding his gaze, she swallowed. "I feel the same way about you."

He gathered her into his arms, taking care to be gentle.

"Hey, there," Doc Taylor said from the doorway. "She needs her rest. You've got the rest of your lives to cuddle. Right now, she needs to sleep."

With that proclamation, Dr. Taylor left the room.

Dade chuckled. "She's right. And I like the sound of that. We do have the rest of our lives."

Settling back against her pillow, Maddie's eyes already drifted closed. "All of our todays and our tomorrows," she murmured.

Her words filled his heart. As he settled in to try and get some shut eye in the chair by her bed, he wished he could somehow thank Grady. The man who'd raised him and loved him and taught him right from wrong had gone and given him one final gift. Dade would forever be grateful. All his todays and tomorrows, indeed.

* * * * *

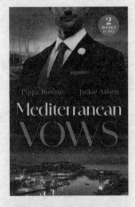

COMING SOON!

We really hope you enjoyed reading this book.
If you're looking for more romance
be sure to head to the shops when
new books are available on

Thursday 6th June

To see which titles are coming soon, please visit
millsandboon.co.uk/nextmonth

MILLS & BOON